THE SUMMER PLAGUE

by Norman Moss

Published in 2009
New Generation Publishing

CHAPTER ONE

T *hey called it a plague but it caused no deaths,*
unless you count one or two murders that
resulted indirectly from the frustrations it
engendered. Its arrival was unnoticed at first.
Its effect was private, its nature insidious. No one came out
in spots, or collapsed on the street. Yet for a time it created
as much anxiety as the Black Death. Only the sufferer knew
he was afflicted, plus, usually, his wife or partner

It attacked sexual behavior, at a time when Western
society was the most sexualized society in history. Never
before was sexual activity so widely recounted and
discussed. Varieties of sexual activity were sanctioned and
even encouraged ,and explained, examined and portrayed
in the media without judgment. People experimented openly
with every imaginable sexual combination, seeking new
forms of erotic pleasure. The practises in other times of the
Roman emperors and their courts and the more licentious
members of the French and British aristocracy were now
available at every level of society. Sex was democratized.
Sexual knowledge was so widespread, in every age group,
that there was a market for kiddie-sized condoms, and one
would not be surprised to find "fellatio" and "cunnilingus"

in a grade school spelling bee (their colloquial equivalents being too easy to spell)..

With the plague, this express train of self-centered pleasure came to a juddering halt. It resumed again later, , after a period of intense anxiety, but some of this anxiety remained. It would never be entirely banished. Men and women had cast off the shackles of traditional morality and the limits on behavior that these imposed. They had set aside rules once said to be passed down from God and made their own rules, each person the master or mistress of his or her own body. .Now their confidence was dented. The power they took for granted could be snatched away from them. Who knew what else lay out there, and in what other ways it could attack this most fundamental part of human life?

For years afterwards, people talked with those close to them about that summer and what it had meant to them. Many people admitted that they were puzzled by their own reactions. Some said it had brought revelation, about their own deepest urges, or about those close to them, or about their relationships. For a very few men, it brought extraordinary, unmatched opportunities. But it would have been insensitive for these to discus this with others

::   ::   ::

Gavin Grove always remembered that it was Bob Black who gave him the first indication. Good old, decent Bob, the small town g.p. who spent three days a week being the campus doctor and always worried through his college patients' problems with them: the bouts of 'flu, the stomach pains and skin rashes, the jock's torn ligament that could keep him out of the game, the girl's anxieties about the pill. Bob was a neighbor; his house was in the next street to Gavin's in Melby Park. As the college infirmary was near the Bliss Institute, they often shared the ten-minute drive to and from home on Bob's campus days.

This time they were driving in Gavin's car along a Long Island freeway, late on an afternoon filled with early April sunshine, past a landscape of prosperity and ease: shopping malls, broad, tree-lined streets, golf courses, small town country clubs with their swimming pools already opened up. Melby Park was not even a small town, more a satellite of the small town of Radford. It had a few leafy streets of houses set back from the road and just enough stores and services to provide a life support system for the inhabitants.

Gavin was telling Bob about some of the optimistic speculation that was going around the Bliss Institute laboratory. He said the work his group was doing on the brain and the autonomic nervous system might link up with a treatment for Parkinson's Disease. Bob was always a good audience when Gavin talked about the laboratory. He had said once that he would have liked to have gone into research.

Gavin finished his account. Bob cleared his throat as a prelude, and said, "You know, something curious has been happening."

He paused and waited, so Gavin said, "Oh yes?"

Bob went on: "I've had five cases of sexual impotence recently. Three of them haven't responded to Viagra or any of the other pills."

"Really?"

"Yes. I don't know about the other two yet. Maybe they won't either."

"Oh. Sounds odd."

"Yes. In any case, the problem goes farther back than not having an erection. There was a total cessation of sexual desire. I wasn't altogether surprised that the pills didn't work."

"Loss of libido."

"Yes. In every case. Usually," Bob went on, "when boys complain of sexual impotence, they're frustrated. This is different. The last boy said, 'I can't get it up, Doc.' Then he said, 'Actually, I don't really want to get it up.' He was worried about what was happening to him."

"Elegant phraseology. He's probably majoring in creative writing," said Gavin, who could be sniffy about some college courses.

"'Can't get it up' is the approved medical terminology," Bob said firmly. "I've had boys worried about being impotent, before, of course," he went on. "Particularly when they're just starting their sex lives. Sometimes I get one or two around exam time. I talk to them about anxiety, occasionally give them something for it."

"But it isn't exam time now," Gavin said.

"It isn't exam time, and the pills aren't working."

"What factors have you checked for?"

"The usual. Psychological factors. None of them show any signs of depression or anxiety. No sign of mumps or diabetes. No sign of abnormality in the testicles. I sent a couple of them to a urologist at Walton General. I've had a report back on the first."

"And?"

"Testosterone and hormone levels normal."

"So it sounds as if it *could* be psychological."

"Well, all I can say is that they show none of the other expected signs."

"That's very puzzling," Gavin said. He was silent while he negotiated the exit to Melby Park. Then he asked, "Do you have any thoughts about it, Bob?"

"I don't know," Bob replied. "I've no specialized knowledge in that area, as you know."

Gavin said, "My cousin was at boarding school. He said the authorities there used to put saltpeter in their food to dampen down their burgeoning sex drives so that they wouldn't get carried away and rape the maids. I don't suppose Holycroft could be resorting to that, could they?"

Bob did not answer. They reached his house and he asked, "Do you want to come in for a drink? I told you I've taken up gardening. I'll show you the camellias. They're just coming out."

"Another time if you don't mind," Gavin replied. "We've got people coming for dinner. One of Martha's oldest friends and her boy friend."

He let Bob out and drove around the corner to his own house. Martha's Volkswagen was already in the garage so she was home from work. He parked his Ford behind it in the driveway. He had no camellias but he managed to keep his front lawn mowed and neat, and a row of petunias would soon be coming up alongside the front path. He felt that was as much as he owed the neighborhood. He took no pleasure in gardening but he liked things to be tidy.

He walked up his front path with the assurance of a man who was on his own ground. He was a cautious man by nature, who moved warily when he was not on familiar territory. He let himself in, found Martha in the kitchen, and kissed her on the lips. "Anything to do for dinner?" he asked.

"It's chicken casserole and it's in the oven. But you can make the salad."

"All right."

"I'm going upstairs to take a shower and change," she said.

"You look fine."

"Oh c'mon. These are the clothes I've been wearing all day with my women. They're not for dinner. And your shirt is pretty grubby."

He washed his hands and chopped up the salad vegetables and shoveled them into the salad bowl while she went upstairs. When they were first married and lived in England, he used to tease her about showering every day or even twice a day, and sometimes get annoyed about it when they were going somewhere and it held them up. He would call it "your antiseptic American cleanliness." But they dropped national adjectives both from their jokes and their arguments as they got used to each other. Their arguments, in any case, were very infrequent.

He went up to the bedroom and changed into his indoor shoes while she dressed. She asked his advice: "This blouse? It's a bit frumpy, isn't it. Maybe the blue dress?"

"It's only dinner with Elaine and Ted, for Pete's sake."

"You can bet she'll turn up looking dazzling."

"And you've always got to compete with her. You told me. She had bigger tits than you when you were young."

"It's not that she had bigger tits, but she had them first."

"And you never forgot it."

"It was important at the time. Weren't you worried about the size of your wang when you were an adolescent?"

"I still am." She turned and punched him in the ribs. "Anyway, now you've got bigger tits."

"I've got bigger everything, let's face it."

"You're well rounded. Cuddly. I keep telling you, fashionably skinny women don't appeal to me."

Before they were married he had made the mistake of remarking to her once, when they were talking about famous beauties, that she was not the most beautiful girl in the world. She was intelligent and was doing post-graduate work at London University and he was surprised at her distress when he said it. Ever since then he had told her often how much he loved her chunky figure, her freckles, her blue eyes and her turned-up nose, all of which was true.

"Elaine's not skinny," Martha said. "And she appeals to a lot of people. Like Ted. She called me at work today for a chat. Ted's quite serious."

"Are they going to move in together? Get married?"

"It hasn't quite reached that stage yet. Anyway, I haven't told you what happened today. One of my clients complained to Grace because I'm terminating her sessions. She's spoiled and self-centered and she just wants to talk about her problems endlessly rather than do anything about them. I'm not doing her any good.. Grace is going to stand by me, I'm sure. But I have to see her about it tomorrow."

Then the doorbell rang "Let them in and give them a drink, will you, while I put my shoes on," she said.

Ted Starowicz was a reporter on the Long Island Chronicle. The Chronicle was a daily newspaper published in a small town nearby, but it was not a small town paper. It had a large circulation and a national reputation and status, partly because many of its readers worked in the big town of New York City and commuted to and from their homes in Long Island. Its circulation area ranged all the way, geographically and socially, from Queens to the Hamptons.

Martha told Elaine once that Ted looked like a hunky orang-utan. He was short, broad-shouldered, dark and hairy, with thick, dark curly hair and heavy eyebrows. Gavin said after their first meeting that he was a bit "over the top." When Elaine said she did not understand that British phrase, he explained and also modified it by saying he had meant that Ted seemed like a man of strong views and strong reactions. In fact, he found him loud-mouthed and egotistic. He was surprised when he learned that Ted had a master's degree from Columbia in French literature, not so much by the degree - he had ceased to be surprised at the kinds of people who had advanced university degrees in America - as the choice of subject. However, after meeting Ted a few more times, he realized that he was intelligent and serious, although he also found him brash and with a casually abrasive manner that sometimes bruised his sensibilities.

He did this as he came through the door, with his greeting. "How you doing, Gav?" he said, using an abbreviation that no one had ever used before Gavin came to America. Elaine greeted him with a warm hello. She had had her light brown hair cropped since Gavin last saw her, and was wearing a silky green pencil dress that clung to her willowy frame. She kissed Gavin on the cheek and smiled at him warmly with her pale blue eyes. When he first met her he thought she was being flirtatious but soon realized that this was her way of saying hello to any man.

Ted did not say much while they chattered over drinks. Gavin had noticed before that Ted had very little small talk. He would be silent while other chatted about nothing in particular, and then launch into a subject that was on his mind, usually one on which he had a lot to say.

When they were seated at the dinner table, Ted raised a story that was on the front page of the Chronicle that day. The story was that Joe Barreras, an industrialist whose activities often got into the newspapers, had bought Biotek Inc, a bio-technology research and development corporation located in the neighboring town of Walton. Barreras owned an electronics company that worked mainly in defense and pharmaceutical companies in America and Latin America.

"Barreras is a bit of a bastard," Ted said. "The story practically made him out to be a white knight of industry. It could have said a lot more."

"What could it have said?" asked Gavin.

"He's played some dirty politics in Central America. According to a piece in the Nation a little while back, he's used his influence to get a monopoly position for a lot of his pharmaceuticals in some countries there. There's no doubt about Guatemala, he was right in there playing footsie with the opposition before the coup."

"I seem to recall reading something about that," said Gavin.

"The Nation article also suggested that when he started out he had help from the mob."

"Okay, so Joe Barreras is a hustler," said Martha. "He's done good things as well."

"Like what?" asked Ted.

"He saved the Van Cortland Museum. That would have gone under and that whole collection would have been broken up and sold if it wasn't for his subsidy."

Ted shrugged. "It's a hobby of his wife's," he said.

"You don't think he might possibly care about the arts?" Martha demanded.

"It's possible," Ted conceded. "He's no Wall Street redneck. He's intelligent. When he testified before a congressional committee about the tactical missile Barreras Industries was developing, he could talk back to them about global strategy. He was on the ball. And he just might care about the arts, our Señor Barreras."

Barreras came from a Mexican-American family in Texas. His first name was "Jose", but although he never concealed or even played down his Hispanic background, he was known almost universally as "Joe."

"You seem to know a lot about him," Martha remarked.

"I nearly had a piece of a rather murky story involving Barreras a little while back," Ted explained.

"This soup is delicious," said Elaine. "How did you get this flavor, Martha?"

"Wild mushrooms," said Gavin. "I got them at the farmers' market in Radford. What story was that, Ted?"

"Well, our Washington bureau had a good story about a CIA operation in Panama a couple of years back that the Government tried to deny. One of the people involved left the CIA under a cloud. He'd been doing some free-lancing, feathering his own nest. Then he turned up as a trouble-shooter for Barreras Pharmaceuticals in Central America. I'm telling you, Barreras is a real operator. The guy was named Philip Carey. He worked out of the New York office and lives in Walton. I was sent to interview him. I thought he might tell me something about the CIA operation."

"Did he?" asked Gavin.

"No. I asked him about his job with Barreras, and he wouldn't say much about that either. Then he or somebody else phoned the editor and asked him not to mention his CIA connection on the ground that it could endanger his life. So the paper left his name out of the story. The editor can be really chicken sometimes. Endanger his life, horse-shit!" Gavin winced inwardly at hearing that word while he was eating,

"Anyway," Ted went on, "it's sort of your field Barreras is moving into now, bio-technology. What do you think?"

"It's certainly a field in which things are happening," said Gavin. "But it's a good way downstream from me. We work in fundamental science mostly. We don't have much to do with applications at Bliss."

After dinner, Martha and Elaine took some things into the kitchen and stayed there for a while, talking quietly, almost conspiratorially. Gavin and Ted sat down in the living room, in front of the brick fireplace that dominated the room. The house was in the style that Martha had dubbed "real estate agent Colonial" when they first saw it. She said it went with her name. They had furnished it to match. She chose most of the pieces and Gavin went along with her choices: dark mahogany furniture to match the black beams in the ceiling, and a deacon's bench in front of the fireplace. She had refused to have a coffee table because it would clash with the style. But she had also refused an offer from her parents of a spinning wheel because she said that would make the place look like a goddamned theme park.

They had made a mistake when they bought the house. The clean lines and healthy appearance had concealed structural diseases which required major surgery soon after they moved in. They had to borrow money from the bank to pay for it and were still repaying the loan. They had thought of suing the surveyor but were told that they would not be likely to gain out of it.

Ted declined an offer of another drink from Gavin because he was driving home and lit a cigarette, first asking Gavin's permission. He was a little uncertain about Gavin. He gave an appearance of being formal and rather staid, as Ted had always thought British people were. His face was usually expressionless. Tall and slender, with a thin face and a smooth complexion, he had a habit of thrusting his head forward when he spoke, like some sea bird. Dark anonymous clothes, thin-rimmed glasses and a clipped manner of speaking added to the picture of blandness. But he was not bland; he would say things that were witty or provocative without changing his expression, so that they came as a surprise.

Everyone at the Bliss Institute knew the story of the time he visited Manhattan with two others on the staff. He went up to the uniformed doorman standing under the canopy outside a restaurant and asked him politely for some directions.

"I ain't no information booth, Mister," the doorman said.

Without changing expression Gavin replied in his clipped British voice, "You ain't no fucking help either," and strolled off, his two companions gleeful.

On an impulse, Gavin said to him, "I've got a story for

you, Ted."

"Oh yes?"

"A wave of sexual impotence sweeping the Holycroft campus."

"Sexual impotence?"

"That's right. And the impotence pills don't work. Think of the headlines. No Lead In College Pencils. Holycroft Emasculated. Epidemic Spreads, Men Flee Campus. New Nuclear Plant Blamed, Long Island Power Sued for Ten Billion Dollars."

Ted looked at Gavin and as usual he could tell nothing from his expression. "Are you bull-shitting me?" he demanded.

"Not entirely." Gavin told him about his conversation in the car, without identifying Bob Black.

Ted considered it thoughtfully. "So Viagra isn't working," he said. "Is it possible that people are building up resistance? The way some viruses are now resistant to antibiotics?"

"No, the pills don't deal with viruses. The pills only deal with failure to get an erection, the mechanism of getting blood to the penis. This seems to be something wrong further back. I've no idea what it could be."

"Whatever it is, it sounds as if it's catching. A spreading case of limp dick."

"There are only a very few cases," Gavin pointed out.

"Could it be psychological?" Ted asked. "An anxiety state?"

"It could, certainly. But normally, that's associated with depression or anxiety. These people don't show any of the usual signs. And the pill usually cures that kind of impotence, the failure to get an erection. We don't know what it is. At any rate, *I* don't know."

"But couldn't it be something psychological that's really deep-seated, that doesn't come out in any obvious signs?"

"Oh certainly, if you're talking about one person. But three cases in a row, maybe more?"

"But a psychological condition can be catching also. It can spread, can't it?" said Ted. "Do these boys all know each other?"

"A good question," Gavin said. "That's just about possible." He reflected that this was something he should have asked Bob Black. Ted was really quite bright, although he often did not seem it. A psychological state could indeed be communicated unconsciously. This was why a controlled experiment with a new drug was always double-blind.

"Anyway, let me know if you hear anything else," Ted said.

Martha and Elaine came back into the living room. Gavin looked at the two women and they seemed to him to be so different that he wondered how they could have been friends for so long, Elaine with her well-groomed good looks and her feline face, listening coolly and attentively, but always in command of herself, always conscious of her appearance, Martha engrossed in what she was saying about a mutual acquaintance who was behaving unwisely, not noticing that one of her cuffs was flapping loosely. Looking at them now, Gavin could see that some men would find Elaine better-looking. He preferred Martha.

The two women talked about their jobs. Martha was a counselor at a local women's health and counseling center. She complained of the deficiencies and inefficiencies of the welfare services.

She also told about a telephone call the center had received the day before from a girl who said she was going to have a baby. She mimicked the telephone conversation, doing the caller in an anxious little-girl voice. "*I'm afraid to tell my parents. They'll kill me.*" "Would you like to tell me your name?" "*Beth.*" "Are you quite sure you're pregnant, Beth?" "*Oh yes. My boy friend and I have kissed five times.*" "I see. Tell me, Beth, how old are you?" "*Nine.*" What Gavin loved about Martha was that she did not laugh at Beth at the end of the story.

Elaine worked for a small advertising agency. She told the others how the director would introduce her to clients as "a member of our design team," when actually she was the entire design team. She designed display ads for newspapers and billboards, usually that were to be seen in the Long Island area. She told them about her newest design, for newspaper ads for a chain of Japanese carry-out places opening at beach resorts. Now she had to do something romantic for a hotel in the Adirondacks which was trying to attract couples for weekends, with the slogan "Have another honeymoon this weekend."

"Suggestions welcomed. Nothing too ribald," she said.

"How about," suggested Gavin, "'Is your marriage getting stale? Try something different with someone different."

"Not quite the idea," Elaine said.

Ted said, "You'll have trouble selling honeymoons if Gavin is right."

"Right about what?" Elaine asked.

"He thinks there's an epidemic of sexual impotence on the way."

"Really?"

"Not necessarily an epidemic," Gavin said. "A few cases. I was just trying to think up a story for Ted."

"It's certainly a good scare story." Ted said.

"Some men wouldn't be scared," Gavin said.

"Like who?"

"Like my Uncle Edward."

"Why wouldn't he be scared?" Martha asked.

"He wanted to get rid of his sex drive."

"Why was that?" Ted asked.

"He wanted to rise above it. He was a Buddhist, you see. He and my Aunt Harriet were both Buddhists. Uncle Edward took it very seriously. He wanted to rise above earthly desires. He said Aunt Harriet, his wife, was a true Buddhist. She had conquered desire and risen above earthly passions, and he wanted to do the same. He said he still had sensual desires. But he tried hard. He tried Mahatma Gandhi's method."

"What did Gandhi do?"

"Gandhi used to take a nubile young girl to bed with him. He'd lie next to her all night to show that he'd overcome his earthly desires. So Uncle Edward did that. He'd get some hooker, a good-looking one, she had to be really good-looking with a good figure if it was going to be a test for him, and spend the night with her in bed in his house. He and my aunt had separate bedrooms by this time, of course."

"Did it work?" Ted asked.

"No. He couldn't overcome his earthly desires. He admitted that to Aunt Harriet. She was very sympathetic. Well, Buddhist teachers say you should keep trying however hard the struggle. So he kept on trying. He would get these young hookers from an escort agency and spend the night with them, and then he'd admit to Aunt Harriet the next morning that he'd failed again. Sometimes he failed twice in one night.

"Anyway, one day my Aunt said that since these girls were trying to help him, it was a bit unfair to send them home without any breakfast. So the next one who came, she cooked breakfast for them. The girl pulled through, she was young and healthy, but the doctors couldn't save my uncle, even with a stomach pump. It turned out that Aunt Harriet hadn't entirely overcome earthly passions."

After a pause Ted asked, "Is that true?"

"Of course," Gavin said. Ted looked into his face but could see no hint of a smile.

The evening ended shortly before midnight, with goodbyes and kisses all around. "For an Englishman, you mix a mean margarita," Elaine told Gavin at the door.

As the car pulled out of the driveway, Ted said to Elaine, "Well, how about having a honeymoon this weekend?"

"You mean," she said, "Looking out on the romantic Adirondacks, where the sunset gives a magical glow to the mountain peaks?"'

"Actually, I was thinking of the view from 4B Hudson Apartments in Radford. The Walmart parking lot, the laundromat."

"I've seen it before. Frankly, it's not the view that's the attraction."

"So this weekend? Friday night to Monday morning?"

"Okay. But we go out to dinner on Saurday."

"It's a deal."

After another minute she said, "Hey, where are we going?"

"The very same Hudson Apartments. You don't think I can wait until the weekend, do you?"

"I told you I wanted to go home tonight. I've got to change for work tomorrow. I thought we agreed on that."

"I changed my mind. It's the way you were sitting with your on the couch. You skirt was riding up and I was looking at your thighs. You'll have to wear the same dress tomorrow."

"But I - "

"Don't argue. It's your fault. You shouldn't have sat like that."

"I don't want to wear this dress to work tomorrow."

"Do you want me to explode with frustration? We can play a game."

After a while she said, "Okay. But not rape. It'll spoil my dress."

Gavin and Martha loaded the dishwasher and raked over some of the evening's conversation. But Gavin was still thinking of what Ted had said, about impotence spreading from one person to another psychologically. When Martha said she was going to bed, he told her, "I'm going to stay down for a few minutes. There's something I want to look up in a book."

"Don't be long, huh?" she said over her shoulder as she walked up the stairs.

His mind was working on the thought that a psychological condition could block the sexual urge and perhaps even transmit this unconsciuously. He wanted to explore this idea. He had been drawn to medicine as a career, he realized after he had already been a medical student for some time, not by a humane desire to heal the sick so much as by an intense curiosity about how a human being works, not just the human body but a human being. It seemed to him to be the ultimate mystery that a material object, the human body, composed of material substances and processes, could be something that also had this other, unique dimension of existence, consciousness, and could think about itself. How did the material become something more than the material? At what point did this transcendence occur? Could the one ever be explained in terms of the other? All the research that he himself had initiated was in the area where physical and mental processes interacted.

He went over to a point in the bookshelves beside the fireplace and took down Sigmund Freud's *Three Contributions to Sexual Theory.* He had given himself a collection of Freud's most important works as a present when he graduated. He looked into the book for ideas but the essays were too abstract and too mechanical, with their accounts of the libido in economic terms, to be relevant. However, he became absorbed in one passage after another as he often did, and when he looked up from the book a half-hour had gone by.

He walked upstairs quietly. The bedroom door was open, and by the light from the bathroom he could just make out Martha's form. She was lying in bed, on her side, her eyes closed. She was weaing the blue sheer nightdress he had bought her last Christmas, and her bare arm was flung over the pillow. He took his shoes off in the bathroom so as not to disturb her and tiptoed into the bedroom. He undressed quickly and got into his pajamas slipped into bed with his back to her.

But she was awake. She snuggled up to him so that he felt

the warmth of her body against his back, and stretched over his shoulder and caressed his cheek, then ran her fingers down his chest. "Hello, darling," she murmured. He kissed her fingers affectionately, and drifted off to sleep.

CHAPTER TWO

Т he Bliss Institute, founded nine years earlier, was already one of the world's leading centers of biological and medical research, an East Coast establishment to rival – although its members would deny any competitive spirit – California's Salk Institute. LIke the Salk Institute. It was named after its founder, and its fo

founder, and its founder, like Jonas Salk, was given the opportunity to create it because he had made a discovery that was of immediate and dramatic benefit to Mankind. Morley Bliss would always be known as the discoverer of the Aids vaccine, but he already had a wide reputation in his own field.

He shied away from personal publicity and he had drawn back at first from having the institute set up by a philanthropic foundation named after him. But he agreed when it was put to him that his name would be an asset and that the institute could reflect his own ideas of what science should be. He also liked the idea that it would be located in the college where he had been an undergraduate.

He believed in science as a disinterested, selfless pursuit that would bring benefits to Mankind. He was a Bostonian, a descendent of generations of Puritans going back to the early days of the New England colony, and although he was not a religious man his friends and admirers saw him as standing in the tradition of the great New England moralists. He had written and spoken out sternly against the involvement of science in politics and in commerce and the submission of many scientists to these interests. .

The Bliss Institute was determinedly international. Its staff was drawn from all over the world. Its discoveries were available to everyone. Under its articles of incorporation, no patent could be taken out on any product arising from work done there. Its facilities, reputation and program attracted leading workers in the field from many countries. So did the presence of Morley Bliss himself at the head. He was almost an iconic figure in the world of medical research, not only for his own work but also for the way he inspired others. He was known to be willing to back new ideas and to involve himself supportively in the work of everyone at the Institute. Since his principles and his outspokenness had made him enemies, there were also those who called him "Saint Morley," pronounced with a sneer.

Three years earlier, Gavin Grove had been a researcher with the Medical Research Council working at the laboratory in Berkshire, just outside London, when he was invited to apply for a post at the Bliss Institute, following two papers he had published on the brain-blood barrier. He was not keen to live in America. An earlier year at the University of California at Los Angeles had been an interesting experience but had left him feeling that England was his home. However, he was attracted by all the things that drew others to the Bliss Institute and he was dissatisfied with the opportunities for original work that his MRC. post was providing for him.

And there was Martha. They had met in London and were drawn to each other right away and started going out together. They enjoyed London life together, shared friends and spent most weekends in Gavin's apartment in a picturesque village in Berkshire, near his MRC laboratory. One Sunday morning shortly before Martha's academic year in England ended they were in bed in Gavin's little apartment. A gale was blowing outside with noisy gusts and slamming icy rain against the window. She said to him, "Isn't it lovely being snug and warm together in here while it's so cold and wet outside."

He said, "No, it's not, it's bloody awful. Because I keep thinking you're going to leave soon and go back to America and I won't ever have you here again, and I can't bear the thought. Oh God, now I'm crying. I'm sorry but I can't help it." She hugged him and buried her face in his chest and said she did not want to be without him either.

When they married she had accepted that this would mean living in England. But he sensed that she was not happy at the thought of leaving America for good, and the idea of at least starting their married life in America was appealing to her, which was another point in favor of moving to the Bliss Institute.

He had made it clear to her that there was no commitment to emigrate when he came and she accepted that the move to America was temporary. But after three years he felt at home. His work was fulfilling and his status was respected. They had bought a house simply because it made more financial sense than renting, not because he wanted to plant roots. But life on the East Coast did not seem as jarringly different from life in England as Southern

California had been and he found that he liked most of the differences that there were. He was earning more money than he could earn in England. He had to admit now that he felt a part of the community of professional people and their families who lived in small towns in that part of Long Island, and he sometimes had to remind himself that he was a citizen of another country.

He was thinking about this now, on a balmy afternoon, as he gazed out of his ground-floor office across at the vast lawn that constituted the central part of the campus, with its inharmonious collection of buildings erected at different times and in different styles, the library, wood and glass and angled flat planes, which he called Holycroft's log cabin, wooden cheek by glass jowl next to the brown stone gothic history and social sciences building, erected at the turn of the century, and next to that the chapel, with its white conical spire pointing up at the heavens like any New England small-town church.

Gavin had spent a hard morning going over a computer print-out containing figures produced in an experiment on chemo-reactions of T lymphocytes, and he had concluded that the experiment was ill-conceived and was not going to produce any useful results. This was going to upset the two young researchers who had devised it.

He pondered this for a while and then, standing by the window, he dismissed the matter and gave way to reflections. When he ignored the college buildings and looked at the lawn and the newly green trees in orderly rows, the scene brought memories of English country landscapes, and summer afternoons on country walks, and then of family holidays on the Mediterranean. Then misty thoughts of possible futures flitted through his mind uninvited and almost unacknowledged, of the children he and Martha would have one day and discoveries he would make. These thoughts were vague and he did not dwell on them. He did not day-dream often. The ringing of the tele- phone jolted him into the present, and he answered it.

"Hello, Gav. Ted Starowicz here. I've got something that might interest you. Do you have a few minutes?"

"I'm rather busy," he said automatically. "But I've got just a moment."

"You know what you were telling me the night before last, about cases of impotence on campus."

"Yes."

"I mentioned it to the L.I. editor. Half-jokingly. Just said it was something to watch."

"Uh-huh."

"I've just been given this. It came in this afternoon. A piece of A.P. copy. Listen, I'll read it to you. Are you listening?"

"Yes, I'm listening."

"It says, 'Twelve cases of sexual impotence with no obvious cause are reported in Providence, Rhode Island by two doctors in the city. In an article in the New England Journal of Medicine, the two doctors, who operate a joint practice, say that in every case testosterone levels were normal and there was no sign of any physical or psychological abnormality.

"'The two doctors, Daniel Freeman and Martin Chung, say they could find no other symptoms associated with the ailment and no features that the men had in common. They say the men ranged in age from nineteen to fifty-six, and included both manual and professional workers.' What do you think of that, hey?"

Gavin paused before answering. He did not think quickly and this item of news puzzled him. "I don't know. I just don't know what to say," he answered, finally.

"Well think of something. I've been told to go ahead and follow up what you told me and check to see if this is happening locally. I'm going to phone some local doctors, and I'd like a nice quote, please, from that distinguished medical scientist Gavin Grove of the Bliss Institute."

"But we're not into that kind of research here. We don't work with people. We work with cells and bits of cells."

"People call in from all over the world to get the view of Bliss Institute scientists, and it's right on the Chronicle's doorstep. That's where we turn to get an informed view."

"Call the Administration, Ted. They're the people to issue statements if anyone does."

"I don't have to. I've got an in. My personal friend Dr. Grove. I'll call you back after I've rung round some doctors. 'Bye."

Gavin was irritated by Ted's aggressiveness, not for the first time, and wondering what he should do when Izzy Rubin walked in to his office. He had come to tell him that he had looked over the figures Gavin had been working on in the morning and he agreed with his negative finding.

Israel Rubin was the head of the Immunology Division and therefor *ex officio* a member of the Executive Council of the Institute. He was a biochemist, small, and oval-shaped, with a bouncy, cheery manner that concealed a busy intelligence, like a teddy bear with an electric motor inside. He had a national reputation as a scientist and a penchant for jazzy clothes. He was the son of a physicist, the grandson of a department store owner, and great-grandson of an immigrant tailor from Poland. He was the only person Gavin had ever met called "Izzy." Gavin had reflected before that if someone in England were unfortunate enough to be named "Israel" he would not be happy to have his friends call him "Izzy."

As division head Izzy had the responsibility for terminating the T-lymphocite experiment. He told Gavin, "You're right. Since the melatin inhibits LH growth, we can't be sure that we're not just measuring melatin." Gavin nodded. "It's partly my fault for authorizing the experiment," Izzy went on, sitting down in the only other chair. "I should have seen this sooner. I don't know why I didn't."

"A post-doc looking for a credit can be pretty persuasive," said Gavin sympathetically.

Izzy said he would explain the finding to the two young men who created the experiment, congratulate them on the ingenuity and industry they had already shown because he did not want to discourage them, and start them on another line of work. He would also tell one of them that he was sending him to the Immunology Society conference in Miami later in the year.

Gavin told him about Ted's call. "A spate of sexual impotence? That sounds very odd," Izzy said.

"It does, doesn't it?" Gavin replied. "But I can't see that it's got much to do with us."

"Mmm. I'd like to know more," Izzy went on, ignoring what Gavin had just said.

"Presumably, we'll hear more if there's anything to it."

"Yes. We'll have to see what the urologists find."

"Exactly," said Gavin. "He wants me to come up with a comment now that the Chronicle can print. I'm not going to, of course."

"I think you should," said Izzy.

"Why? What can I say?"

"You should say something. The Institute's under a bit of pressure at the moment. The National Science Foundation has been leaned on not to push any work our way. We're not sufficiently all-American. Did you know that?"

"No."

"And some members of the Holycroft Board of Regents are saying it shouldn't be on the campus. Also because we don't fly the American flag."

"I gather some of them have been saying that since it started. Anyway, what's that got to do with it?"

"Come on Gavin, get wise. Any reminder to local people that it's nice to have us here would be all to the good. That they've got this powerhouse of brains in the neighborhood. Particularly if somebody thinks we might actually be some use."

"You mean like giving some men their balls back," Gavin suggested.

"If that needs doing they'll be interested, you can bet on that. Why not say something about how some of our work is relevant to any medical problem that might exist?"

"What work?"

"Use your imagination. Your own work on the autonomic nervous system. Ahmed's with hormones. Say you haven't looked at the question, but if there is a problem, then some of the work we're doing here on glands and the nervous system could have some bearing on the matter. That'll satisfy them."

Gavin hesitated. "Come on," Izzy urged him. "This is

no time for modesty. It's a good idea politically to get all the positive publicity we can now."

"I thought the Institute was supposed to be above politics."

"It is. And you've got to play clever politics to stay that way," said Izzy, grinning as he got up from his chair.

   ::   ::   ::

In the Chronicle newsroom, Ted Starowicz spent an hour-and-a-half telephoning g.p.s. in nearby communities. The first one he telephoned said, "Yes, as a matter of fact, two men have come to me complaining of it in the last week and have said anti-impotence pills have had no effect. Why, has anyone else reported the same thing?" Ted told him about the New England Journal of Medicine article.

The second said, "Now that you mention it, yes. I've had three cases that haven't responded in the first instance. I've referred them to the hospital for further tests. But look, I know what newspapers are like, particularly where it's anything to do with sex. I don't want you to make anything out of this."

Seven out of the eight reported cases of men saying they were impotent and were not responding to pills as they should. As the pattern built up Ted searched around in his mind for a possible cause of this outbreak in the area, or even for somewhere to look for one. At every point, he came up against the fact that it was not all that localized, that it was also happening, if it really was happening, in Providence, three hundred miles away.

He also remembered suddenly a conversation he had overheard a week earlier. It was at a diner around the corner from his apartment, where he was eating supper. Two young men sat in a booth across from him. They were both wearing open-neck shirts with t-shirts underneath, one wearing sneakers, the other loafers with thick athletic socks. One was leaning back in a posture of I-don't-give-a-shit cool with his legs stretched out into the aisle, the other was leaning forward over the table, his body tense.

The cool one said, "You're telling me, old buddy, that you got Linda Bolovsky up to your room and all you did was, like, show her photographs?" The other one said, "That's right, old buddy."

"But what got into you? I mean, didn't you even, make a move, you know?"

The other seemed to tense up even more. "I don't know what got into me. That's what I'm trying to tell you, old buddy. I don't want it any more. This is just between you and me, huh?"

Ted became aware that something new might be happening, some new disease, and he could be one of the first to find out about it. This could be a good story. He had gone into journalism hoping to be involved at some time in important things. His idea of what were important things had changed over the years.

Ted came from Jersey City, where his father was assistant manager of a furniture store and his mother pursued, doggedly but hopelessly, a dream of gracious living. She would try out recipes for chilled soups or colorful salads, which she would serve the family in summertime on their tiny patio on a table decorated with a spray of flowers. His father would not notice the finer points of the meal, talking over supper about the trouble he had from a customer who wanted to return a sofa bed that had had God knows what depravities wreaked upon it for a month. Ted's mother encouraged him to play tennis and discouraged bowling, and on a few occasions took him to classical concerts along with his sister Susan, two years older than him. Ted had played some tennis, but more importantly he had pitched for his high school baseball team, which pleased his father.

When he was seventeen his older sister Sue, who was at junior college, gave him some relief from parental ambitions by becoming pregnant. She had all their parents' attention and she enjoyed this. After prolonging the crisis for some time she married t baby's father, who went on to finish his accountancy studies and then moved with Sue to Houston.

His mother was delighted when Ted went to Rutgers, and still more so when one of his majors was French literature. He realized that she had a vague image of a world of sophisticated and stylish *belles lettristes,* a literary equivalent of Martha Stewart dinner parties. Actually, it was the post-World War Two French writers carelessly labelled "existentialist" who drew him to the subject, and in his post-graduate year at Columbia he wrote his master's thesis on Camus' plays. These writers appealed to him because of the way they wrote, sometimes harshly, about life on the edge, "the literature of extreme situations". Writing about the point of living, or sometimes the pointlessness, they stirred a feeling in him that life should be spiritually adventurous, that the conditions of life should not be accepted unquestioningly.

He knew by the time he got his master's degree that his attraction to the subject had little to do with scholarship, and also that he was not going to be a creative writer. Unlike some of his friends, he was not writing a novel. So he gave up the idea of an academic career and turned to journalism. One of its appeals was that it might be a way to observe at close hand some extreme situations, perhaps a war, watching other people on the edge, so to speak. Later this thought became entangled with the journalist's normal ambitions for big stories, big bylines and exclusives.

Now he saw that something was happening which could be strange and new and for the moment it was his story. He picked up the telephone to call Gavin again. He reflected that he might have been more tactful when he spoke to him before. His usual response to Gavin's British reserve was to blast his way through. But Gavin made no difficulty about giving him a quote. He even let Ted read it back to him:

"It's too soon to say anything concrete about the problem, or even that there is a problem. But if this is some new disease, the first approach to it would be to look for possible dysfunctions of the glands and the autonomic nervous system."

"Has this work being going on at the Bliss Institute?"

"Yes, we've published a number of papers in this area. As it happens, I myself have done work on the autonomic nervous system."

"Can you think of a possible cause, Dr. Grove?"

"No, it would be foolish to speculate this early. As I say, we're not even sure that there is a problem. I'm just saying that if there is, these would be the areas to look into."

Ted thanked him and rang off. He was excited now. "Right. A new disease wiping out men's libido could be a good story," he told himself. "If it's worldwide and it means that men can't reproduce and the human race is going to die out, that will be an even bigger story. Let's make sure I keep hold of it. If I don't watch out they'll hand it over to the science correspondent, Charlie Smith, who should have been put out to grass years ago, or the national desk. This is going to be my story!"

He squared his shoulders and marched across the newsroom to the office of the managing editor, Tom Manning, but he could see through the windows that it was empty. He turned to Manning's secretary. "He's with the publisher," she told him before he could ask her. "He said he'll be back by five o'clock. Can I help?"

"No thanks," he replied. "I'll come back."

He sat down to start writing the story, keeping one eye cocked at Manning's office. Ten minutes later, he was lecturing himself in his mind. "Steady. Just for once, don't storm in there arguing that you should have the story. Just for once, see it from the other person's point of view. Manning thinks you're a bit of a wild man. He doesn't assign you the big stories. If you go charging in there, it will reinforce his view. So be cool. You can't demand too much. This time, don't demand anything. Write the story, follow it up tomorrow, see how it develops. You're starting out in front. Be a Taoist for once, for God's sake. Let things happen." He often lectured himself, although he did not always listen to his advice. When he was alone, he sometimes talked to himself, softly but moving his lips.

He resolved now that he would not say anything to the Managing Editor but would just wait for him to react. "I won't go to see him. I'll write the story and let him send for me," he told himself. "I'll force myself to be patient. I'll chain myself to my fucking chair if I have to."

The Chronicle ran the story down a single column on the

front page. "Doctors Report an Increase in Impotence Cases," the headline said soberly.

Ted was sitting at his desk looking at the front page with satisfaction when Dan Meltzer, an editor in the features section, came over with his usual bouncy, nervy walk and the grin he often carried on his face. "That's quite a story you've got there," he said. "I think we should do a survey in the office, find out if anyone here is affected."

"Really?" Ted said dryly.

"Yes. It ties in with an idea for a story I've had for some time."

"What's that?"

"The influence of occupation on sex life. Start with the media, because that's where we are. See whether there's significance in the sexual predilections of particular jobs. Radio reporters and oral sex. Editorial writers and masturbation. Copy editors and – "

"Tell you what," Ted said, because he found his company tiring, "why don't you do just what you said. Go around the office asking people whether their dick is working."

"Maybe I will," David said, and Ted had a horrible idea that he might.

"Don't," Ted said. "I was only kidding. Look, Dan, you're one of the cleverest guys on this paper, as you keep telling everyone, but you can be an ass-hole. If you go around asking people about their sex lives, you'll be an unpopular ass-hole."

Dan was irrepressibly talkative and often embarrassing. He could be funny until people got fed up and sent him away. He never knew when to stop. Another staff member had been present when Meltzer had run into Tom Manning and his wife in a downtown drugstore. Meltzer had wandered over to the counter where condoms were on display and then called across the store, "What flavor did you say you like, Mrs. Manning?" Manning was not amused. Nobody ever said Dan Meltzer was careerist.

The wire services carried the story about impotence cases in Long Island and got on to regional bureaus to follow it up. The result was astounding. Many doctors all over the country reported cases of sexual impotence that were not responding to the usual medication. The most cases were found in the New York-New England area. The indications were that the disease had started in the Northeast and was already spreading across the country.

The new disease left men with no sexual impulse but unimpaired in every other way. Their testosterone level, normally the measure of sexual potency, was normal. Even their sperm count was normal.

Television and radio reporters talked in those first days about the new virus that beats the pills, suggesting that the clever viruses have built up resistance to the anti-impotence pill. Medical writers rushed in to point out that a new virus and Viagra and its cousins had nothing to do with one another, that these pills did not block the effect of a virus. But some commentators still said that was needed was a new super-Viagra.

Medical men said they could not understand why this was happening if testosterone levels were normal. They explained the problem on television and in the newspapers, with diagrams and pictures. Editors agonized over those diagrams and pictures. The pictures were usually of internal organs rather than external, the diagrams fuzzy in the outlines but nevertheless they tested the limits of what can be shown in a family newspaper.

Gavin's statement was repeated and since he was the first medical man to be quoted on the subject, newspapers and television and radio stations called him over the next few days. He refused most TV and radio requests but, remembering what Izzy had said, he did go on two local TV stations and trotted out again his comments on his work on the autonomic nervous system and the functioning of the sexual organs.

As soon as the disease was identified, it was found to be on the increase. Every day brought more and more cases. By the end of the first month the spread of impotence was an established fact and the Sunday newspapers speculated on the number of men affected. The best guess was that it might be ten to fifteen percent of the adult male population. They all reported, not merely an inability to perform, but a lack of any sexual desire. There were no reports of an equivalent affliction among women.

The news came as a shock to Americans, a unique shock, more than the assassination of a President or the start of a war. It was not some public drama on the world stage but something that had grown up among them, a part of the private lives of individuals. When they saw the news on their television screens, or read it in the newspapers - and once this story had broken it dominated the news media - they were hearing and reading about themselves. Every man, every couple, felt threatened. The sense of shock mounted. First there was the presence of an entirely new disease, then it was spreading, then, suddenly, it was an epidemic.

Some writers suggested that the trouble was psychological and speculated on the cause: the changing roles of men and women in society, the alleged feminization of America, or perhaps the changing role of America in the world. Commentators pointed to social trends that were already tending to make men economically and socially redundant. Psychologists talked and wrote about the transmission of anxiety states, but others said no psychological dysfunction could spread this rapidly. Some European commentators suggested that it was mass hysteria, to which, they suggested, Americans were prone.

Ted did the follow-up stories in the Chronicle. He called Gavin and asked him whether people at the Bliss Institute had any special thoughts on the subject. He caught him in a benevolent mood and Gavin invited him to join a few members of the Institute for a drink after work on Friday at the Holycroft Faculty Club to hear what they had to say. People at the Institute were honorary members.

He asked Denise Springer, a Canadian biochemist, to come along, and she cavilled at first at spending time talking to a newspaperman. "I can't be bothered," she told Gavin. "When I read in the newspapers about some new miracle cure I usually find either that it's wildly exaggerated or it's something every g.p. has known about for the last ten years." Denise was slender and stringy, with a strong jaw and an acerbic manner; she reminded Gavin of the young Katherine Hepburn. He pointed out to her that the one newspaperman would be outnumbered by scientists she respected and she agreed to come.

Although a few women were members of the faculty club its furnishings were masculine. Like most such clubs, it aimed at an atmosphere of exclusiveness and luxury that flattered the members. There was a leather-fronted bar, but the men from the Bliss Institute sat in leather armchairs around a heavy oak table in a corner of the lounge. They were discussing over drinks what was overwhelmingly the number one subject of conversation in America that weekend.

They went over key questions: Was there any pattern among those afflicted? Was race or climate a factor? Was it on the increase? Did it affect the blood vessels and nervous system? Would it eventually have an effect on the testes?

"That's the most important question, the testes," Izzy remarked. "If it does affect them, then men will become sterile, and then we're going to see a sharp fall in the birth rate." The others nodded. "On the other hand," he went on, "it may not be as bad as we think."

The others looked at him inquiringly. Someone said, "But there are a lot of cases."

"But very few that have had the full examination so far," Izzy said. "There are bound to be more cases of impotence reported now anyway. A lot of guys will have thought, 'Well, maybe I'm a little tense, things are tough at work, the wife and I aren't getting on too well at the moment, it'll pass.' Or more likely, they just don't think about it for a while. Then they read these stories in the paper and think, 'God, maybe I've caught this illness, whatever it is.' And they rush to the doctor."

Lee Hsiu, a tall, skinny microbiologist from Taiwan, said, "Single men will report their impotence before married men. The ones with active sex lives, anyway. They're likely to be aware of it first. For a single man, assuming he doesn't live with his girl friend, going to bed with a woman is normally synonymous with having sexual intercourse with her. This is not true of the married man."

Ted took up the point. "Sure, that's right. If a bachelor goes to bed with a girl it's because he's going to bang her. The married man goes to bed with his wife every night anyway. That's where he lives." Gavin went cold and did not hear the next couple of comments.

"Meanwhile," said Izzy, "the newspapers are already coming up with some wild explanations."

"You expect that of newspapers," said Denise. "On the other hand, what's wild? If this thing is happening, do we have any sensible hypothesis even? Something like this that has no other effects? Can you really be sure it's not something that some terrorist has squirted into the air to make Americans impotent? Or some kind of radiation that affects the brain? Or something from outer space?"

"Anyway, one thing's sure," said Izzy. "If this is happening, giving ten million American men their sex drive back is going to be the top priority for American medical science."

The next week endocrinologists at Johns Hopkins Medical School located the problem and answered the question that had puzzled medical scientists: how was it that the testosterone levels were normal? The testosterone receptors, that are found in the body cells and that normally inter- act with the testosterone to allow it to function, were not working.. The testosterone were there but were rendered ineffective. This also explained why the sperm count in the men affected was normal.

Once again scientists were hurried before TV cameras,

this time to explain testosterone receptors and to speculate on a virus that might have affected them. Once again Gavin went on the local TV and radio stations and took calls for newspapers.

Some of what the scientists said was alarming. They pointed out that the testosterone governs, not only the male libido, but secondary sexual characteristics as well. In time, men would see a waning of these. The physical characteristics that distinguish men from women, such as a deeper voice, facial hair and firmer muscle tissue, would diminish. Not much was said about this in the media at first. The idea that a large number of American men might become sexually impotent was difficult enough to take in, without contemplating the prospect of them all being smooth-cheeked effeminates with treble voices.

Over the next few weeks, all the indications were that the disease was spreading rapidly. Newspapers would report the spread of the affliction with a headline giving simply a percentage: "Now It's 30 Percent." Nobody needed to ask what the figure referred to. Newspapers would make their own guesses about regional percentages. "One-Third In Colorado" was the headline in the Denver Post. "40% In The Country, 30% In Florida," headlined the Miami Herald, evidently determined to find some good news. But it was difficult to get an accurate figure. Because impotence is a negative condition, it is not always easy to recognize.

Bob Black, on another drive back from the campus, told Gavin, "They're coming in to my office all the time now. There's one man, eighty-one years old, who told me he's experienced a loss of sexual desire. That was the way he put it. He's single. Divorced. I asked him when he last had intercourse and he said fifteen years ago. But he wagged his finger in my face and said, 'But I think about it a lot and I could still do it until last week.' At Holycroft boys have come to me who are virgins and are worried because suddenly, they're no longer sexually frustrated. I don't know what the hell to tell them."

A month after the first reports, an extraordinary picture was emerging. Evidently, the condition had been spreading before it was noticed, but even taking this into account the increase was remarkably rapid. Based on extrapolations from reported cases, it was estimated that between 40 and 50 percent of the male population of the United States was now sexually impotent. The number appeared to be increasing. No disease had ever been known to spread this rapidly before.

Wild speculation abounded. Mostly, people sought human agencies to blame. A favorite one was that this was germ warfare, a cunning terrorist attack on America. Others included additives to the food, radioactivity, a recombinant dna experiment that had gone wrong, the Aids vaccine. There were sensible reasons for ruling out most of these. Any additive in food or water would have been acting on the body for years and it would not have had affected so many people suddenly in such a short space of time. This applied also to radioactivity. As for the Aids vaccine, a few people had not been vaccinated and it was already established that some of these were impotent.

Morley Bliss, although weakened by a recent stroke, made himself available to the media. His thin, erect figure and his shock of white hair became familiar to TV viewers. He said the testosterones still created sperm but not sexual activity, so the sperm could only be extracted from the male and inserted into a female egg by artificial insemination. "The seeds of future generations are there," he concluded. "However much this spreads, the American nation won't die out. It just won't have so much fun."

Other countries looked to see whether they also were experiencing similar phenomenon. There was an increase in Canada that paralleled that in America. There was some in Mexico, although this was difficult to gauge because of poor medical reporting and cultural taboos. There was no sign that the disease had taken root in countries outside North America.

Those affected commercially were among the first to react. The prostitutes' pressure group HART, Hookers Amalgamated for the Right to Trade, appealed through the Press to American science, calling on it to give top priority to finding a cure. Porno movie theaters reported a drastic falling-off of business.

A planned goodwill visit by three Italian Navy ships to New York and other East coast ports was cancelled. No reason was given, but a wise man at the American Embassy in Rome suggested that goodwill was not likely to result. He pointed to the likely reaction of longshoremen and American seamen in their present condition if they saw concupiscent Italian sailors swarming ashore to engage in the pursuits that sailors traditionally engage in, and extending to American women the invitations that Italian men traditionally extend to women.

Although every aspect of sexuality is usually a constant subject for humor, there were few jokes about this. This was not something that was happening only to other people, or at any rate that anyone could be sure would happen only to other people. The deprivation was too central to men's sense of their identity and women's of their needs to make jokes about it.

The publicity made it easier for men to talk about it, and admit to it. Quite soon men were saying freely, and even casually, "Well, I've got it. Have you?" Or, as time went on and it continued to spread, "Have you got it yet?" The fact that the affliction was a shared one made it easier for men to bear it. It was not only a private deprivation which each individual had to suffer alone. It was also a national problem, therefor, the feeling was, it would have a national remedy. Somebody would do something.

Some congressmen and commentators said the President should address the nation on the subject and treat the matter as a national crisis and criticized him for his inaction. Yet it was difficult to imagine President Masterson, with his heavy, jowly features and serious demeanor, going on television to talk to the American public about sex.

One leading political columnist usually hostile to the Administration sympathized with the President in his failure to give a lead. "This hesitation in speaking out does not reflect any shortcoming on the part of Mr. Masterson," he wrote. "The sudden emergence of this most intimate aspect of individuals' lives as a major public issue is

unpre- unprecedented. Even after the extraordinary airing of intimate matters during the Clinton presidency, this is not an area that the White House can easily address. The greatest of our national leaders would also have difficulty dealing with it. Who can envisage George Washington, or Thomas Jefferson, or Abraham Lincoln, addressing the American people on the difficulty of getting an erection?"

Eventually, the President took note of the seriousness of the situation in a statement issued by the White House. The statement said that a medical problem was now so widespread that it had become a national issue. It did not spell out the nature of the problem, nor did it use any words like "crisis" or "emergency." It said the problem required the co-ordinated scientific resources of the nation to tackle it. It announced the establishment of a Presidential Commission to co-ordinate these resources, and said this commission would appoint a committee of scientists to lead the scientific work.

CHAPTER THREE

A reporter from the Chronicle telephoned Gavin Grove at nine o'clock the next morning, Saturday, when he and Martha were eating breakfast, both in their pajamas. The reporter asked him whether he would comment on the White House statement.

"This is getting ridiculous," he said. "I don't have anything of consequence to say about it."

"Would you serve on the Presidential commission if you were asked?" the reporter asked him.

"I don't expect to be," he replied. "Why don't you talk to Morley Bliss? That's a little more likely. Ask him."

He went back to the breakfast table and told Martha who the caller was. "You're getting to be their tame pundit," she said.

"Bloody silly," he muttered, finishing his coffee.

Bob Black and his wife Barbara were also having breakfast in their pajamas. Bob had just been on the telephone reassuring an over-anxious mother about her son's 'flu, and he returned to his granola. Their daughter Debbie, a high school senior, came down to the kitchen.

"You're up early for a Saturday," Barbara remarked.

"I couldn't sleep longer," Debbie explained. She poured herself a cup of coffee from the percolator and sat down at the table. "I've been thinking," she said. "I'd like to ask Karen and maybe a couple of other girls to come over this evening. Just to talk, and maybe watch a video. Is that okay with you guys?"

"Sure," Bob said. "Is Jimmy away then?"

"I'm not seeing Jimmy this evening," Debbie said casually, sipping her coffee.

Barbara shot Bob a cautioning glance across the table but it was too late. "Any special reason?" Bob asked.

"Oh, he just said our Saturday evenings were getting to be too much of a habit," Debbie said lightly. She picked up a section of the newspaper and started to read it. Then she burst into tears and ran out of the room.

Israel Rubin and his wife were also in their pajamas, sitting up in bed with breakfast trays. Sarah Rubin taught a full schedule of courses in American history at Holycroft and took care of the house and children with only part-time help, so on Saturday mornings Israel brought her breakfast in bed. When he joined her in bed he was silent, and stared at the wallpaper for several minutes while she munched a croissant.

She turned and said, "What are you thinking about?"

"Huh? Oh. Just approaches to the impotence problem."

"And?"

"Damned if I know. Find out where things go wrong. We've got to do that first. Then see what we can do about it."

"Think of something, please," she said. "There haven't been any stains on Mike's sheets lately."

"I want Mike to have a happy life too," he said.

"I want grandchildren," she said.

Ted Starowicz and Elaine were in Ted's apartment, and they were also in bed. They were not wearing pajamas.

She was saying, "Ted, *again?*"

He said, "Honey, we'd better make hay while the sun's still shining."

At lunchtime they went from the bedroom into the living room and turned on the television to see the news. Before the news, they found themselves watching with awed fascination an evangelist who had recently acquired a weekly spot on a number of TV stations. He spoke quietly, but in a tone that was sombre even for him.

"When God's message comes, it's clear. You don't have to be clever, to be a scholar, to understand what He means. Because he doesn't talk only to intellectuals. He talks to ordinary men and women. For years now, we've been hearing that God didn't really mean exactly what he seemed to mean. Clever folk have been telling us that we should use our bodies any way we wanted for pleasure. Enjoy yourselves, God wants you to be happy, that's what they told us. Fornication isn't a sin. Oh no. That's an old-fashioned idea of what religion is all about. God didn't really mean that you shouldn't covet your neighbor's wife. Only simple folk think He meant exactly what he said. The Bible didn't really mean that sexual perversion was an abomination. That's only a narrow, literal interpretation. That's what we were told."

The preacher's voice rose. Evidently, what had gone before was a prelude, and now he poured drama into his tones. "Well now God has made His message plain! For those who wouldn't understand before. Do they understand *now*? Has there ever been a time in the history of the *world* when God spoke more clearly than this? Are we all going to get down on your knees and beg forgiveness for our loose living and our sins and our perversions? Beg forgiveness and promise that if He gives us back the precious gift of sexual reproduction, that this time we'll use it as he intended and obey his commandments?"

The news program concentrated on reactions to the White House statement. Leading figures in the medical and scientific worlds welcomed it, and so did congressional leaders. The medical and scientific people talked about sexual impotence. The senators and congressmen talked about "the medical problem" and "this thing that's afflicted so many Americans."

After the main news, a reporter for the local station interviewed Joe Barreras and asked his reaction, as the new owner of Biotek Inc. Barreras said he welcomed the setting up of a national commission, and promised his full support.

He was a lithe, slender man in his early fifties. His face was angular: a pointed chin and high cheekbones formed a triangle. He had dark eyes that darted with interest when he was engaged in an exchange and black eyebrows, and curved eyelashes that many women would envy. His hair was greying at the temple and he wore rimless glasses. He was dressed with elegant casualness, in a tan blazer and a bolo tie that identified him as a Westerner. He spoke with confidence, but also with a touch of modesty, with no captain-of-industry self-importance.

"As you know, I'm new to Biotek Inc.," he said. "Not entirely new to research in this area, but new to Biotek. That's going to be our top priority, beating this thing. Our top, top priority. I'm going to be spending a lot of time in Walton." He spoke softly, emphasizing his words with occasional gestures with his hands.

"Do you know in which area you'll be concentrating your search for a cure?"

"I'm not a scientist. We've got a team of very good scientists at Biotek. We're going to add to it to make it even better. I want us to be world leaders. My role is simply to spell out for the team the objectives, give them the right spirit - not that that's a problem - and see that they have everything they need."

"You certainly took over Biotek at an interesting time, Mr. Barreras," the interviewer said.

"Oh yes, didn't I just?" Now Barreras leaned forward with enthusiasm. "You know, this is a terrible thing that's happening, God knows. But as it is happening, I'm glad I just turned out to be in a key position to tackle it, to do this thing for America. Can you imagine a more exciting challenge? What was it that the British poet Rupert Brooke wrote when the First World War broke out? 'Thank God for He has matched us with this hour.'. That's how I feel. I'm glad God has matched me to this hour."

Ted turned to Elaine and remarked, "That son-of-a-bitch might do it. He usually does what he sets out to do."

"If he does do it he'll be the most popular man in America," said Elaine. "He could be President of the United States if he wanted to be."

Ted shook his head. "Not his style. The President is constrained by the Constitution. Jose Barreras likes to make his own rules."

"Why do you call him 'Jose' when everyone else calls him 'Joe'?" Elaine asked. "It sounds racist."

He thought for a moment and then said, "I don't know. I

suppose 'Joe' sounds too friendly."

The following Tuesday at the Bliss Institute, Morley Bliss himself turned up for the weekly meeting of the Executive Council. Although he was still director he had rarely come to these since his stroke and he did not come into his office every day.

Now he was in the chair when the others arrived, still tall, slender as a reed, blue veins ridging his bony hands, a lock of his white thick hair hanging down over his forehead. The others had not been permitted to see him walking in arduously, leaning on his cane. His secretary sat beside him. The others waited expectantly for him to speak.

"Good morning, ladies and gentlemen," he began, his voice thin but firm, his vowels broad and Bostonian. "I know there's an agenda for today's meeting, and we'll get to it eventually. But I think myself that we might make the first item the extraordinary spread of sexual dysfunction, and whether we should try to contribute to finding the cause and a possible cure."

"Of course we should," said Izzy. "There's a need. We have the facilities to tackle the problem. Surely no one here is going to disagree with that?"

"There is room for discussion about the priority to be given it," said Monika Van Doorn, the Dutch microbiologist. "My department for one is stretched to the limit."

Jim Eisgrau, a burly Afro-American who was head of the Genetics Division, almost exploded: "For God's sake, this is an extraordinary emergency! We don't know what it's going to do to this country. And it's not only this country. How can we call ourselves a medical research outfit and not throw everything we've got into this? Every other institute in the country is going to go all-out to tackle this thing. The President has called for a national effort."

"I don't think we should let that influence us," said the Assistant Director, John Visconti. "We're not here to compete with other institutions, and we're not here to answer Presidential calls." Visconti, the only non-scientist on the Executive Committee, regarded himself as the guardian of the Bliss Institute's purity.

Morley Bliss chimed in: "I respect what John has just said. But considering the President's age, I don't think he's so desperate that he's asking for help only with a personal difficulty." The others chuckled.

"In medicine," he went on, "there's no sharp distinction between the theory and its application, between fundamental and applied science. This goes back to first principles." The others settled back. Morley Bliss liked going back to first principles and was clearly going to talk for a while. It was clear from his tones that he leaned in favor of tackling the impotence problem although he drew back instinctively from joining the ranks marching behind the commander-in-chief. It was clear also that he was stimulated by the problem, and he took the lead in suggesting lines of research.

After some more discussion, the council decided that they would give the subject high priority and department heads would work out a coordinated research plan. Some other projects would have to be shelved. They also agreed that the Institute would be represented on the President's commission if it was invited.

During the next few days, the question of whether other countries were afflicted was aired constantly. There was no doubt about Canada and Mexico, although the degree of spread in Mexico was not clear. In several countries there were some reports that the affliction had affected people, but expert commentators said that considering the anxiety attached to this subject, these reports could not be confirmed. However, they said that because of the amount and rapidity of international travel it was likely that the disease would spread beyond North America if it had not yet done so.

The World Health Organization in Geneva declared that this was potentially a global crisis and said it would set up a committee for co-operation in tackling the problem. The U.S. Government immediately promised full participation.

One afternoon, Mohsin Ahmed walked into Gavin's office. Like most of the offices in the Institute, his was small, with a desk, a chair, bookshelves and just enough room for one more chair. Mohsin dropped into the spare chair without waiting for an invitation. The two men had worked together and had exchanged visits in the evening with their wives.

Mohsin, generally known as Mo, was a cheery, excitable, Pakistani with jet black hair, a handsome moon face and a bounding enthusiasm for whatever he was involved in. Gavin thought it was probably this quality that made him attractive to women. He had spent most of his youth in the United States because his father was a United Nations official, and had returned as a graduate student and took a PhD at Cornell. Gavin gathered that when he was at Cornell he had a cut a swathe through female students and some of the faculty as well. It surprised everyone when he brought back a bride from a visit home to Pakistan, a young and pretty Pakistani graduate student who adored him and ruled their home with a firm hand. He had just returned from a visit home for his brother's wedding.

"How are things back home?" Gavin asked him.

"They're all talking about what's happening here," Mohsin said.

"Are they worried that it'll spread over there?"

"Worried? They're terrified."

"Really?".

"Some people are laughing at America but it's a very nervous laugh. You know, I met my maths teacher from high school on the street. He must be at least a hundred years old. He stopped me and grasped my sleeve tight and asked me whether as a scientist I thought this thing would spread to Asia and whether a cure would be found before it did. The man sounded desperate! It was as if his wife, who also must be a hundred, was going to kill him if she didn't get laid regularly. My mother didn't want me to come back to America in case I can't give her grandchildren."

"But you came back anyway."

"It's too late. I've got it. I couldn't bear to tell my mother. I've never in my life discussed sex with my mother."

"I'm sorry," Gavin said.

"Yes, I've become an honorary American. And how about you, eh? Are you an honorary American also? How's your love life?"

Gavin was often put out by Mohsin's directness. "Pretty quiet on that front," he said, because he could not think of a way to avoid the question..

"Pretty quiet on that front, eh? That's a very British way of putting it. All quiet on the Western front. Me too. I gather we're being mobilized here to tackle the great American problem."

"I don't think Morley would accept the term, but that's pretty much the size of it. Got any ideas?"

"A bacteria," Mohsin suggested. "A virus. A totally new chemical reaction."

"A virus couldn't possibly spread that quickly," Gavin objected.

"And it can't be bacteria because bacteria couldn't affect this function and no other. And it can't be a chemical effect because no chemical effect could be universal. You can prove that it's impossible. Then where are you? It's happened."

"That's true. We can't rule anything out," Gavin admitted.

Mohsin went back to his own office. Gavin knew he would be thinking about how to tackle the problem. Mohsin was the most ingenious and doggedly persistent experimentalist that Gavin had ever known. He had once spent twenty-four hours without a break at a laboratory bench supervising an experiment with viral proteins. Then he decided that the experiment had failed because of a .01 percent impurity in one of the chemicals used, so he synthesized some himself and spent another twenty-four hours watching over the same experiment. The second time it worked.

A week later, on a Friday, several scientists from the Institute sat around an oak table again in a corner of the Holycroft Faculty Club in the early evening. Now the nature of the disease was known and a program of exploratory research had been worked out.

"Monika's still holding out against turning her lab over

to it," said one.

"Maybe we should have a talk with her husband," said Jim Eisgrau.

"That's enough of that. I like Monika even though she can be a stubborn Dutch mule," said Denise Skinner.

"I don't altogether blame her," said Lee Hsiu. "I've waited for weeks to use the Tricarb 5000."

"National emergency," said someone else. "Do we know what the latest figures are?"

Gavin had brought Ted Starowicz along again, and Ted spoke up now: "A.P. estimates the latest score at 90 percent in America. U.P.I. says it could be 95 percent."

"By the way," said Denise, "I had a call from Biotek today."

Everyone looked at her. "Oh really? Saying what?" Izzy Rubin asked.

"Just would I like to come and look around their laboratories."

"Sounds like a job offer coming up."

"I told them right away I wasn't interested. But I bet they'll float a few more of those invitations around now that Barreras has taken over. He's set himself this big task now of solving the impotence problem. He'll want to expand his staff."

"There'd probably be more loot there," someone said.

"I'll go on working for the good of humanity and the greater glory of Bliss," said Denise.

"It's not just Biotek," said Izzy. "Every big pharmaceutical company will be buying up all the brains they can. Christ, think what it would mean to a company to have the cure for this thing."

"I've had an offer from Kingsland Chemicals," said Jim Eisgrau quietly. They looked at him and he shook his head. "Not for a moment," he said.

Then they talked about the disease, and Ted Starowicz who was sitting next to Gavin, asked him in a low voice: "Do you think you could take time out and explain some of this to me some time? I'd like to have an idea of what's going on. The biology of sex for eighth graders, something like that."

"I'll try to give you a crash course," said Gavin. "How about this evening? If you're not doing anything for supper come back with me. We'll find something for you to eat. We can talk about it afterwards."

The meeting broke up soon after that and they drove to Gavin's house. Gavin had not had a chance to telephone Martha in advance but Martha was easy-going and he knew she would not worry about an unexpected visitor. She had made stuffed fish for two and they had a brief discussion about which of them would have the ready meal she took from the freezer.

Then Gavin poured them all drinks and they sat down in the living room and he told Martha a little about the faculty club discussion.

"It occurs to me," she said, "that biologists and people like you are the most important people in the country now. In the world. Everybody's watching to see what you come up with."

"The man who discovers the cure is going to be man of the year," Ted agreed. "The man of the century. He'll be providing what all men want most now."

Martha went into the kitchen to prepare dinner. "It won't be long," she said. "Don't start about what's gone wrong with the male sex drive until I get there."

"I've explained it to you already," he called out to her.

"Yes, but I'm not sure I understand it all. I want to hear it again."

Gavin began when they all started eating. "The sexual reproduction system," he said, "starts in the brain, with the pituitary gland, where I've spent a good deal of my professional life. This gives the orders."

"You mean like telling you to get an erection," Ted said. "'Get it up!' like."

"Well, yes. But there's a chain of command. In the normal system, the pituitary gland orders the nervous system to produce gonadotrophin, which are hormones. The gonadotrophin produce testosterones, and testes, and these produce sperm. You know about sperm, I take it."

"I think I know what they are," Ted acknowledged.

"Well this system has broken down," Gavin said.

"So the people who say we need a super-Viagra have got it wrong," Ted said.

"Completely wrong. Viagra and Cialis and all those are irrelevant. They ensure that when the sexual stimulus is there, blood flows into the penis to create an erection. That isn't where the trouble is."

"You mean the system isn't producing the gonad-whatsits," said Ted, who had his notebook out now. "And how do you spell that, by the way?"

Gavin spelled it for him and then went on, "No, it is producing them. The break is further down the road. The gonadotrophin are there. And they're producing testosterones. If there weren't enough testosterones the cure would be easy. You could simply give people more, by injections. But testosterones, like other hormones, work by interaction with cells. The cells have receptors which take them up, let them do their stuff. The cell's testosterone receptors aren't working.. So the testosterones are dud. That's why men don't feel anything."

"Is it too soon to ask why the cell receptors aren't working?" asked Ted.

"Yes it is. There are several possible explanations, all equally implausible."

"Could it be a virus?"

"Could be, although it would be a virus such as no one has ever imagined before. For one thing, no virus has ever spread that rapidly."

"Are you looking for a virus?"

"Like crazy."

"How do you look? With microscopes?"

"Not ordinary microscopes. A virus is too small to see. You use an electron microscope. It bombards it with electrons and you can pick out the outline. We're looking in blood samples."

"Why blood samples?"

"If it's a virus it'll go right through the bloodstream, even though only the testosterones are affected. You'll even find it in the saliva. But we're looking for other things as well."

Martha chimed in. "Do you think it could have been a piece of genetic engineering that went wrong? That's what's been suggested."

"I honestly can't see how."

"Or even a terrorist plot?"

"They'd have to be bloody clever terrorists, who can do things with biotechnology that nobody else has done."

"Has anyone ever tried?" asked Ted.

"That's a good point. Probably not," Gavin said. "All the same, it would seem to require an extraordinary ability to manipulate at the micro level."

"But it's so new," insisted Martha. "So different from anything that's ever been before. I don't see how you can have something that different happening naturally."

"Remember Aids?" said Gavin. "That was certainly different. Before it came, most people would have said that was impossible. 'A virus that attacks the whole immune system? That's ridiculous. Couldn't be.' So no, I'm not sure it isn't caused deliberately, by some bunch of people somewhere who've worked on this for years. I'm not sure of anything and neither is anyone else."

"I thought men weren't sterile, that they could still produce babies," Ted said. "How can that be if the testosterones won't work? Aren't they the things that produce sperm?"

Gavin said, "They have some sperm but - would you rather I waited until we've finished eating?"

"You can go ahead so far as I'm concerned," Martha said stoutly.

"They have some testosterones which make some sperm," Gavin continued, but not enough for normal sexual intercourse. You can get some out and inject it into a woman by artificial insemi-nation."

"How would you get them out?" Ted asked.

"With a hypodermic needle."

"You mean sticking the needle right in the, er - "

"Yes."

"Ouch!"

"It wouldn't be too bad, with a local anesthetic. It's nothing to what women go through to produce babies."

When Martha had served dessert, Ted said, "Tell me, Martha, is this thing affecting your work at the counseling center? Do you get women with problems because of this?"

"Too soon to tell. Of course this situation will affect women in all sorts of ways. Occasionally sex is the answer to a problem. but not very often. The woman I was with this afternoon, my last client, it may actually help her."

"How's that?"

"Well perhaps not, really. What I was thinking of is, she doesn't get enough sex anyway. Well, any woman can get enough sex if she isn't particular. She doesn't get enough attention from men. I think it may be easier for her if everyone else is in the same position."

"Why doesn't she get enough attention?" asked Gavin.

"Because men are stupid. They think she's not attractive. Well, I suppose she doesn't have conventional good looks. She's rather plump and - well, dumpy. Though she says now she's going to diet. That will help. And she has to wear thick glasses because she's short-sighted. But she's got some very pretty features, and a lovely smile. And she's a really nice person. She's warm and caring and witty, and has some good women friends."

"And not being attractive is a big thing in her life, I suppose."

"Oh God, it's knocked her self-esteem to hell. In high school, she didn't have a date for the senior prom. She never got over that. Men are so damned stupid!" Martha said again with feeling.

"And worse. She has men friends. They turn to her when they're in trouble. She's said that. That's what gets me. Some even tell her their troubles with other women. She's befriended several men. They're pals. A couple have been friendly enough to go to bed with her, for a short time. But when they want someone to take to a party or to take out, they go for someone who's conventionally good-looking . And she feels betrayed. It makes me mad."

"Martha often comes back from her counselling angry at men," Gavin told Ted.

The next day, Gavin went into his office and found a memo from the Executive Director asking him to become a member of the Presidential Commission's Scientific Committee, representing the Bliss Institute. He marched into Israel Rubin's office carrying the memo in his hand. "Izzy, do you know about this?" he asked.

"Yes," replied Izzy, turning in his swivel chair to face him.

"What do you think? Isn't it a crazy idea?"

"I don't see why. They want two people from Bliss. I'm also going to be on the committee."

"Putting you on makes sense. Putting me on it doesn't. What about Morley?"

"He's ruled out for health reasons. And he really is. You've been quoted in the Press quite a lot. Your name has become known."

"But that's just media stuff, for Pete's sake. Nobody takes that seriously. I don't have the sort of position you have. I'm not even a division head here," Gavin insisted. He was still standing and was suddenly aware that he was looming over

Izzy so he sat down.

"Okay, so you don't like administration. You don't like bossing people around. Your work is known outside this place. Don't sell yourself short."

"I don't want the appointment."

"Why?" Izzy demanded.

"It means jumping over the heads of a lot of other people here, and upsetting people. Somebody else could do it better."

"Come on, Gavin," Izzy said, getting to his feet now. "It's not a big promotion. Most people won't mind and if anyone does he's a jerk. Think about it before you reach a decision."

Gavin was genuinely troubled by the idea. He was not falsely modest. He thought he was a good scientist with some achievements that were creditable. But these achievements were beyond dispute. He did not have to argue for them. He had never liked argument and drew back from situations that would expose him to criticism. He was worried now about being appointed to a high-profile position because of the accident of his being quoted widely in the Press rather than indisputable merit. He had no enemies in the Institute and he did not want to make any.

He told Martha about it over supper, explaining some of his anxieties. She assumed at first that he was going to accept it anyway and wanted her to nudge him into it after a display of reluctance. So far as she was concerned, this was a wifely duty and she was ready to go along with it. But when she told him he should accept and he argued, she sensed that his arguments were genuine and he really would turn it down. Now she knew she would have to push him.

They took it up again in bed that night as they lay side by side, both holding books because they liked to read in bed. She listened as he explained his feeling that no one really wanted him to serve on the committee, that he felt he was being asked to do so only because he was now known in the Press. She thought that being on the committee would make him better known and could mean advancement but she was not going to put the case to him in these terms.

"Look, the Institute wouldn't have put your name forward if they didn't think you would be good on the committee," she said. "It would make them look foolish."

"Maybe," he replied, doubtfully. "But whatever they think, I'm not sure I belong on the committee."

"Morley Bliss must have gone along with the idea," she said. "Perhaps he even originated it. It would be a bit of a slap in the face for him if you turned it down." She sensed that he was weakening.

"I don't think it was his idea."

"He certainly accepted it. Nobody forced it on him. Come on, you shouldn't fight with them."

He was silent for some time, and then he said, "Okay. I guess I'll have to be a committee man."

"Good. You're doing the right thing," she told him.

She put her arms around him and kissed him, on the cheek and on the mouth. He kissed her back. She turned off the light.

Then she pulled back a fraction and did what she had decided earlier in the day that she would do. She took his hand and moved it over her body. He knew what she wanted. He rubbed his cheek all over her body, kissing as he went, giving her love with the kisses. He kissed and licked her nipples until they hardened, and then slid down to kiss her belly. Then he kissed the inside of her thighs, rubbing his cheek on the place between them with its tuft of hair. She murmured gratefully, breathing harder.

He lifted his head away and started to rub her there gently, his hand following a familiar path until it came to rest.

"Yes," she said. "Like that. That feels good."

He stroked with the tip of his finger, and as the little thing became damp and erect she gasped and said, "Ah, good, good! You're so clever! Ah!" He could always get her going that way. Then there were no more words, just her hard breathing and then whimpering, the sounds he knew and enjoyed hearing.

Her body felt contented and tired. She knew he enjoyed pleasing her, as she enjoyed pleasing him. But she found it difficult to take in that during all her bodily excitement he felt nothing at all. This was distant. It was not a sharing. It was as if he had sent her a present in the mail.

Martha wanted a sharing. She had always needed some kind of a relationship in order to enjoy sex, or even to endure it. She had discussed this occasionally with woman friends who would go to bed with a man on very short acquaintance if they were attracted, or even just if they were feeling horny. She said she could never do this. One woman had even criticized her as anti-feminist, and said she was supporting an old-fashioned double standard. She said a woman had just as much right to get physical satisfaction from a man's body without making any emotional commitment as a man had to get his rocks off with some pick-up. Martha had replied that she did not question a woman's right to do this, she simply could not enjoy it herself. The other woman had sneered, "You're just an old-fashioned romantic."

What she needed, she had decided, along with good old erotic friction in all the right places, was intimacy. The relaxed closeness with Gavin was the best part of their sexual relationship. It allowed them to laugh a lot and tease one another and joke about what they were doing to each other in bed. Lying next to him now as he slept, she wondered how close they would remain without a full sexual relationship. She wondered whether she would still need Gavin as much, and whether he would need her as much.

::   ::   ::

Ted Starowicz was working at his desk when the Managing Editor, Tom Manning, called him into his office. Ted walked over warily, telling himself not to argue whatever Manning said, or at any rate not to argue too aggressively. He already had in his mind several reasons why he should stay with the impotence story and he was wondering how many he could put forward.

Manning beckoned him into a chair and said, "You've been doing a pretty good job on this story, Ted."

"Thanks," said Ted.

"How would like to take it over from now on? Do that and nothing else."

"That would suit me fine," Ted said.

"You'll have an assist from Charlie Smith as science correspondent where necessary, and some others from time to time. There are a lot of aspects to this story."

"Fine," Ted said. He wanted to say more but he told himself to shut up.

"Good. We've got to treat the subject delicately, you know. Do you have a summer holiday coming up?"

"I've got one due in July. But I haven't made any plans and I can put it off," said Ted.

"It may be an idea. We'll see when the time gets closer. In the meantime, you won't be given any other assignments. And when reporters do other aspects of the story they'll check with you. Okay?"

"Okay." Ted did not trust himself to say anything else. He had been patient for one of the few times in his life and it had worked.

Nearby, two young women on the staff were chatting at the water cooler. "How's life?" said one.

"If you mean what I think you mean, pretty dull," said the other, who had been married for just three months.

The first made a grimace. "Uh-huh. You miss it?"

"Of course, don't you?"

"I'm beginning to. Do you notice they don't even look at you now when you walk by."

"That's right. I never really noticed it much before. That they looked. I'm not a great beauty, let's face it. Now I notice that they don't."

"It's a relief sometimes."

"Oh yes. Not to have Jerry on the door leering when you walk in in the morning."

"Yes, things like that. Bob's father always used to look at my tits when he talked to me. He came around last Friday and he didn't look at my tits. Come to think of it," she added reflectively, "he didn't talk to me either."

"But still, I sometimes miss them looking," the other said. "I find I've taken to swinging my ass. But of course, it doesn't make any difference."

"Here comes Shirley, swinging her ass as usual." Shirley, a newsroom secretary who always showed off her figure with tight clothes, a short skirt and a sexy gait, walked along the length of the room carrying a sheaf of papers.

"And there's someone who's still looking," said the first young woman, nodding in the direction of Ted Starowicz, sitting at his desk now.

Absently, Ted watched Shirley's hemline bouncing up around her thighs, following her with his eyes for a few moments, unaware that he was doing so. An editor standing in the doorway of Manning's office, watched the two young women looking at Ted.

"I think that's one lucky guy," he said to Manning, through tight lips..

Ted took Elaine out to dinner that evening. They had not seen each other for several days. They had a drink in the cocktail lounge before going into the restaurant and he told her he had missed her. Over the meal they talked about their jobs.

"At least our creative director, Mr. Male Menopause, doesn't brush against me every time we pass in the corridor any more," she said. "But we sure picked the wrong time to tell people to have a second honeymoon in the Adirondacks."

"That campaign's not going too well, huh?" Ted said, sympathetically.

"Are you kidding? Honeymoon? You said that the first night I heard about it."

"I was joking then. You'll have to think of something else to pull in the couples. Card games, maybe," Ted suggested.

"Card games."

"Sure. Bridge Between Lovers. Put Your Passion Into Pinochle."

"I don't think it'll fly."

Ted told Elaine about the Holycroft faculty club meeting, and the conversation with Tom Manning that morning.

"So you're full time on that now," she said.

"Yes. I'm the paper's specialist on drooping dongs."

"Guess you're feeling pretty chipper these day."

"I'm enjoying the job at the moment, it's true," he agreed. "Hell, it's the big story."

"And you're in demand."

"But it's not as if I know anything about biochemistry. If I fell under a bus tomorrow they'd get someone else to pick up the story."

"I don't just mean as a reporter."

"What do you mean?"

"Oh c'mon, Ted. There aren't that many sexy men around any more. You have a certain scarcity value."

He considered this in silence for a few moments, and then shook his head. "Look, honey, don't make problems where there aren't any. I'm not even thinking about anyone else."

"You must be. Women know there's something different about you and you know it."

"I don't know it. How do other women know? I haven't got a permanent bulge in my pants "

"They know. It's the way you look at women. And not only that. Didn't you see the way women reacted when you were holding my hand in the cocktail lounge?"

"No."

"You haven't noticed the looks our waitress has been giving you?"

"No."

"And the things she's been showing you?"

"I noticed that she's wearing her sweater low-cut, if that's what you mean. I could hardly miss that cleavage."

"She's putting on a display for you. When she bent over I thought she was going to drop one of her boobs in the salad. You must have noticed other things."

"I haven't."

"Ted, I've always said you're self-centered, that you don't notice other people. You don't even listen to other people half the time. I sometimes wonder how you can be a reporter."

"Most reporters are self-centered and don't listen to people," he said. "They're all egotists."

"Sometimes you don't know when women are flirting with you. I've seen that in the past."

"That's true. I've missed some great opportunities."

"Now you can have a lot of women for the asking."

"Anyway, I don't want a lot of women, I want you."

"Yes, I'm at the front of the line. For tonight. I suppose I should count myself lucky."

"Oh, don't be so stupid."

"I'm not stupid," she said coldly. "And I'm not blind either."

"You damned well are stupid!" he snapped suddenly.

"And you're getting more so."

They did not talk a lot during the rest of the meal, and Elaine seemed to Ted to be irritable. Over coffee, he put his hand on her arm and said, "We could go on for a drink or two, but I'd rather go straight back to my place."

"I'd rather not go back with you tonight. I don't feel too well. I suppose I'm just not in the mood."

"You're sure?"

"I really don't feel like it tonight. My tummy's a bit upset. If you don't mind too much."

"All right," he said coolly. He was not surprised after their exchanges over dinner, but he was puzzled again, and disappointed. He paid the bill without looking the waitress in the face and when they left he walked through the dining room looking straight ahead.

They said nothing as he drove her home and then kissed her goodnight. His body itched with frustration. He had looked forward to having her in his bed and had thought about what he would do with her. He went to bed with a book instead of Elaine, *The Double Helix*. He had decided to read it when he started on this story, since it was a classic about a major discovery in biology, the double helix of dna. The openly competitive spirit among scientists surprised him, but he understood it better than the molecular structure. He would try to read those passages again some time.

He smoked several cigarettes as he read. He never smoked in bed with Elaine because she did not like it but he did not bother to argue with her when she said he should give it up. He had acquired the smoking habit from the wrong people when he was a teenager. He knew it was unhealthy in the long run but he reckoned that given the lack of caution in his temperament, it was probably the least dangerous of the vices he might have taken up. If he threw his suppressive energies into giving up smoking he might start drinking to excess, or racing motorbikes. He admitted to himself that this might be rationalizing the fact that he did not want to give up cigarettes.

He and Elaine saw each other again a few days later and they went back to his apartment and spent the night together. Neither of them said anything about what had gone before. He enjoyed sex with her, but found she was often tetchy. He did not have much spare time these days and could not fix a specific time to see her again. He wanted her to make a date for whatever time he finished work. She did not accept this, and he did not press it.

::   ::   ::

That Friday at the President's news conference, President Masterson spoke about the success of the economy and the new education bill, but reporters asked questions about the impotence plague. Could it be, several wanted to know, the result of bacteriological attack on the United States.

"We have no evidence to support such a suggestion," he said.

"But medical scientists say it can't be ruled out, that nothing can be ruled out," one reporter pointed out.

"No, nothing can be ruled out," the President agreed. "Our scientists don't know yet what is causing this."

The reporter pressed the point. "Scientists also say they know of no way of no this could happen naturally. Doesn't this suggest a Man-made biological mechanism?"

"I repeat," the President said testily, "we have no evidence to suggest that this has been created deliberately."

One reporter pointed out that several foreign terrorist groups and foreign governments were believed to be working on bacteriological warfare. "What will you do if there is evidence that this was deliberate?" he asked. "Would you regard it as an attack on the United States?"

"Obviously, we would take appropriate action," President Masterson said. "But I repeat, we have no evidence that this is the case." He refused to be drawn further.

Several reports of the news conference led on these exchanges. One began, "President Masterson said today that the Government has no evidence that the present plague affecting men is the result of a bacteriological attack on the United States by a terrorist group. But he added that the Government would take 'appropriate action' if this proved to be the case."

The next week, Gavin and Izzy flew down to Washington on Sunday evening for the first meeting of the Presidential Commission on the Medical Problem, as it was called euphemistically.

They assembled on the Monday morning at a large meeting room in the blockhouse on stone pillars that houses the Department of Health, Education and Welfare, sixty scientists from academic institutions and industry, several secretaries and a note-taker. They all sat at two long tables. The Surgeon-General read out a message from the President couched in elevated tones, welcoming the scientists and telling them that the hopes of Mankind rested on their endeavors.

After this had finished, Gavin said softly to Izzy, "All this stuff about the best of American science and American talent. I feel like a spy who's here in disguise."

"You're an honorary American here," Izzy assured him. Gavin chuckled and told him about Mohsin's use of the term "honorary American."

When the meeting broke for coffee Gavin saw an old friend across the room, Alan Carling. They had met when Alan spent a year doing post-graduate research at the Hammersmith Hospital in London. He was from Georgia, from an old plantation-owning family that had played a prominent role in the Confederacy, and he had once explained to Gavin what this meant in the South. Gavin, who had never been to the Southern states, imagined one of Alan's ancestors as Leslie Howard in *Gone With The Wind.*

Alan was chubby with a chubby baby's face, its shape emphasized by the round glasses he wore. Gavin thought that he probably had ambitions beyond his abilities, like many scientists. Now he worked for Biotek Inc. Gavin made his way over to him and they greeted one another, got their coffees and sat down at a table together.

"I've been seeing your name in the papers," said Carling. "You seem to be rated pretty highly on this problem."

"Come on, you know better than that," Gavin replied. "That's just newspapers."

"The Bliss Institute sent you here. That's more impressive."

"And Biotek sent you here."

"Yes, I must admit I'm quite chuffed about that." Carling had picked up a lot of British colloquialisms during his time in England and scattered them through his speech. To Gavin, they sounded odd in his deep South accent. "I'm in line to be head of a department," Carling went on. "There are changes at Biotek, as you probably know."

"What's it like working for Joe Barreras?"

"He came across at first as a bit of an arrogant bugger. We're his team now so we've got to be the best. But he went around and talked to each department about its work and its problems. He's a fast learner and he's sympathetic to scientists. And he's putting in more cash and hiring more people."

"To work on the impotence problem."

"That's about all there is now, so far as we're concerned."

Gavin hesitated, and then asked, "How are things with you and Caroline?"

"Definitely over. Definitely." He drained his coffee and put down the empty cup as if to illustrate the point. "Divorce pending. Hey, the next session's starting, we'd better get back. Let's get together some time."

Gavin and Martha had attended Alan's wedding but had not met them together since. They had both decided that the couple seemed ill-matched. Alan was patently proud of his tall, good-looking wife who sculpted. She, marrying for the first time at thirty-five, seemed to regard him even at their wedding reception as little more than a useful accessory. "Did you notice that she kissed the best man more enthusiastically than her husband?" Martha whispered to him. They felt confirmed in their view when they learned that the Carlings were now living apart.

In the sessions that day, all the current findings were laid out. Almost certainly it was an auto-immune disease: somehow, antibodies had been created that attacked the mechanism and prevented it functioning as it should. The speculation was that this was brought on by a virus, which must be much more powerful than any other since it created its effects so rapidly and so universally. A few people suggested that the work at their institutes would be speeded up if they could have more computer power, or a newer machine, or more research assistants. Everyone knew that some institutes would try to use the crisis to get more funds.

Izzy was invited to have dinner with some old friends, and he took Gavin along. They talked shop, and personalities, but not much about the conference. Afterwards, as Izzy and Gavin taxied back to their hotel together, Gavin asked Izzy what he thought of the presentations.

"I have the impression that a lot of people are playing their cards close to the chest," he said. "I'm not saying they have anything to tell, but I suspect that some of these places wouldn't give much away if they did."

"I was wondering about that," said Gavin. "They want to make the discovery themselves."

"Some of them," said Izzy. "Also, I've noticed that a few places haven't sent any of their top people, just second-team men. They can show the flag, but not really give anything away." Gavin wondered if Alan Carling came into this category.

"What are we going to do?" he asked.

"Oh, you know that. Play it straight. Tell anything we find as soon as we find it, to extend scientific knowledge. That's the Bliss way."

There was only a morning session the next day. At this, a representative of the Surgeon General's office gave them the latest picture. He impotence was definitely spreading in Mexico and Central America; the best estimate was that a quarter of male Mexicans were affected. Doctors in Europe reported an increase in impotence but there were no statistics yet and no one was sure that this could not be explained simply by anxiety. There was less certainty in Asia and Africa; presumably, the disease had not had sufficient time to spread there, although it also seemed possible that the tropical climate might blunt its effectiveness.

In America, he said, the incidence of the affliction was now virtually 100 percent. Then he explained what he meant by "virtually." It seemed that a few individuals were immune to whatever had brought on this condition. It was estimated that there was one of these among every 400,000 men.

CHAPTER FOUR

A s Spring turned to summer that year America changed, and watched itself changing. The change was heralded by scientists who told the country, in television interviews and newspaper articles, that in all the mammals a diminished libido is accompanied by a reduction in aggressive behavior. The public were told again and again that laboratory mice injected with drugs that reduced their libido are less inclined to fight one another for food, and that rats similarly treated will not bare their teeth despite flagrant provocation.

People were led to expect a change in behavior that paralleled that of the rodents in laboratories since men's testosterones seemed to be dud, and some were ready to find what they expected. Some sports writers reported.that baseball games were not being played with the same manly vigor as in other years. They said umpires were having an unnaturally easy time, with fewer outraged challenges to their decisions. Other people claimed to see a different tone in the nation's bar-rooms, with arguments often conducted with genteel restraint rather than a pounding of the bar with fists. Some reported a modification in behavior on Wall

Street, with fewer aggressive take-overs, although the level of financial activity remained the same.

As the weeks went on, changes appeared that were measurable and indisputable. There was a marked drop in violent crime as shown in the statistics of muggings and armed robbery. In inner city areas police reported that they were having a quieter time than they ever remembered. They noted that there was not this year the usual summertime rise in warfare among street gangs, and also in unplanned killings and woundings that usually accompany a heat wave - the domestic row that ends in a beating or knifing, the quarrel in a tavern in which someone pulls a gun. Curiously, the general reaction to this news was not satisfaction but rather, anxiety.

In one of the few Administration comments, the Vice-President declared in a television interview with a panel of reporters: "We are in danger of losing those qualities that have made America what it is." Replying to criticism, he said that he was not speaking about violence on the streets but about the fall in enlistments in the Marines.

Men also committed less violence against animals. There was a fall in demand for hunting licences and ammunition, and the deer and some smaller creatures had a less worrying time. Attendances at boxing and wrestling matches fell off.

Attention was drawn now to the physical changes that might result in men, and particularly in growing boys, if the plague continued. Newspaper articles pointed to what medical scientists call the secondary sexual characteristics that are controlled by testoterones, the physical features that distinguish men from women.

Parents scrutinized their pubescent sons anxiously,

sometimes peering at them indecently in the bath. Men tended to wear their shirts with the top buttons undone displaying more of their hairy chests than was customary before. They looked at themselves in secret, standing bare-chested in front of the mirror, rubbed their muscles to see if they were turning to subcutaneous fat, and listened anxiously to their own voices. Yet there was no reliable sign that so far, men were losing the distinctive physical features of their gender.

The advertising industry, which prides itself on reading the public mood, floundered for new directions. A conference for the industry addressed by leading advertising figures and psychologists was called "How Do You Sell a Sports Car to a Man Who Doesn't Want a Mistress?" The industry as a whole suffered a decline. Manufacturers of many products from after-shave to swimsuits did not know how to advertise their products now that there was no use tickling the sexual instinct, so they just stopped trying while they thought things over. Others just kept going in the only way they knew how. The same billboards featuring the same beguiling female smiles and female forms dotted the nation's highways, like religious icons in a nation of unbelievers.

Hollywood set about revising its schedule of productions, and some in their early stages were cancelled entirely. Variety headlined a story on two of these canceled productions: "Sex Comedies Now Ex-Comedies." Fashion commentators forecast that the trend in women's clothes in the fall would be to business-like suits and padded shoulders. An editorial in *Women's Wear Daily* said: "For the moment, an age-old argument has been settled. This season, women will be dressing for other women."

Some monthly magazines shortened production times and revamped editions. The August issue of *Marie Claire* advertised an article on 'Men Without Macho'; Another women's magazine, more daring, carried on its cover the headline: "Cunnilingus - Tell Him It's Not An Irish Airline." Cosmopolitan carried a series of articles on 'Life After Sex'.' A girl from *Redbook* telephoned Gavin and said the magazine was planning a long article in several parts called 'Alternatives.' She asked him whether, as a medical expert, he could suggest alternatives to sexual intercourse. "Cold showers," he told her.

Cures were touted. Federal laws restricted the advertising of medicines, but the downmarket magazines carried advertisements for regimes of exercises, many adopting the language of Tantric Yoga, with its Sansksrit words for genitalia, sperm, and various sexual acts.

The fact that the plague came with the advent of warm weather led to speculation that it was related to climate, and would disappear when winter came. One newspaper commentator came out with the bizarre suggestion that the plague might be a seasonally recurring phenomenon, lasting only for the summer but returning every year, so that Americans would henceforth restrict their love-making to three seasons. "It gives a whole new meaning to the term 'summer holiday,'" he wrote.

In the circles in which Gavin and Martha moved, little changed in social life. At a dinner party people still invited a spare man to pair with a single woman and vice versa. In the first part of the summer, at least, marriages remained marriages. Occasionally someone would make a momentary reference to the situation in relation to themselves. One woman complaining to the Groves about her teenage daughter's behavior remarked, "Well at least I know she's not going to come home pregnant." And when a woman told a story at a dinner party about having to walk home anxiously through dark streets after her car had broken down, her husband said, "You didn't have much money in your pocket book and that's all anyone is going to want from you these days, honey."

In the private part of their lives people were affected in different ways. Just as people are different in their sexuality, so people were different now in their lack of it.

On one typical Saturday night in July, a warm, balmy night on Long Island, a little before midnight, people came home from other people's homes and from movie theaters and concert halls and restaurants, and turned off television sets and put down books and magazines and got ready for bed, and in none of them was there any sense of anticipation. In the little towns around Radford, the silence of the night was punctuated only by the sounds of cars drawing up and pulling out, signs of an evening's socializing coming to an end, and by the faint bumps of frustrated mosquitoes hurling themselves at the screens that protected doors and windows.

In the only Italian restaurant in Radford, a young man and woman lingered over liqueurs and a second cup of coffee. It was their second evening out together. Most of the diners had left, the check was in front of the man and the waiter was hovering.. Over dinner they had talked more and more intimately about themselves, and now he found he was reluctant to see the evening end. He talked to the young woman, awkwardly, jerking out words as if they were not the ones he wanted to use but the only ones he could find.

"I know I should take you home now. But - this may sound silly, but - would you like to come back to my place for the night? I don't mean - I mean I won't - well I'm not special. I'm like everybody else. But I'd like - I'd like to sleep with you. I'd like you to be there in the morning."

"It's not silly, it's lovely," she said. "And yes.I'd like to." She leaned across the table and kissed him on the lips. He was surprised at how thrilled he was at her kiss.

In the presbytery of a Roman Catholic church in a blue collar neighborhood on the edge of Queens, a priest was kneeling by the side of his bed, in a bare room furnished only with a bed, a chair, a table, a small bookcase, and a crucifix on the wall. The priest had an expression of intense concentration. He was praying, trying somehow to send a part of his soul heavenward, across dimensions - for he had taught himself not to think of heaven, God's abode, in spatial terms, as a place up above - to where God was present all about. He was thanking God for releasing him from the sin of betraying his priestly vow of chastity.

Mohsin Ahmed had been in bed for some time, reading a novel. Now his wife Karmi joined him and he put down the book and switched off the light. He kissed her tenderly. "I love you," he told her, in the dark.

"I love you too," she said.

"I'm sorry I can't do anything," he said.

"You're an idiot," she said. "You can do *something*."

"Oh, I see."

"Good. Now come here." She put her hands on either side of his head, kicked off the bedclothes and moved his head downwards. She was not wearing pajama bottoms. "I've prepared myself. I read about this in an American magazine," she said.

"Whiskey!" he exclaimed.

"Bourbon. Your favorite. Oh yes, good man. Oh, yes!"

At the same time, Tom Manning, the Managing Editor of the Long Island Chronicle, was getting into bed with his wife, Millie. The Mannings were in their late forties and had been married for twenty-two years. They had spent the day packing for their summer holiday, which was to be spent in Italy. He always made sure that whatever happened they had this two-week summer holiday together. He felt he owed her this. Millie often said that her husband was married to his job (he considered it a professional failure that he had never been able to edit out the many clichés that littered his wife's conversation). He was aware that his job absorbed most of his energy and attention and that he spent less time with his wife than most men.

During their holiday they would make love more often than when they were at home, particularly now that their children were older and no longer came with them. Occasionally they even made love in the afternoons, which they had not done since they were much younger, emerging from a hotel room at the cocktail hour. This was on his mind now and he knew it must be on hers. He always had to say what was on his mind and he said, "I'm afraid it won't be the same as other times in one way."

"Do you mean what I think you mean?"

"Yes," he replied.

"That doesn't matter," she said lightly. "To tell the truth, it hasn't meant all that much to me anyway, not for years. I pretended I enjoyed it more than I did to please you."

"Oh," he said, and lay there on his back, staring up into the darkness. He tried to digest this and knew it would take him a while.

Millie also lay awake, excited by what she had just dared to say. She knew it would hurt Tom and she was glad. He had it coming to him. She reckoned that she had a lousy marriage. He took her for granted and did not bother to relate to her feelings. She had brought up his children with very little help from him, she kept a good home and entertained his friends, and in return he would present her with his company every now and again, or an evening out, or sex, as if it were a gift for which she should be grateful.

Ted Starowicz was at a party. He had come with Elaine but she had been crotchety with him all evening as she often was these days and now she was in the kitchen talking to some other women. He was out on the porch with Dan Meltzer and another man from the Chronicle, all of them with muscles and inhibitions loosened by alcohol and the Saturday night party spirit. Meltzer was sprawled on a swing sofa and Ted and the other man were in cushioned bamboo armchairs.

Meltzer speaking slowly in a fuzzy voice, asked the other man, "How do you feel these days?"

"You mean," the other said, "Without sex?" He was embarrassed. Ted saw that Meltzer was being his usual self, blundering ahead.

Meltzer hesitated before replying, as if he was not sure what he did mean, then replied, "Yeah."

"I don't exactly want it. At first that bothered me. Now it doesn't any more." He waved his hand as if signalling that the discussion was finished.

But Meltzer pressed on relentlessly. "It's okay with Estelle?"

"Maybe it bothers her a bit."

"It doesn't bother you, not wanting it?"

The other man finally gave in to the interrogation. "I don't think so. It worried me for a while because I thought I didn't want the other things I wanted. Like, to get ahead, things like that. I mean, I still wanted them, but I thought maybe not as much. But I don't think so now. I want the other things as much. When I play squash I still want to win. I want promotion. Does it bother you?"

Meltzer was ready to unburden himself. "You want to know the truth about how I feel?"

"No," murmured Ted.

"I hadn't been getting much anyway, quite frankly. Since I split with Lisa. I know there's plenty out there but I was feeling low. Too low to chase women. So I was really horny. I used to look at women, stare at them. Particularly when they were wearing short skirts, or on the beach. I was hurting."

"So now you're not horny."

"Now I'm not horny. The itch has gone away. But somehow - I don't know - I miss it. Something's gone. I miss the hurt. I miss the hunger."

They were both silent after this confession. Them Meltzer asked him, "How about you, Ted? How are things with you?"

Ted affected a drunken mumbled and said, "I got to get another drink," and lumbered off into the house.

Meltzer said, "Just like I thought. I reckon Ted's still got it. He's not like the rest of us."

"Really?"

"That's what they say. You'd better watch your wife when he's around."

At just about the time that all this was happening, on the Holycroft campus, a security guard making a quick tour around in his car spotted a prowler at the Bliss Institute. He jumped out of the car and called out, and shone his flashlight on the building, but the figure disappeared into the darkness. He checked the bushes and then the outside of the building. A window had been forced open. He called a caretaker, and the two of them checked inside; nothing appeared to have been stolen. "He was probably disturbed him before he could take anything," the guard said, when he reported the incident to the director on the Monday.

A memo was circulated to staff reporting the break-in and saying that nothing had been stolen. The memo reminded people to lock doors and windows before leaving.

During those months, nearly everyone at the Bliss Institute was working on projects connected with the impotence problem. Some of the staff agreed to postpone their summer holidays in order to press on. Gavin and Martha put off their plan to hire a camper and tour the Colorado National Park, telling each other that they would still do it another time. Gavin liked scenery on a grand scale, and he was disappointed at giving up the trip. The soaring mountains and plunging canyons of the Rockies, as he envisaged them, would be a change of vista from the featureless Long Island landscape.

He did not give over his whole life to the laboratory. He played tennis two or three times a week on the Holycroft courts and improved his backhand. He and Martha went into

New York City for a weekend at the end of July, staying at a hotel uptown, going to the theater and visiting friends, Bloomingdale's and the Museum of Modern Art.

Walking along Lexington Avenue in the forties, Gavin looked at the tawdry store fronts and the garish neon signs, and the dirty streets with garbage blowing around them, and the steam rising up through a manhole cover like an invalid's bad breath, and he remarked, as he often had before, that this was a really ugly city. Ten minutes later and four blocks away, he stood with Martha on Fifth Avenue and looked along the avenue, at the glittering lights on the stores, the elegant store windows, the rampant foliage rising up several stories behind glass, and the burnished sides of skyscrapers glowing gold and copper with the reflected light of the setting sun, and he remarked, as he often had before, that this was a really beautiful city

That Monday, after the Groves' weekend in Manhattan, the news burst upon America that the virus had been found. It had been isolated, not in an American laboratory, but at the Pasteur Institute in Paris.

Ted telephoned Gavin. "Does this mean that a cure is around the corner?" he asked.

"Not at all," Gavin told him. "It's a first step. But there's no knowing how long the rest will take. It's an autoimmune disease, remember."

"Ah yes. I'm trying to remember our science correspondent's explanation in the paper of what an autoimmune disease is. Something about cells staging a mutiny."

"I remember it," Gavin said. "He explained that the antibodies, which normally fight off invading viruses, turn on the body themselves. He said it was like soldiers mutinying and starting to pillage the place they're supposed to defend. People often use military similes in explaining medical science to the layman, as you've probably noticed. Lots of attacking and defending the body."

"Are there any other autoimmune diseases?"

"Sure. Rheumatoid arthritis is a common one. Graves' disease is more like this. The antibodies inhibit the effect of thyroid hormones. Testosterone is also a hormone."

"Does this mean that the plague isn't Man-made? That it isn't part of a terrorist plot?"

"There's no more evidence one way or the other. As you know, I always found that pretty hard to believe."

Ted paused to absorb this. Then he asked, "So now that they've isolated the virus, what's the next step?"

"The next step is to produce the virus in quantity, so that we can work with it."

"Why do we have to produce more of the viruses? I thought the world was crawling with the goddamned things. Surely that's the problem."

"They're bumping about in people's bloodstreams but it's difficult to get them out. And we want hundreds of grams, kilograms of the thing to work with. That's a lot."

"What do you do with the viruses when you've got them?"

"Try to create an antibody to it. An antibody to an antibody."

"And how are you going to do that?"

"God knows."

"Have you got his phone number?"

"Look, I'm sorry but I shouldn't have started on this now, I'm just on my way to a meeting. If you need any more of the scientific background, call me this afternoon."

Then Gavin went to Izzy's office to talk about his dna project. He would be working on the dna of the molecules of the new virus. If he could crack it, replicate the dna pattern, they might take that route to removing its sting. He knew he would be absorbed in dna from now on and needed to know what laboratory help he could expect.

Ted put down the phone. He was not expected to write the science background piece but he needed to be sufficiently familiar with the subject to recognize progress when it came. He was jotting down some notes of what Gavin had said when Tom Manning's secretary came over to say that Manning wanted to see him.

In Manning's office he found several of the senior staff standing around in an informal conference. Ted noticed that they accepted his presence among them easily, which they would not have done before he started working on this story.

Kate Lestrange was among them. She was the editor of a section of the weekend edition called Living. Manning was complimenting her: "That was nifty feature in your section about the singles bar closing. That girl you've got did a good job on it. She has a nice light touch."

"I'm glad you liked it," Kate said. "I thought she did a good job too."

"Also," Manning said, "you might like to know we're going to take ads for vibrators from now on. Change of policy. We're following the Times."

Then he turned to Ted. "Is this French discovery pretty certain?" he asked him.

"They seem pretty sure it is at the Bliss Institute," Ted replied. "They say the Pasteur Institute is a top-flight place and wouldn't come out with an announcement like this unless they were certain."

"Ed here," Manning said, "wants to write an editorial pointing out that for all the talk of the Presidential Commission and the efforts of American science, it was the French who made the breakthrough, although it's America that's most affected. Do you think that's fair?"

"It seems fair to me."

Manning made no sign that Ted was to leave but he turned back to Kate Lestrange and they talked about some pieces for the next week's Living section. Kate wanted a feature on how women's problems had changed. Ted mentioned the counselling center where Martha worked. Kate said she had heard of the woman who ran it, Grace Whiting, and would try an interview with her.

Then she told the others, "You know, Ted and I go back a long way."

Ted was surprised. Years earlier, when he was at Columbia doing his master's degree, Kate was at the Columbia School of Journalism, and they had lived in the same building on the campus. They had not seen much of each other. Kate moved with a more sophisticated New York crowd while his social life was mostly limited to students. She had never referred before to their knowing each other earlier.

"Really?" asked Manning politely.

"That's right. Ted was doing his master's in French literature. Specializing in the postwar French novelists, right?"

"Playwrights," Ted corrected. He was surprised again, that she remembered what he was studying. He could recall only one conversation they had when he had told her what he was doing.

"I knew Ted was at Columbia," said Manning. "I didn't realize you two were there at the same time."

Kate was tall and conventionally if not strikingly good-looking, with full lips and brown hair which she wore short. She had a cool manner that commanded respect and could be intimidating. Even those men on the staff who usually discussed women in anatomical terms did not talk that way about her. She was, as one of them put it, "a serious lady." It was common knowledge that she had had an affair with a senator and used to go to Washington on weekends, and some of her colleagues speculated at one time that she might marry him and move to Washington. Ted and Kate left Manning's office together. "You've done some good stories on this," she told him.

"Thanks," he said.

"Tom thinks so, you know."

"Glad to hear it," he said, noting her familiarity with Manning's opinions.

"I often thought you were one of the brightest guys in the newsroom," she went on. "I hoped they would give you a really good story to get your teeth into. It seems that now they have. You're on your way, so far as the top brass here are concerned." With that she left him at his desk and went on walking to her office.

Ted was gratified by what Kate had said. She did not give out compliments lightly and was certainly not one to soft-soap people. With his story finished, he sat down to tie up some loose ends. He read all of the long cover story in Newsweek titled "The Loss of the American Libido," and noted some local angles that might be followed up. A major pharmaceutical corporation was experiencing a big setback because its biggest product was contraceptive pills; the corporation had a plant in the locality employing several hundred people. The business section was bound to be covering that but it seemed like a general news story also.

A Long Island congressman said the Government should take more seriously the possibility that the plague was engineered by Muslim fundamentalists who had poisoned the water systems of the Western world. He noted that there were no firm reports of the plague in Arab countries. The Chronicle had already run an interview with him and he had nothing new to say on the subject.

Brothel-owners in Nevada, where brothels were legal, were asking for Federal emergency aid, saying this was a national emergency and they were victims. Ted wondered whether he could do a story on the plight of a local brothel, known to its customers, of whom there were a few on the Chronicle staff, as the Waldorf Towers. He presumed it had closed its doors and wondered whether he could write about it circumspectly and whether he would be allowed to be sentimental.

He made a note of some leading scientists in medicine and biology who were working on this problem. He thought he should know who they were and look out for their names, and one day he might go around the country talking to them.

He was putting away his notes and clippings when Kate Lestrange came up to his desk. "Ted, would you do me a favor?" she asked.

"Sure. What?"

"Would you give me a lift home? My car's being repaired,

and I can't seem to get a cab. They're all busy. I'm not far away."

He hesitated, and said, "I've got to finish up some things. It'll take me ten, fifteen minutes."

"That's fine," she said. "Will you come by my desk?"

Well, well, he thought, that's what happens when the managing editor says nice things about you. In the car she directed him to her apartment house, which was actually several miles away. When he stopped the car, she said, "Come on up. I've got something that will interest you. From Washington. About your story."

The apartment house was smart, with an awning across the sidewalk in front and a uniformed porter. It had a long lobby, with two sets of elevators for the different wings. She lived on the tenth floor. Her apartment was furnished with tubular metal furniture and abstracts and posters of art exhibitions on the walls. Modern style for a modern lady, he thought.

He accepted a Scotch on the rocks. When they stood next to each other he noticed that she was the same height as him. She gave him a letter and he sat down on a couch to read it. It was from a friend of hers who was a staffer on a Congressional committee, and one paragraph referred obliquely to scientists lobbying for funding.

It did not have much to do with his story. Ted was trying to think of something polite to say when Kate sat down on the couch beside him, put her hand on his shoulder and said, "You know, as well as thinking you were one of the brightest guys in the newsroom, I also always thought you were one of the dishiest."

She kissed him gently on his ear lobe. Surprised, he

turned to her and she was looking straight into his eyes with a directness that was not so much an invitation as a command. He kissed her on the lips. She kissed him back. She was pressing against him, calmly, in control. Her body was warm under her blouse and he felt her breasts pressing into his chest. They had their arms around each other and he felt the warmth of her hand on the back of his neck.

Perhaps if Elaine had been nicer to him in the past few weeks, he might have broken away and told her he was being faithful to his girl friend. At least, that's what he told himself the next day. Or if Kate had not been such a serious lady, so that this offer from her was difficult to turn down. As it was he kissed her again and opened his mouth and she opened hers and their tongues played with one another. Then they pulled away from one another and she put her hand on his thigh and he felt its warmth..

There was something he wanted to know. "Do you really think I write well?" he asked.

"Oh yes, really," she said, as she slid her hand up towards his crotch.

He let his quickening pulse take control, and when they stood up he took her hand and let her lead him into the bedroom. They started to undress and when he put his hand between her legs she lost her cool and started to pull off his clothes. He found her wanton urgency exciting, so that he tore a button off his shirt as he ripped it off. Soon they were on the bed and he was on top of her thrusting, and she was gasping, her breathing fast and frantic, and then turning into shrill little cries.

Afterwards he smoked a cigarette lying beside her. He could not help making comparisons. Kate was quicker than

Elaine to take the lead and quicker to come. Her flesh was smoother than Elaine's, her breasts smaller and firmer, her movements more jerky.

She kissed his shoulder and murmured, "That was good. I need physical sex sometimes."

He raised himself on his elbow and looked down at her. "I'm glad I could be of help," he said dryly.

She picked up his chilliness and said quickly, "Oh, I'm glad it was you, Ted. I really like you." He dozed off. When he awoke she was still beside him, reading a book about Government and the Press. She put it down when she saw he was awake. The bedside clock showed him that it was almost midnight. "Kate, honey, I've got to get back home," he said.

"No you don't," she said. She moved quickly, and catching him by surprise she sprang up and climbed on top of him, straddling his chest, squeezing him with her thighs and pressing down on him so that he could not get up.

"Christ, you're strong," he gasped.

"Weight training," she explained. She edged back a little, then bent over and kissed his penis, then rubbed it against her vulva. Soon it was hard and she eased it into her. Afterwards they had cold chicken and salad and white wine from the fridge and then went back to bed.

Lying next to her, Ted thought about sex. He always liked the Old Testament term for a man having sex with a woman: he "knew" her. "Abraham knew Sarah, and she conceived." With good sex, you know someone, in a very special way.. Penetration had an element that was more than physical. Sometimes, you only knew them a little. He knew Kate a little because he heard the sounds coming from deep in her being, but he heard them from a distance, as it were. He knew Elaine. They both approached sex together eagerly, and she gave herself to him. They looked into each other's eyes when they made love, if the position allowed it. He was not sure how much he liked Elaine, but he knew her. He did not think he would ever know Kate as well.

They left together the following morning. She was going straight to the office and he was going home, so he waited with her in the lobby while her cab came. He went with her to the door of her cab. She did not say goodbye but kissed him lightly and slid her fingers down his chest, as if to guard the memory.

He was vaguely aware that a woman was at the far end of the lobby outside the other elevator watching this goodbye scene, and that even at that distance she seemed familiar. When he got into his car, he realized who it was: Naomi James, a girl he had dated briefly when he was at Columbia. He looked back but she was gone. He remembered Naomi James.

Back home, his telephone answering machine was flashing. He turned it on, and there were several messages from Elaine.

The first said: "It's eleven o'clock. I just feel like saying goodnight to you. I haven't seen you for nearly a week and I miss you. Let's meet soon. I want to talk about things." The second said, "It's twelve-thirty and I can't sleep. I just hope you're out with the boys." The third said, "It's eight o'clock in the morning, and you're not there. You bastard, Ted. You bastard! Just don't call me again."

He telephoned Elaine at her office wondering what he would say to her but she was out.

::   ::   ::

At the Bliss Institute, Gavin pinned copies of the pictures of the guilty virus that the Pasteur Institute had circulated on his office wall and was soon immersed in its molecular structure. Occasionally, he would remind himself that all these molecules together, in their intricate mathe- matical patterns, added up to a human being. This was the great mystery that still fascinated him. It required an effort to make the connection, and indeed, some scientists did not do so. At the Medical Research Council in Berkshire he had written a paper about some molecular protein reactions observed in a human body and added as a postscript, humorously, as he thought: "The man got a headache." The laboratory head said only that he doubted it.

One evening, he and Martha were sitting in their living room after supper, and she asked him how his work was going. He told her something about his efforts she asked, "Are we going to find a cure?"

"Yes. If it doesn't die out by itself."

"Why should it die out by itself?"

"Because the body will develop its own cure. That's what usually happens with plagues. Even the Black Death died out eventually. But yes, I think we'll find a cure. Fifty years ago I wouldn't have been so certain. Maybe even twenty years ago. But now science has the resources and the manipulative abilities to beat it."

"I haven't got all that much time. I'm thirty-three," Martha said. "We should have started a baby already."

He was surprised, and he turned and looked across at her; her face was taut. Suddenly, this was no longer a discussion about a disease and other people. They intended to have children.

"That still gives you plenty of time," he said. "Besides, women can be impregnated by artificial insemination."

"Sure," she said. "Taking the sperm from you with a hypodermic needle." She almost spat out the words. "We could do it all that way."

They were sitting in separate armchairs, but now he got up and went over to hers and sat on the arm and put his arm around her. "I'm sorry, Martha" he said softly, because he had tossed out the thought lightly. "Does that idea frighten you?"

"I'm not sure what frightens me," she said. "But I'm frightened." She leaned into him

He spent the rest of the evening thinking hard about the problem. Now it was something that he had to do to protect his family, his wife and the family he might one day have. A recollection came into his mind, a paper published two years ago that might be relevant to the work that was being done, albeit not his work, on chemical denaturing.

He decided to tell Izzy about it and the next day he went to the upper floor to look for him. Izzy was at a meeting, but he found Mohsin, who took him into his office and started to tell him about the cultures he was having prepared.

Gavin listened to him for a couple of minutes and then cut in. "I was going to tell Izzy something, but I'll tell you," he said. "Have you ever read a paper by a man named Emilio Meriacci?"

"No."

"No reason why you should, I suppose. He's an Italian biochemist. The paper was given at a conference I attended once, and I was interested because it was about an experiment with the pituitary gland. But one thing in it stuck in my mind. He obtained some biochemical reactions by the use of selenium in a culture."

"Selenium? Unusual."

"Yes. I was thinking about it, and it struck me that there was a similarity with the reactions we're looking for. I don't remember the details but you can probably find Meriacci's paper on-line."

"Thank you. I'll look it up."

The next afternoon Gavin saw Izzy in the corridor, hurrying along as usual. When he saw Gavin he stopped. "Mohsin told me about your idea about selenium," he said. "He says you could just be on to something. He's very keen."

"It wasn't my idea," Gavin said. "I just referred him to a paper.. I couldn't even remember the details."

"Well Mohsin looked up the paper and he says it could very interesting. He and I are setting up some experiments using it."

"Already?"

"You know Mohsin when he gets on to something. It's all systems go. I think it's a good idea."

Gavin was pleased but he was getting into a phase of his own dna calculations that required a lot of concentration and he did not give much attention to any other line of work. This lasted three days, and then he put the work on a computer and lifted his head.

That morning, he got a telephone call in his office from a man he had been friendly with during his year at UCLA, a biochemist called Michael Rasmussen who was now at Stanford. "Hi. I'm in your neck of the woods," he said. "I thought I'd give you a call and see how you are."

"I'm fine. How long are you here for, Mike? Can we get together?"

"Afraid not. I've got to go back this afternoon. It's been a very quick visit. I'm just about to check out of my hotel and I've got a half-hour to spare. Anyway, how are you, Gavin? Are you working on the big problem?"

"Trying to figure out how to do so. What brings you here?"

"Same thing, really, A job possibility with Biotek Inc. in Walton. They wanted me to come for interviews. Sent me a ticket."

"So how did it go? Did you get the job?"

"They offered it to me but I turned it down."

"Any special reason?"

"Well, just between you and me, there was something nasty there."

"Really?" Gavin suddenly remembered that at UCLA, a mutual colleague had described Mike Rasmussen as "a real straight arrow guy." He remembered because he had never heard this American term before and he had to ask what it meant. He said to him, "A number of people are being offered jobs at Biotek. If there's something nasty in the lab there, I'd like to know.

"Oh, it's not the guys in the lab," Rasmussen said. "That's not why I turned the job down. It was something else. In fact, it was so nasty that I think I really ought to tell you. Somebody ought to know." Rasmussen sounded angry. "It's the guy who calls himself the Administrative Director. Name of Philip Carey. He talked to me about the job. Do you know what his idea was?"

"What?"

"That I should stay where I am for a little while longer. Then come to Biotek and bring along all the papers I could find on work that our department had done in the meantime on the impotence problem. Indicated that there'd be a bonus in it for me."

"That certainly is nasty."

"Damned right. I asked him whether he expects me to steal the papers. He said no, but there must be a photocopier there. I told him to shove his job."

The idea made Gavin angry also. He knew the world of science was not above greed for recognition but he felt it should be free from outright criminality. Also, the name of Philip Carey jogged something in his memory. He searched his mind, but he could not recall what it was.

The talk of Biotek reminded him of Alan Carling, his Georgia friend from London who was now at Biotek. When they met in Washington, he had promised Alan he would invite him to dinner. It would be interesting to get his view of things at Biotek. After consulting with Martha that evening he rang him with an invitation for Saturday.

Alan was very pleased to come. He was in the throes of the divorce and lonely. They had drinks on the patio, looking at the little lawn that Gavin always called, in the British way, his garden. Carling had the appearance of a man who was not taking care of himself. His shirt was unironed, there was a button missing from his jacket, and his plumpness was becoming flab.

He talked unhappily about the divorce. His wife, as he

told it, was unstable and very selfish. They had been unhappy almost from the beginning. When Martha went inside to finish cooking the dinner, he told Gavin that he was sure she had had at least one affair with another man while they were together. He could not prove it. Now he would have to pay alimony. He was in a mood to pour out his heart. He drained his glass several times before dinner.

At the dinner table, they talked about the work on the impotence problem. "We're trying all sorts of things," said Alan.

"Us too."

"A lot of it originates in the San Diego lab."

"What's that?"

"Barreras Pharmaceuticals has a laboratory in San Diego. Now that Barreras owns Biotek, they feed us ideas and work to follow up."

"Is it a big lab there?"

"I don't know how big it is, but it seems to be a real powerhouse. We've had several memos asking us to look into this or that, following up something that was originated in the San Diego lab."

"Serious ideas?"

"Could be. I got one yesterday. There was a paper about the pituitary gland. It seems to have some relevance. I've got to look it up."

"Not the one by Emilio Meriacci."

"Yes, that's the name. Do you know it?"

"We've got somebody looking into that at Bliss."

Carling put down his knife and fork and looked worried. "Oh God, Gavin, I shouldn't have told you. You know we're supposed to stay shtum on everything that goes on in the lab."

"Well, I shouldn't really have told you that we're working on it at Bliss. So we're even." Gavin tried to sound reassuring. "Scientists aren't very good at keeping secrets anyway. Everybody knows that. Do people from San Diego come on visits?"

"I haven't seen any. The memos all come from our new Administrative Director. Philip Carey."

"Philip Carey?" Gavin repeated.

"Yes. You know him?"

"No, but as it happens, I heard a story about him earlier this week. From somebody he offered a job to. Something rather sleazy."

"I'll tell you something else about him," said Alan. "He's just been appointed to the Presidential Commission. He'll be Vice-Chairman of the Industry Committee. That's Barreras' influence, you can bet."

"What's the Industry Committee?""

"Representatives of the industry to advise on what the industry needs and what it can contribute." Gavin wondered again where he had heard Philip Carey's name in the past, before that call from Mike Rasmussen. He knew he had heard it somewhere else.

Alan went off to the toilet, and while he was gone Martha made fun of his accent. "Wheyah's yowah bayethroom, please?" she mimicked. Then she said, "He's giving you the poop on Biotek. Let's give him some more to drink and get him talking some more."

"Come on, he's our guest," Gavin protested. "That sounds underhand."

"You're so proper," she said. "I'll give him more drink and

you just listen."

Carling went on drinking, but all he told them about Biotek was that he was dissatisfied. He burbled on about other things that were making him unhappy. There was the prospect of cutting his living standards to support Caroline, his former wife and present enemy. They murmured sympathetically.

"First we quarrelled about love," he said. "Can you quarrel about love? I think we did. Then about sex. Now it's about money. And she's got a lawyer."

After this he leaned back in chair and closed his eyes for a few moments. Then he opened them and said, "What were we talking about? My problems, as I recall. I must be boring the shit out of you both. I apologize. I think it's time I was going." They called a taxi for him.

"Poor Alan," Gavin said to Martha, as they got ready for bed.

"Yes, the poor man is quite sweet," she agreed. "In other circumstances, I suppose I'd be looking for a girl friend for him."

"You might think about it anyway," said Gavin. "A woman's warmth can still be comforting to a man when you're feeling low. Or even when you're not." She kissed him on the cheek, and when they got into bed she snuggled up to him. He went to sleep like that.

When he woke up the next morning, he thought he remembered where he had heard the name of Philip Carey before. He often found that he solved simple puzzles in his sleep. He would go to bed pondering a question and wake up with the answer. As it was Sunday he waited until mid-morning before telephoning Ted.

"Ted, do you remember that night that you and Elaine came over to dinner, and we all talked about Joe Barreras taking over Biotek?" he asked.

"Yup."

"And you told me about some man involved in Barreras industries who had left the CIA after doing something dodgy. You went to interview him."

"Yup."

"What was his name?"

"Philip Carey," replied Ted.

Gavin told him about Carey's job at Biotek and about his friend's story about his suggestion. "I really don't like that kind of thing," he explained. "It's so damned dishonest."

"Carey's a hundred percent fink all right," Ted said. "Would your friend Michael Rasmussen talk to me?"

"I think he might talk to you off the record."

"I'll see," said Ted. "I'm going to follow this up if you've no objection."

"None at all."

"By the way," Ted said, "I'm coming to the Bliss Institute tomorrow morning on the way to the office. I'll stop by and say hello if you're about."

"Sure, do. Who are you seeing?"

"Nobody exactly. I mean, I'm not coming as a reporter."

"Why are you coming then?"

"Er - I thought you knew. They want to run some tests on me."

"Tests?"

"Yes. Some more tests. They've already taken blood and done some. You see, I'm - well I'm not affected. You know, everybody who isn't affected has been asked to make themselves available for testing."

"Oh. Oh, I see. So maybe I'll see you tomorrow."

::   ::   ::

Ted was nervous on the way to the Bliss Institute, not so much at the prospect of further tests as because of the little plastic bottle he was carrying. He hoped that a man and not a woman would take it from him. If it were a woman he would find it hideously embarrassing. She might ask him for a date on the spot.

He had demurred at first when it was requested. "I can produce a sample of urine but this is different," he protested. But the man at the Bliss Institute pressed him on his duty to science and to his less fortunate fellow-Americans, and he finally agreed. They wanted it to be fresh, produced within the last few hours. He had thought he would ask Elaine's help but he could hardly do that now. He was not sure what her response would have been anyway. He had had to rely on his imagination, and to his surprise it seemed for a time not to be up to the task. He thought he might have to go out and get a dvd to help him.

He drove slowly and very carefully from his home to the Institute. He envisaged being stopped for speeding, or because he had bumped into another car, and a cop spotting that bottle and asking whether it contained liquor and whether he had been drinking, and he explaining what it was, and the cop saying, "It's *what*? Well I'll be - hey, Al, come and see what we've got here. There isn't much of this around these days, and this guy's giving his away!" And he would be telling them that he was in a hurry, that the stuff would get stale and lose its - well he was in a hurry.

To his relief, it was a male laboratory assistant who whisked the bottle away and labelled it. Then they took some more blood and urine samples and let him go. He did not feel like calling in on Gavin just then. He wanted to get away from the Bliss Institute.

Besides, he wanted to follow up on the story he had started on yesterday, about Carey. Turning his thoughts to this and away from what he had just delivered to the Bliss Institute, he grinned in anticipation, feeling what he imagined a foxhound felt when he got a scent of the fox. He would consult Manning. With Carey's connections it would be wise to get some backing before he went further.

Manning was just back from his European vacation and he seemed glad to see him and to deal with editorial problems. Ted told him about the story, and said, "I spoke to Rasmussen, this scientist friend of Gavin Grove, on the phone yesterday."

You've spoken to him already? On a Sunday?"

"Yes. I called him at his home in Los Angeles. He confirmed the story. He doesn't want me to quote him but he insists it's true. My friend Gavin Holder assures me he's very reliable."

"Good work."

"And I reckon," Ted went on, "that if Carey made the suggestion about copying documents to him, he made it to others also."

"Seems probable, doesn't it?" Manning leaned forward in a businesslike stance. "We'll get on to the Washington bureau and see what they can find out about Carey's CIA connection. Perhaps you'd like to talk to Washington yourself."

"Yes, I would."

The Washington bureau turned up a little material on Carey but it was less than he already knew. Ted telephoned Biotek and asked whether Mr. Carey was in. "Yes, he is," a secretarial voice said. "Who shall I say is speaking?"

He hung up, left his desk and hurried down to his car in the car park. He drove over to the Biotek building in Walton, eight storeys of concrete and glass rising straight up above a flat lawn with a parking lot at the side. Ted walked into the lobby and started for the elevator but a security guard barred his way, so he asked for Philip Carey at reception, giving his name.

He sat for a while on a couch in the reception area, waiting for the receptionist to tell him he could go up, next to a large potted fern hat loomed over him. He looked through copies of a pharmaceutical magazine and the *Wall Street Journal*, and watched a few people come in, mostly neat-suited men who he guessed to be salesmen selling anything from scientific equipment to carpeting. Sometimes someone flashed a pass and walked right through. When the door opened bringing a breeze, the sharp end of one of the fern leaves moved slightly and tickled the top of his head. He thought that he might to have a plant like this in his apartment to brighten it up. Then he decided that its size would create psychological problems for him, like having a wife who was a more successful journalist than him.

He was not invited to go up but Carey came down. He was a powerfully-built, barrel-chested man with a bald dome, about fifty years old, in his shirt-sleeves. Apart from his horn-rimmed glasses he could have been an ageing wrestler, and he advanced on Ted like a wrestler coming out of his corner. Ted stood up to face him.

"You're Ted Starowicz from the Long Island Chronicle?"

"Yes. Mr. Carey?"

Carey did not answer but said, "I remember you came and asked me questions once before. What do you want now?"

"I understand you're to be Vice-Chairman of the Industrial Committee of the Presidential Commission," said Ted, politely.

"That's right."

"Well, I'm covering this situation, so I'd like to ask about your background."

"What do you want to know?" asked Carey. He did not make it sound inviting.

"Well, what you were doing before you joined Barreras Pharmaceuticals."

"I was in the Government service."

"Does that mean the CIA?"

Carey peered into his face for a while as if it were a newspaper he was trying to read in a poor light. "You asked me about that before. What's with you?" he demanded. "Are you political? Or are you just after a headline?"

"Since you've been appointed to this committee, I'd just like to know about your background."

Carey's tone changed, and became almost conciliatory. "Perhaps I'll talk to you about it some time later on," he said. "I have served our country in a number of interesting capacities, and I was doing so while you were still in school."

"Could you tell me why you left the CIA?"

"I resigned to go into private business," said Carey. "That's all, if you don't mind." He turned to go.

"One thing more, Mr. Carey."

"Yes?"

"I've been told that you've offered scientists jobs at Biotek Incorporated if they would bring with them confidential information from the laboratories where they're working."

"You've been told *what*?" The last word cracked out like a rifle shot.

"I said I've been told that you've offered - "

Yes, I heard you. That is totally untrue. It's a vicious lie. If you print anything like that, you'll hear from Biotek's lawyers." He turned on his heel and walked away.

Ted went back to the office and reported the encounter to Manning. "Carey denies it, but we can get proof so fuck him," Ted said, grinning. Manning agreed that now they could use Carey's career in the CIA. He insisted, however, that Carey's denial of the story must go in the second paragraph, before details of the accusation or any background.

Ted wrote the story. He could not get to Manning to show it to him personally but he gave it to the national editor and told him it involved policy judgments. When he read it in the paper at home the next day he was pleased to see that it was almost unchanged.

At the Bliss Institute, Gavin sauntered into Izzy's office with a copy of the Chronicle in his hand and dropped into a chair. Izzy was on the phone and whispered in an aside to Gavin that he would be some time, but Gavin signalled that he would wait and read the newspaper. When Izzy had finished his conversation and turned his attention to him, Gavin asked him, "Do you know a man named Philip Carey?"

"I've seen his name somewhere. Let's see. Oh yes, he's a Biotek man, Vice-Chairman of the new Industrial Committee of the Presidential Commission. Right?"

"That's the man."

"What about him?"

"I've been hearing things about him," Gavin said.

"What have you been hearing?"

"That Mr. Carey is - let's see, how can I put this delicately - a shit."

Izzy grinned. "I see. Could you be more specific? Not that I'm doubting your judgment."

"It's in here, in the Chronicle. The story's true." He showed him the paper and told him what he knew.

Izzy read the story, and then commented, "I think this should go a little further."

"That's what I think," Gavin told him. "You can take it from here." He went back to his office.

Morley Bliss was in his office so Izzy took the newspaper to him. "Hmmm. This Mr. Carey," Bliss said after reading it, "seems to have an unpleasant background, and an unpleasant foreground too if this is how he behaves. He doesn't seem like the sort of man scientists should be working with on an issue of such national importance. It doesn't sound as if we can trust his disinterested pursuit of the goal we all share. What do you think, Izzy?"

"I quite agree," said Izzy.

"Of course, we can't simply accept something just because it's in the newspapers," Bliss said. "But I think somebody should look into it. You don't happen to know where this story comes from, do you?"

"As it happens I do," Izzy said.

" Yes, I thought you would, somehow."

"And it's accurate."

" Hmmm. Of course, I'm not on the commission. But this institute is represented on it."

"And you do know people on it, Morley. You can make your views known. You do have a certain influence."

"Do you think so?" Bliss seemed to ponder this as if the idea that he had influence in the scientific community had never occurred to him before. "Perhaps I do. How do you feel about working with a man who behaves like that, Izzy?"

"Not too happy. And I'm prepared to say so."

"Good. This seems to me one of those times when the world of science should stand up for its standards. Perhaps I'll have a talk with one or two people. If you have views, you have my full backing in letting them be known."

Two days later, Philip Carey resigned from the Presidential commission, saying that pressure of work prevented him from giving the post the attention it deserved.

Ted got the news in his office and telephoned Carey to ask for a comment. The secretary was telling him that any statement would have to come through Biotek's public relations department when a voice in the background called out: "Is that that little bastard from the Chronicle?"

He heard Carey snatch the phone from her and his voice came down the line: "You've got yourself a headline but you've caused a lot of trouble. You're going to be sorry one day!" And Carey slammed down the phone.

CHAPTER FIVE

Early one Friday evening, Martha Grove was in her kitchen with Grace Whiting, her boss at the counselling center, and Elaine. She had driven home with Grace, and Elaine had called in. Martha poured sherries for all of them.

Elaine was saying that her advertising agency had acquired the account for a local travel agency that was going to run women-only group tours to Europe. They wanted some display advertisements quickly.

"It's obvious what the selling point is," Martha said, "even if you don't come right out and say so. Penises that work. I can't think of any way you can advertise it that that isn't pornographic."

"How about," suggested Elaine, "a brawny Scotsman in a kilt, with, you know, those big muscular thighs, beside a trout stream, holding up a troOOOOOOOOOOOOOOOOOOOOOOOOOOOOOOOut, and the heading "The Fishing's Good."

"It would be banned for indecency," said Martha.

"It sure will if men have anything to say about it," Grace chuckled.

"We might be more subtle," Elaine suggested. "Use a

few images. The Eiffel Tower. The leaning tower of Pisa."

"Oh shut up, Elaine," said Martha laughing.

Grace was brown-haired and stocky with intelligent grey eyes, dressed today as most days in shapeless trousers and sweater, and chain-smoking. There was a leathery toughness about her which belied the sympathy she could show towards women and even men in difficulty, and which Martha knew well. Martha had come to like Grace more and more in the two years that she had worked at the counselling center.

"Whatever the ad says," Grace went on, "I guess most women know now they're going to have to get on a plane and go somewhere if they want any sex life with a man. You gals must be having a thin time." She looked inquiringly at Martha.

Martha shrugged. "There are ways and ways," she said. "What used to be the *hors d'ouevre* is now the main course." Then, feeling disloyal for saying even this much, she added: "Gavin and I still love each other. It hasn't made any difference to that."

"Ted's still okay," Elaine said. "I mean, the thing hasn't caught up with him yet." The other two looked at her in surprise. It crossed Martha's mind that Gavin must have known and had not told her.

"Lucky you," Martha said.

"Not really. I've just about given him up. A million women are after him now. He can pick and choose. And I have to get on line with the others. I can't stand that."

"You've given him up?" Grace asked. "You mean you've given *it* up?"

Elaine shrugged. "I get itchy sometimes but I'm not

desperate."

Grace looked at her watch. "Georgina Mills is going to be on the Dan Nelson show about now. I'd like to see what she has to say. Okay?" she asked. They agreed and went and sat down in the living room.

Georgina Mills was an associate professor of English literature and a feminist who had won a minor reputation as a lesbian proselytiser before the present plague began. Now she expounded her views on the present situation as the three women sat around and watched, with fresh glasses of sherry in their hands.

"You say this is a crisis. I see it as an opportunity," she said to Dan Nelson, who had put on his interested face. "It would be a crisis for the nation if the disease wiped out the male sperm. That would be a crisis for the whole human race. But human reproduction can go on. Thanks to our clever scientists, women can still be impregnated, babies can still be born. It's a psychological problem for the male sex. A lot of males are going to have to confront some of their hang-ups." She was tall and angular and very positive. She wore a smart two-color suit and heavy rings on both hands.

"Do you really think, Professor Mills," Nelson asked, "that women can get along contentedly without sexual activity?"

"Not most women, no," Georgina Mills said. "But I think they can do without sexual intercourse with men."

"I don't think most women would agree with you," Nelson said. He was speaking cautiously. His program was built around showbiz celebrities, but he had a national political figure or an author on every now and again to show that he could deal with serious issues. These usually played the game and were genial chat show guests. Georgina Mills was unpredictable and looked as if she could eat television interviewers for breakfast.

"You're quite right, Mr. Nelson," she said, and the relief showed on his face. But then she went on, "Most women do think today that they need sexual intercourse with men. They've been conned for centuries into believing that they need penetration by the male member to achieve full sexual satisfaction. More and more women are realizing that this is not the case."

"Right on," said Grace.

"It is sort of nice," murmured Martha.

"This has been the basis of male domination for millennia," Georgina Mills went on. "That's why I say that the present situation is an opportunity for womankind."

Dan Nelson wanted to steer the discussion away from the anatomical with this talk of "penetration by the male member." This was, after all, early in the evening. "But what about the effect on the family?" he asked .

She dismissed this with a wave of one heavily-ringed hand. "The modern family is only one possible form of social organization for bringing up children," she said "And it's one that has proved detrimental to the development of women as full human beings.

"You mean the conventional two-parent family," Nelson said.

"Yes. I'm not against children having two parents. I'm not even," she added mischievously, "against one of them being a man. If a woman wants to share her house and the upbringing of her child with a man, I won't say she mustn't. But she shouldn't be forced to do so by conditioning and the social pressures that support a male-dominated power structure, nor by the supposed need for a male sexual partner. It may well be that this plague, or whatever you want to call it, will have had the beneficial effect of ending the period of human evolution in which male-female sexual intercourse with the woman the passive receiver is the most common form of sexual activity and the usual method of human reproduction."

The program turned out to be devoted to what Nelson called "the broader issues of the current biological crisis."

The next guest was a popular writer who had just written a magazine article about male-female partnerships in the present crisis. She had intended to talk about emotional bonding and loyalty but following Georgina Mills she seemed to feel that she had to compete and expand the conventions of early evening television. She was soon talking about what she called the physical factors.

"Physical sexuality is a part of a loving relationship between a man and a woman. It's what distinguishes it from other loving relationships, after all," she said. She was small, black-haired and chubby, and wore a jacket that splayed out at her hips. She spoke rapidly and earnestly, with the assertive confidence of one accustomed to addressing an audience about intimate matters whether in print or in person.

"And when physical sexuality isn't there, what's left?" asked Nelson, barely glancing at his cue card. "Isn't there love?"

"Oh yes. But I don't accept that physical sexuality isn't there."

"But surely, for men nowadays - "

"Women still have sexuality. In a loving relationship, each partner wants to please the other. A partner in such a relationship has an obligation to satisfy the other partner's sexual needs, quite apart from his own. He should want to do so. If a man really loves a woman he'll want to do so as much as he can." She was in full flow now. Her dark frizzy hair fell over her eyes from time to time and she brushed it back without missing a syllable

"We accept that," said Nelson. "But where it's not possible to satisfy a partner's physical needs, surely there are other ways in which love can be expressed." He wanted to get to something that was uplifting.

"But it is possible," she insisted. "Or at any rate, a man can do a great deal. We have to recover a recognition of polymorphous perversity. Erotic pleasure isn't limited to one part of the body, and certainly not to one act. A man can use his hands in all sorts of ways to give intense sexual - "

"I understand, but we don't need to hear - "

But she was in full flow. "There are things he can do. He can use his hands. He can use his mouth. He can use his fingers, his toes - "

"His *toes*?" repeated Nelson, startled out of professionalism.

"Certainly," she said. "There's a lot that a sensitive man can do with - "

" You've had some interesting things to say about the emotional bonds," Nelson cut in, using all his authority to regain control. "I'd like to hear a little more about that." He managed to keep her talking on this level, and the viewer could almost see him making up his mind that he was not going to have any more goddamned women like these on his show.

The next guest was a psychiatrist who had written a popular book about sex in modern society. His square rimless glasses matched the square shape of his face. He was as bland in his manner as Georgina Mills had been abrasive, as judicious as the two women had been forthright. His speech was carefully crafted and was full of cautions and temporizings, of "One will have to wait and see whether..." and "It will be interesting to observe how..."

Nelson asked him: "Do you feel this is altering the psyche of America? That is, do you think we are becoming, in a broad sense, a less manly nation?"

"The definition of what is manly is different in different cultures," the psychiatrist replied. "The characteristics that a culture associates with manliness are not necessarily connected with sexual activity, or even with the male gender. We'll have to see whether the things that our culture associates with manliness, like strength, bravery, an adventurous spirit, are any less prevalent as time goes on. They may prove to be just as prevalent. Homosexuals have sometimes exhibited all of these characteristics. Although, of course, homosexuals have been affected by this plague in the same way as heterosexuals.

"We can look for changes in our national character if this plague, or whatever you want to call it, continues. It will be interesting to see what these will be. Certainly there's no reason to suppose that all the positive characteristics of our society will disappear. In past times, eunuchs have proved to be creative and have contributed to the societies in which they lived."

Nelson winced to hear American males, presumably

including himself, depicted as eunuchs. Then he asked: "You've written about sex and marriage. Do you think men will continue to seek a permanent relationship with women?"

"Again, this will be something fascinating to watch. Hardly any marriages are taking place at the moment, but this may be just because we customarily think of a married couple, and particularly a newly married couple, as sexual partners. If this situation continues, we may come to think of marriage as, not merely something more than this, which it is now of course, but as something other than this. Men are drawn to women for many reasons and on many levels, starting with a child's relationship with its mother. We don't know how much of this is related directly to the adult sex drive. This is something we may find out a little more about."

At just about the time that the three women were pouring their first glass of sherry, Gavin was in his office tidying up before leaving.for the day. He had closed the desk drawer and had his hand on the doorknob when the telephone rang.

"This is Dean Hoffmeister," the caller said. "As you may know, I'm the scientific director of Biotek."

! Gavin had heard of Hoffmeister. Scientists talked of him with respect "Yes, I know your name. Hello," he said.

"I'd like to invite you to come and visit us some time soon," Hoffmeister said. "I'd like to show you our facilities, introduce you to some of our people here,"

. "It's kind of you, but I'm very busy right now, and I don't think I could take a day out," said Gavin.

Hoffmeister persisted. "Actually, we've heard of your

work and we're thinking of offering you a position at Biotek. I'd like to discuss it with you."

"That's flattering, Dr. Hoffmeister, but I'm not considering changing jobs now."

"I think we could offer you a substantial increase in salary."

"Thank you, but I'm really very happy here at Bliss."

"I see. Okay, Gavin. If you want to think again about the matter at any time, do give me a call."

"I will." He hung up wondering whether he should have called the other man "Dean" instead of "Dr. Hoffmeister." They had never met, never even spoken before, but Hoffmeister had called him by his first name. He was still not completely in tune with American manners.

Izzy stuck his head in the door and said, "Coming over to the club?" They walked over to the faculty club and went straight to what was becoming the Bliss Institute scientists' regular Friday evening corner. Several others were already there.

Others at the club had come to regard the Friday evening group with curiosity and interest. As he and Izzy walked towards it one man at the bar, probably emboldened by an early start to an evening's drinking, called out, "When are you guys going to come up with something that'll give us back our love lives?"

"We've got the cure but we're keeping it to ourselves," Izzy told him.

Izzy and the others exchanged shop talk: about the work, prospects and personalities. Several of them reported getting job offers connected with the work on impotence. Since others spoke out, Gavin said that he also had had a call from Biotek. Nobody gave a figure but they all knew that the offers would include higher salaries.

"So why aren't we all leaving Bliss?" asked Denise Springer. "I'm not suggesting that we should," she went on, "I'm just wondering whether anyone has got any ideas as to why none of us has done so. After all, some of us are getting better offers than we're ever likely to get again. But no one has left Bliss since these offers started to come in."

"I guess most of us are happy working here," Carl Eisengrau said. "That's worth a lot. Not many places give you this much scope and this much freedom."

Izzy took this up. "I think Morley himself is largely responsible for the atmosphere here," he said. "He's created this tradition of choosing individuals carefully and then backing them all the way on almost anything they want to do. Also, we all have our gripes, but he's created an institutional spirit."

"He's a marvellous man, and it's a marvellous place!" Mohsin said simply. "I was in Moscow a while ago and somebody quoted to me a Russian saying, 'Better to make ten friends than a hundred roubles.' Here we are all friends. That's important. And Morley himself."

His enthusiasm embarrassed the others slightly. Denise Springer said, "Yes. Morley gets on my nerves at times with his moralizing but I guess he is one big reason I'm here and why most of us are here."

Then they talked about other institutions. Gavin told the others about his evening with Alan Carling. "Biotek seems to be working on that Meriacci paper, same as Izzy and Mohsin," he said, for Izzy had joined Mohsin in this work.

"I'm surprised that they've come up with that idea too. It's not an obvious one," somebody said.

"I was surprised too when he told me," Gavin said. "He probably shouldn't have told me, but he's a talkative guy. And they're also working on a melifulin b culture."

"They're working on that at Salk," said Eisengrau. "A friend of mine there told me."

"Biotek apparently get a lot of these ideas from Barreras Pharmaceuticals' lab in San Diego," Gavin said. " They've produced several ideas that Biotek are following up. It sounds like a high-powered place."

"Balls," said Denise.

"What?" Gavin asked, surprised.

"Balls," repeated Denise. "Balls that the Barreras lab in San Diego is a high-powered place pouring out a lot of ideas. Have any of you ever seen it?" There was silence.

"Well I have," she went on. "I was offered the job of running it once. It's got maybe half a dozen scientists, a technician and a cat. It's working on improvements in manufacturing methods, that's all. It came with something Barreras bought and he hasn't got around to closing it down. That's one reason I wasn't interested in taking the job. They're competent guys there, but it's a very small outfit, and it's not doing interesting work."

Gavin shrugged his shoulders. "That's what Alan told me," he said.

"Did your friend Alan go out to San Diego?" Denise asked.

"No, I don't think so. He said they just get memos with ideas that are supposed to have originated there."

"I don't know where they come from," Denise said.

"But you can bet your ass they don't all come from that little lab in San Diego."

Over dinner that night Gavin told Martha about the call from Biotek. "That must have pleased you," she said.

"Yes, I must admit it did," he acknowledged.

"And you're not even considering it?"

He shook his head. "To tell the truth, I haven't even thought about it. I'm quite happy where I am."

Martha decided to wait until later, with all questions of his salary forgotten, before bringing up her difficulty, and they watched some television after dinner. Then, near bedtime, she said, "I had trouble today. The Volk's been acting neurotically again. I'll have to take it in to be checked over, and I'm afraid it may need repairs yet again."

"What's the trouble?"

"I have trouble starting it."

"Something wrong with the starter?" suggested Gavin, who did not know anything about cars.

"Perhaps. I think this time we may decide it's not worth spending more money on it, and it might be time to trade it in for a new car. We've had it a long time."

"We won't get much for it," Gavin pointed out.

"We may have to buy a new car anyway."

He paused and made some umming sounds before replying. "I don't know that we can spend that kind of money right now. Not while we're still paying off the loan for the repairs."

"We can if I need a new car. What do you expect me to do, go into Radford by bus every day?"

"There are buses, and other people do."

Her voice became sharp. "All right, I'll take the Ford

and you can go the Bliss Institute by bus."

"Come on, there aren't buses that go to Holycroft."

"There are."

"Not from Melby Park."

"There are from Radford, and you could get a bus from here to Radford."

"Don't be stupid."

"Why is that stupid? You think you're going to have a car when I spend half my day traveling around on buses?"

"You're a bit spoiled, you know," he told her, in what he thought was a soft, reasonable tone, "It's not the end of the world if you have to use public transport. I know you weren't brought up to it."

"Don't start that crap about my rich upbringing," she retorted. By now she was on her feet and taking the dishes off the table, slapping them together so hard that Gavin thought they would break. Her parents were comfortably well off and wealthier than most people he knew, but not what she would call rich. She stomped off to the kitchen with the dishes and he put the rest of the things away in silence.

Gavin was annoyed because he had somehow got himself in the wrong. He did not really think she should travel to work every day by two buses. Since coming to this country he had often noted the reluctance of the Americans he knew to use public transport. He was only trying to make the point that having to travel by bus occasionally was not a great hardship and he was aware that he had not made it very well.

In bed that night, he was the first to say it: "I'm sorry we had that row. I said some stupid things."

"I'll take the car into the garage on Saturday and see what they can do with it."

He kissed her, and she nuzzled his neck, and put her arms around him. He stroked her breast, and moved his hand downwards. "No, don't, please," she said. "Not now."

"I'm sorry," he said. "I know it's not the same."

::   ::   ::

Ted Starowicz spent an afternoon doing a story on a local hospital that carried out artificial insemination, and had let it be known that they were now prepared to extract sperm from men donors. The director told him they had had a big increase in queries but only a small increase in the number of inseminations actually performed.

"Why do you think that is?" Ted asked him.

"It seems to me," the director replied, "that a lot of people want to hold a.i. in the background as an option, in case this thing goes on. But they're not ready to accept yet that it will go on. I don't suppose any of us are."

"That makes sense," Ted said. He questioned him closely about the procedure, and came away pleased. This would make a nice story.

He got back to his office in the early evening, and there was a message to say that Naomi James had called, with her telephone number. He remembered getting a glimpse of her at the other end of Kate Lestrange's lobby, and was surprised that she had seen him and recognized him at that distance. It had been quite a few years since they had last seen each other. He called her back right away.

"I'm sorry if I seemed to ignore you the other day," he told her, "but you were at the other end of the lobby and by the time I realized it was you, you'd gone."

"That's all right. It's been a long time," she said. He knew from mutual acquaintances she had married and had a teaching job at a small New England college.

He had dated her briefly at the end of his year at Columbia and before he went to Paris on a six-month fellowship. Talking to her now, he pictured her as he had last seen her and it was still a picture that appealed to him. She was short, with heavy black eyebrows and lustrous brown eyes and a touch of olive oil in her complexion. This all indicated forebears from the Mediterranean, despite her name. She had black hair which she wore, he remembered, in a page-boy cut that framed her pretty face. Like him, she came from New Jersey, from Hackensack.

He had enjoyed their evenings out, even though she poked fun at him. He remembered her saying, when he was talking about going to Paris: "You're a few years too late, Teddy. You really want to be there in 1948. Post-war, that should have been your time. Spending the afternoon at the Café Deux Magots discussing existentialism with Sartre and suicide with Camus, and then going off to lay Juliette Greco."

She would not go to bed with him. She said he was going abroad soon so there was no future in it. "It would be like a one-night stand, and you're worth more than that," she told him. It occurred to him later that this was a good trick, turning him down but making him feel good about it.

Now he asked her, "Are you living in Cedar Hill Apartments?" "Yes. I've just taken a small apartment there."

"By yourself?"

"I'm divorced now."

"I'm sorry."

"I'm not."

"And you've moved out here?"

"Yes. Starting in the fall, I'll be doing a PhD at Holycroft in American lit. And I have a teaching job there. And I hear you're doing very well in journalism. And not only in journalism."

"Meaning what?"

"I saw you were visiting our mutual friend Kate Lestrange." Naomi had been no more Kate's friend at Columbia than he had. "She's pretty classy. Always was."

"I always liked classy ladies, if you remember," he said.

"Anyway, I thought I'd call you. You've been to see her apartment. Why not come and see mine?"

The invitation was so direct that it startled him for a moment. But then he said, "Okay, yes."

"I didn't quite mean that. Not the way it sounds. I mean, since we're sort of neighbors now, perhaps we could have a drink somewhere." Evidently, she had startled herself with her boldness and was drawing back. "We can catch up on each other."

"Or dinner," he said. "Tonight. Have you had dinner?"

"Yes, and I've just washed my hair. Another time?"

"Tomorrow night?"

"Okay."

"Fine. I'll call for you at seven-thirty." Then he envisaged the embarrassment of meeting Kate Lestrange in the lobby. "Well actually, that might be difficult. Perhaps we could meet at the restaurant. Do you know the Radford Inn?"

She still had a page boy haircut. They were nervous with one another over drinks, each of them laying out disconnected bits of their lives over the past few years, but over dinner they talked more easily and gradually revealed themselves. With the straight biographical details over, where they had lived and where they had worked, they started to tell each other more.

He told her something of the truth of his time in Paris, rather than the usual version he trotted out for people: that somehow he had not been ready to make the most of the experience, and he had not found either friends or intellectual enlightenment. He hinted at what he was now realizing, that he had begun to grow up only after he returned. He told her how bad he had been at the beginning in his first job in journalism, on a small town paper in Massachusetts. "I had a lot of pretensions left over from my undergraduate days that got in the way," he explained. "I find it embarrassing even to think about the way I was then."

She told him how and perhaps even why she had married the wrong man for the wrong reasons; she was still trying to work these out, it had something to with her father's weak character. She said his competitive drive and careerism had shut her out of his life. His brief fling with another woman only three years after they were married had caused her a lot of pain and was a good enough reason to break it up. "I don't think I could ever fall for someone like that now. I hope not," she concluded. They were both aware that sharing these confidences was something special.

When she closed the door behind them in her one-room apartment, they kissed, and neither of them spoke. They undressed, kissing and fondling one another as they did so. Then they lay down side by side on the bed. He started to stroke her body and kissed her all over. She ran her hands over him, and handled his sensitive parts tenderly.

They travelled slowly along the path to a climax, and he used his skill to linger along the way. When they made love she looked up into his eyes, until she reached her climax, when her eyes first widened and then closed. As pleasure filled his body she dug her nails into his back and cried out his name.

Lying together, their bodies touching from shoulder to heel, she said thoughtfully, "I wish I hadn't seen you and Kate in the lobby that day."

"Then we wouldn't have met again, and I wouldn't be here. You're sorry?" He was upset to hear her say this.

"Oh, I don't quite mean that," he said, and pressed her face into his shoulder.

"You're glad you're here with me?" He wanted reassurance.

"Yes. I just wish it had happened differently."

"You mean you wish I'd called you instead of you calling me?" he asked. "I probably would have."

"I wanted you here for the wrong reasons," she said, slowly. She paused for a while, collecting her thoughts.

He caressed her again. He kissed her shoulder and, turning her over, he stroked her back and her small buttocks, taking pleasure in the feel of her skin, studying with his hands the textures and skin tones. She pulled back and went on. "What I mean is this. You know, at Columbia, Kate always seemed to be one of those girls who was a cut above the likes of me, in looks, in sophistication, in everything."

"She was a cut above the likes of me," he said. "I was just a kid from Jersey."

"I saw that Kate had you. You were leaving in the morning. And I guessed that you were - well, you know, you were still male in that way. So I suppose I thought I should have you too. Maybe some of Joe's competitiveness has rubbed off on me. It's a pretty lousy reason to go to bed with someone."

"You mean you wouldn't have otherwise?"

"No, I probably would have eventually. That's it." She was talking slowly, working out what she was saying as she went along. "I mean,. I wish there wasn't that reason. You're worth more than that."

"You said that to me once before," he said, and kissed her."

They left together in the morning, since she had to go out. As they walked through the lobby he glanced around a little anxiously. He did not particularly want to meet Kate Lestrange. It occurred to him later that Naomi would have been pleased if they had.

He thought about Naomi during the day, and his body remembered her. Towards the evening he telephoned her. He got an answering machine and he said, "Just thought I'd call. I miss you already. I'll call again." He meant to call her again but then the weekend edition wanted a long summary of develop- ments to date and he had to write it with Charlton Smith. Then there was another story to do, and he did not get around to calling Naomi that week, although he thought of her often.

When he did think of her again, he thought of other women also. If Kate and Naomi, then why not others, since he was in this extraordinary position through an accident of nature? Could he have any woman he liked? Not quite. But a lot of other women, to be had easily. Perhaps most other women. It was a staggering idea. It was even sexually exciting in itself.

He tried to grasp it. He thought of all the women about whom he had had carnal thoughts. Not the long-term, considered, serious lusting, month-in, month-out unrequited carnal passion. He had never known this, not because he had always had any woman he wanted but because he gave up easily. Rather, he tried to capture the casual, transient lust, unconnected with any serious ambition.

When he was twelve years old, his uncle Max, who lived in Canada and was said to be wealthy, had come to visit them, and had given his sister and him as presents the unheard-of sum of two hundred dollars each to spend. Like most twelve-year-olds he was a materialist. He used to spend a lot of time looking in store windows and catalogs at things he would like to own: a really good baseball glove, a whole number of video games, a mobile phone that did everything shaped like a football. He did not so much covet them as simply think, in an abstract way, how great it would be if he could have them. Now, suddenly, with his uncle's present, he could buy any of them. All sorts of things were possible. He had gone back over the store windows and the catalogs with new eyes. He recalled this feeling now.

He thought of women he knew, even slightly, who sometimes aroused a faint feeling of sexual desire when he saw them, a feeling so everyday that he hardly noticed it, any more than the brush of wind on his cheek or the pressure on his body of the seat belt in a car. He dredged up these thoughts. Could all of them now become realizable ambitions? He tried the more specific, more anatomical thoughts that sometimes slid through his mind when certain women passed by: I'd like to clutch that ass, kiss that breast, stroke that thigh. Maybe he could do it all. Maybe all women were available to him.

The first woman who swam into his mind and stayed there was Shirley, the newsroom secretary who always showed off her body as she sashayed about. He always looked at her when she walked by and fleeting thoughts of her naked sometimes came into his mind. Was she available? Could he ask her out and make a play for her? Would she leap at the chance? Or would she just give him the brush-off? The trouble was, they had been around each other for a year or so without either of them paying any particular attention to the other. It would be an abrupt move for him to ask her out on a date. Also, she was just a cute young secretary and he had to admit that it would be a come-down if she turned him down, particularly if it got about. The thing to do was wait for a situation that threw them together, say, if they met by accident on the street somewhere, and he could then suggest that they stop off for a drink, without having to commit himself by formally asking her out on a date.

There were others, women he knew and women he saw all the time and did not know and women he had glimpsed just once. Images came to his mind, of cleavage, if angora wool over breasts so soft that he wanted to stroke it as he would stroke a kitten, of a tall cool blonde with white pants tight over her ass, and a jolly plump brunette who threw back her head and laughed a sexy laugh, of a walk, of a look in the eye, of the way this one carried herself and that one of carried a plate of sandwiches.

He had always been shy with women at first. He was not shy in the bedroom. Nor was he shy in talking to women. But he was shy in the early approaches to a sexual relationship. His step in the foothills was sometimes hesitant and faltering, and he would often draw back or stumble. At a party occasionally, he would make conversation with a girl he found attractive but hold back from making advances, only to watch someone more sure-footed and confident carry her off. He had once read an interview with some writer, and the writer was asked what he knew now that he would have liked to have known at eighteen. He had replied, "Girls like it too." He also would have liked to have been more aware of that when he was younger. He sometimes reminded himself of it now.

He was also self-conscious about his body. He was shorter than the average, and sometimes shorter than women he met. He was hairy. He knew some women found this attractive but this seemed to him to be a perversion. Sometimes, when his hairy skin rubbed against a woman's skin it would leave a red bare mark, and on those occasions he felt he was violating her.

He would wait and see whether he met Shirley by accident, and then be ready to take advantage of the situation. As it turned out he met Anne, who lived two floors below him in Hudson Apartments. She seemed to be in her early forties, and was tall with dark brown hair and a soft plump moon face, given to wearing slinky, body-hugging clothes. He had decided when he first saw her that he liked her slightly overripe shape. He had met her when she was struggling through the lobby with several packages and had helped her up in the elevator with them to her apartment. She thanked him and said she had just moved in and they had introduced themselves. He remembered her first name only. He saw her several times after that, sometimes with a man a little older than her.

They met at ten o'clock in the evening, as they were both going into the elevator, and they smiled and said hello as always. He recalled that he liked her shape and had only an empty bed waiting for him and he told himself, "Well, this is it. Let's see."

"Hello Anne, how are you?" he asked casually.

"Tired. I've had a difficult week," she replied.

"Maybe you need to relax," he suggested. "Do you feel like coming in to have a drink?" She hesitated and he added, "And maybe watch a late-night movie?"

"No thanks. I think I'll turn in early," she said. The response came out automatically. Then she saw that he was eyeing her up and down and she returned his look.

She and paused as she was about to get out of the elevator, then said, "Maybe I will come in for a drink. Okay," she said, and let the elevator door close. She continued to look at him curiously, not quite sure what she was seeing, until they got out at his floor.

As they went into his apartment, she asked, "Are you hitting on me?"

"I'm intending to," he said.

"In the old-fashioned way?"

"I'm an old-fashioned guy."

"Well, that's something. There aren't many of those around," she said, brushing her hair from her forehead and straightening the hem of her dress. She went in and sat down on the sofa. He was conscious of the untidiness and picked up some newspapers and a coffee mug from the floor and took them out of the room before sitting down beside her. He offered her a drink and she asked for Scotch, and he poured drinks for them both.

"I've been admiring you from a distance for some time," he told her.

"That's nice to hear. It was from a distance."

"Do you really want me to turn on the TV?" he asked,

"Not unless it's an absolutely fantastic movie."

He started to put his arm around her, and hesitated, awkwardly. "This is silly. We're neighbors, we ought to get to know each other a bit. I'm afraid I don't even remember your second name."

"Broadley," she said. "Yours?"

"Starowicz. You're not married?"

"Divorced. Years ago."

"I thought I saw you with a man from time to time. Grey hair, distinguished looking."

"He was a boy friend, but not for a little while now."

"So what do you do, Anne?"

"These days I mostly just sit around and think about it. Oh, I see what you mean. I'm a buyer for the Willow group of stores. Soft furnishings."

"Been doing it long?"

"I was with Macy's but I got tired of my Manhattan

cubby-hole. What do you do?"

"I'm a reporter. On the Long Island Chronicle."

"What do you report?"

"All sorts of things. I'm not a specialist."

"It must be an interesting job."

"Yes, you meet a lot of interesting people. That's such a cliché. This is even sillier."

"Isn't it?" She leaned forward, and now he put his arms around her and kissed her. He was amazed at his audacity, and amazed at how easy it was.

Her flesh was soft, as he had imagined it, giving him a feeling of almost decadent sensuality. He had never been to bed with a woman as old as her before. In bed, she was wildly appreciative, gasping as soon he touched her pubic hairs.

Afterwards she said, "God, I was an easy lay, wasn't I?" They were lying side by side.

He tried to think of a polite reply. "Enthusiastic. I like that," he answered, finally.

"I'm not always like that, but this is a special situation," she said.

"I know. I guess I'm lucky," he said.

"I'm pretty lucky too. You're just two floors above me."

"I'm not here all the time," he said. "I have a lot of work and I've got - "

"Don't worry," she interrupted, and smiled at him. "I'm not imagining I can claim special rights. Just once in a while, huh?"

"Once in a while would be great," he said, relieved.

"I'm not usually this forward, I promise you."

"I believe you," he assured her.

"I don't usually come on this way. I can relate to men in other ways. In fact, I get pissed off at the men I meet in business, from out of town, who think that just because I'm single I must be   - you know. Good for a night's entertainment. But lately, it's been different. There hasn't been anything. And you turned me on the way you looked at me in the elevator. Nobody's looked at me like that for a while."

"So how do you feel doing without sex?" he asked her. He often wondered how women felt these days.

"I don't like it," she said. He murmured sympathetically. "But quite honestly," she went on, "I think it's only because I'm used to it. With my boy friend. In the past I've done without it for quite long periods before."

"So you could do without it?"

"Yes, if you hadn't turned up. What a woman wants just isn't just sex. I mean, it is sex but not just screwing. It's something else. What I want anyway."

"What?"

"Oh, it's being recognized as a woman. You want the occasional man to look at you in that way, to touch your arm, hold your hand, even kiss you. You want there to be a spark there sometimes. That kind of connection. That's sex."

"Uh-huh."

"You still feel that about a woman, Teddy boy. And that's what women want from you. Not just a stiff cock. Not that I'm knocking a stiff cock," she said, and reached out and touched his, which was not stiff but soon would be.

::   ::   ::

At the Bliss Institute on Monday, Gavin had a frustrating morning. Some chemical solutions he needed had not been prepared; then he spent an hour explaining to a junior colleague why an idea the other had for a line of research was mistaken, and some of the other's dismay and disappointment stuck to him. He decided he was not going to accomplish anything right now and went up to the canteen for an early lunch.

He had not yet started eating when Izzy Rubin came in, and he asked him to join him. Izzy got his food and talked about his work with what he was now calling the Meriacci reaction.

"It's yielded something," he told him. "No doubt. The virus is showing signs of multiplying. I'm trying to work out where to go from there, along with Mohsin." Izzy was outlining the possibilities when Denise brought her tray over to their table.

"May I join you? she asked.

"By all means," said Izzy. "Very pleased to see you. I was telling Gavin here about some work on the Meriacci reaction which he initiated. But there's another problem I've been thinking about. You brought it up last Friday, Denise."

"I did?" she asked.

"Yes."

"What problem is that?"

"Things that don't fit. There's this tiny laboratory in San Diego that's apparently pouring out a lot of work, more than that little lab could possibly do. This friend of Gavin's gave him two examples of that work."

"He probably shouldn't have told us so much," said Gavin. "He was in an unhappy mood, because of his divorce and things. Please don't mention his name again. I don't want him to get into trouble."

"Okay, I won't. He gave us two examples of the work. Both of them are things that other places are working on. One Salk, the other us."

"So?"

"So. You say the lab at San Diego couldn't be doing all this work themselves. Doesn't this suggest something to you?"

"What?" asked Gavin.

"What it suggests to me is theft. They can't be doing all the work themselves because that lab is too small. And it's an extraordinary coincidence that two projects that the San Diego lab supposedly initiates are things that other labs are working on. Maybe material is being stolen."

"Do you think so?" Gavin asked.

Izzy did not reply directly but went on, "And there's one person who might be capable of organizing this. This Philip Carey. CIA background, he left under a cloud, and he apparently tried to get people to leave their jobs for Biotek and bring confidential papers with them. That's pretty sneaky."

The others paused to consider this. Then Denise said, "Okay. But he's here on Long Island. The other guys are in San Diego."

Gavin added, "Maybe I'm being naive, but it doesn't seem likely to me that the San Diego lab are really a band of scientists dedicated to stealing ideas from other labs."

"Unless he's staffed San Diego with his own people," said Izzy. "A team of people who do nothing else but steal material."

"But how would they go about it?"

"I said I'd been thinking about it," said Izzy. "I didn't say I'd solved the problem. I'm inviting collaboration. Do either of you have any ideas?"

They ate in silence for a while, each thinking purposefully. Izzy ate in spurts, pushing food into his mouth and then pausing and frowning down at his plate. You could almost see his thoughts starting off in one direction, then stopping and starting off in another. Denise chewed hard, as if the act of masticating were connected to the act of ruminating, and more energy put into one meant more output in the other. Gavin seemed to be concentrating on his food, occasionally looking intently across the table at a space just above the others' heads.

Once Denise said, "Computer hacking. If they could hack into everbody's computers."

"Maybe," Izzy said.

Eventually, Gavin said, "Suppose somebody did steal scientific secrets, like Carey was trying to get that other man to do. What would they do with them?"

"What do you mean?" Izzy asked.

"What does Carey do with them? Just give them to the people in the labs and say, 'We stole this from this place, that from that place, here, work on them'?"

"That doesn't sound very plausible," said Denise.

"No it doesn't. The scientists at Biotek wouldn't all go along with that. They may be competitive but they're not a bunch of crooks. But suppose Carey or somebody did steal ideas, and they wanted people to follow through with the work. They could say they came from the lab in San Diego. The San Diego lab would be their alibi."

There was a pause. "Now that is an idea," said Izzy. "You've gone way ahead of me."

"It's only a theory," said Gavin. "But it does seem to fit the facts."

"But," Denise said, "whoever organized the theft of secrets, how would they go about it? Spies? Spies in several labs? A spy here at Bliss?"

"That is a nasty thought," said Gavin. "I don't like to think about it."

"Maybe we won't have to," said Izzy. "There are electronic spies."

"What do you mean?" asked Gavin.

"Electronic eavesdropping. Remember that break-in a few weeks ago, when nothing was stolen? On a Saturday night?"

Denise whistled. "Hey, yes. Somebody could have planted a bug."

"Exactly," said Izzy. He thought for a while, and then announced: "I'm going to ask the Executive Council to have the place swept for bugs."

When the council met, he encountered opposition at first from Morley Bliss. "We just shouldn't be playing that kind of game," he protested. "Our work is open. We've decided that again and again."

"But not totally. Not while it's in progress," argued Izzy. "We don't want someone else to capitalize on it and exploit it."

"That's true," said someone else. "And we want to be sure we can at least talk in private. Do we want to the director of some other lab to be able to listen in to our council meetings?"

After more discussion, Bliss sighed, "I suppose it's the world we live in. Okay, let's do it." The vote was unanimous.

The Deputy Director, John Visconti, was assigned the task of finding a private investigation agency. He did, and the agency sent a man along who spent a whole day sweeping one room after another.

The agency sent in a report saying there were no electronic bugs, and this was reported at the next Council meeting.

CHAPTER SIX

In July, the Administration came under pressure to act because of what became known as "that cartoon." The cartoon was in an Egyptian newspaper, and it depicted an international meeting at which representatives of several countries were holding out their flags horizontally while the Stars and Stripes dangled from a drooping flagpole.

The cartoon was reprinted in some American newspapers and created public fury. The Secretary of State had to agree that it was an insult but said the United States could not bomb Cairo in retaliation, or even change its Middle East policy. Nonetheless, newspaper letter columns and radio phone-ins resounded with the fury of ordinary Americans. The cartoon also strengthened the view that was being heard more and more, that Islamic extremists were responsible for the plague and that the United States should take retaliatory action without further ado.

Things were made worse by the fact that the phrase "American droop" made its appearance in the language. In several languages, in fact. The French Foreign Minister, Yvonne Tardieu, criticizing Germany for what she said was a weak-kneed stance in the European Union's trade dispute with Japan, said the German Government seemed to be suffering from "American droop." She later apologized for what she said was a hasty and ill-chosen phrase. In Israel, a right-wing opposition leader, mixing metaphors ingeniously, accused the Foreign Minister of approaching negotiations on a new peace plan "carrying a Neville Chamberlain umbrella with an American droop."

America's balance of payments suffered as tourist visits from overseas fell to virtually zero. A Treasury Department spokesman said, "We hope this will prove to be temporary. In any case, there is no medical evidence that short-term exposure to the American environment will affect the sexual fun0ction."

The first all-women tourist groups came back from Europe with disappointing reports. Inter- viewed by reporters, some admitted to hoping that what they discreetly termed "romance" might have been a holiday bonus. But men all over Europe had shunned them, for fear of catching "the American disease." A reporter asked one member of the group what she had hoped to be doing on the trip and she replied, "I won't tell you that but I'll tell you what I did. I saw a lot more museums and cathedrals than I'd expected to."

In some Third World countries, the rumor spread that any contact with Americans could bring on the disease. American cars were stoned on the street, and the State Department advised American citizens in some countries to leave, or if they remained, to travel about as little as possible. Some African governments barred Americans from entering the country.

It was a shock to Americans when Australia followed suit. The disease had not spread there and was not known to be present and some members of the Government thought it might be possible to prevent it entering. The Government rushed through Parliament a bill barring Americans, Canadians and Mexicans unless they had been away from home for at least eighteen months. Medical commen- tators said this would be unlikely to be effective since the virus must be present in many parts of the world now and could come from anywhere. Whereupon some members of parliament proposed a more drastic measure still for the defense of Australia's manhood: a self-imposed quarantine that would isolate Australia from the rest of the world. This could be achieved easily since Australia has no land frontiers. It was calculated that by strict rationing of many provisions and relying on stockpiles of raw materials, Australia could survive for a year or more without imports..

The World Health Organization announced that it was calling a conference of leading bio-medical organizations around the world to discuss approaches to the problem. The Director-General suggested that such meetings should be held regularly until a cure was found.

A leading British Sunday newspaper considered the situation in a thoughtful editorial. It said that for reasons that were not understood, the disease had reached a near-100 percent level only in America, and that it did not seem that it would reach this level anywhere else. The newspaper held out the possibility that the American nation would be without masculinity, in the sexual sense, for a long time.

"Artificial insemination will become the norm," it said. "The next generation of Americans, one and all, will be fathered by hypodermic needles. It will be something new in the world: an entire nation of people whose conception and birth have been separate from the physical act of love, all of them the product of planning and technology. Furthermore, it will be a nation of men who, while not quite androgynous, will lack some of the normal masculine physical characteristics. What kind of nation will it be? And how numerous? How many people will want babies in this way? And how many babies? This will be a new race of people in the world."

The wire services carried quotes from the editorial. Tom Manning read out parts of the wire service story at the morning conference in his office on the Monday. "I'm going to get the full text of this editorial," he told the others. "I think we might carry it on the op ed page. Let our readers know what some people think is in store for us all."

"It'll scare the shit out of them," one of his deputies said.

Manning shrugged. "It scares me," he said. "But if that's what's coming, maybe we ought to be scared. It's not our job to keep bad news from our readers."

When the others left his office, he brooded for a while about his marital position. In twenty-four years of marriage he had never been unfaithful to Millie. When he thought about this, which was not often, and considered other men he knew, he decided that this was unusual. All the more so as he was not unattractive. His sister said he had the face of an Irish pugilist but he was well-built, with steel-grey hair which was thinning on top and blue eyes, and an air of authority that went with success. No doubt it was a factor that his career in journalism had been almost all as an editor rather than as a reporter so that he was rarely away from home. Also, adultery meant a number of things that were alien to his nature: lying, concealment, emotional complications. He had never wanted sex with anyone else strongly enough to offset this. Unlike some of his colleagues, he did not regard sex with a number of women as a natural reward for success in his career.

But now, after what Millie had said to him the other night, he felt that he ought to commit adultery. He owed it to himself. It was a wife's duty to satisfy her husband's sexual needs, and *vice versa*. A man needed to feel that he was pleasing a woman as well as having pleasure himself. If the woman did not enjoy sex with him, then she was failing to satisfy his need. In that case he had a right to seek a satisfactory relationship elsewhere. Not to do so was to be something less than a well-rounded, mature human being leading a full life. He considered that he was a mature human being, and he ought to be well-rounded and lead a full life.

He looked across through the window of his office and saw Kate Lestrange striding across the news room. In the rare moments when the idle thought of an extra-marital affair entered his mind she was often a partner in the imagined affair.. She was young enough and good-looking enough to compliment his virility, and she matched him professionally and socially. But now he had nothing to say to Kate. Whatever moves he made, whatever her response, he could not follow through. He ought to have an affair now and ideally he should have one with Kate. But he was cheated of even the possibility. He scowled at the thought.

Kate stopped by Ted Starowicz's desk and she put her hand on his shoulder and exchange a few words with him. Manning watched closely, and before she walked away from him she gave his shoulder a gentle rub. She did not just leave her hand there, she rubbed his shoulder. It was a

friendly gesture, but since when were Kate Lestrange and
Ted such good friends, goddammit? And that rub was more
than friendly, more than affectionate even. It was *sensual.*
Only now did he recall that someone had told him that he
thought young Starowicz was one of those rare men who
were not afflicted like everyone else. His scowl deepened.

He remembered that he had to say something to Ted, and
called him over. "I thought you should know that I want to
run a profile of Joe Barreras soon and I'm having somebody
else do it," he told him. "It's your territory but I don't think
you'd get much access."

"No," Ted agreed. "Biotex won't roll out a fucking
welcome mat for me after my story about that prick Carey."

Manning nodded, indicating that he was through. Then,
almost without intending to, he said, "One more thing, Ted."

"Yes?"

"I personally am getting a bit tired of your language, and
you sometimes use it when ladies are present. It's always
'That prick' and 'Fuck this' and 'Fuck that.' .I was telling you
about a serious editorial matter and your language was
inappropriate."

Ted was surprised. He knew that he was often
intemperate in expression, but the language in a newspaper
office was traditionally highly charged and often coarse. He
just nodded and turned on his heel and walked away.

He decided to follow up, as a lightweight story, the
escort agency, Playgirl Escort Service, which, surprisingly,
had started advertising. Ted called the owner, a John Dallas,
and asked if he could come and see him. Dallas agreed
enthusiastically.

The Playgirl Escort Service was located over a realtor's

office in Forest Hills. The office was small, and shabbily furnished, with an armchair that barely contained its springs and a large desk with the varnish wearing off. Two pictures on the wall showed, respectively, a speedboat against a background of luxury skyscrapers and skiers on a fir-fringed ski slope, presumably representing the Playgirl Escort Service's view of the good life, and about the world a customer entered when he hired a Playgirl escort. A receptionist sat at the desk, young and dark-haired and with frizzy hair and large teeth. Her sweater was pulled tight over her breasts which were pushed into a conical shape, reminding Ted of the nose cones of guided missiles.. Ted wondered whether they moved. An album of photographs was on the table in front of her.

She told Ted that Mr. Dallas was busy on the telephone and would see him in a moment. While Dallas finished a telephone call he sat in the armchair and they exchanged a couple of remarks about the character of the neighborhood and the difficulty of getting to work, and then Dallas called him into the next room.

He was a small, narrow-chested man with a beak-like nose. He moved in short, jerky motions, like a sparrow, and talked in nervous bursts. Evidently, he was not sure how to talk to a represen- tative of the Press. He had a message for Ted and his readers, something he had apparently been working out in his mind since Ted called.

"A lot of people don't come to us because they got the wrong idea about what we're offering," he said. "They think we're some kind of call girl agency." Ted did not know whether he was supposed to look shocked. "We're not selling sex," Dallas said, carrying on with his prepared patter.

"We're selling companionship. Our girls are good at being companions. They're sophisticated girls, you can take them anywhere. They've been to college, some of them. They can talk about what's in the newspapers, all sorts of things."

"Business is bad, huh?" Ted said, trying to sound sympathetic. He was feeling genuinely sorry for Dallas, trying to earn a living selling social companionship now that his previous line was wiped out.

"Well, yes, it's fallen off a bit," said Dallas, looking away at the corner of the room and focussing on an electric kettle and two dirty cups.

He went on with his message: "A lot of people got the wrong idea about what we're doing here, as I say. But there's a real need for our services. I mean, say you're a visitor from out of town. You're doing business here, maybe. After the day's business is over, you don't want to spend the evening alone, right? Like, in your hotel room watching TV. So you'd like a female companion for dinner maybe, perhaps to go into New York and take in a show. Or maybe you're going to an affair and you want to take a lady along. You can call on us. Our girls know how to behave. Or maybe you're not from out of town, but you're single, maybe just divorced. A guy gets lonely. It's not good for a guy to be alone a lot. It's not healthy. Doctors say that. He should have somebody to talk to."

On his way back, Ted thought about how he could write up the story as a plaint for a dead industry, slightly making fun of John Dallas. But when he sat down at his desk he realized that this would not work. It might have if Dallas had sounded very funny. He shelved the idea. Maybe he would follow it up later and talk to some of Dallas's girls.

He was reading through a press handout from a local drugstore that was now selling vibrators   when   the telephone rang, and it was Dallas. "Mr. Starowicz, I want to ask you something," he began.

"Yes?"

"I understand that you're a potent. That you've still got balls. Is that right?"

"Who told you that?" Ted demanded.

"Trish. My secretary. She said you were looking at her in that way." Ted was not aware that he had been looking at her in that way. "Well, are you?" Dallas demanded.

Ted hesitated, caught off guard. "Well, er - "

"You are, huh? Okay, Mr. Starowicz, I've got a proposition for you. How would you like to come on my books?"

"As what?"

"A male escort. It's a new line I want to start up. You're not a bad-looking guy. And you're – well, you're a guy. My girls can get – o.k., let's face it, it ain't always only company they supply - they can get a hundred and fifty dollars an hour. They used to, that is. That's after they've paid me my share. You've got something special to sell. I can get you three, maybe four, hundred dollars an hour. And a lot of hours. Because sometimes, you've got to be a companion too, an escort for the evening."

Ted was amazed. "Four hundred dollars an hour? As a male escort?"

"That's right. I'm talking about physical companionship. How about it?"

"No. I like my work."

"Okay. You can still be a newspaperman, you won't have

to quit. You get days off, don't you? You get evenings off sometimes. Some of my girls do other work."

"No, Mr. Dallas. Definitely no."

"Definitely, huh?"

"Definitely, definitely."

"Okay, Mr. Starowicz. Let me know if you change your mind, huh?" Dallas said. Ted hung up, and shook his head in wonderment.

Kate came on to Ted again, letting her know that she wanted him, and Kate wanting him was sexy. So he went back to her apartment and went to bed with here, satisfying her with physical sex, as he put it to himself ironically. The second time was more enjoyable, as the second time usually is, because they were more relaxed and knew each other's responses better and they were more forward in trying different ways.

He also went to bed with Toni, from systems. He had always liked Toni. She supervised the computer systems for the newsroom and she served the editorial staff like a waitress seeing that her customers were well fed and satisfied. She was a pleasantly plump blonde, usually smiling and always placid even when she was surrounded by electronic chaos and fraying tempers. Ted, like most of the other men in the newsroom, had exchanged banter with Toni that was friendly and mildly flirtatious but never serious. "I like you, Ted, because you don't bring me problems," she would say when he stopped by at her desk. A couple of times he was eating a bar of chocolate when he passed her and he stopped and fed a piece into her mouth, and she closed her eyes and uttered an "Mmmmm" of pleasure.

Now, as he passed her desk she was putting down the phone, and she looked up at him and said in her usual whispery voice, "Oh, damn!" He looked at her inquiringly. "My girl friend was coming over to supper this evening and now she says she can't come," Toni explained.

She could have made this remark at any time in the past and it would have had no significance. But now she went on looking into his face, and it left a question hanging in the air.

He thought to himself, "Maybe this also is it." He said to her: "Well all I'm looking forward to is a carry-out pizza. If you can beat that, you could invite me as a substitute."

"I can do at least as well as a carry-out pizza. And you'll do as well as my girl friend," she said.

"Great. I'll pick up some wine."

He went back to his desk thinking about how her thighs would feel and made some telephone calls. He tried to work out how he could do the story about the brothel closing down.

Then the telephone rang, and John Dallas was on the line. "Say, Mr. Starowicz, I had another thought."

"Mr. Dallas, I'm really not going to go along with your proposition. I'm sorry."

"No. I'm not thinking of you. But do you know any other potents?"

"Other potents?"

"Yeah. Do you know any?"

" Oh sure. We have a club. We meet on the first Tuesday of every month."

"Really? That's great. Could I come along to one of the meetings maybe, and make my pitch?"

"I'm only kidding, Mr. Dallas," he said. "No, I don't

know any others." John Dallas was certainly a tryer, he reflected as he hung up. His doggedness was a tribute to the spirit of free enterprise.

Toni's plump flesh was firm, not soft like Anne Broadbent's, the flesh of a milk-fed shepherdess in a painting by Watteau. In bed she was as calm and steady in her movements as she was in the newsroom. They caressed for a long time and he enjoyed the feel of her skin. When he was aroused and started to climb on top of her she pushed his shoulder back down gently and climbed astride him, then eased his member into her.

She moved up and down and rocked backwards, and said, "Mmmm, mmmm," in appreciation, much as she did when he put a piece of chocolate into her mouth. As he thrust up into her the sound moved to a pitch of mild intensity and then changed to a sigh. If she had an orgasm, it was a gentle one. He enjoyed it but he would have liked more of a response from her. What the hell was she doing sounding calm when his dick was inside her?

She lay beside him and they talked in the dark. "I always liked you, Toni."

"But you managed to contain your feelings until now."

He was discomforted. "Oh, I was otherwise involved," he mumbled. On an inspiration, he added, "Besides, I thought you were." He knew nothing of any boy friends of Toni's.

"I always liked you too," she said. "Now I suppose I go on your list of women."

"It's not such a long list. Does everybody know about me?"

"Women do talk. And yes, it's pretty obvious, I'm afraid,

if one's around you. I guess you've had Kate Lestrange."

"No comment."

"I'm sure you're doing all right. You can have a lot of the girls in the office just by going like this." She made a beckoning gesture with her index finger. "Though I probably shouldn't tell you that, since I hope you'll come back to me occasionally."

"I will, Toni."

"You'll have to take me out to dinner next time. A girl's got to have some pride." He smiled. He found it relaxing being in bed with Toni and decided to come back for more soon.

"How about Saturday night?" he suggested. "Including dinner."

"That sounds good."

"I don't really want every girl in the office," he said.

"I didn't say you could have all of them. Not everyone takes to you. I don't want you to get *too* much of a swelled head."

On Saturday morning he did some shopping for provisions and then had lunch at a burger and salad place he knew near the Holycroft campus, sitting on a gleaming pine chair at a pine table. In term time it would have been full of students but now it was nearly empty. His waitress was a girl he had noticed before, a tall, pretty girl of nineteen or so who went in for sexy clothes and flirted with the students. Watching the scene on previous occasions, he had guessed that she met a lot of boys there and went out a lot,but there would not be many dates for her these days.

She knew him by sight and greeted him with a friendly smile. She was wearing a low-cut peasant blouse with a suede mini-skirt, and she bent low over the table when she put a glass of water in front of him. He gave her his order, and then he watched her moving among the customers, most of whom were finishing their meals, smiling at the men,. He decided that she had learned early on, probably when she was a cute little girl, that smiling and showing how pretty she was produced results and she had never bothered to learn any other tricks. He could imagine her being presented to an archbishop, or the Pope, and fluttering her eyelashes and bending low to show some cleavage and giving her cute smile.

Then he contemplated her swaying ass as she walked among the tables and her lithe young body and he thought, "Why not?"

She was a lot younger than him and in normal times would probably regard someone of thirty-three as too old to have any potential, an inhabitant of a different sexual universe. But these were not normal times. When she brought him his order, he said, "That's a very fetching outfit you're wearing."

"Thank you," she said.

"Sexy, too."

She pouted a little. "That's not something most people notice these days."

"I notice it," he said. "You're very noticeable, you know."

She looked down at him curiously. "You're not very busy," he said. "Sit down for a minute or two." He got up, walked around the table, and pulled out a chair for her. She looked surprised. Clearly, she was not used to this kind of courtesy even at the best of times, and these were not the best of times

She called out to the other waitress, "I'm taking five," and sat down.

"You're a reporter on the Long Island Chronicle, aren't you?" she said to him.

"Yes."

"I remember your saying that once. Gee, that must be an interesting life. You must be clever." And she looked into his face with wide brown eyes, leaning over the table. This was the only game she knew and, old as he was, he was the only player in town.

"It is interesting sometimes. I'd like to tell you about it," he said. "What time do you get through here?"

"Two-thirty. Two forty-five if it's busy."

"It's a lovely day. Would you like to come out for a drive and see some countryside?"

He had to play the game. In the car, he told her that she was beautiful in a very unusual way, and asked whether she had ever thought of photographic modelling as a career. He said he knew one or two people in the modelling business. Later, he said he knew he should not make serious advances so quickly, he knew she was not the kind of girl who went to bed with every man who took her out, but she was so beautiful that he could not help himself.

In his apartment after a couple of hours in the car, however, he made her play his game. He got her to undress before he did, so that he, fully dressed, could look down on her body as she lay on his bed. It was slender and firm, and rubbery to the touch. He had not held a body this young for years. It took him back to his undergraduate days.

"Come on, you too," she urged him, tugging at his belt,

but instead he ran the tips of his fingers lightly over her, tickling her breasts and belly and thighs and just the tips of her pubic hairs, looking down on her and teasing her. He stroked her all over again and again, making her wait, feeling her getting wet, hearing her say with what almost a plea, "Come *on*," until he could not tease any longer and tore off his clothes and threw himself on her.

Afterwards, when he had dressed and explained to her that he had a professional engagement that evening, and she had made clear her disappointment, there was just time to take her home and Kiss her warmly to show that their encounter had meant something and then go back to his place and shower and change before picking up Toni.

They did not linger over dinner. They were back in Tonis's apartment well before midnight, and they were undressed and on the bed a few minutes later.

He recalled her gentle-sounding orgasms, and he wanted something more in the way of a response. He kissed and caressed her, and stroked her between her legs enjoying the silken feel of her skin. Then he said, "Not on the bed," and pulled her off the bed.

" Where then?"

"This way," he said, and made her bend over the edge of the bed. He grasped the front of her thighs and entered her from behind, ramming hard until she cried out. He was not sure whether her cries came from pleasure or pain and he did not care. It was a response and he wanted one..

He woke the next morning, the bedroom curtains still drawn and the room still dark, he, and heard Toni in the kitchen making coffee: He murmured to himself, "Pretty good. Two in one day." He smiled with satisfaction. Then he said, "You, Ted, are in danger of becoming a locker room Lothario. A real ass-hole. Watch out!"

"What did you say?" Toni called out from the kitchen.

"I was talking to myself," he said. "I was just saying how lucky I am to be here."

With an abundance of women suddenly available, he ran his mind over the women in his life, working backwards from the present, quickly, like a videotape reversing. There were not all that many. He went through Elaine, the time they met and the first time they went to bed together, and sexy Sue before her. She was a pain in the ass and had no more brains than her cat but he used to get an erection even thinking about her. He went over his few brief affairs, and a girl who loved him in college, and a lonely wife in his first job who was also in love with him, skipping the heartbreak one that had him wracked with pain.

The videotape stopped at one whose name he could not even remember. She was not a woman but a girl. He knew her when he was a boy and had not yet kissed a girl except when they played kissing games at parties. She was in school with him but they were not in any of the same classes. They both took part in a square dance exhibition as part of a Thanksgiving program. As she danced across from him, skipping from side to side, she smiled and her blue eyes sparkled with pleasure, and her pale brown curls bobbed up and down, and her tiny breasts bobbed under her pink soft wool sweater. She was so pretty that he could not take his eyes off her, and when she returned his gaze he blushed scarlet.

When they did a reel her arm would link through his briefly and he would touch her bare skin and it felt marvellous. He got to the point where he would say hello to her when they passed in the corridor, with his heart thumping against his chest. She would reply, "Hello, Ted," and smile and it was a thrill. The next year the family moved away and she left the school. No carnal thought regarding her had ever entered his mind.

With all the sexual pleasures he had experienced since then, and the cornucopia of pleasures that awaited him now, he was vaguely aware of something missing, something that flitted about like a half-seen vision, as she had skipped from side to side in the square dance where he could see her but not quite reach out and touch her, something just beyond the edge of his consciousness.

::   ::   ::

At the Bliss Institute Gavin was thinking of dna patterns and studying a computer print-out so intently that he did not even look up when Izzy walked into his office. Izzy had to speak to him to get his attention. "Sarah says she's not seeing enough of me these days," he announced.

Gavin looked up now and said, "Uh-huh."

"She says I'm working too hard at too many different things." Gavin wondered why Izzy had come into his office to tell him this and gave him another "Uh-huh."

"She's right, too. Trying one selenium culture after another with Mo and checking, and everything else in the division also. And now I've got to prepare a report for the commission meeting in Washington next week."

He paused. Gavin decided he had to say something so he asked, "Do you find the report is a lot of work?"

"Oh no, not a lot," Izzy replied. "But on top of everything else it's a bitch. So for next week I'm asking you to do it - oh come on, Gavin, please. I'm up to my neck in lab work and administration both. Please take this over. You can handle it."

Gavin talked to the different departments about their work and prepared his summary for the Washington meeting carefully, and went over his notes on the plane as he and Izzy flew down together.

He gave his report at the morning session of the conference, when people were reporting on progress in their institutions, mentioning the selenium culture only briefly. He threw in a couple of humorous asides and these witticisms were successful, delivered as they were dead-pan, in his clipped English voice. It all went down well. He found that he enjoyed the experience. A couple of people complimented him at lunch..

When they broke at the end of the afternoon session Izzy came over to him and mentioned a friend of his who was one of the great figures in bio-chemistry, a Nobel laureate now at Berkeley. Izzy asked him to join them and their party for dinner. "You go ahead," said Gavin. "I don't mind not joining you. He's an old friend of yours and I won't be offended."

"No, no, he asked me to bring you along," Izzy insisted. "He was impressed by your account of our work. Let's meet in the hotel bar at seven o'clock, and we'll go over to join him at the Mayflower. Okay?"

Gavin got down to the bar early and sat at a table with a drink and a newspaper. A lot of people from the conference were staying at the hotel and as the bar filled up some of these came in and he greeted a few by name. He became aware at one point that a small group of men at another table were looking over at him and talking among themselves.

Then one of them threaded his way across the room to his table and addressed him. "We haven't met before but we've talked on the phone," he said. "I'm Dean Hoffmeister, of Biotek Inc." Gavin stood up and they shook hands, and then Hoffmeister said, "Would you care to come over and join us for a drink?"

Gavin did not want to get involved with them but he also did not want to be uncivil. "Thank you, but I'm just waiting for a colleague and we're going out to meet some others for dinner," he said.

"Just for a few moments, then," said Hoffmeister. "Joe Barreras would like to meet you."

"He's here at the conference?"

"He's not attending the conference but he's here now. He was in Washington and he came by to take a look and see who's here."

Gavin went over to their table taking his drink with him, and Hoffmeister introduced him to Barreras and two other men who he took to be his senior executives. A chair was brought over for him. Barreras was dressed in conservative grey, with his dark hair slicked back. There was nothing in his manner that indicated the power that he held, but the deference of the others at the table was evident.

He said, "I understand that you gave a very interesting presentation today, Dr. Grove."

"Thank you."

"I understand also that Dean here has tried unsuccessfully to interest you in joining Biotek."

"I was flattered at the suggestion, but I'm happy at the Bliss Institute," Gavin said. "I like the work I'm doing and I like the people there."

Barreras nodded approvingly. "It's a good place," he said. "I admire Morley Bliss and what he's done." Barreras spoke softly and he made no unnecessary movements. He was a man who did not waste any energy or time.

Gavin decided that one did not meet a man in Jose Barreras's position often and it would be wasting an opportunity to confine the conversation to polite platitudes. "I'm interested to hear that you admire Morley Bliss and the Institute," he said. "Surely what the Bliss Institute is doing is very different from what you're doing, Mr. Barreras."

"Oh? Why do you think so?"

"You're aiming at commercial success. And you've certainly achieved it. The Bliss Institute isn't commercially orientated. Our area is pure research, as I'm sure you know. It's unusual for us to be working for a specific application like this."

Barreras seemed pleased to have a serious interlocutor. "In the case of the effort that we're all involved in," he said to Gavin, "it's not just about commercial success. It would be small-minded to reduce it to that. We all want to find a cure."

"But you'd like Biotek to be first."

Barreras leaned back in his chair. "This thing is too serious to play competitive games with it. I promise you that if a cure is discovered at Bliss or anywhere else and it works, I'll stand up and cheer. Mind you, I'm not pretending that I won't be proud as hell if a team at Biotek finds it."

"So in this instance, you're operating in the same way

that we are?"

"No, I wouldn't quite say that, Gavin. I've always operated in the world of commerce. I know how to motivate people financially. Perhaps I'm pushing forward in a different way to the way Morley Bliss would. But there are similarities, of course. I'm a manager and I'm managing a scientific institution. I manage people and systems."

"And if you succeed in this endeavor you'll make a lot of money."

"Oh yes. But I've got a lot of money anyway. I don't need more that much."

Just then, Izzy came into the room, and after brief introductions he said they had to leave now or they would be late, and Gavin said his goodbyes. As they waited outside for a taxi, Izzy remarked, "You've got some interesting friends."

"Just acquaintances," Gavin said.

Gavin enjoyed dinner, particularly as the company included several of the big names in biochemistry. A couple of people complimented him on his presentation, and asked his opinion of others and of the way the conference was going.

The next day he attended all the sessions and took notes on several new approaches to denaturing to report back. People talked about dna but nobody had anything to show yet. Some were trying interferon. A few others were trying to create anti-antibodies. He saw Alan Carling at one of the sessions and they arranged to have dinner with him that evening, since the meeting was to go on the following morning. "I know a quiet place, away from this crowd," Carling said.

When Gavin got to the restaurant, Carling was already there. "Have a drink. I'm a couple ahead of you," he said and he clearly was. He seemed in better spirits than he had been that evening at his house.

"I hear you met my esteemed leader Joe Barreras last night," he said when Gavin sat down.

"Yes. Where were you?"

"Oh, I was admitted into his company only once here. I don't rate very high in the Biotek scheme of things." Strangely, Carling was grinning as he said this, as if at some private joke that only he understood.

They talked through the meal about people at the conference and Carling drank most of the bottle of wine they had ordered. By the end his voice was slurring. Gavin wondered how many drinks he had had before he arrived. Carling returned to the subject of Joe Barreras and Biotek.

"You know I told you I thought I was going to be promoted."

"Yes."

"Well I've been passed over."

"I'm sorry."

"For a couple of guys who aren't as good as me. One of them from another of Barreras's pharmaceutical companies. What the fuck does he know about fundamental research?"

"That's too bad."

Then Carling smiled again. "They're going to have to pay more attention to me now," he said. "I've figured out a way forward. An important way forward."

"You have?"

"Well, I'm advancing some of the work that a couple of other people have done. But I see the next step which they haven't seen yet."

"Good. That should improve your prospects."

"Yes, and not only at Biotek. If they don't give me what I want I can go somewhere else. I've had an offer. I can take my work with me. And those other guys' work too, since I've advanced it."

"That would be unethical, Alan."

"Like Joe Barreras cares about what's ethical. That cunt." Carling looked into the corner with a wobbly, drunken stare.

Gavin did not like the idea of Alan taking Biotek's secrets to another company but remembering what he had heard about Philip Carey's activities, he reflected that it would serve them right.

::   ::   ::

The next day, on the shuttle flight back to New York, while Izzy dozed beside him, Gavin looked out of the window at the blue sky and the fluffy, milky clouds like balls of cotton, and rehearsed in his mind how he would tell Martha about the conference. He would tell her that everyone was still in the dark about the way to a cure. He would tell her what others had said of his talk, and he would tell her about the scientists he had met with Izzy. "Do you know who I had dinner with the night before last?" No, that smacked of name-dropping. "My report went down pretty well, I think." Too vain. He would wait until she asked him and let her prise it out of him. 0

He arrived home at six o'clock. Martha was upstairs making the bed, which was unusual. "Didn't Rosa come today?" he asked, after he had kissed her.

"Yes, but I came back early and took a nap," she said.

"Why? Are you feeling okay?"

"Sure. I just didn't sleep well last night. I miss you." He smiled at her. "Supper will be ready in a few minutes."

They went into the kitchen and talked while she cooked. There were cigarettes in the ashtray. "Grace came back with me and we stayed chatting for a while," she explained, as she emptied the ash- tray into the garbage pail. "How was the meeting?"

He told her about the progress that was reported, and told her that he and Izzy believed some people were not reporting in Washington all the work that was going on in their laboratories so that they could stay ahead of the competition.

"Okay, now tell me what I want to know," she said.

"Meaning?"

"How did you do? How did your report go?"

"Actually, it went down well. Several people told me so." He grinned sheepishly despite himself.

She looked across at him and saw that grin, and the embarrassment at the display of pride that made him look like a schoolboy, and she loved him. She remembered now that when she first fell in love with him she had thought of him as a grown-up schoolboy, and wanted one day to have little boys who looked like him. The recollection was strong and for the moment she felt about him just as she had in those early days. She wished they could make love and the fact that they could not was painful. Then she wondered whether she would ever have those little boys.

After dinner they sat on the deacon seat and watched the

television news. The newscaster said there were signs that the impotence plague was spreading in Europe now. There was no mistaking the satisfaction on his face as he summed up by saying: "So it seems that Europeans' hopes that this is purely an American disease are being dashed."

"He doesn't seem too unhappy about that," Gavin remarked.

"Quite right," said Martha. "If we're not having fun, why should everyone else?

The newscaster went on to say that there was still no sign of the disease appearing anywhere in what he called the Arab or the Muslim world. "There are no reports of the affliction in the Middle East, or in Pakistan or Afghanistan," he said. And he added, "Several congressmen have pointed out that this still leaves open the possibility that this is a terrorist attack on the West by Islamic extremists."

"Did you notice his voice?" Martha said to Gavin.

"You mean the way he made the point about it not being in the Muslim world sound sinister."

"Oh, do you think that was it?" Martha said. "I got the impression that he was just trying to make his voice sound deeper."

Then there was a story about the delegation from Hawaii who had gone to Washington - all-women, since no men could be found to go - who were lobbying for a halt to flights from the mainland. "We don't want to secede from the Union," explained the delegation leader. "We're still loyal Americans. We just want to restrict the physical connection with mainland America for the time being." A Senator from Hawaii was interviewed and took a fence-sitting stance. He was in a difficult position The women from Hawaii said they wanted all their representatives in Washington to stay there.

The big local news story was the Yablonsky killing. Gene Yablonsky was a 29-year-old bachelor, a warehouseman who lived in a small town nearby, and, it seemed, one of the tiny minority of American men who had retained their sexual potency. Last evening, which was one of the hottest of the year, as the reporter emphasized, Yablonsky was in a local tavern. After several drinks, he started telling some of the others about what a great time he was having with women. Some angry words were exchanged and he left.

One of the other men, a frequent bar-room companion of Yablonsky's who had also drunk a lot, brooded on what Yablonsky had said. He decided that Yablonsky had aimed his remarks at him and that his wife had been one of Yablonsky's women. He went home and accused his wife, who denied the charge, and he hit her. Then, on his own admission, he took his pistol and went to Yablonsky's apartment, and when Yablonsky opened the door he fired three bullets into his head at close range, splitting open his skull and splattering some of the contents on the wall behind him.

The man was charged with murder. His court-appointed lawyer said immediately that he would ask to have the charge reduced to manslaughter because of the aggravating circumstances.

A TV reporter interviewed a number of Yablonsky's neighbors. Gavin and Martha, watching the program, both remarked that they were amazed at the interviewees' sympathy for the killer. One said: "He did what a lot of people would want to do. A guy that's like Yablonsky should keep his mouth shut." Another said darkly: "I reckon that maybe Gene knew the secret of how to beat this thing, and dint tell anyone. I heard he had a cousin who was a scientist or sump'n." Another said: "After what Yablonsky was saying, if they try to send Bill to the chair for shooting him this whole town will march on the jail and burn it down."

Ted Starowicz watched the same program, sitting alone in his apartment, and he too was surprised at these comments.

He was thinking about these when he went into the office the next day. As soon as he sat down at his desk, a young reporter who had only recently joined the paper came over and asked him, "Have you got a moment to spare?"

"Sure," Ted said. He thought he was going to ask his advice.

"I'm doing a follow-up to the Yablonsky killing story. I want to talk to a potent, to get his reaction. See what his experiences are of other people." He had obviously rehearsed this request.

"A potent," Ted repeated. He remembered that John Dallas had used this word.

"That's what people call - I've heard people call - someone who's still sexually – well, you know - normal."

"And?" Ted gave him a hard stare. He did not feel like making it easy for him.

The young reporter stumbled a bit. "Well, Ted, as I said, I gather - people say you're - you're still potent. So I thought I'd interview you. Have you found women behave differently towards you? Do you fjnd some men are hostile?"

Ted relaxed his gaze. "Come on, give me a break, huh? Find some other ''potent'."

"Come on, you give *me* a break," said the other. "Potents are one man in four hundred thousand. Where am I going to find another one locally?"

"I'm afraid that's your problem, fella. I like to be helpful, but I'm not going to be interviewed about my sex life in my own paper. Or any other paper for that matter."

"Well bully for you! You're sitting pretty, aren't you?" the reporter snarled, and stalked off.

Ted was upset at this resentment. If the reporter had not been so unpleasant he would have apologized again. He thought of going to the Long Island editor and explaining his reluctance to be interviewed, which he was sure anyone would understand. But then he wondered how sympathetic the man would be. How sympathetic anyone would be. He tried to imagine how he would feel if he were impotent like the others, and one other person were not.

There were a lot of letters to the editor in the paper about the Yablonsky killing over the next few days. One said there was no excuse for murder, but it would be both wise and decent for potents not to advertise their condition and to stick to their own wives or girl friends. Another said Yablonsky's killer had done a serious disservice to the American nation, since potents were so few and the health of American women and possibly the future of the American nation depended on them.

The paper carried an editorial on the Yablonsky case, warning against a witch-hunt atmosphere over potents. Ted noticed that Tom Manning avoided his eye the next day. He wondered sourly whether he was expected to thank him personally for the editorial. He felt both irritated and dejected when he left the office.

Well, he thought, the hell with them. Eating dinner by himself at a local restaurant the evening before, he had started talking to a girl in the next booth who was also alone. She called herself Didi. She was petite, shorter than him and slender. She had honey-colored curls, blue eyes and large, shiny teeth, which prevented her from being a conventional beauty but gave her face a cute, schoolgirl quality. She told him as soon as he started talking to her that she was a dancer, opening soon in the chorus of a Broadway show, and she lived in Queens and was out this way visiting her parents because she couldn't afford her own apartment.. He had taken her phone number.

Now, smarting from the irritating encounter with the young reporter, and from Manning's remarks about his language, he phoned her and arranged to take her out to dinner that night.

Over dinner, Didi talked at length about her dance teacher and her hopes for her, her singing teacher, who was psychic, and the part that she should have got, and her taste in food. Her career and those involved in it and her life-style seemed to be her only topics of conversation. She was so self-absorbed that she did not notice his behavior and was surprised back at her apartment when he put his arms around her and kissed her.

"So are you - ?" she said.

"Yes."

When the fact that he wanted to go to bed with her penetrated her mind, she agreed readily and her athleticism made it memorable for Ted. Afterwards she asked, "Will you take me out to dinner again?"

"Yes. Okay."

"I mean in Manhattan, not Queens. A restaurant I know off Broadway in the 40s. It's not terribly expensive," she added. He guessed that a lot of her friends went there.

He promised to call her. But he did not call her the next day, he Naomi James. He wanted to see a French movie much praised by reviewers that was showing in Walton and he decided she was the right person for that kind of evening. He phoned her and made a date for three days later, which was the first evening she could make it. He resolved to remain celibate for the next three days.

They enjoyed the movie and talked about it over coffee and cake afterwards and decided that it was a film worth talking about seriously.

They talked some more about themselves. He told her about his story on Philip Carey, and how it had forced Carey to resign from the Presidential Commission. She told him about her plans for her PhD thesis, which was to be about the changing image of marriage in the American novel. He felt warm and relaxed as they walked back to her apartment, and decided he liked her more and more.

They held hands, and paused at the little green opposite her apartment house to look at the stars. "It's a marvellously clear night," she said. "There's the whole Milky Way."

"Yes. You can make out the constellations."

"I don't know anything about the constellations," she said. "I don't know where anything is. Not even the North Star."

"You don't? Well there's the Big Dipper. Over there. You see those three stars make the handle - those three in a broken line." Then he showed her how one side of the big dipper pointed to the North Star. "You've got to imagine patterns in the sky," he explained. "Straight lines going from one star to the other. They're all arbitrary. You can draw your own pictures. But those are the ones that have been drawn." They held hands as they walked back to her apartment and up in the elevator.

"I really like being with you," he said, as she searched in her pocketbook for her key.

"I've enjoyed it too, Ted," she said. "Really. I hope we'll do it again some time soon." She found the key and opened the door and kissed him on the lips.

He said, "But aren't I coming - ?"

She put her hand on his chest and held him back from the door. "Not on the first date," she said primly. "A rule of mine."

"But this isn't our first date," he protested.

"It's the first time *you've* asked *me* out," she said. "The other doesn't count because I asked you. I have enjoyed it." She put her arms around his neck and kissed him again, and closed the door.

He stood there feeling stunned, and then disappointed, and then angry.

Inside the apartment, Naomi leaned against the door and exhaled slowly. It had been difficult. She had thought about Ted a lot during the past two weeks. Sixteen days, actually.

"Most women would say I'm crazy," she said to herself. "Maybe I am crazy. I've settled for a lot less than I want too often. Now I know what I want but I don't want it that way. I want it the way I want it."

CHAPTER SEVEN

Throughout most of August, Gavin and Denise Springer worked together on dna samples of the virus. They had separated several strips of amino acid to insert into the dna of the virus. Denise was a demanding partner and at times a difficult one, stubborn when they argued about which tracer to use. But she kept him up to the mark.

Morley Bliss called in to discuss their work with them, something he had not done often with the Institute staff since his illness. Characteristically, he did not just drop in casually and chat so that it was merely a stroking session. He made an appointment and listened carefully as he and Denise gave an account of their work and looked at their results. Characteristically also, he understood their work immediately. Neither he nor Denise said anything to each other after he left but they both knew they felt encouraged.

Denise invited Gavin and Martha home to dinner one Saturday and they met her husband, a young lawyer. They had been married for less than a year. His obvious pride in his wife's work and standing and her obvious affection for him, expressed in small physical gestures, was touching. Gavin saw Denise, tough and acerbic, who made him nervous with her acid tongue, in a new light.

In the car on the way home Martha said to him, "It's so nice, the way they feel about each other."

"Without a sex life," he said.

"That's a very limited idea of a sex life," Martha said. "They have a sex life."

"What do you mean?"

"Their life together is a sex life. So they don't engage in intercourse."

"But it's not a normal sexual relationship. None of us have that."

"It is a sexual relationship," she insisted. "Do you think he'd feel the same way about her if she were a man? They have a sexual relationship. Look at the way he looks at her. We have a sexual relationship."

"I suppose so," he said thoughtfully. "Men still like women."

She was silent for a while and then she said, "Speaking of that kind of thing, I'm worried about Helen."

"Helen of Troy? Helen Masterson, the First Lady?"

"One of my clients. I told you about her. She's the one who's never had a proper boy friend."

"Oh yes, the one who's so unattractive. Who didn't have a date for the prom. Thick glasses and all that."

"She's not really so unattractive, I told you. And she's slimming down now and it improves her. Anyway, she has one now."

"A boy friend?"

"Well, a boy friend the way other people have boy friends these days. It's a man she's very fond of. They like each other. That's what I mean. She tells me they spend a lot of time together and they talk very intimately. It's good for her.

She really enjoys being with him. He seems to enjoy being with her."

"That's fine."

"Not entirely. She's terribly insecure in the relationship. Understandably, given her background. She's worried that if or when he gets his sex drive back and things get back to normal, things will go back to normal with her also. This guy will drop her and go after some conventionally good-looking girl. Not that he's such a catch from the sound of him, he's not exactly dashing. She confessed to me that sometimes she sort of hopes the plague will continue."

They had reached home now and as they walked in the front door she said. "God, in some ways I think life is simpler without the male sex drive, but in some ways life is just as complicated without it."

The next day Mohsin Ahmed walked into Gavin's office grinning broadly. "We're getting results, we're getting results!" he exclaimed gleefully.

"What results? "

"The combination of selenium and hydrochloride and the right temperature. It was Izzy's idea to try it that way. The virus is in a log phase. You can see the antibodies. You were right, Gavin, about that Meriacci paper. Selenium may be the key to the whole thing. Come and see the gelplates."

"I'll come and see what you've got this afternoon, okay? I've got some things to finish off this morning." He found himself half-hoping despite himself that Mohsin was wrong. Now that he had gone this far he would have liked to have created the new antibody by the manipulation of dna.

A half-hour later he passed Izzy in the corridor on the way back from the washroom. "I've just had a visit from Mo,"

Gavin told him. "He says your culture is working. The virus is in the log phase."

"It looks good, doesn't it?" Izzy said. "It's his, principally. He's doing all the work. I haven't even seen his latest results. But I'm sure he's right. I've just been up at the Council meeting telling them about it. We might even get some positive results in time to report them to the WHO meeting. That would be nice."

"The World Health Organization meeting? Is that set?" Gavin asked.

"Yes, didn't you know? It's October 4th, in Geneva. At the WHO headquarters there. I'm going as one of the American delegation. You're an alternate."

"What do you mean I'm an alternate? What are you talking about?" They were still standing in the corridor.

Izzy explained, "Eight people are going from America, all people from major institutes who have attended the Washington meetings. I've agreed to be one. I was asked to name an alternate from Bliss in case I fall down and break a leg, and I named you. You've attended the Washington meetings, you can represent Bliss. You can give an overall picture if you have to."

"Very flattering and all that, but you might have asked me."

"I'm sorry but I was very busy. I was going to tell you."

Gavin said, "Anyway, how can I be an American representative at the conference when I'm not an American?"

"That doesn't matter, you'll be representing an American institution. But don't worry, I'll be careful and I won't fall down and break a leg and you won't get to go. I've never been to Switzerland and I'm looking forward to it."

"You have a rather cavalier way with my career," Gavin said testily. "I suppose one day I'll open a newspaper and find that I've become an American citizen and I'm running for Congress."

"I promise I'll tell you that first."

Gavin strolled back to his office and considered this. What surprised him when he thought about it was that it had not occurred to him to refuse, as he refused at first to represent the Institute at the Washington meetings. He had enjoyed attending the meetings, enjoyed the congratulations he had received on his report, enjoyed being at the center where many paths met. He was not going to become one of the politicians of science but he was finding this world congenial.

He sat at his desk and found that he was thinking about the next Washington meeting as much as about dna, what he would say there, who he would meet. This was a bad sign. He slapped his wrist mentally and picked up his notes.

His telephone rang and it was Ted. As usual Ted got right to the point. "I remember you mentioning a medical scientist called Alan Carling?".

"Yes. Why?"

"He's disappeared."

"What do you mean, disappeared?"

"Vanished. Missing from home. Nobody knows where he is."

"Since when?"

"Four days ago."

 "What happened?" he asked Ted.

"He just didn't turn up at the office one day. Eventually someone went around to his apartment and called the police. He'd gone No sign of him. One of the editors passed it over to me because it seems that Carling was working on the impotence problem. How well do you know him?"

"Fairly well," Gavin said. "I met him when he was working in England. We've seen each other a couple of times recently."

"Did he have any problems?"

"Yes."

"Can you tell me what they were?"

"No."

"Oh. Do you reckon he might have committed suicide?"

Sometimes Ted's insensitivity annoyed Gavin. After all, Alan Carling was a friend of his. He terminated the conversation.

He was upset about Alan Carling and he wanted to talk to someone about it. He called in at Izzy's office and suggested that they have lunch together. In the canteen he took him into his confidence and told him all about his recent meetings with Carling and Carling's suggestion in Washington that he might go over to another company with some Biotek research..

"Alan was sort of going to pieces," he said. "His setbacks were getting him down. What with his divorce and everything. Then, as I say, he told me he thought he was really on to something, that he'd found this way forward. Well, it might be, but given his state of mind I had doubts. He might well have given himself too much hope."

"I see that," Izzy said.

"I think myself that he's going through a crisis and has gone to earth somewhere. Maybe gone to hide away with his family in Georgia for a while or something. He's got all these troubles, money and so on, and perhaps he kidded himself that he'd made a great advance and he realized he hadn't. And it was all too much."

"That sounds likely," Izzy said. "But for Pete's sake don't let it get out that he thought he might be finding a cure."

"Why?"

"Can't you imagine it? A lot of cranks will say that the cunning terrorists who have done this to America have now eliminated the man who was about to find the cure."

"God, that's a thought. Some of this paranoia seems to be developing."

"On the other hand," Izzy said, "I'll say something that may also sound paranoid."

"What's that?"

"Didn't you say he implied that he might move from Biotek and take some of Biotek's work to another company?"

"Yes."

"Well that wouldn't please Biotek. In fact they'd be pretty damned angry about it. Maybe somebody decided he mustn't be allowed to do it."

Gavin stared at him in disbelief. "My God, Izzy, do you really think they're capable of that?"

"I don't know about 'they'. Joe Barreras owns Biotek now. I have the impression that he plays hard ball. And even more this Philip Carey. And Barreras has picked up some pretty rough associates along the way. The mob, according to some report I read somewhere."

Gavin was amazed. What Izzy said had to be taken seriously. He knew the world of American science. Gavin had always been frightened by violence. At school he got into a fight once and ran away and became known as a coward, and this upset him. He thought he lived and worked now in a world in which this did not matter. Now he was frightened by the suggestion that violence might have intruded into this world, that a scientist could be murdered because of what he was doing. He almost shivered at the idea.

Izzy went away with his tray and came back with dessert. "I might as well have some today," he remarked. "I'm not going to have much supper tonight. Sarah has taken the kids to see her parents and I can't be bothered to cook for myself."

"Come home with me and have some supper," said Gavin.

"No. it's kind of you but I can't stick myself on your wife at this short notice," he protested.

"No trouble. There's bound to be something to eat. We'd like to have you. Martha will be very pleased. Don't go home to an empty house." He meant it. He liked and admired Izzy

Gavin called Martha at the Health Center to warn her but the secretary said she had gone home early. This surprised him. Martha took two afternoons off a week but this was not one of them. He called home but there was no reply. He meant to call again but then Mohsin called in to remind him to come up and look at his gelplates.

He looked through the microscope and saw a cluster. "There's certainly some agglutination there. Your treated virus is producing something," he said.

Mohsin grinned with pleasure. "Go tell Izzy. He'll be glad to hear you say that."

"Where is he?"

"He went into the council room withLee."

The council room was down the corridor on the same floor. It was a large room dominated by a polished oak table at the center. People sometimes used it when they wanted to talk in private on neutral ground. Gavin and Mohsin went there and found Lee Hsiu venting to Izzy his irritation at one of his co-workers. Izzy promised to look into the cause of the conflict, and then, as Lee left, he turned to Gavin and said, "Well, what do you think of Mo's gelplates?"

"It looks good," said Gavin. "I've been looking through everything. It seems to me that's the best bet so far."

"Perhaps. But the dna route is still a possibility. Don't slow down. I'm not even sure that Carl with his t-cells won't come up with an anti-antibody."

Gavin picked up Izzy at the end of the afternoon. In the car they talked over some details of the denaturing process. Gavin was impressed with the way that Izzy deferred to Mohsin's work although he was senior to him in status and had clearly been an equal partner in the enterprise.

When they went into the house Gavin called out a "Hello," and Martha called back, "We're out on the patio."

They walked through and found her sitting there with Ted, both of them with cold drinks. Martha was laughing at something Ted had just said and was wearing a thin summery dress in rainbow colors and she looked to Gavin particularly sunny and appealing.

"Hi," said Ted getting up from the garden chair. "I've just arrived. I was passing this way and dropped in. There's something I want to ask you about. Martha said you'd be back soon."

Martha welcomed Izzy and Gavin said to Ted, "I think you've met Israel Rubin. At the faculty club." Ted greeted him respectfully.

As they both dropped into chairs Gavin asked, "Any news of Alan Carling?" Ted shook his head. "Oh. I thought that might be what you had to tell me. Did you hear about Alan, Martha?"

"Yes. Ted told me. It's worrying, isn't it. I hope he turns up soon."

Gavin took orders for drinks. Ted stubbed out his cigarette in an ashtray that was already overflowing and said, "My news is that I'm going to visit some other big institutions that are working on this problem. The editor has okayed the trip."

"Where are you going?" Gavin asked.

"I've already talked to people at Columbia and Sloane-Kettering. Now I'm going to Harvard, Washington University in St. Louis, L.T.S. Industries in Albuquerque, UCLA and the Salk Institute at La Jolla. Any other suggestions?"

"I think that covers the most important places," Gavin replied. "Don't you, Izzy?"

"Most of them, probably," Izzy agreed.

"When are you going?"

"Sunday. We decided that if I'm going to go I should go soon."

"How long will you be away?"

"The whole trip should take about two weeks. I'll be back by Labor Day."

"I'll give it some thought," Gavin said. "We'll talk before you go."

"Thanks," said Ted. Then he asked, "How are things coming along at Bliss?"

Gavin did not reply because he did not want Izzy to think he talked freely to a reporter who was his friend, but Izzy said, "Things are happening but I can't be sure where we're getting to."

"Finding the right antibodies?"

"We can't talk about it just yet."

"I thought the Bliss Institute had an open-file policy," Ted said.

"Not completely open," said Izzy. We don't talk about work while it's in progress. Allow us a little confidentiality, please. After all, there's fierce competition in this area as well as cooperation."

"Is there? That's one of the things I want to talk about before I go," Ted said.

"We had a bit of a scare about leaks a few weeks ago," Izzy said. "We've even had the place swept for electronic bugs."

"Really? Who did it?" asked Ted.

"A private investigation firm. They sent along a man with a whole suitcase full of equipment and he swept the places. It took him all day. He didn't find anything."

"Can't be done," said Ted.

"What do you mean?"

"You can't tell on a one-day visit whether a place is being bugged. I did a feature on a local company that's one of the top firms for counter-surveillance. They said there are a lot of people in the field who do a slapdash job."

"Does this sound like a slapdash job?" asked Izzy.

"Yes. Apparently, it's virtually impossible to detect a sophisticated, well-placed bug when it's not operating. The people who planted it probably have it timed, or else they target one particular room. Also, they might know when the place was going to be swept and turn it off. They can do that by remote control."

"How would they know?"

"I don't know. Didn't anyone discuss the date with other people? Didn't they arrange the appoint-   ment by telephone?" Izzy was silent.

"There are supposed to be ways of detecting a transmitter when it's not working by a kind of radar," Ted went on. "But that's far from foolproof. Particularly if the transmitter is hidden among other pieces of transmitting equipment, like a telephone. There are all sorts of ways to hide it - I don't remember all the technical details. If you really want to make sure that a meeting is not being overheard, you sweep the place while the meeting is going on. Even then you need very sophisticated equipment." Gavin was often surprised at Ted's pockets of knowledge. He supposed that it came from his job, looking briefly and intensively into many different areas.

Izzy said, "So it's possible that we're still being bugged and our conversations are being over-   heard?" Izzy asked.

"It is if the guys doing it are clever operators," Ted replied.

"Where would the bugs have been planted?" Gavin asked Izzy.

"We reckoned the most likely place was the council room. But they swept the whole place," Izzy said. "Mind you," he went on, turning to Ted, "we don't know that anything was bugged. It's just that some people seemed to be doing the same thing that we were doing a short time after us and it got us a bit worried."

"What's doing the same thing? Finding the antibodies?" asked Ted.

"Finding the right ones," Izzy said.

"To kill that particular virus, you mean," Ted said.

"Yes."

Gavin said, "A great-uncle of mine, a doctor, discovered an anti-body that killed a virus."

"Really?" Izzy asked.

"Yes. He hoped it would make him famous, but it didn't."

"Why was that?"

"Well you see, he discovered the virus also. His name was Donald Grove and he got the virus recognized officially as the DG virus. But it had never been found outside the laboratory. If it was ever found outside and it caused an outbreak of a specific disease, then he had the cure. He'd invented it. So he was always looking for the disease. The DG disease, caused by the DG virus."

"Is this true?" Izzy asked.

"Of course. Anyway, he would read in a medical journal of a new kind of plague in Brazil, or West Africa, or Greece or somewhere, and he'd say, 'I think they've got an outbreak of DG disease.' He dreamed of being hailed as a benefactor to humanity who had saved millions of lives and getting a Nobel Prize.

"The disease has never been seen yet. But it became an obsession with him. He'd occasionally act as a locum for a g.p. Someone would come in with a sore throat or pains in the joints and he'd examine them and say in a grave tone, 'This could be serious.' Then he'd call the local Health Authority and tell them to prepare for a spread of DG disease, and he'd go home and get ready to tell the world he had the cure. The medical authorities got tired of him. He had to retire eventually.

"He died shortly afterwards. He had a heart attack and was taken to the local hospital. One of the doctors there was an old friend of his. He could see that he was dying. He bent over him and said, 'I'm afraid I have bad news, Donald. You've got DG disease.' A smile came over his face, and he died a happy man."

Izzy chuckled. Ted asked, "Was he from the same branch of the family as your uncle who was a Buddhist?"

"Same branch," Gavin said

Martha said, "I'm constantly finding new things about your family, Gavin."

Ted said, "Anyway, do you mind my asking, have you got any ideas about what I should be asking about and who I should be seeing on this trip?"

Gavin gave Ted the name of an old friend still at UCLA who he thought would probably be working on the problem, and Izzy suggested a line of questioning for LST Industries which might bring out some things they had been keeping quiet about, and contributed a name at the Salk Institute. Ted thanked them both and said he had to leave because he had a date. "Enjoy your travels," Gavin said to him.

The other three went into supper and Gavin asked Izzy, "What are you going to do about debugging after what Ted said? Have it done again?"

"I don't know," said Izzy. "I'll raise the subject at the next council meeting. My feeling is that the steam has gone out of the issue now."

They talked about Alan Carling because he had been eating dinner at this table only a short time before. Gavin repeated his theory that he had retreated somewhere to sort himself out. Izzy did not mention again his earlier suggestion that Carling might have been murdered

As Martha served a defrosted blueberry pie for dessert, Gavin and Izzy told her that things seemed to be going well at the laboratory and she asked, "What's the next stage?"

"Check that it really has produced antigens in the culture," Gavin replied.

"What does that mean?"

"The antigens will produce a new antibody, the antidote. If it produces it in the culture, see if it has the same effect in animals, and then in humans."

"How?"

Gavin explained, "You try it. You inject it into animals. If that works, inject it into people. Perhaps even make it into a pill.".

"And that will make the cell what-do-you-call-its work again?"

"The cell receptors, yes. Then the testosterones will function normally and the whole system will be back on course again."

Izzy finished his pie, wiped his mouth with his napkin, and said, "There's another possibility. The new antibody might build up defenses against the virus but not kill it. The virus may be too well entrenched."

"Then what?" asked Martha.

"Then we'll have a vaccine but not a cure."

"So that'll mean there'll be no cure?" asked Martha. "Everyone who's got it will always have it?"

"Exactly. We'll be able to prevent it but not cure it. Future generations can have sex lives, but not ours."

"Golly," said Gavin. "That's something to think about."

"And I've been thinking about it," said Izzy. "Not just about us. Consider my children. Mike's fifteen, Gail's fourteen, Tommy is ten. Mike's got it, so there'd be no sex life for him. Mike hasn't reached puberty yet, he hasn't started producing gonadotrophin and testosterones, he can be vaccinated. He'll be okay. As for Gail, she'll find when she grows up that she's attracted to younger men. And she'll have a lot of competition in her age group."

"Do you really think that's likely, that we'll have a vaccine and not a cure?" asked Martha.

Izzy raised his palms in a gesture indicating infinite uncertainty. "It's possible. But it's also possible that we're nowhere near either a cure or a vaccine. You know, we can't imagine this thing going on and on so we assume that a cure is just around the corner. But it may not be. After all, it was pretty unimaginable that it would start in the first place."

After he left Gavin said to Martha, "I'm sorry I brought Izzy home without giving you notice. But I called you at the center to tell you and they said you'd gone home early. Then I couldn't get an answer here. What were you doing?"

Martha was stacking dishes in the dishwasher and she shook her head. "I didn't come home early."

"The secretary said you did."

"Well she was mistaken," Martha said lightly. "I went out to get something and she must have thought I'd gone home for the day."

She turned back to the dishwasher and then said, "Anyway, there's something I want to talk to you about. I had a call from Louise today. She and Michael asked me to come on holiday to Acapulco with them in the fall, since we've postponed our summer holiday." Louise was Martha's older sister and her husband was something successful on Wall Street.

"But we've got the money set aside for a holiday, and we'll have one some other time," Gavin said,

"I'll be their guest. That's their idea. I'd go along with them and - well, just be their guest," Martha said nervously. Gavin pursed his lips with an expression of worried thoughtfulness. Martha looked at him expectantly. He knew she knew what he was thinking. Eventually she said, "Only for ten days." Still he did not say anything. She said, "I haven't spent any time with Louise for a long while. And I'll be able to help her with the children. And Acapulco isn't the sort of holiday you'd enjoy. Lots of lazing under palm trees by the swimming pool. I'll probably get bored myself." She tailed off weakly.

"We couldn't afford to go there together anyway," he said finally. "Certainly not until after we get this loan paid off. Not the kind of place they'll be going to." He could have kicked himself for saying that.

"Oh Gavin, don't be like that. Louise and I are sisters. I'd do the same sort of thing for her. We've entertained them here."

"Yes, but we haven't taken them to a posh hotel," he said, and started scouring the saucepan.

She said, "You know how the family looks up to you. You're the scientist." He did not say anything. "Anyway," she went on, "I didn't say yes. I said I'd think about it. And talk to you."

::   ::   ::

When Ted left the Groves' house he drove for nearly two hours, through Long Island exurbia and then Queens and across the Triboro Bridge. Coming from New Jersey and living in Queens, he was used to looking at Manhattan across a river, and the vista of skyscrapers had always seemed to him a challenge. Sometimes, as now, he had a sense as he drove across the bridge that he was storming an enemy-held island like in the films of World War Two. He gripped the steering wheel and as he charged Manhattan's ramparts he sang under his breath the Marine Corps hymn: *From the halls of Montezuma To the shore of Tripoli...* Manhattan here I come!

He drove to a parking lot near Times Square, where he speculated that the cost of parking his car would probably be the cost of dinner for two. It would have been quicker and cheaper by train but he wanted to be mobile, to be able to drive Didi back to her apartment in Queens or else to his apartment. Then he went to meet her at the restaurant she had chosen.

It was down a few steps, a place that was a bar at one end of the room and a restaurant at the other with red check tablecloths. The waiters and waitresses all wore expressions that said, "I'll take your order but this isn't the real me. The real me is an actor/script writer and one day you'll be seeing me/reading me." Little Didi was already there, wearing Capri pants and a fluffy sweater than seemed to double her size, talking to a woman at the bar. She greeted him with a whoop of delight that made people turn around and threw her arms around his neck.

As Ted expected, there were people Didi knew in the bar area. They took a table and during dinner one or two others came over from time to time to chat with them. She did not so much introduce him as exhibit him, putting her hand on his shoulder or his thigh possessively. He played his part by fondling her, stroking her arm tenderly. She enjoyed the attention they were getting. After dinner they had drinks at a table in the bar area.

One person who called at their table stayed, a German girl called Ingrid, also a dancer, tall and Junoesque, with rounded hips and sumptuous breasts. Ingrid seemed captivated by him and was quite open about it. She directed her conversation mostly at Ted, and focused big dark eyes on him with open envy. Ted looked at her and wondered whether making a date with her when he was out with Didi would be bad manners. He could do it surreptitiously but he decided that if he whispered a suggestion to Ingrid that they might meet some time she would be likely to stand on a chair and make an announcement about it.

She and Didi seemed to be good friends, and gradually another idea formed in his mind, an idea that excited him. An opening came when Ingrid said to Didi, speaking across him, "Didi, I like your friend Ted."

He said, "I like you too, Ingrid."

"That's nice," she said. "We all like each other."

"Yes, we do," he said, and made it sound like a statement of some significance. "We don't really have to end the evening, do we?" They both looked at him. "I mean, we could all stay together."

Ingrid beamed. "What a luffly idea," she said.

Didi looked doubtful. Ingrid leaned over and put her arm around her shoulder. "Come on, Didi darling," she coaxed. "In zees times, you must share your luffly man. And we can all haff a good time together."

Didi still looked worried. Ted turned to her and said," It would be an experience. Have you ever done it before?" He leaned towards her and put his hands on her knees, looking straight at her and shutting out Ingrid for the moment. He reckoned he was giving her a chance to refuse. He owed her that. She looked back at him and then shrugged.

They went to a hotel on the next block, the Charles. Ted had stayed at the Charles for a night once, and had mentioned it to Gavin and Martha when they asked about an inexpensive hotel in Manhattan. It was hardly a romantic setting, with its large, drab foyer adorned only by two tired potted palms but it was nearby. The three of them walked up to the desk together and Ted booked a double room from a bored room clerk who looked as if he would rent a room to two dwarfs and a bear without showing any interest.

.The women's two bodies made a marvelous contrast: the slender suppleness of Didi's, with her firm little breasts, muscular belly and tight ass, and Ingrid's voluptuous curves. Ingrid's breasts spread like firm gelatin when she lay back, and when she bent over Ted they hung down like church bells. Didi got into the spirit of the occasion and Ingrid was there from the start, eager to try anything, not wanting to be left out.

He played with them both for a while. Ingrid expressed delight continually, in murmured words of appreciation, gasps and exclamations. *"Ach! Ach!"* she cried when he penetrated her. He and Didi took this up as a joke, teasing her, giving out *Ach Ach*'s when a sensitive part was touched, all three of them laughing.

Didi and Ingrid joined together using hands and mouths to arouse him, and when he was gasping with delight they pulled away. "Don't stop now!" he pleaded, and they made him say "Please" and then "Pretty please," and then *"Bitte, bitte!"* which Ingrid explained was German for "please" before they would let him come, and he almost yelled out when he did..

At one point Didi tickled Ingrid and then he pounded her into the mattress bringing her to a moaning, shuddering orgasm. Then, after a short break, he climbed on top of Didi and went into her. Ingrid seemed exhausted but she recovered quickly and soon she was straddling his back and he felt her fleshy thighs against his side and her pubic hairs rubbing against him like a brush. Didi, underneath him, her legs stretched out on either side, looked over his shoulder and asked him curiously, "What are you doing to Ingrid?" and he replied, "Ingrid's doing it herself."

The next morning he drove Didi back to Queens and then drove back to Radford, grinning with remembered pleasure. He knew he would have these memories for a long time. He also knew that as they remained in his mind the details would be rearranged slightly, airbrushing out certain things: the awkwardness of all their bodies together, with parts colliding as one of them moved over or around another, even raising a bruise; and the smells, of bodies and sweat and sex, in what seemed like a confined space, so that sometimes he was gasping for clean air.

Was it, he asked himself, the most exciting sexual experience he had ever had? Certainly the most unusual. It was something new. There were others that were good in a different way. He thought of making love to Elaine, which he enjoyed. He thought of Naomi. His loins were sleepy now, but he wanted to be in bed with Naomi.

He thought some more about Naomi, and found that someone else entered his thoughts. He remembered the teenage girl with corn-colored curls who skipped from side to side in a square dance, and small breasts that bobbed under soft wool, and blue eyes, who made his young heart miss a beat whenever he saw her. He could not remember her clearly. She was an indistinct figure who bobbed about at the edge of his awareness as she had bobbed about in the square dance. And with her a thought hovered on the edge of his consciousness, also indistinct and not fully formed, containing regret for something that he had lost in the process of growing up, and developing the extra layer of skin that came with adulthood. He knew that that something that was to be valued, and worried that it might now be getting further away still.

::   ::   ::

That morning Gavin Grove, poring over computer analyses of dna patterns in his office, received a telephone call from Dean Hoffmeister of Biotek. "I'm calling to repeat our invitation to come and visit our laboratory and perhaps join Biotek," Hoffmeister said.

Gavin was surprised at his persistence. "It's very good of you - " he began but Hoffmeister interrupted him. "I'm in a position," he went on, "to offer to double your present salary. And I think you'd find your situation and working conditions here more than satisfactory."

Gavin was surprised. He asked, "Do you know what my present salary is?"

"No," said Hoffmeister. "But I've been instructed to tell you that whatever it is, we'll double it."

"That's a very gratifying offer," Gavin said. "What makes you think I'm worth it?"

"It's simply that we're trying to get the very best people around to work on the impotence problem in our lab," Hoffmeister replied. "We know your work is good. Also, Mr. Barreras met you the other day, and was impressed."

"How could he be impressed? I hardly said anything."

"He asked about you. I told him a little about the work you've done and he said he'd like to have you on our team."

Gavin said again that he did not want to leave the Bliss Institute, and Hoffmeister said the offer remained open if he should change his mind.

When he got home that evening, Martha said to him, "I've told Louise I can't go to Acapulco with them. I wouldn't enjoy it without you."

"You didn't have to do that," he mumbled. But they both knew that she did have to, and also that some damage had been done which would need repairing.

After a pause she went on, "They've asked us to come and visit with them on Fire Island on Labor Day weekend. Dad and Mom will be there. I said I thought we'd go but I'd check with you. That's okay, isn't it?"

"Of course. That's fine." He was glad they could make an alternative arrangement, although he did not relish the idea of a weekend with them. In most circumstances he got along well with Martha's mother and father, but now they would be praising his brother-in-law's expensive vacation house, expensive car, expensive boat and two expensive children. And his brother-in-law would ask him heartily about life in the world of science. He would also probably ask when medical science would give men back what, uh-hum, they were missing, apart from a few lucky bastards.

He set the table and over supper he told Martha about Hoffmeister's call. He said Biotek had offered to increase his salary but he did not say by how much. "They seem to be very anxious to get me," he said,

"How interesting that the call should come at just this time," she remarked.

He was surprised that she should say this. "Yes. I suppose if I took the offer we could afford to have a holiday in Acapulco with Louise and Mike if we wanted to."

"No, no, that's not what I meant," she said. "Not at all. I mean how interesting that it should come just when you think that the Bliss Institute may be on the way to cracking the problem. Very interesting."

"What do you mean?"

"Well, Ted was explaining to us the other day that the place could still be bugged. Izzy says Mohsin is on the way to getting the answer now. You said you agreed with him. In fact, it seems to be a line of work that you suggested. Didn't you say so out loud at the Institute?"

"I suppose so." He was also remembering that he and Izzy had talked about it in the council room.

"Well then, maybe it was overheard. They think you might know the answer. And they want you."

"I hadn't thought of that. It seems a bit far-fetched."

"I don't think so. Did you really not see the connection right away?"

"No," he admitted. "Besides, if that's what's on their minds, why aren't they making the offer to Mohsin also?"

"How do you know they're not? Don't you remember that you told me once, more than once, how great scientific discoveries are made? Seeing connections between things not obviously connected? Darling, you may be a good scientist, but you're not always good at making connections outside science."

After supper he sat down with that day's Long Island Chronicle and read the profile of Joe Barreras. It was a picture of a super-achiever, but also a man with many sides to him. A number of things in the article surprised Gavin. Barreras had not studied business administration at Princeton but modern history and economics. He told the interviewer that he had at one time considered an academic career. He had played varsity tennis at Princeton, and later had employed a world-class player to coach him and keep up his game.

It recounted his meteoric career. How, three years out of Princeton and a junior executive with an electronics company, he had bought a patent that the company did not want, had an engineer adapt it to missile guidance, and set up his own company. His move into pharmaceuticals came a few years later when he bought an ailing company in

Mexico, expanded its manufacturing plant and moved its head- quarters to the United States.

He had founded a chain of multi-ethnic community organizations and an arts foundation in which his wife was active. She spent most of her time in their home in San Antonio. He also had an apartment in New York and a summer place in Maine. The article hinted that he played a role in Central American politics, and one of the photographs that illustrated it was of Barreras with the man who had led the recent coup in Guatemala.

Then Gavin turned to the news pages. There was a report that last year's Miss Kansas was now living with one Wilbur Nash, a clerk in a farm feed warehouse who had left his wife to move in with her. He was a bespectacled, weedy-looking man, to judge from the photograph. The former beauty queen told reporters, "He's a wonderful man and we're in love."

Mrs. Nash confirmed that her husband seemed to be immune from the impotence virus. She was being held by police because she had gone after her husband and his new companion with a hunting rifle. The police said they would release her if she promised not to commit an act of violence. She said she would promise no such thing.

The op-ed page was taken up mostly with two opinion pieces on marriage and divorce, setting out opposing viewpoints.

One said that adultery by a wife should no longer be grounds for divorce. Through no fault of anyone's, the vast majority of men were unable to provide women with what law and tradition recognized as their conjugal rights. If a woman was able to obtain these rights elsewhere, she should not be judged to have offended against the institution of marriage by doing so.

The other article said that adultery in the form of sexual intercourse between a man and someone else's wife should be made a criminal offense, for the man if not for the wife. The writer argued that a potent's possession of attributes which other men now lacked gave him the possibility of special access, rather as doctors have special access to female patients. "A doctor's special access to a woman's body imposes special obligations upon him. He is not allowed to have sexual intercourse with a woman patient and he faces severe penalties if he does so. In the same way a potent's special access imposes obligations upon him," this article said.

Gavin could see both sides of the argument but his liberal instincts recoiled from accepting the second. It implied that women were not responsible and, like children, needed protection from their own instincts.

He went to sleep thinking about it, and about Wilbur Nash and a beauty queen, and about a young and virile doctor looking at Martha naked. He woke early with a worry nagging at the back of his mind, like an itch that he wanted to scratch. In his sleep he had been working on questions he did not even know were there. An exchange with Martha came to him and would not go away.

"I didn't come home early."

"The secretary said you did."

"Well she was mistaken."

He had not wondered about this at the time. He was not used to wondering whether Martha told the truth. Now, lying in bed fully awake, he found his mind moving purposefully.

That exchange with Martha. And there was something out of place. Not anything that was said but something that looked wrong. What was it? Yes, the ashtray. Ted said he had not been there long. But the ashtray was full of cigarettes. Ted smoked. Martha did not smoke. He did not smoke.

Something else, some time before. Yes, he had come back from Washington and found Martha making the bed at six o'clock in the evening.

"Didn't Rosa come today?" he had asked her.

"Yes, but I had a nap this afternoon," she had said. But Martha hardly ever took naps in the afternoon.

Things not obviously connected. A bed that needed to be made at six o'clock in the evening. Ashtrays full of cigarettes. A secretary who said Martha had gone home early when Martha said she had not. Ted sitting there on the patio saying he had just arrived and an ashtray full of cigarettes. Martha saying she had not gone home early when someone else said she had. Why would Martha say that? *She was having an affair with Ted!*

The conclusion came to him as a surprise, catching him off-guard. Hot tears welled up in his eyes before he could even reflect on it. He leaped out of bed and rushed into the bathroom and locked the door so that Martha would not wake up to see him crying. He sat on the toilet lid and sobbed silently. When he had regained control of himself he washed his face, went back to bed, and lay there thinking.

He could talk to her. "I can't really blame you. I always said you were sexy. That's one of the great things about you You did that just to satisfy a physical need. Probably most women would. It doesn't end our marriage, I understand that. We have a deeper partnership. If I were a soldier stationed overseas during wartime for a long period, I'm sure I'd have sex with someone else, but it wouldn't mean that I didn't love you. I understand."

He would yell at her, "It's only been months, weeks even! You didn't have to jump into bed right away like a farmyard animal! Is that all our marriage means to you? Is that all that *I* mean to you? You bitch!" And he would slap her face, knocking her across the room, so that she would know what she had done to him.

Feelings boiled up in his mind turbulently, one replacing the other and then two or three bubbling up together: misery, anger, bitterness, jealousy, self-pity, sympathy. He kept thinking of Ted, his vigorous stride, his hairy arms. He had entertained that bastard in his home. He had treated him as a friend. He hurried through breakfast, barely talking to Martha, and went to the office early. When he was there he managed not to think about Martha and Ted, but his world today was not the same as it had been yesterday.

His mail at the office included his credentials as an alternate American delegate to the WHO conference in Geneva. He should not really be an alternate delegate, he decided. For one thing, if the selenium culture really was going to produce a breakthrough, and Izzy for some reason could not report it to the conference, then Mohsin should be the man to do it. He was doing the work. If he, a Brit, could be an American representative, then so could Mohsin a Pakistani. After all, Mohsin had spent half his life in America, which was more than he had.

At least this gave him something to talk about when he got home. He was tense and bottled up. Martha said to him, "You seem worried, darling. Is anything wrong?" He told her he had run into a difficult period in his lab work. When he thought of talking to her about what was really on his mind, he pulled back in fear. She might walk out on him.

He found after a few days that he could talk to her again. He always tried to be honest with himself about his feelings, and he knew now that whatever she might be doing, whatever lies she might be telling him, he was happier with her than he would be away from her. He also knew that having to lie to him would be causing her pain. He did not know whether he should be pleased about this or ashamed of wanting to stay with her whatever she was doing.

::   ::   ::

Ted found that he was becoming one of the best-known reporters on the paper. His byline appeared often on the front page and on longer inside-page articles. He sensed a more respectful attitude to him in the office. But there was not a more friendly attitude. He was invited out less these days. He used to play poker with some men in the office from time to time when someone got up a game, but if they had played lately no one told him about it. He wondered whether he had been too aggressive in his expression of opinion at one session. He explained himself afterwards, saying to his host, "I didn't say you were a fucking fascist. I said these were the sort of opinions I would expect to hear from a fucking fascist."

When Caspar Kelly, a sober, decent editor on the business desk of the Chronicle who he usually found rather boring, invited him to come with him and his family to the Radford Country Club on the Saturday before his cross-country journey, he accepted. This was principally because hardly anyone invited him anywhere these days. He did not particularly like the country club. For one thing, although he enjoyed swimming he did not like it as a form of display, which it tended to be there. For another he felt that it was for different age groups, either teenagers who could meet their friends and flirt or older, family men and women, usually these kids' parents.

He sat with the Kellys for a while, watching the Kelly children splashing about in the shallow end of the pool and chatting about local life and the news of the day. Then Caspar said, "I'm going for a swim before lunch. You coming?" His wife got up to join him but Ted begged off and said he would leave swimming until the afternoon.

He remained behind because he was interested to hear the conversation of the four boys sitting behind him, which he had picked up only in snatches while the Kellys were talking. Now with the others gone he could eavesdrop seriously. He leaned back in his deck chair so that he could hear better and held a newspaper in front of him pretending to read it.

"Hey, look at young Karen there."

"Which one is she?"

"The one sitting next to the diving board, in the blue two-piece."

"Oh yeah. That's a great pair of hooters. I remember her when she didn't have any."

"Are you really interested in tits?"

"Are you?"

"C'mon, we're all the same way. Unless one of us is a potent."

Another voice that Ted had not heard before spoke up. "Well actually, I didn't want to tell you guys because I thought you'd be jealous."

"Sure, Jim."

"Still, there's one good thing about it."

"There is?"

"Yeah. We can sit around saying, 'Aw gee, if it weren't for the plague I could score with this one and that one.' We can kid ourselves."

"'The plague!' What kind of language is that?" A voice rasping with scorn.

"That's what people call it."

"'The plague!' You mean our dicks are on the fritz."

"That's right. The language of the people. American demotic." This was the one called Jim. "The President ought to cut that crap about 'a medical problem' and go on TV and say, 'My fellow-Americans. All our dicks are on the fritz.'"

Ted did not want to draw attention to himself by turning to look at the boys but he had a picture of them in his mind. They were at college - not Ivy League - and back for the summer. They were good friends and had gone through high school together and many of the experiences of adolescence, the first this and the first that. One was cocky and aggressive, the leader when they were younger because the boldest, the one who poured scorn on the word *plague*. One was more troubled and honest about it. One of them, Jim, was more self-aware, humorous, ironic. One was just happy to be part of the gang, a natural follower.

"There's Walt Geiringer. Wasn't his kid sister your girl friend?"

"She still is my girl friend." This in an indignant voice.

"No shit. What do you, neck?"

"Yeah." Defensively. "We sort of neck."

A silence followed. Then, "Didn't her mom and dad split up?"

"Long time ago. She's with her mom."

Three girls came by. "Hi, Gene," one of them said. "How's college?" There were some introductions, for not everyone knew one another, and an exchange of small talk about Francie and Bonnie and Bernie and Marv.

The conversation petered out with the next stage unspoken, like a tune with the last few bars missing. No one said anything for a few moments. Then the girls said their so-longs and went on their way to the other side of the pool.

One of the boys behind Ted said," "I thought of saying something to them about this evening, but why?"

"We all thought of saying something."

"We could have asked them to out with us anyway."

"You should have. We could do with some female company. Except Marty here, who's got his girl friend."

"I don't know. I think I'd rather just futz around with you guys."

A pause. Then, "Well, somehow I felt bad when they went away."

Betty Kelly came back from the pool rubbing her hair with a towel ear and Ted could not listen to the boys any more. She was accompanied by another woman who Ted took to be somewhere in her mid-thirties. He took in her chunky body, her thick black hair and the faint blue lines of veins on her thighs. She was wearing a swimsuit that showed a lot of cleavage and flab. She stood over Ted and he got to his feet.

"This is Pauline Day," Betty said. "I think you've met."

"At a party at the Patels," Pauline said. "Last year. I was with my husband."

"Yes, I remember," he lied.

"My husband and I aren't together any more."

"I'm sorry."

Did the Kellys know about him? he wondered. Caspar was on the Chronicle. Did everyone on the paper know? Had Caspar told Betty? Had Betty told all her friends? How many people here knew? Pauline sat down next to him without waiting for an invitation, perching herself on the edge of a deck chair. While the Kellys rounded up their children they made small talk.

After lunch he swam for a while and then lay on the grass beside the pool to dry off in the sun. Pauline came and sprawled out next to him. For something to say he told her his views of the Masterson Administration. She tickled his ear with a blade of grass and he brushed it aside irritably.

He got up and went to the toilet. Two men were there, both in their forties. He knew one of them vaguely and nodded to him. He was in advertising and commuted to Manhattan. The two broke off their conversation for a moment when Ted walked in. Then the man who was in advertising said to the other, "So now my wife's living with this fucking woman in Texas. And she's got the girls with her." Ted glanced over at the man as he turned away from the urinal and walked over to the wash bowl. His eyes were hurt and angry.

"That's awful," the other said sympathetically.

The man spoke again, in a harsh tone, "I was just reading an article about potents. You know? What should be done with them."

"And?"

"This woman writer says they should be put in reservations. Kept as studs."

"Oh yes?"

"We could send the women in there, in turns, and they would service them. Once each. How do you like that?" He glanced over at Ted as he finished drying his hands, and then flung the towel into the bin with a violent motion.

"Great life for the potents," said the other.

Ted was appalled at their hostility. If they had been younger he would have been worried that they might beat him up.

When he got back to the poolside another woman was with Pauline, younger than her. Pauline introduced them grumpily. The other woman, who was lowering the strap on her swimsuit said hello and sat down without waiting for an invitation.

Ted felt that people were staring at him. He could not stand it any more. He said quickly, "I'm afraid I have to leave now. I'm going out this evening and have to go a long way. It was good meeting you. I'll have to say goodbye to the Kellys." He hurried away.

He was nervous driving home and drove badly, turning a corner too widely once so that he came out in front of a line of traffic, getting an angry beep on a horn. He found himself wondering whether the other drivers knew about him and whether they were all hostile. Were they honking some damned potent? This is crazy, he told himself, you're getting paranoid.

When he got home there was a message on his answering machine from Anne Broadley to say she would be home all evening if he would care to come up two floors. He thought of Anne Broadley and said to himself. "The hell with it." He turned on the television. But later in the evening he felt too nervous to read and there was nothing he wanted to watch on TV so he phoned her and said he was coming up. It occurred to him that he could almost certainly be in bed with either Pauline at the swimming pool or her younger friend, but he had only thought of getting out of there.

"I'm glad you came, honey," Anne told him when he walked into her apartment. "It's not just for bed. I like you."

CHAPTER EIGHT

T he next Friday evening, Gavin dropped in to the faculty club and headed for the Bliss people's usual corner. He was waylaid at the bar by a member of the English department called Ernest Green, a smallish, prematurely balding figure who usually had a worried look. He did not know Green well, but e warmed to him because it was evident that he cared deeply about his subject and about his students.

"Hello, Gavin, come over here and have a drink," Green said.

"I won't right now if you don't mind. I'm just on my way to join some colleagues," Gavin said, but Green seemed ill at ease so he stayed with him for a few moments and asked him about the book he was writing about Robert Frost.

Green said it was coming along and then said, "And how's your work going? That's a lot more important."

"I wish I could tell you. There's no way of knowing until someone gets there," Gavin said.

Just then Morley Bliss walked by them with Israel Rubin and headed for the Institute's corner. A Holycroft faculty member at the bar called out, "Hey, Izzy. Are you guys going to come up with the cure?"

"We've got the cure but we're keeping it to ourselves,"

Izzy told him.

Bliss Institute people stood up to make a place for Morley and welcomed him warmly. He had not come to one of the Friday evening sessions before. Several people had remarked that the challenge of dealing with the plague problem seemed to have invigorated him.

"Morley Bliss knows as much about the work as anybody," Gavin told Green, nodding towards him. "And I'm sure he doesn't know."

"I've been thinking about the plague lately," Green said.

"Who hasn't?" Gavin replied.

Green seemed ill at ease and Gavin did not want to abandon him so he said, "Why don't you come over and join us then." He went over to the corner and took a chair and Green followed with his drink and took another chair on the edge of the circle. He seemed ill at ease, and Gavin realized now that he was a bit drunk.

They talked about the fact that so many laboratories were now duplicating one another's work, and about some of the wilder theories that were being aired in the media, and then about reports from abroad. There was a pause in the conversation, and Ernest Green spoke up. "Are you people really sure you should be putting back the male sex drive just as it is?" he asked.

"Most people seem to want it," someone replied.

"Do you have any other ideas?" someone else asked.

"Well, the sex drive has caused an enormous amount of trouble," Green said.

"What kind of trouble?" Gavin wanted to know.

"Several kinds. For one thing, there's the aggression that goes with it." Green seemed to warm to his theme now..

"The point's been made that the streets are safer for women now. They're also safer for men. That's an improvement in quality of life. Macho men like to fight one another rather than love one another."

"But the sex drive is natural," objected someone from the Bliss Institute.

"So is smallpox," Green retorted. "We vaccinate against it." He had left behind any diffidence he had in joining the group. Things seemed to be spilling out of him, as if he were not totally in control.

Carl Eisgrau said, "The male sex drive keeps the human race going. It's been designed by Nature to do that, and Nature's taken millions of years to do it."

Green said, "Okay, it works biologically. It's kept the show on the road. I understand that. But Nature doesn't give a damn how much suffering it causes along the way. After all, it's a pretty slapdash way of doing things."

"What do you mean slapdash? It seems to me amazingly efficient in the way it works," Eisgrau said. "The way things fit into other things. And the way instincts push us that way. An engineer couldn't have designed system better. And the chemistry is astonishing."

"I suppose it is if you look at it as a mechanism, but it causes a lot of trouble," Green insisted. "It goes in all sorts of odd directions. It makes a man marry the wrong woman. You know, the man who marries a girl because she's got great tits and finds he's married the rest of her as well."

Gavin looked across at Green, his face red, gesticulating with the hand holding the drink, and decided that he was feeling some kind of personal distress.

"But that's how it works," Eisgrau said. "He'd never

marry her if it weren't for those tits. And the human race wouldn't be kept going."

"But that doesn't make for sensible marriages," Green responded. "And that's apart from people who get fixated on odd things, like rubber wear or artificially enlarged breasts. Or schoolchildren." Green was the focus of the conversation now.

"But you're talking about aberrations," Gavin said.

"Not unless you consider that the majority of the population is aberrant. Look at our thriving pornography industry."

"That's true," Denise Springer said. "People have become rich catering to the errant ways of the male sex drive. That's not to mention some very nasty things that are actually done."

"   "For all that, we can only try to give men back their normal sex drive," Izzy said. "What else can we do? We're scientists, we're not inventors. Do you want us to invent a new mechanism? The normal male sex drive is all there is."

"But I can't say the normal sex drive is a source of unfailing happiness," Green replied. Then more boldly, "Have all of you always been happy about the direction in which your John Thomas has pointed you? Hell's bells, mine gave me agonies when I was an adolescent."

"Yes, adolescence can be awful, we all know that," someone agreed.

"Didn't you do things that you were ashamed of the next day?" Green demanded. "*Think* things you were ashamed of? And not only in adolescence."

The question hung in the air, and in the silence that followed Green suddenly seemed alone and vulnerable, like an officer in battle who has gone too far ahead of his men.

Unexpectedly Lee Hsiu, usually reticent, went to his rescue. "Yes, I suppose we all have," he said. "I used to go to prostitutes. I'd always feel bad about it right afterwards. I don't know why, there was nothing really to be ashamed of, that's what they were there for. But I did feel bad. But I went on going."

"Copies of Hustler under the bed," someone volunteered as his contribution..

"What are suggesting we do?" Izzy asked Green, who was now the center of attention

"Couldn't you scientists find some way to start again from scratch? Create some substitute for the sex drive that would get the job done, and perhaps give us some enjoyment, and wouldn't have all these attendant disadvantages? Do you have to create again the same Goddamned thing to hang on us all?" .

"You exaggerate our creativity," Morley Bliss said. "As Izzy said, we're not inventors. What we're trying to do is remove a blockage in the mechanism that's already there."

"Well please think twice before you do," Green said. "Have a sense of responsibility."

This sounded pretentious. Green suddenly realised how freely he had been talking. He was just sober enough to be embarrassed. He mumbled, "Anyway, I must have some sense of responsibility to my family. My daughter's coming back from camp today and I promised to get home early."

He hurried out of the faculty club, annoyed with himself for letting so much spill out. He was almost crying with embarrassment as he realised how he had sounded, and at his frustration. Walking across the campus, he found that his wife's words of the night before were still echoing in his mind, as they had been all day: "Believe me, it won't hurt me. It's not too big. Use it. Please!"

There was some more discussion and then the participants drifted off, to wives, children, dinners, visits from in-laws or friends, reading students' papers. Some were going to homes that were less happy and harmonious than they had been. There was no consistent pattern of change in domestic life, but one thing that provided happiness and satisfaction was now missing. In some homes, a wife was tetchy and edgy, in others a husband was quick to anger. In many others, something that was a means of repairing a breach in married life was now missing, and discontents emerged snarling and barking. There was less marital violence during this period, but as the months went on, more couples parted.

Gavin found that he was in no hurry to go home to Martha and he stayed on until the last remnant of the group broke up. He was walking across the campus towards the parking lot, along a dark pathway lined with oak trees, when Mohsin bounded up behind him and greeted him with a slap on the shoulder so exuberantly that he thought for a moment that he was being mugged.

"Gavin, my friend, it's going well!" he exclaimed. "We've come to the next stage."

"You're just coming from the lab?"

"Yes."

"You're working late."

"With our little culture. The antigens are spreading, in a log phase. We'll be ready to inject it into mice very soon. And I think it's going to work."

"So you reckon you're home and dry."

Mohsin suddenly became more sober. "Not quite. It can always be different in animal tissues, you know that. Let's say we're rounding third base and home plate is in sight." Mohsin's familiarity with American idiom often surprised Gavin.

"But we're on the right road now," Mohsin went on, and in his excitement his walk turned into something like a skip. "And it feels good. Oh, when things are like this I want to go home and make love to Karim," he groaned. "I mean, I don't want to, but I want to want to. I wish I wanted to."

"Yes, I know," said Gavin. Then he said, "Tell me, if it doesn't work, or even if it does, have you got any ideas for an alternative sex drive?"

"What do you mean?"

"Something that'll keep the race going, give us all a desire to procreate, but work in a different way. Somebody was just saying we should have this."

Mohsin stood still and contemplated this for a moment. "Something from the plant world, maybe? Asexual reproduction?"

"No, that's not what I was thinking of," he said. "I mean a sex drive in humans, but something over which we'd have more control."

"You mean a cock with a brain?"

"Or at least a GPS. system. Something a little more discriminating than the present set-up." Mohsin stood considering this. Then Gavin slapped him on the shoulder and said, "Don't worry, it's just something somebody said. It set me thinking.""

He walked on, slowly. He had not worked out fully all

his feelings about Martha's infidelity but the anger lodged in him like a piece of undigested food. He would not apologize for getting home late, or even offer an explanation if she asked him. He would just scowl.

Martha was finishing her supper alone. She asked him where he had been and he just said he had been at the faculty club. She told him there was some meat and vegetables in the kitchen that he could warm up. He turned on the television while he ate. Well, Martha thought, I was wondering what effect this will have on us. He doesn't seem to hurry home to see me. She forced herself not to say anything to him about it. One more victory for the plague, she told herself.

When he had finished his supper she asked him several times how his work was going. Eventually, he started talking. "Mohsin Ahmed thinks they're going to crack it."

"What do you think?"

He found he could not help carrying on the conversation. Talking to her was a habit. "I've got a lot of faith inMohsin. He's excitable, but in the lab he's painstaking. He says they're almost at the next stage."

"What's that?"

"Inject it into mice. See the effects on testosterone."

"And then?"

"Inject it into rabbits, and then into humans."

"So if he's right, how long will it be before it's available as a medicine?"

"It'll take a little time to go through these testing procedures. You've got to make sure that even if they're producing the right antibodies that fight off the virus they don't do anything else awful at the same time."

"Is that really a possibility?"

"Oh sure. I mean, once it's gone through mice and rabbits and hasn't done any harm, then it's probably not going to harm people. But it is possible. When they tried out the first attempt at a 'flu vaccine, they found it gave a number of people diphtheria."

She was pleased to be talking to him but upset that she had had to make the effort. She had hoped that they would be just as close without sex. Maybe he was just distant this evening.

::   ::   ::

Ted Starowicz, on his travels, reflected that one trouble with this trip was that all the laboratories were doing essentially the same things with only minor variations. Writing about them was like writing about several different train journeys along the same route. So he wrote about the personalities, and people's forecasts of what would happen and when, and the atmosphere in the different laboratories. He tried to describe the almost apocalyptic pessimism of the man at Harvard, and the clean-cut, very earnest young men at Washington University who looked like members of a college chess team and thought someone was going to beat this thing and they wanted to be first, and the seminar under the orange trees at UCLA.

The trip was memorable particularly for the women. At home his position and the hostility it aroused was giving him anxieties. But once he got on the plane he felt liberated and bold.

There was Anna, the flight attendant on the shuttle to

Boston, who was chunky and buxom and had short curly red hair. When she asked him routinely on her way down the aisle whether he would like to purchase a drink he said he would like one with her afterwards in the bar at Logan Airport, and he did and they went back to her apartment, where she got excited almost as soon as he touched her and practically had an orgasm when he kissed her nipples and gave out wild cries when he penetrated her.

There was Helen, smart, svelte, Afro-American, who taught creative writing at Washington University and who sat next to him on the plane to St. Louis, and - only later did he connect this with her vocation - was unceasingly verbal when they made love in his hotel room, talking throughout, saying how good it was and not there but there and that's right and faster please and yes and now she was going to come soon.

There was Melanie, the assistant manager of the hotel in Albuquerque, who was witty and exchanged banter with him in the lobby and then came up to his room and gave a squeal of delight when he pushed her on the bed, and was chubby and plain but had all the usual things in the usual places, including big ripe buttocks on which his fingernails raised welts when they went down on each other.

And there was Bobby, his introduction to California. Tall and sinewy, wearing a long dress slit up to the waist, seated at the bar of his hotel with a high-heeled shoe dangling off one foot. Bobby came on strong. Ted had barely sat down when this husky voice spoke to him. "You a visitor to the West coast?" When he acknowledged that he was Bobby said, "I thought so."

"It shows?" Ted asked.

"It does. You haven't got that deep California tan, sweetie. We'll have to expose you to some healthy California living."

"I think I'd like that."

"And you've got an uptight Eastern way about you. We'll have to do something about that also."

There was some more of this banter in Bobby's husky drawl, and when Ted suggested another drink the reply was even more forward that he had expected. "I've just love another drink. But you know what, sweetie? Since you're staying in this hotel, why don't we have it in your room where we can admire the view?"

Once in his room Bobby's arms were around him. Firm lips nibbled his ear and then kissed his neck. A predatory hand stroked his ass. He smiled and stroked Bobby's ass and they fell back on the bed. He heard a clunk and then another as two high-heeled shoes hit the floor. A clever hand was rubbing his thigh and touching his penis into hardness and then two hands were unzipping his fly. He moved his hands over Bobby's belly and thigh and then between the thighs and felt – what? He was so shocked for a moment that he did not know what was happening. He was feeling something between Bobby's legs. It was something hard! Bobby had a penis.

He leaped off the bed flinging Bobby off him so violently that he fell on to the floor and before he knew what he was doing he kicked him in the ribs.

"Hey, you don't have to turn nasty," Bobby complained from the floor. "Just because I'm not what you thought, it doesn't mean we can't have some fun."

"Get the fuck out of here!" Ted yelled almost incoherently, zipping up his fly. "Get out or I'll brain you with a chair I swear to fucking Christ!"

"All right," said Bobby, pouting as he stood up and rearranged his dress. "You really are uptight.." Then, "You sure you don't want to try it?"

"Get *out*!".

At the door Bobby said, "You don't try something new, sweetie, you don't know what you might be missing."

After that there was cuddly, cute, dimpled Liz in La Jolla, who accepted his invitation to show him a good Mexican restaurant, and talked with him about John Updike and Vikram Seth and adopted an expression of intense inward concentration as he pounded her into the mattress, and then told him that he had come too soon in the resentful tone of a diner complaining to the chef that the *canard á l'orange* was a trifle under-seasoned.

There was Judy, departmental administrator at UCLA, tall and slender with long straight brown hair that reached halfway down her back and small firm breasts. Judy seemed insatiable. She woke him again and again during the night and kissed him all over, and when he said he could not do any more made cooing, encouraging sounds, and stroked him until he found that he could.

In the morning, she was brushing her long straight hair in front of the mirror as he dressed, and she stopped and turned to him and said in her soft, breathy voice, "Darling, last night was marvellous. Couldn't you possibly stay over another night or two?"

"Not possibly," he told her. "I'd love to, but I've got a plane to catch and appointments at the other end."

She turned back to the mirror and went on brushing her hair. She seemed to have switched something off. "Pity," she said, half to herself. "The dates get better as this week goes on."

"What do you mean?" he asked, puzzled. "You're not into astrology, are you?"

"Hell, no, I mean my fertility period."

"What are you talking about?"

Her tone changed and she spoke sharply. "What do you think this has all been in aid of, buster? I want to get pregnant."

Most remarkably, most memorably, there was Marie Zamora. She was one of the stars of a popular soap opera on television, and it was accepted that a lot of people watched it - men, anyway - because she was in it.

Marie Zamora oozed sex. She had large round brown eyes and a body that was likened to that of the Venus de Milo. She wore clinging clothes of soft material as strokeable as a kitten's fur. She had lustrous lips and a low, purring voice, and she could pronounce a man's name as if she were chewing the word slowly and enjoying the taste. On the TV screen when she bent over low in front of the camera, exposing most of the beauty of her full, firm breasts, millions of men in front of their television sets groaned with longing. Sometimes Ted was one of them.

It was the Chronicle's Los Angeles stringer, Robert Rozhak, who suggested that Ted meet her, when they had dinner together. He had already perceived from an exchange of sparks with the waitress that Ted was not like other men were these days. He said Ted might interview Marie Zamora for the Chronicle. He said she liked talking to journalists who were not showbiz writers and he had contacts in the studio who might be able to arrange it. He hinted that she might like talking to a potent. Ted agreed and the next day an appointment was made for the following evening at her home after she finished work. He had arranged that no studio publicist would be present.

He was excited at the prospect and the possibilities. During that day, when he was interviewing people or being shown around the UCLA laboratories, he found his mind wandering back to the appointment he had after dinner.

He was almost surprised to find that she was real. At the back of his mind was the idea that Marie Zamora was a construct, something created by the artful use of the resources of television to convey sex appeal rather than someone who breathed and ate breakfast and went to work. But she was here, just as beautiful and desirable as she was on the screen, sitting opposite him on a sofa covered with white angora, talking to him, smiling at him.

. He had to create an atmosphere, encourage her to talk frankly about herself, allow her to go off the record and sound off about the casting couch producers of her early days in the business and some of the fools she had to work with. He told her that he had always thought she was very beautiful but in a very special way, and now saw that she had a vitality which television still had not used to the full. She beamed with approval. He wondered briefly at one point whether she could talk about anything besides the TV business and herself but decided that it was not worth trying.

He had to make the moves, over to the sofa she was sitting on and further, but she let him make them, until they were kissing. Then she seemed to melt in his arms, and she took him by the hand and led him into her bedroom. Her bed was king-sized bed and covered in a bedspread that was also soft white angora. She stood beside it, tall and voluptuous, an inch taller than him. As she undressed for him, slowly and sensuously, allowing the silky garments to slide over her body to the floor, Ted was almost breathless with excitement.

Then she was lying on the bed and he started to kiss her all over and caress her body enthusiastically. But she said sharply, "Not there," and then, "Careful, mustn't leave a mark," pushing his face away from her shoulder, and "Gently!" These admonitions were a chilling breeze on his ardor. He pulled back and after a few moments raised himself up.

He looked down on her, stretched out on the bed with her honey blonde hair spread out on the pillow, her nipples pointing upwards, her thighs spread slightly apart so that he could see the tuft of hair below the swell of her belly. His passion was stirred again and he reached out towards her. She took his hand and placed it on her vulva, with the authority of a movie director moving a prop to its rightful place. She moved his hand up and down. He followed her instructions and rubbed her until she became damp down there. Then she reached between his legs and moved his member towards her. He followed her directions and penetrated her, and she immediately clamped her arms and her thighs around him and started jerking her pelvis upwards. After that she did it all herself, while he, locked in her quadri-limbed embrace, was carried along to an insipid climax. She reached her own, and remained with her eyes closed for a while, and then turned and smiled at him. He smiled back, out of politeness.

He was not cruel, and what he had to say he said silently, to the ceiling above his head, as he stared upwards in the early morning light that seeped through the curtains: "Marie, after Paris, you've been the biggest disappointment of my life."

At her request he left early in the morning before the studio car came to collect her. He walked along the oceanfront boulevard until he found a coffee shop one block from the beach where he got some breakfast, and then walked some more.

The night had left him feeling flat and empty and he did not have the energy to think about the work he was doing. He spent a while looking around and savoring the fact that he was on the other side of the country. Compared to Long Island, and to New Jersey, the townscape was lush. Greenery seemed to sprout everywhere: tall palm trees along the road, fruit trees in the gardens, cactus-like bushes on street corners. If there were a crack in the sidewalk, he thought, some huge exotic plant would spring up through it. He tried to see some difference in the people as he passed them on the street, hurrying off to work, or in a few cases, watering their front lawns. But this was still America and they were the same: the beautiful ones, the ugly ones, the ordinary ones, the crazy ones.

After a while he took a taxi back to his hotel and showered and shaved. He had a little time before his next appointment and he decided to telephone Gavin Grove to chck on what was happening at Bliss. It would be early afternoon on the East Coast. He remembered that Israel Rubin had said that exciting things were going on. Having cultivated Bliss Institute people and followed the story from the start, it would be galling to be beaten if the big story of a breakthrough came from Bliss and others got it before he did.

"Please tell me, Gavin, is anything big likely to come out of Bliss soon?" he asked.

"Very unlikely," Gavin said. He sounded as if he did not want to talk.

"Really? Not soon?"

"That's right."

"I've seen a couple of the guys you mentioned out here and it's been very helpful." He waited to see whether Gavin would ask him any more about the trip but he did not. He decided this must be a bad time to call and said his goodbye.

::   ::   ::

Gavin fumed inwardly at his inability to be really rude to Ted. It was his middle-class English upbringing, he thought. He did not want to talk to him, to chat in a friendly way as if Ted had not made love to his wife. Actually, Izzy was standing next to him when he took the call and he could not have been rude to him anyway without some explanation. And he could not have told Ted anything of importance about the work at Bliss because he was still staggered by what Izzy had just told him.

"I just can't believe it," Gavin said.

Izzy, sitting in the chair in his office, was grim-faced. "I was amazed myself. Still am. But Mohsin's the man and he says so. He and I have been on the wrong track. We've been getting it wrong."

"Wrong?"

"Totally wrong. That's what he says."

"But h told me you were ready to start injecting it into mice."

"I thought we were but I was going on what Mo said. He came in here over the weekend. Said he suddenly thought of somewhere he could have gone wrong, and came in and checked."

"What was wrong?"

"His analysis of the antibodies. He says they weren't antibodies at all. They were just a mutant version of the virus."

Gavin thought about this for a moment. It seemed just possible but it was not the sort of mistake he would expect Mo to make. He said, "I saw an agglutination on his gelplates. Are you sure that's what it was?"

"I'm not sure. I haven't checked. He's sure. And it's not the kind of thing he's likely to be wrong about. He also says the mistake goes way back. That the whole idea of using the selenium culture didn't work out."

"Where are the cultures?"

"Mohsin's destroyed them."

"What? Why did he do that?"

"I don't know."

"It was a crazy thing to do!"

"I *know*," Izzy said unhappily. "It sounds as if he was in a crazy mood. He admitted it, actually. He's taking this very badly."

"You say he's at home?"

"He said all this in a letter for me. Said he needed a few days' rest. I called him at home. He said he was so upset that he didn't want to talk. He actually said he might quit the Institute and go back to Pakistan."

"God. Could this get to him like that?"

Izzy went on, "I wrote to him, told him to take some time off, come back whenever he felt like it. It's my failure as much as his. I chose the line we took. I left the detailed work up to him. I should have followed it more closely. Checked."

"You had other things to do. Why did he destroy the culture for God's sake?"

"I suppose he was upset. Mohsin is a very emotional guy. I don't *know*, I tell you!" Izzy was clearly upset also. There was no point in pressing him further.

"I'm going to try to talk to Mo," said Gavin.

Mohsin's wife Karim answered the phone, and said Mohsin would not talk to him. "He will not speak with anyone, Gavin dear," she said. "He nearly won't speak to me. He's very, very upset. I am very worried. I think it is a nervous breakdown.".

"Look, do tell him that I called, please. Is there anything I can do to help?"

"I don't think there is. I know you are a good friend."

For the next few days, Gavin's thoughts kept going back to Mohsin's work. He still could not accept that Mohsin had gone so far down the wrong road because he had read data incorrectly.

Then Izzy came into his office and said, "Mohsin seems to have taken his notebooks home with him. They're missing, the key ones, anyway. I wanted to find out where we went wrong."

"So you can't check?" Gavin asked.

"No, not without going back to the beginning. When he gets over this, I'll talk to him about it and get the notebooks and go through them. But if he says we were wrong, I'm sure we were wrong.""

"He's really behaving very strangely. It's worrying."

"Yes, it is. Look, Gavin, this thing, the plague, is causing a lot of anxiety. Different people react in different ways. A lot of people have difficulties at home, apart from anything else. Who knows what kind of strain it's creating for Mo?"

Gavin telephoned Mohsin's home again. Karim did not know anything about the notebooks. He asked her to ask Mohsin. He called back and she said Mohsin would not say anything. She said again that he was spending most of his time in the bedroom and would not see anyone. She was worried and wanted to call a doctor but he would not let her.

Gavin could not get on with his dna work for thinking about the denatured virus. He was not convinced that Izzy and Mohsin had gone wrong. He asked Izzy to start down the same road, trying out the same temperature and chemical changes, but Izzy shrugged off the idea. Gavin saw that he just did not have the heart to go over the ground again.

He went up to the laboratory where Mohsin had prepared his virus culture and talked to his laboratory assistant, a PhD student called Maggie. "Did you keep your own notes on the cultures you prepared?" he asked her.

"Not my own. I wrote them up for Dr. Ahmed."

"How well do you remember them?"

"Pretty well. I wouldn't swear to every last detail."

"Tell me, Maggie, could you make up the same culture again?"

She thought for a moment and then said, "Yes, with a bit of time and a bit of trial and error."

"Could you do it for me?"

"If I had authorization I could, yes."

He went into Izzy's office and told him he proposed to have Mohsin's last virus culture made up and asked him to authorize it, since Maggie and that laboratory was in his area of responsibility.

Izzy was reluctant. "Other people are using that lab to break new ground," he said. "Why repeat old mistakes?"

"I'm not convinced that it was a mistake, or at least that it was that particular mistake. I think it's worth the trouble to find out."

"You're got your own work, Gavin, and that's important."

"This is worth doing," Gavin insisted.

"Well, I'll have to get the approval of the Exec Council," Izzy said doubtfully.

Now Gavin knew he was stalling. "Executive Council approval for something like this? Come on. This isn't a policy decision."

"All right, Gavin, you can have a week with Maggie in that lab. And I'll still mention it in the council meeting this afternoon."

"A week's not a lot of time. I don't know that we can produce anything in a week."

"Well there's a demand for lab space. That's all I can give you."

Gavin told Martha about it that evening. Ted was still away and he wondered now whether Ted would come to see Martha again when he got back. He was still angry, and his feelings boiled when he thought about her and Ted. But he could not get out of the habits of married life. They made plans for the three days on Fire Island with her family, what they would pack, what he would wear. He told himself he must be nice to her parents and to her sister and brother-in-law.

Later that week the telephone rang early one evening. A woman's voice said, "Is that Dr. Gavin Grove?" and when he said it was she said, "Mr. Barreras would like to speak to you."

Gavin was startled but Barreras came on the line before he could think about it. "Hello, Dr. Grove, this is Joe Barreras. We met in Washington three weeks ago, do you remember?" The modesty was affected, no doubt, but even the show of it was impressive.

"Yes, of course I remember."

"I'd like us to get to know each other a little. I was wondering whether you and your wife would like to come and spend part of Labor Day weekend with me?"

"I'm awfully sorry, but I'm afraid we're going away for the whole - I'm not sure. I'll have to consult my wife. Can I call you back?"

"Of course. I was thinking you could come up to my holiday place at Bar Harbor in Maine. There'll be one or two other friends there. My plane would bring you and take you back."

"Thank you for the invitation."

"And?"

"As I say, I have to try to arrange something with my wife. I'll call you tomorrow if I may and let you know. I hope you don't mind."

A lot of thoughts were running through his mind. He was worried by the invitation. Barreras did not waste his time, so what did he have up his sleeve? Presumably, he wanted him still to join Biotek. His guess was that this would be a recruiting weekend and there would be other potential Biotek recruits there also.

He would have turned down the invitation normally. Although he would be interested to meet Barreras again he had no intention of leaving Bliss, and his sense of social morality told him that to go would be accepting hospitality under false pretences. But this was an opportunity to get out of the Fire Island weekend with his in-laws. They would not only accept the excuse, they would be impressed by it. "Gavin is so sorry he can't be here," Martha would say. "He's spending the weekend at Joe Barreras's summer place in Maine. Barreras wants him to join his laboratory, but I think he'll probably decide to stay at Bliss."

He talked it over with Martha, although not in these terms. Martha would not drop Fire Island. "I'd jump at Barreras's invitation normally out of curiosity, you know that," she said. "But it's not often that Mom and Dad and Louise and I all get together, and they'd feel badly let down if I didn't come. You know, Dad's been ill and all that. But I think you should go."

"I must admit," he said, "that I'd like to see the man at close quarters."

"And who knows, you might end up joining Biotek? It's not impossible. He may not be such an ogre."

"I don't think he's an ogre. Anyway, there'll be other scientists there with their wives. I won't have him all to myself. My guess is that this is a recruiting drive he's conducting personally."

"Then you should be flattered that he's including you."

"Perhaps."

They were talking over supper, between mouthfuls of food, and she put down her knife and fork for a moment and said, "Don't be tempted just by a higher salary. You'll go where you can work best, be a good scientist. That's where you belong."

He smiled and thought what the hell, she did not care that way about Ted, maybe he would be able to put that behind him..

He telephoned Barreras's office and accepted the invitation for himself, explaining that his wife would not be able to come. Arrangements were made. He would go to JFK Airport, and a company jet would fly him and a few other people to Bar Harbor. He would be brought back to JFK on Monday morning since unfortunately, Mr. Barreras was not able to entertain him on the Monday as well. He was advised to bring a swim suit, and a tennis racket if he played tennis. Martha fussed about whether his summer clothes were smart enough and insisted that he buy a new pair of casual shoes.

On the Thursday of that week the Volkswagen, the smaller of their two cars which was always designated Martha's, broke down on the way from Radford. Martha got a jump start from a friendly driver and arrived home an hour late. "I'm not going to take it out again," she said.

He telephoned their usual garage and then another one and got the same answer. "No one is going to look at it until after the Labor Day weekend," he said. They postponed the discussion about what to do if the car needed to be replaced.

He drove her into Radford on Friday evening, and put her on the train for New York. She would go from there to Fire Island. On the platform, he kissed her. "I'm sorry I'm not coming with you," he told her.

"Liar," she laughed. "But I'm sorry I'm not coming with you. Have a good time."

He went back and watched television, wrote a chatty e-mail to his brother in England, and renewed a subscription to a professional magazine. Early on Saturday morning he drove back into Radford and left the car at the station. He had arranged with Martha that when he came back from the airport on Monday morning he would take a taxi home, and leave the car for her to collect when she arrived back from Fire Island on the Monday.

A limousine called at Radford Station on the way to JFK Airport. He was waiting for it outside the station when Denise Springer and her husband drove by. They stopped for a moment. He had not made much of the weekend invitation at Bliss but Denise had been there when he was telling Izzy about it. "Just off?" she called out from the car. He nodded.

"Take a long spoon," she said, grinning, and waved as they drove off.

CHAPTER NINE

Gavin was welcomed aboard the executive jet by Julia Hayden-Browne, who said she was Joe Barreras's personal assistant. She was about thirty and British, with straight brown shoulder-length hair, a turned-up nose and pale blue eyes, and a coolly confident manner.. He was surprised to find that there was only one other passenger on the plane, a square-built man in his fifties in a light summer suit. Julia introduced him as a vice-president of Barreras Industries.

The plane took off at 11.30 and was soon at cruising altitude. They unbuckled their seat belts and sat in armchairs around a coffee table. A white-coated steward appeared. "Would you like a glass of champagne?" Julia asked Gavin.

"I'd rather have some coffee, thanks," he said, determined not to be impressed. The steward brought his coffee, opened a split of champagne for Julia, and brought mineral water for the vice-president.

He and Julia talked during the flight. The other man had little to say. Julia came from Winchester, her father was a judge, and she had come to America originally to work for Sotheby's. Working as Joe Barreras's assistant was demanding but it was also interesting and rewarding, she said. She asked about him and seemed interested in everything he had to say.

It was a hot day and everyone had boarded the plane in shirtsleeves. Inside the pressurized cabin it was cooler and Gavin reached for his jacket. As he put it on he realized that his wallet was missing. He knew where the wallet was. He had put his jacket on the seat beside him in the car when he drove from into Radford. The wallet had fallen out of his pocket on to the floor and he had picked it up and put it on the dashboard. On days when he walked around in shirtsleeves he kept his money in a billfold on his belt so he had not noticed that his wallet was missing when he paid for the limousine to the airport. There were credit cards and an identity card in it but no cash. He shrugged and did not mention in to the others. It would still be in the car when Martha picked it up at the station and she would find it. He would not need his credit cards during the weekend.

The plane followed the coast most of the way and just off the Maine shore it circled Mount Desert Island, their destination. Gavin had a good view of the patch of green and russet brown in the gray, foam-flecked sea before the plane landed at the island's little airport. A station wagon was there to meet them. The Hispanic driver greeted them and took everyone's bags, implying with his warm words and friendly manner that there was absolutely nothing he would rather be doing on this particular morning. When they arrived at the estate Joe Barreras welcomed Gavin with a strong handshake and greeted the others. His clothes were smart and casual: a blue polo shirt, gray slacks, gray canvas shoes.

The driver took their bags into the house. "I guess you're about ready for lunch," he said. "If you want to freshen up in your rooms I'll see you downstairs in a few minutes."

Gavin knew vaguely that Bar Harbor had been a favored resort of the rich around the turn of the century, rivaling Newport, and the house seemed to be from this period. It was a pink brick mansion with gables along the sloping roof and a long wooden porch. It was set in grounds that stretched back as far as Gavin could see, separating them from other summertime visitors, with a mountain peak rearing up behind.

Gavin's room was decorated in lilac and gull gray. The *en suite* bathroom had gilt faucets. The room was cool, presumably air-conditioned, but by a mechanism so unobtrusive that Gavin had to listen carefully to hear a faint hum and could see no visible sign, so that one had the impression that the climate was determined solely by the pastoral shades. The room had the tranquil loveliness of a beautiful woman with pale, delicate features, so that any eruption of the crude elements, such as heat, cold or rain, would have seemed like a violation. The tall, lace-curtained windows gave a view of a long lawn with circular flower beds and, over to one side and glimpsed through some trees, a swimming pool.

A copy of *The Times* – what Americans persisted on calling the *London Times* - was on the bedside table A nice touch, Gavin thought. He had not seen it for some time and he flicked through it.

Lunch was served on the porch. Apart from Julia and the vice-president from the New York office there were three other guests: Michael Barreras, Joe's brother, who was also something in Barreras Industries; Stephen Johns, who Gavin remembered vaguely was a Deputy Assistant something at the Department of Defense, and Suzy. Suzy was small and lithe and very pretty, with long straight blonde hair and sloe eyes. She wore a minimal beach suit. She seemed to belong to Joe Barreras. She gave him most of her attention and he responded by flashing her a smile every now and again or patting her on her perfectly-shaped little rump.

The lunch was cold: avocado salad and a dish composed mostly of lobster and shrimp, with a combination of flavors in the dressing that Gavin could not place but that he found delicious, and white wine.

They talked for a while about the state of the nation and the world, and several times Barreras asked Gavin's opinion. Stephen Johns, a tall, slim erect figure with steel-grey hair, said at one point, "It looks as if Jesse is going to get his present."

"You mean the MZ2?" Barreras said.

"Yes. It's gone up to Masterson and he said we can have it anyway." Gavin had read in the newspapers about the controversy over the MZ2, a new anti-aircraft missile. He guessed that Jesse was Jesse Morgan, the Secretary of Defense.

"Even without the Saudi deal?"

"State stood firm against that and won. That's why it's a present," said Johns.

Gavin could not remember reading anything in the newspaper stories about the possible sale of the missile to Saudi Arabia. He decided to say so; there was no point in pretending to be in the loop on Administration matters? Barreras explained that the Defense Department proposed to sell the missiles to Saudi Arabia before they went into production to reduce the unit cost but the State Department blocked the plan. After some lobbying in the White House it seemed that the President now intended to give the green light to the missile without any pre-production sales abroad even thought this would cost more. Gavin enjoyed hearing this insider background.

The others asked Gavin about his feelings about coming to America and the differences between life here and in England. He trotted out some of his standard conversational comments. He said he thought it significant that American houses have porches in the front while British houses have theirs in the back, indicating that Americans relax in the public gaze, nodding to neighbors as they pass, while British people relax in private.

He said that looking back on his time at UCLA, it seemed to him that going from the East Coast to Southern California was more of a change than going from London to New York. "As a Westerner, I think I'd go along with that," Barreras said, "Even coming from Arizona, I feel as if I'm going overseas when I cross the Rockies." They all laughed. Gavin felt relaxed, more than he thought he would.

After lunch as the others went off in different directions, Barreras led Gavin away from the table to a corner of the porch. "Let's have a talk," he said as they sat down in white wooden armchairs. Gavin was beginning to realize that there were no other scientists here and wondered whether some might be coming tomorrow. So far, the recruiting drive seemed to be aimed solely at him. He did not have a chance to try to work out why he was so important to them because Barreras was talking to him.

"Dean Hoffmeister told you some time ago that we'd like you to join Biotek," he began. "I'm telling you now that I also would like to have you join us."

"Why me in particular?" he asked.

"Because you're an intelligent guy in general terms, which is important to me, and specifically somebody who might be able to do valuable work on the impotence problem."

"But I told you, I like it at Bliss. I like the work I'm doing and the people."

"The work you're doing would be similar, except that you would have more control over it than I imagine you have now. I envisage your being one of the senior people there. Maybe you feel sometimes that you'd like more control over your work." Gavin thought of Izzy giving him just a week to duplicate Mohsin's work. Yes, sometimes he would like more control.

"And we have good people at Biotek," Barreras continued. "I think you'd find the atmosphere congenial."

"I know you have good scientists there," Gavin replied. "But you told me when we met in Washington that you didn't blame me for wanting to stay at Bliss. You said you admired Morley Bliss and what he had created."

"Yes, I do, I certainly do. But it seems to me that it's a bit like a monastery. Are you sure you belong there?"

"A monastery? That's not quite the way I would describe it."

"I'm not suggesting that you guys are all like monks. I mean in its function," Barreras explained. "It preserves the pure values of scientific inquiry. It keeps itself apart from the values and the bustle of the society around it. That was the function of the monasteries in the Middle Ages. They preserved scholarship, the knowledge that had been gathered in the past, behind the monastery walls. Outside the walls, it may have been all mayhem and bloody wars.

"The Bliss Institute is dedicated to the pure pursuit of knowledge, okay, following Morley Bliss's ideals. It's shut off in the same way from the mainstream of American life, the pushing and shoving that's a part of a dynamic society. I'm not sure that's necessary today. After all, science has flourished in America. It doesn't need protecting. Some scientists may need protecting but that's a different matter. That's okay if they need it. But are you that kind of a person? Do you need to be shielded from the rough old world?"

Barreras paused long enough for Gavin to consider what he had said, but also to wonder why he was making this pitch to him in particular. Then he remembered that the lab might be bugged. What if Barreras Industries knew he was duplicating some of Mohsin's work? What if Mohsin really had created the denatured virus only for some reason he did not realize it, and somehow - God knows how - they knew this also? This could explain why they wanted him.

"Tell me something, Mr. Barreras - " Gavin began.

"I'd rather you called me 'Joe' if you don't mind," said Barreras.

"Joe. Let me ask you something. Are you asking me to come and work for you and bring with me work that was done at the Bliss Institute?"

Barreras answered slowly and carefully. "I'm asking you to come and do your very best to help us solve the problem."

Sitting on his porch, talking to him as an equal on first-name terms, Gavin decided to come out with the question. "You know, some people think we're being bugged at Bliss."

Barreras nodded. "That sort of thing goes on."

"Have you bugged our lab? Our phones?"

Barreras was silent for a moment, and then asked, "Do you know how to plant an electronic bug?"

"No, of course not."

"Neither do I."

"Come on, you know what I mean. Have you had our place bugged?"

"Certainly not. I tell my people what I want done I don't usually tell them in detail how they should do it."

"Does that include finding out what goes on in other laboratories?"

"We want to know what others are up to. Just as they want to know what we're up to, and they try to find out. It's a competitive business."

"Do you expect your people to do anything at all to get the results they want? No limits?"

"Not no limits, no, certainly not. I absolutely don't expect them to break the law." Gavin thought for a moment of Alan Carling. Barreras went on, "You know, Gavin, compared to Europe, America is a very goal-orientated society. People tend to go for the goal. They judge by what's achieved, by the result, not so much by the style in which it's done. Like it or not, that's how we've become the wealthiest society in the world and achieved a pretty decent way of life also."

"Not for everybody."

"No, not for everybody. You don't have to tell me there are people who are left out. I'm a Hispanic.. I'm not going to give you a sob story about it. I didn't grow up in a *barrio*, we weren't poor. My father owned a store. But I was still a Spic, a Dago. Life had its difficulties for me. But if there wasn't a red carpet laid out for me, it wasn't impossible for me to get ahead

"As I say, we Americans are goal-orientated. When a man runs for President of the United States, he wants to win. That's his goal. He doesn't stuff the ballot boxes. He doesn't have his opponent murdered. But do you think he says to his campaign managers, 'I want you to make sure above all that if people vote for me they're doing so for the right reasons?' No, he talks to them about how he can get the most votes. Because he wants the job and he thinks it's important that he gets it. That's the American way. Get there and do the job, that's what counts. 'The bottom line' is a rather crude way of putting this attitude, but it sums it up.

"And talking of the bottom line, I'm going to tell you something in confidence. I'll be announcing it soon but I'd like you to keep it to yourself until I do. I'm going to offer a prize of five million dollars to the person or persons in my company who discovers the cure for the impotence plague. If you joined the company and worked on the impotence problem, that's what you'd be shooting for. Five million dollars. And if you came up with the answer, produced a substance that contained an antibody to the virus and could be used, that's what you'd get."

"Five million dollars to one of your employees?"

"That's right. Or more likely, to be shared among two or three, if they find the cure. If you came over, you'd be in the running. My guess is that you'd be somewhere in the lead."

"And if I left Bliss right now and got that prize, I'd lose all my friends in the process."

"Do you think so? Really?"

"Well, probably. Most of them. I'd have walked out on the team right in the middle of the game, just for money."

"Nonsense. You'd have changed jobs, that's all. Scientists are always changing jobs, just like other people. Your friends know you're a person with integrity, if they're your friends. And do you think people at Bliss would really turn against you if you discovered the cure at Biotek? Think of it, Gavin. You'd be the most famous medical scientist in the country. And probably one of the richest. Do you really think your old friends wouldn't want to know you? You think they'd turn down invitations to come and see your new home? Apart from anything else, their wives wouldn't let them."

He paused to let all this sink in. Then he leaned back in his chair and said, "Let's drop this for a while. You're my guest and it would be inhospitable to batter you with business. I notice you've brought your tennis racket. Do you feel like a game a little later on?"

"That sounds fine."

"Good. It's too hot for it in the middle of the afternoon. I'll see you at, say, five-thirty. Okay"

"Sure."

"I have to make a few family phone calls. Do you mind entertaining yourself for a while? You might want to take a dip in the pool. I noticed Julia going down that way. Or you can talk to my brother about an Englishman's view of America.

::   ::   ::

Gavin opted for the pool. He swam for a while, and then floated on his back, feeling the gentle warmth of the sun, and thought about what Joe Barreras had said to him. A little while earlier, when he and Izzy talked about Alan Carling's disappearance, he learned that someone could be killed - it was possible that someone could be killed, at any rate - because of something he was doing as a medical scientist, an idea that was totally new to him. Now he had learned that one could acquire five million dollars, or perhaps a half-share in it, by working as a medical scientist, and this idea also was new to him.

He did not day-dream often and he had never thought before about having five million dollars or about what he would do with this kind of money. Now he thought about it for a few minutes. He would not be one of the very rich, people who talked in billions rather than millions. But he would be rich in a way he had never thought of being rich before. However, he did not have five million dollars, he reminded himself, and he had no intention of leaving the Bliss Institute for Biotek so he was not going to have it, so he had best forget about it. There were other things he would rather do, anyway.

His reveries were disturbed by a splash. Julia Hayden-Browne appeared beside him in the water, grinning beneath her bathing cap. He swam for a while, and afterwards he lay on a sun lounger on the lawn by the pool drying, and she joined him on another sun lounger

They talked about England and America and their lives. She had an apartment on Staten Island overlooking New York harbor, and she liked New York life and the theater and jazz and Sunday brunch on Central Park South. He said he and Martha sometimes spent a weekend in New York City. Then he decided it was too hot and he would cool off with another spell in the pool and she said she would join him and they swam side by side, and then dried off in the sun again

He went up and changed for tennis and came own to the court just as Barreras appeared, a small, lean, lithe figure. His gleaming white tennis shirt and shorts showed up his dark skin coloring so that he looked more obviously Hispanic. They agreed that they would play one set.

Barreras served first, with hard, fast serves, so fast that Gavin missed several altogether and lost the first two games on this. He recalled reading that Barreras had played varsity tennis at Princeton and had kept up his skill with the help of a -coach. He started returning the serves but Barreras still won the third game although it was close. Gavin looked across the net at Barreras and reflected that considering that he was probably twenty years older than him, he was doing pretty well.

Gavin got the hang of those serves, or at any rate they did not seem so fast, and he won the next two games. Then Barreras won one with two brilliant shots, one into the far corner away from Gavin and one lob just over the net when Barreras was at the back of the court. Gavin ran forward for the second one, did not get it and crashed into the net. He felt the sting of the rope mesh and made a mock grimace. Barreras grinned and said, "I like to win."

Gavin was breathing hard and his arm was still stinging and he suddenly felt competitive. "So do I like to win," he told himself. The score was now four games to two in Barreras's favor. It would be difficult to catch up but not impossible. It was his serve and he started slamming them in wildly. Two were out, then two landed squarely in the right place and Joe missed them. Then he thought he double-faulted but Barreras swung at his second serve and missed. "Wasn't that out?" he called, but Barreras shook his head and called out that it was just on the line. "Well, he likes to win honestly," he thought to himself. He won the next two games and then lost one, so that the score was now five games to four against him.

He was still playing aggressively, standing in a crouch, ready to spring. Barreras seemed to be tiring, which was not surprising. He landed a couple of good shots just out of Gavin's reach but flagged in the volleys. Gavin found he was playing more wildly and double-faulted a couple of times. "Calm down if you want to win," he told himself, and went back to his normal style, so that his first serves were hard but not too hard. He was pleased that Barreras missed several returns anyway and lost the next two games, so that the score was now six games to five in his favor. The next game would be a clincher if he won it. If Barreras won the game would go on.

Barreras was serving but his serves were slower now and Gavin was returning them easily. When a couple came right to him he slammed them back so hard that he barely felt the impact of the ball on his racket. Once he thought he had over-reached himself, aiming the ball at the corner away from Joe and missing the boundary line, but Barreras called out, "It was in."

"Are you sure?" he demanded, because he also liked to win honestly, and Barreras nodded vigorously. Then there were two fierce volleys, each ending with Barreras hitting the ball into the net. Gavin was tiring and wiping his sweating brow with the back of his arm between the volleys, but he knew he was playing his best. Barreras hit an easy serve, Gavin returned it with a hard back-hand, to the right side of the court where Barreras could not reach it, and the game was his. He was sweating and breathing hard and happy.

"Jesus, that was good," Barreras said to him, slapping him on the shoulder, as they walked off the court. "You're a damned good player, Gavin. And I'm not as good as I was. We must play some more. It does me good to be beaten sometimes." Gavin grinned.

Back in his room in the shower he felt like singing. Winning that tennis game had done something for him. He felt quite equal now to Barreras, and the wealth and power that he and this house represented. He decided that Barreras was a stimulating partner, on the tennis court and in conversation, although he disagreed with a lot of what he said.

Dinner was clam chowder and roast beef, lean and tender. It was served at a polished table in the dining room set with gleaming silverware. In other rooms there were modern paintings or New England scenes, but here there were a set of Mexican woodcuts. They seemed to show that Jose

Barreras, Mexican-American, was not only in occupation of this piece of old Maine but in possession.

They talked about British and American education and their own days at school and univer- sity. Then Stephen Johns cleared his throat as if he were about to make an announcement and said, "Gavin, Joe tells me that you're a distinguished medical scientist. Do you have any idea when we're likely to find a cure for this plague that's affecting us men? And affecting women too, I suppose" - this with a glance at Julia and then at Suzy.

"There's really no knowing," Gavin said. He explained the different approaches to the problem, taking care to keep his explanation general and not referring to any work going on at the Bliss Institute. He talked about the invading virus and the defending antibodies and said as he had said before, "The military metaphor is inevitable. As a Pentagon man, I imagine you'll feel at home with this." Johns chuckled appreciatively. He threw in one of the jokes he had made at the Washington conference and it went down well.

Johns said, "I notice it was the Pasteur Institute in France that located the virus. Do you think an American laboratory is going to find the cure?"

"Well, American laboratories are certainly putting the most effort into it," Gavin replied. "But that's no guarantee."

"Some people in Washington think it's very important that it should be an American institute that discovers it," said Johns.

"Why?"

"Because the cure, once its discovered, will be a source of power if the plague spreads across the world."

"Do you mean," Gavin asked, "that the American Government might not share it with the rest of the world if it was discovered in America?"

"The company that found it would hold the patent," the Vice-President of Barreras Industries pointed out.

"I see so an American company would refuse to share it. That would make America really popular," Julia chimed in sarcastically..

"Not that, but I've heard some pretty strange thoughts kicked around," Johns said.

"Could the Government keep it secret?" Barreras asked.

"It would be difficult to give a medicine to the entire male population of the United States without somebody else noticing," Gavin pointed out..

Johns said, "We had a group brainstorming it, coming up with any wild ideas they could think of. It's been suggested that we might put something in the water supply to counteract the disease here. But that's fantastic. Of course, the Administration would be happy if the cure were discovered in America, just for the prestige."

"Of course. That we can all understand," said Barreras. "But what if it doesn't spread to the rest of the world? What if it turns out that it's limited to North America, or perhaps North America and Europe? That's what seems to be happening now?"

"That's where we come in," Johns said.

"What do you mean? Who's 'we'?"

"The Pentagon," said Johns. "We're looking for evidence that this was done deliberately, that it's a germ warfare attack on the United States. Then we'd have to respond."

"But it doesn't seem likely," Gavin said. "And how would you respond? And against who?"

"We'll find a way to respond, don't worry," said Johns grimly. "If people even think this might be an attack on the United States, we'll have to hit back at somebody."

The night was warm and after dinner they all went out on to the verandah. It was lit by a string of little lanterns, but there was a full moon and a cloudless sky and Barreras turned off the lanterns. They sat in the moonlight sipping port and talking. Johns regaled them with entertaining gossip about Administration figures. Gavin enjoyed this and remembered a couple to pass on. The Vice-President from the New York office gave his opinion on the economy. Michael Barreras recalled early life in the Barreras household and their father's foibles. Then, while others were talking, he said quietly to Gavin, "I hear you may be joining our company." Gavin shrugged this off saying it was only a possibility, nothing more.

They agreed that it would be nice to take a turn around the grounds before going to bed, and strolled across the lawn to a line of fir trees and a rocky shoreline. Gavin had not realized that the grounds extended this far. There was a dock with two boats beside it, a substantial motor launch and a speedboat. They all stood silently for a few moments looking out on the dark surface of the water, the trees glinting yellow in the moonlight, the only sound that of crickets and the water lapping softly against the rocks. Barreras put a hand on Gavin's shoulder and another on Johns'. He did not say a word but his face showed a satisfied smile. He seemed pleased as a host that his guests were enjoying the scene, his lawn, his view, his night, his moon, his stars.

When they started back to the house, Barreras fell in beside Gavin, and asked him, "Have you thought some more about what I mentioned earlier today?"

"You mean about changing jobs? I don't know. As I think I said earlier, I'm not sure it would be right ethically to move at a time like this." He felt now that he could talk to Barreras frankly.

"Do you think it would delay finding an answer to the impotence problem?" Barreras asked.

"I don't suppose so."

"That's the only ethical question, surely. To let the plague go on like this longer than necessary would be unethical, immoral. I wouldn't countenance it for a moment, and I don't suppose you would. But if it's only a matter of who finds it - well. If you find it for us and release it to the world, you'll be very famous and you'll be rich. If you and a number of other people find it at Bliss, you won't be so fa00mous and you won't be rich. That's the only difference."

They had reached the house now and they stood talking outside the door. Barreras said good- night to the others as they went inside, but he gave no indication to Gavin that their conversation was at end. The doorway was flanked by two tall white Doric columns that gleamed in the moon-light and Barreras, as he said his goodnights, was leaning against one of them, with one hand in his pocket. It seemed to Gavin that he might be posing for a photograph as the epitome of American opulent elegance, a photograph that could be published in *Homes and Gardens* or *Vogue*.

When the others had gone inside he beckoned Gavin over to the verandah and they sat down, and Gavin returned to the afternoon's conversation. They took up Barreras's point about the reward. Gavin asked, "But what if I work out what turns out to be the way to the cure, only it's not really me who's discovered it? If it's somebody else who's found it but he doesn't say so?"

"Why wouldn't he say so?"

"Because, perhaps, he doesn't realize he's found it. Say he started on a line of research and then dropped it because he thought he'd gone the wrong way. But in fact he'd gone the right way."

"I don't understand you. If he doesn't know he's found it, then he hasn't found it. If he's stumbled on something and doesn't recognize it, that's not scientific discovery, it's just luck. Like Christopher Columbus. He got the credit for discovering America but he was just a dumb sailor who went on until he hit land. He didn't know what he'd discovered. He thought he was in China."

Gavin paused to absorb this. Then he said, "I like it at Bliss. I like the atmosphere, I like the people, I like the way the place works."

"Okay. If you like it enough, you'll stay there. I think myself you deserve recognition for the standard of your work. Not necessarily for making a great discovery, but more than you're getting. Bliss is a good place in its way. But there are a number of people there who rallied around Morley Bliss when the place started and they're going to stay at the top there, and everyone else will be in the second rank at best. Are you really going to spend the rest of your life there? And if you're going to move, why not move now? There'll never be a better time.

"I tell you, I'm making the laboratory at Biotek into one that can look any in the world in the eye. We'll be getting some of the very best people - we're getting them now. So I'm offering you a chance to join us and earn a lot more money." He stood up. "Anyway, sleep on it." He gave Gavin a nod that said goodnight, and they went inside.

In bed, Gavin read some of the articles in *The Times* and thought that maybe he did deserve something more in life than he was getting. If Mohsin was wrong he was wrong. He had terminated his line of work. If he, Gavin, began it all over again at another laboratory, then it was his intellectual property, and any results that came out of it were his. And anyway, he was the one who had suggested treating the culture with selenium. Could he envisage working somewhere other than Bliss? Yes, he could. It wasn't his whole life. He had worked at the MRC in England with some success. But on the other hand....He went to sleep thinking of the on-the-other-hands.

When he came down to breakfast the next morning Suzy was already there, eating a bowl of granola. He helped himself to coffee and warm rolls from the sideboard. Suzy told him that she had an English girl friend when he was in junior high school, and asked him whether he thought Camilla Parker-Bowles would be queen..

Joe Barreras came in. "There are some lovely walks near here," he said. "Frankly, a lot of the island is given over these days to rather tacky tourism but some woods near here are one of the pleasures of the place. We can go for a walk this morning - nothing too energetic, not a hike or anything.

Or if any of you prefer, you can sit around here and have a swim in the pool."

"What about another game of tennis?" Gavin suggested. "Give you a chance to get your own back."

"I'd love it but to tell the truth I've got a pain in the arm. A kind of tennis elbow. Some other time, yes."

Gavin said he would like a walk, and Julia and two of the others went along. Strolling through woods and past aromatic apple orchards, they swapped bits of life history. Gavin told stories of being a medical student in London, and Joe Barreras told a story about an encounter over one of his missile projects with a congressman who, he said, confused ICBM with IBM. Julia talked about the difference between working for Sotheby's in London and in New York. The Vice-President told a long story about an episode in college which he evidently thought was funny but no one else did.

Barreras told them a little about the history of Bar Harbor, about the fishing industry that had supported the island in the last century, and the French-Canadian villages, and the influx in the early years of the century when it became a fashionable resort, when wealthy families came with their servants and built summer homes and laid out gardens. Then they deserted it so that he, Joe Barreras, who loved the island's rugged landscape and did not follow the fashion, was able to buy this house from the family of the railroad magnate who built it.

Lunch was served on the verandah again. Gavin noticed that the white-coated man who served it was the one who had cleared the table at breakfast-time. He was almost relieved to find that the size of the domestic staff was not unlimited. Afterwards he found himself alone with Joe

Barreras in a corner of the verandah. Barreras recalled his first visit to England, on holiday with his wife, the only time he mentioned his wife, who, Gavin presumed, was otherwise engaged this weekend. Then Barreras asked conversationally, "Do you get back home to England often?"

Gavin shook his head. "I've only been back once since I came to America four years ago. That was for my mother's funeral. We're thinking of going back on a visit next year."

"Any special reason why you haven't been?"

"Not really. But there was no necessity. Oh, I'd like to see some old friends, of course, and the place again. My brother came over on a visit last year. But there's a lot of America I still want to see. And we'd have to stay in a hotel in London."

"You mean money's the reason?" Barreras looked surprised.

"It's a factor."

"But travel is so cheap today. Can I ask how much you earn at Bliss?"

"If I take up your offer to double my salary, then I'll tell you," Gavin replied..

"I have some idea of the salary levels there," Barreras said. "You really should be doing better. You shouldn't have to count pennies."

"Come on, I don't have to count pennies. Dollars, maybe."

"It seems to me that you deserve more," Barreras said. "That you're worth more. And please don't tell me that there are other ways to value things besides in money terms. I know that."

"I wouldn't try to tell you that, Joe, it would be insulting. But I do think that you care about money more than I do. I'm not pretending that I don't care about money, of course I do, but perhaps not as much as you."

"Probably you're right. But I've seen the way money changes people and changes their lives, mostly for the good. It doesn't change people for the bad. If somebody nasty has money, then it helps them behave in a nasty way because it gives people more power, but it doesn't make them nasty. Money determines partly the way you live, what you can do, the choices you have." Barreras was standing close to Gavin now and looking into his face. He was talking about what he had learned from life, as one might talk to a son or a daughter.

Gavin said curiously, "Since we're talking about money, did you set out very early on to make a lot of it? Do you mind me asking this question?"

"No, I don't mind. No, I didn't at first," Barreras said. "It may surprise you to know that at Princeton, I thought I wanted an academic career. I planned to go to get a higher degree and teach at college. I wasn't even sure whether I wanted to teach economics or modern history. Economics interested me for a while, the attempts to match theories to practice., the relation between maths and people's behavior.

"If I could have simply gone smoothly from under-graduate to graduate study I probably would have done so. But my parents had saved up so that I could go to college and they hadn't reckoned on my wanting a master's degree. So I would have to work while I was getting my master's, or more likely take a year off and work and save money. I could have done it. Hard work never scared me. But the prospect made me sit back and think about how much I wanted an academic career and what I really wanted. And I realized that I had a lot of pretensions but that I would really like to be rich. To be rich means you count for something, and I wanted to count for something. If I wasn't rich I would always be sorry.

"I'd never admitted this before. I suppose it was partly being a Hispanic. I wanted to shit on some of the people who'd been shitting on me. But no, mostly it was the good old American dream. Most of the other things I wanted that I thought would come with an academic career would come with being rich, leisure, a chance to influence things in this country. Not being rich would always be second-best. So if I was going to have to work hard, then I thought I might as well work hard for what I really wanted.

"You're different, Gavin. You have a serious contribution to make as a scientist, and that's your primary goal. Am I right?"

"Yes, I suppose you are, but that doesn't make me unselfish, a sort of saint. I like money, of course, and I'd like to have more. But when I became a scientist I set out after different rewards. For one thing I really enjoy my work a lot of the time. When I was - oh, maybe fifteen, I read a book about how the body works and found it fascinating. I've been fascinated ever since. When I was accepted by the Medical Research Council in England for my first research post, I was over the moon. If somebody had said to me, 'Look, you can earn a lot of money doing something else,'which I don't think I could, by the way, I'd have said 'Not interested.' In fact, I could have earned more practicing medicine privately. Even now, I'm enjoying trying to solve the problem I'm working on. Although as always there are frustrations, the chance, the likelihood even, that I'm on the wrong track. But solving problems, looking for cures, is not principally what I'm about. I like doing fundamental research. That's where I've done my best work.

"And there are other rewards. Scientists are just as selfish as other people, and just as egotistic. You must have been around scientists long enough to see the jockeying that goes on to get someone's name on a paper. Or a professorship? One wants the respect of one's peers. One's name attached to discoveries. Even, perhaps, the occasional prize. There's that kind of reward. In England they dole out knighthoods and honors, which is the same sort to thing."

Barreras considered this. "Yes, you should be a scientist and have the rewards of a scientist. If you discovered the cure, you'd certainly be famous. But anyway, a scientist is a member of our society, and like it or not, one of the expected rewards for good work in our society is money. We don't give people knighthoods in America, we give them money. At Biotek you'd earn a lot more, which seems to me to be right and proper. And you'd have a chance, perhaps a good chance, of earning that five million dollar prize I mentioned yesterday. Tell me honestly, are you ever going to have five million dollars any other way?"

Gavin shook his head. "It's most unlikely," he admitted.

"We only live once," Barreras said. "If you don't have it in this lifetime, you won't get another chance. You'll be missing it."

"What am I missing?"

"Comfort, for one thing. It's more comfortable traveling first-class. And it's a way of living. When you go into a restaurant, do you look down both sides of the menu, to see what things cost?"

"I suppose so, yes."

"I don't. Haven't done for years. Never will again. My father did, to the end of his days. Didn't know what it was like not to. He wasn't poor, but he had to look on both sides of the menu. Michael, my brother, took over our father's store. He sold the store and he has a job in my company now and he has a good salary, but he'll never get away from looking at both sides of the menu. Same with a hotel. If you're going away and you choose a hotel, you look to see what it costs first, right?"

"Uh-huh."

"With five million dollars, you won't have to think about how much it costs. Without it you'll never know what it is not to. It's a different way of going through life. It doesn't guarantee that you're going to be happy. Nothing can do that. But at least you won't have to worry about piddling little things. I'm saying all this because I like you. I think you belong among people like us. It irks me that there are two-bit bond salesmen - car salesmen, for God's sake - who don't have a fraction of your brains and aren't contributing anything to society who earn more than you. And probably look down on you because of that."

He settled back, evidently finished with this part of the discussion. Then he looked across at the pool and asked, "How you do you like Suzy? She's cute, huh?" Suzy, in a yellow bikini, was lying on a towel soaking up the sun, with a nose shield over her nose.

"Yes. She's beautiful." Gavin said it as a polite compliment to his host, as he might compliment him on a new car.

"She was a *Playboy* centerfold, you know that?" said Barreras. "When I was a kid I used to jack off to *Playboy* centerfolds. Did you? No, all right, you English don't like to talk about personal things. But tell me, have you ever laid anyone who looked as good as that? Probably not. You're married, I think."

"Yes, and happily."

"Good. But don't tell me that if you think about it, you wouldn't like to have fun with some- one like Suzy once in a while. Suzy and I are going to part company soon. You could probably have her for a little while."

Gavin said, "What do you mean I could have her? You make her sound like a second-hand car. In good condition, one previous owner."

"Oh no, not like that. Suzy's not for sale. She's a sweet thing. But she likes men with money because she likes to be given presents. She also likes you, I can tell you.. The idea doesn't do anything for you now, I know. We're all in the same boat. But when your juices get going again, you could probably find yourself thinking a lot about what you passed up."

"I can imagine that might be," said Gavin truthfully. Actually, he was thinking at that moment about Ted Starowicz. A little bit of infidelity on his part with a gorgeous little thing like Suzy was no more than Martha had coming to her.

"How about Julia?" Barreras went on. "She's a different proposition, isn't she?"

"Quite different," Gavin agreed.

"She's a good-looking chick. And a very bright lady. You two seem to be getting on very well. How do you feel about her?"

"I like her. Are you going to tell me she'll be bowled over by five million dollars?"

"Hell, no. But she's a healthy girl, I can tell. She's had boy friends, she needs her oats. If you discovered the cure, it would take time to turn it into a medicine, time to manufacture it, even if we passed on the formula to the world, which we would. There'd be samples made in the laboratory first. You'd have access to them before the general public. You'd be a potent. If Julia likes you now, and she does, as I'm sure you can tell, she'll like you a hell of a lot more then. Are you going to tell me that that thought doesn't do anything to you?"

"No. Once again, it's an appealing idea."

"After all, it won't make any difference to America, or to the world at large, if you or somebody else is hailed as the discoverer, or if it's found at Bliss or Biotek of anywhere else. But it'll make a difference to me and it'll make a difference to you. I'd like to have you on my team, Gavin. I enjoy your company. We could have more weekends like this one."

"I've certainly enjoyed the weekend," said Gavin truthfully. "I'll think about it very seriously."

"You'll think about it very seriously?" Joe's tone was just a fraction sharper. "What are you, a Congressional committee? I'd like to have you at Biotek, Gavin, but Biotek can live without you."

Gavin retreated a little. "Of course, I know that, Joe. But it's a big move and I want to talk it over with my wife. She's away and I'll be back home tomorrow evening. I'll let you know in two or three days. Will that be okay?"

Joe's tone softened again. "Sure. I'll be here for the next two days. I have some business entertaining to do but I'll be here. After that I'll be in Walton."

Gavin felt buoyant at supper and felt he was sparkling in the conversation. Stephen Johns told some more Government stories and when the meal ended he told Gavin to call him at his office when he was next in Washington for one of the commission meetings. He put questions of the future out of his mind when he went up to his bedroom but he felt that he belonged among these people. Forgetting about Julia and Suzy for a moment, he wished Martha could be here with him.

He was due to fly back the following morning with Stephen Johns, who was going to visit his brother in Connecticut, and the Vice-President from New York. Julia was staying behind. Johns wanted to get there early in the day so they had breakfast early and then got into the station wagon with their cases for the short ride to the airport. Barreras came out to say goodbye and so did Julia.

"Do call me next time you're coming into the city," she said looking him directly in the eyes. It seemed to him that with her direct look the invitation was deliberately ambiguous. The "you" could mean him and his wife or it could mean him alone.

Gavin kept looking at his watch and wondering what time the plane left. He had to remind himself that the plane would leave whenever they wanted it to. He and Johns did not talk much on the flight back and shook hands and parted at JFK. "So maybe I'll see you again in Washington," Johns said as they parted.

At the airport, the scorching heat reminded Gavin that he had flown south. It had been warm at Bar Harbor but here it was fiercely hot, one of the hottest days of the summer. He took the airport limousine to Radford. He got a taxi from Radford Station since he had promised Martha that he would leave the car at the station so that she could drive home, and it was just before noon when he got back to the house. Then he remembered that he had intended to pick up the wallet that he had left in the car. He had forgotten that.

His answering machine said:. "Hi, it's Izzy. Would you call me when you get in?" But he did not want to phone right away. He sat in the armchair to do some hard thinking.

He realized that this past weekend could be a turning-point in his life. The possibility of a new way of life opened up before him. He deliberately shut out the idea of five million dollars, which would probably not happen, and thought simply of a doubling of his salary, which was a direct offer. They could repay the loan for the house repair within the year. Biotek was nearby so they would not even have to move house.

He used to tell himself, and tell other people when the question came up, that he was quite happy with the salary he earned. He could do with some more money - who couldn't? - but he was not actively discontented. Now he thought about what he could do with twice the salary. He could put aside the first month's extra money and say to Martha, "Let's go on holiday to Hawaii with Martin and Louise." They probably wouldn't, they would go on vacation somewhere else, to the Rockies or to England and the Continent. But they could afford to do either. They could loosen up, look a little more only at one side of the menu, go into New York and go to smart restaurants pretty much whenever they felt like it.

He would hold a leading position in Biotek. He would see more of Joe Barreras, who was certainly not an ogre. He and Martha would be invited to Bar Harbor again and meet the kind of people who were entertained there. Martha would enjoy that, he was sure. There was a whole world there of people who knew what was going on in the Government, who traveled to Europe as a matter of course and did not worry about whether they could afford this or that restaurant.

There was also the very real prospect of fame and five million dollars. He could let that into his mind now. Joe was right: he would never have another chance. And he thought about Suzy and Julia and all that. Other men enjoyed girls like Suzy. Why shouldn't he? Because as a scientist he was only interested in higher things?

He was already working out how, if he did decide to go, he would tell Morley Bliss. Morley would not try to hold him back. Some at the Institute might make a few snide remarks but not Morley.

He did not want to tell Izzy what was on his mind and he thought at first he would avoid him until he had spoken to Martha. He wished Martha were here now. But it would be rude not to respond to Izzy's message so he dialled his number, determined to say as little as possible about the weekend.

CHAPTER TEN

Izzy answered the phone immediately. "Have you heard?" he asked. "Or have you been out of touch?"

"I've been out of touch all weekend," Gavin replied.

"Morley's had another stroke," Izzy said.

"Oh no. When?"

"Saturday afternoon."

"How bad is it?"

"He died on Saturday evening."

"Oh, God."

Gavin was shocked, and surprised immediately at how shocked he was. Izzy was silent for a while, letting him absorb the news. Then he went on: "The funeral's tomorrow. The Institute will be closed."

"What time?"

"Three in the afternoon. It's a blow, isn't it?"

"Yes. To all of us."

Then Izzy said, "Look, Gavin, I'd like to talk to you. Can you come over here this morning? Is it a lot to ask?"

"I don't have the car. I left it at the station for Martha. But it's all right, I can get a cab."

"No, don't bother to do that. I'll come over there, if that's okay."

"Sure. You want to come now? I'm not doing anything."

"Fine. I'll see you soon."

Gavin put down the telephone and found he was leaning back against the kitchen wall as if he had been struck a blow. He realized now how big a space Morley Bliss occupied in his world. Now he had to grasp that he would never again sit down opposite that man with his shock of white hair and his Uncle Sam figure and explain to him excitedly the work he was doing, and wait anxiously and hopefully for Morley's comments. There was no one else whose comments meant as much. He would never again see Morley grinning happily at the achievement of someone in the Institute, or commenting acerbically, in his broad Bostonian voice, on some piece of blatant self-aggrandizement in the world of science. Maybe Barreras was right and he was a father-figure. Well, he would miss him as a father.

He was surprised that Izzy wanted to see him. Certainly he would want to share his feelings, share the sense of loss, but his wife Sarah had also known Morley Bliss. Izzy and Sarah often had Bliss, who was a widower, over at their house.

After a while, Gavin tried to think about what difference, if any, Morley's death meant to his own future. It should not make it more difficult for him to leave the Institute if he wanted to. In fact, it removed one link binding him to it. Yet somehow, he wanted Morley's acceptance of the move, he wanted him there to assure him that this was ethically quite all right.

When Izzy arrived, Gavin poured them both iced coffees from the pitcher in the refrigerator. They sat at the kitchen table and drank slowly. Izzy told him about

Morley's second stroke and how they learned about it.

"Any idea what will happen at the Institute now?" Gavin asked, more to break a silence than because he thought there was anything to say.

"There'll be a meeting of the Board of Trustees soon to discuss the choice of a new director," said Izzy.

"Will they choose someone from the Institute or an outsider?"

"I don't know. Could be either. They won't move in a hurry. I think the important thing now is for all of us to keep the work going"

"Sure." Gavin felt uncomfortable at this.. He was holding out on Izzy, not telling him that he was contemplating moving.

Then Izzy said, "Morley's death isn't the only shock I had this weekend."

"Really?"

"Mohsin came to see me yesterday. That's what I really came to tell you about."

"Oh. How is he?"

"Awful. He told me the most amazing thing." Izzy paused, and seemed to take a deep breath before continuing. . "Mo said he was on the right track with the denatured virus. He lied in saying he was on the wrong track."

"He *what*?" Gavin almost rose out of his chair in astonishment.

"That's right. He lied about it."

As always when confronted with a phenomenon he did not understand, Gavin stood back from it. He thought, and could not make any sense of this. "I don't understand," he said finally. "Why on earth would he do that?"

"He was forced to."

"He was forced to lie to us? What do you mean?"

"He told me the whole story under the impact of Morley's death. He was in tears. Literally in tears. He said he couldn't go on lying now. He was being blackmailed. His family has a Taliban connection."

"Taliban? Mohsin?"

"One branch of his family is Taliban, he told me. His uncle is a Taliban commander in Afghanistan. And he has a couple of cousins he reckons are probably on a CIA list.

"You know, the Institute is regarded as a bit un-American anyway. This guy must have been pretty persuasive. He asked Mo whether he'd told Morley Bliss about his Taliban uncle. Well, he hadn't. He hadn't told anybody. It's not the sort of thing you go around telling people, I suppose.

"And Mohsin was convinced?"

"I guess if you're in his position, you're a Muslin living in America it's a sensitive point. I suppose Mo was vulnerable. This guy persuaded him that if this came out now it could damage the Institute's good name, and it would be a terrible blow to Morley himself. He also said we wouldn't get any more funding himself. He threatened to tell the newspapers unless Mo dropped his work on the selenium virus culture. And made sure I dropped it also.

"Mo said he couldn't bear the thought of hurting Morley that much and damaging the Institute, and he gave in. He told us he was on the wrong track."

Izzy paused, to let Gavin absorb this story. Gavin muttered, "My God."

Izzy went on,, "Mo was in a terrible state. He had to

tell me this twice before it sank in."

"My God," Gavin said again. Then, "What did you tell him?"

"Of course I told him that nothing that was said about his family could harm the Institute. I said he should tell this guy to go fuck himself and we'd all stand by him. I tried to persuade him."

Izzy shook his head as if still in shock at the story he was telling. He went on as if he were talking to himself: "Persuading Mo that he could do serious harm to the Institute. It was driving him into a nervous breakdown! God, I'd like to get hold of that son-of-a-bitch." He clenched his fist.

Gavin asked, "Did Mo say who it was who was blackmailing him?"

"A man who called himself Bob Smith. He wouldn't say any more. But I've been thinking about this." Izzy leaned across the table towards Gavin and spoke more quietly and quickly: "It's somebody who knows who's in the Taliban? And whose job is it to know that?"

"The CIA."

"Right. So it's someone who in the past has had access to CIA files. Or perhaps has friends in the agency now who would do him a favor and find out Run a check on the Ahmed family."

"My God. You think it was Philip Carey?"

"It does look like it. Philip Carey. Working for Barreras Pharmaceuticals." He leaned back now that he had reached his conclusion, and shook his head slowly. "Boy, that's some outfit. When Joe Barreras took over Biotek, he brought quite a bag of tricks with him. There's competition

and competition. I've thought again about your friend Alan
Carling's disappearance. I must say that however - Gavin,
are you all right?"

"Yes, I'm okay."

"You really are upset about this."

"Yes, I am." Gavin had not realized how much his
feelings showed. "Remember, I've just spent the weekend
with Joe Barreras."

"Oh yes. How was he?"

"Charming."

"That figures. I know there are some dirty tricks played
in business, but I wasn't prepared for this kind of thing. And
coming on top of Morley's death."

They talked some more, but Gavin was fidgety. His
picture of the world had been transformed abruptly, and he
wanted to be alone to work out what had happened. He was
waiting for Izzy to go. Izzy seemed to sense this and he left
soon, saying he would see Gavin at Morley's funeral the
following day.

Then Gavin sat down and tried to make his whirling
thoughts stay still. He thought back on the weekend, and
everything seemed different. Was it possible that Joe
Barreras was the man he said he was, and that he did not
know about any of this? No, it was not possible.

Barreras himself did not go around bugging places and
blackmailing people. He did not make people disappear. But
he hired Carey to get results and he did not care how he got
them. Presumably Carey had told him the position at the
Institute, had told him that he had stopped Mohsin but that
he, Gavin, was going on with the work. So Barreras decided
he wanted to get him on his side. He would have gone about

it with the same ruthlessness that he went about everything else.

All that stuff about science and ethics and friendship was a lot of rubbish, designed for the purpose of winning him over. It was said intelligently because Barreras was an intelligent man. Probably, Barreras had told Julia and the others who worked for him to butter him up. His whirling thoughts settled down now and the kaleidoscope became a still picture. What had been friendship he now saw as seduction. The promise of money he saw as bribery. He cursed himself for having been so foolish and, much worse and more surprising, vulnerable to temptation. He thought he had ethical standards, he reflected ruefully, but he had turned out to be a pushover.

He might have changed his job and found himself helping a bunch of crooks become even richer and more powerful. He was ashamed. By even considering it he had betrayed Morley Bliss and his friends at the Institute. He had betrayed Martha. She cared about his work, she believed in him and his standards. Damn his brother-in-law for making him want more money. Damn Ted Starowicz even more. He wasn't sure why but damn Ted Starowicz anyway. He deserved it.

And damn Joe Barreras! Damn him to hell twice and three times because he had made him succumb to his intelligence and charm. He hated Barreras for this. He hated himself also, for what he had contemplated doing.

He had promised Barreras he would give him his answer after consulting with his wife. Well, he would not need to consult with Martha. He would give him his answer right away. He rehearsed it several times. "I've just been hearing about your Philip Carey. I really don't think those are the kind of activities I want to be associated with." He thought of different ways of phrasing it. Then it occurred to him that Mohsin may not want it known that he had spoken about the blackmail and it was not up to him to tell Barreras that he knew. This was still confidential. He decided he should say as little as possible at this point.

He telephoned the number at Bar Harbor, and waited while the servant who answered went to find Barreras. He envisaged the servant going in search of Barreras, roaming the estate in his mind, and then handing Barreras the white cordless phone on the veranda, or by the swimming pool, or at the waterfront looking out on the sunlit ocean. Eventually, Barreras answered.

"I haven't consulted my wife yet," Gavin said, "but I've reached a decision on your offer. I don't want to work for you." He made it personal deliberately, "you," not Biotek.

"I see. You're definite about that, are you?" Barreras said.

"Absolutely." He gritted his teeth grimly when he said it and hoped this showed in his tone.

"That's a pity." It was clear from Barreras's tone that he had accepted Gavin's decision and was on the point of dismissing him.

Gavin wanted to know one thing more. "Tell me something please. You could have won that game of tennis, couldn't you?"

"Yes," Barreras replied. "I was being a good host."

When he hung up he still felt dissatisfied. He had spent too long enjoying Barreras's company, basking in what he thought was his friendship, preening himself on having earned his approval. One telephone call in a rather sharp tone was not enough to expiate this.

Biotek might still find the antidote to the impotence plague before anyone else. If they really knew what Mohsin had been doing, they would follow the same route and they had a good chance of getting there first. Izzy and Mohsin were ready to inject mice two weeks ago, but stopped. Biotek might have done that already. Izzy and Mohsin might not catch up. Then plagiarism, blackmail and perhaps murder would win. If only he could do something about it, something to put the Bliss Institute ahead. He owed the Bliss Institute something for even thinking of joining Barreras.

Suddenly, he thought of what he could do. He jumped out of the chair with excitement. It would be uncharacteristically dramatic but it just might steal a march on Biotek. If Izzy and Mohsin were really on the right track, and he trusted their judgment, then this could underline the point. Could it do harm? He had to admit to himself that it was possible. He was normally not one to take risks but this was not a normal situation. He telephoned for a cab. Because it was Labor Day he had to wait for half an hour and he was impatient. He told the driver, "Take me to the Bliss Institute. That's on the Holycroft campus, I'll show you when we get there. Then I want you to wait about fifteen minutes or so, and bring me back here. Okay?"

The weather was still hot and he was perspiring when he arrived at the Institute. He hauled the janitor away from baseball on the television to get him to let him in. "Gee, Dr. Grove, you got to work even on Labor Day?" the janitor said, as he unlocked the front door of the building.

"Just something I have to check on, Andy."

"I was real sorry to hear about Dr. Bliss," he said.

"Yes, it's a great loss. We're all sorry," Gavin agreed.

He used his own keys to let himself into the laboratory he wanted, and then into the closet where equipment was kept. He was out in ten minutes and back in the taxi and0 on his way home.

He wished that Martha were home now. Not that he would tell her everything that happened over the weekend, that he had been so taken in by Barreras and his friends that he was ready to join Biotek. He would tell her that over a period of time, although he would never tell her about Suzy. He just wanted her here, wanted her love and the reassurance of her company and the decency she repre-   sented. He thought how lucky he was to have someone like her. The thing with Ted Starowicz hurt a lot but he loved her anyway. And maybe she had not slept with Ted, maybe he was wrong about that. He would hug her when she came in, hug her tight.

Martha said she would be back after supper so he ate his supper early as if this would make her come back sooner. The package meal from the freezer did not have much taste; he recalled the meals at Bar Harbor.

He went upstairs to the bedroom to find some things to tidy and the telephone rang. It was Denise Springer. She had been away for the weekend and had just come back and heard about Morley. Denise was near to tears; he could hear that on the telephone. This was the Denise he had seen in her home with her new husband rather than the tough, gritty figure that colleagues who saw her only at work knew. "Bob used to tell me I had a crush on Morley, and he was half-right," she said.

"I just learned when I came back this morning," he told her, without telling her what else he had learned.

When she had finished, Gavin thought of Lee Hsiu, who lived alone and did not have anyone at home to share the loss with, and would be reticent about calling other people. He wanted to talk to someone anyway. He telephoned him.

"I'm glad you called. I've just been talking to Carl," Lee told him. "It's a blow, isn't it?"

"I don't think we realized quite how remarkable a man he was."

"I knew from the first time I met him." Lee recalled their first meeting, at a scientific confe- rence in Bombay. They exchanged reminiscences and sentiments for ten minutes. Gavin was talking in the bedroom, sitting on the edge of the bed.

When he got off the phone after the second call, he felt relief at the silence, and then emptiness. He realized how much he wanted to see Martha, to have her there to hug her. When important things happened, he needed Martha. He picked up a magazine and scanned it idly. Then the doorbell rang. He ran down the stairs feeling a surge of love for her and opened the door.

"You're an inconsiderate fucking pig," she told him. She stood there with her overnight bag on the step beside her. Her forehead was damp with sweat and a lock of her hair hung down and stuck to it.

He stood still. "What do you mean?"

She walked by him into the house talking furiously as she did. "You were going to leave the car at the station for me to come back! You forgot that. I called you to come and collect me, but the phone was busy. It was busy all the time."

He picked up her case and followed her in. "I was on the phone. 0But the car - "

She was unstoppable in her rage. "Do you know what it's like trying to get a cab in Radford on Labor Day? In the evening? I had to wait forty minutes! In this heat."

"But Martha, honey - "

"You left your Martha honey stranded in the station. I was feeling sick from the heat and I had a drunk who was throwing up on the floor for company. Why the hell didn't you do what you were supposed to do? Why couldn't you remember? I suppose a weekend with the rich set drove it out of your mind." Her face was ugly with anger.

"But I did."

"You did what?"

"I did leave the car there."

"Where?"

"In the station forecourt." Now he reacted to her anger. "I left it there as I said I would. What the hell do you mean by coming in like that?"

They glared at each other for a moment, then she said, "I'm sorry. Please, do me a favor and get me a drink."

She collapsed into an armchair, and he went into the kitchen and made her a vodka and tonic with lemon and a lot of ice. When he brought it to her she spoke more quietly. "I swear the car wasn't at the station," she said. "The space isn't all that big. I couldn't have missed it." She took a long drink from her glass, then looked up at him and asked, "Did you really leave it at the station."

"Yes, of course."

"But it wasn't there this evening. I promise you."

"Then it's been stolen," he said. They both were silent for a while, at this conclusion.

"I'm sorry darling," she said finally. "I'm sorry I came in like that and called you those names. But I was getting hotter and hotter and more and more tired and working up to it. Come over here and let me kiss you." He sat on the arm of her chair and she kissed him, and he ran his hand through her sweaty hair and she said again that she was sorry.

He said, "We'd better phone the police and tell them the car's been stolen."

"Sure. Would you do it? I'm wiped out."

"Okay. And I've just remembered something else. I left my wallet in the car. Something else to report."

He telephoned the police, and explained that the car could have been stolen at any time during the past two days. The policeman said they would log it, but the computer was down, so it could not be reported statewide until the following day. Gavin telephoned two credit card companies and reported the lost cards.

Then he told Martha about Morley Bliss, and a little about the weekend. She knew immediately how much Bliss's death would affect him. She had the next day off anyway and said she would come to the funeral with him.

In bed, he told her he loved her deeply, and was very lucky to be married to her. She hugged him. "I love to hear you say that," she whispered. "It was nice with Dad and Mom and Louise again, but I missed you a bit when I went to bed at night." They kissed. He went to sleep with the thought that things were about as good as they could be in the circumstances.

::   ::   ::   ::

They got up late and she made a late breakfast of scrambled eggs and bacon. "I like this kind of meal but I don't like to eat first thing in the morning," he said, telling her what she already knew, as he often did. "We could have breakfast at this time on the weekends sometimes."

The mail came while they were eating, and his new driving license was among the items. "Just as well, since my old one was in my wallet," he remarked.

Now he told her what else he had learned that day, about Mohsin halting his work under threat. He found it difficult to make it convincing. He felt as if he were recounting the plot of a television crime drama rather than something about people he knew. "To think I've just spent a weekend on friendly terms with that bastard," he said in conclusion.

"Do you really think Barreras himself knew what was going on?" she asked him.

"Oh yes. I think he countenances that kind of thing, yes. It makes sense. They forced Mohsin to stop the work. Then, because I was going to go on with it, they wanted to neutralize me by getting me to work for them. I think he's responsible."

She shook her head. "I can't believe it. He wasn't exactly one of my heroes but I never believed he could do that kind of thing. In fact, I'm amazed that that kind of thing can go on."

"So am I," he said.

He did not tell her about his visit to the Bliss Institute

laboratory. They went upstairs and dressed, discussing what each of them would wear since they were going to a funeral. He did not have a black tie. "Perhaps I should stop in Radford and get one on the way there," he said.

"No, it's not necessary. Just a dark tie," she said. "My blue suit, yes?"

"Sure. That looks fine."

Martha was dressed first. She was downstairs in the kitchen when the doorbell rang. A policeman and a policewoman were on the doorstep, both in shirt-sleeves.

She assumed they had come about the car. The policeman was tall, gawky and fresh-faced, and looked to her like a high school basketball player. What was that about knowing you were getting old when the policemen looked younger? The policewoman was a stocky woman with short, straight hair, with three stripes on the shoulders of her shirt, insignia of rank. The young policeman spoke. "Mrs. Grove?"

"Yes."

"May we come in, Ma'am?" He was extremely deferential. She moved aside to let them in and saw now that they both had grim expressions and seemed nervous. The policewoman was clenching her lips tight and was avoiding her eyes.

The policewoman spoke. "Your husband is Dr. Gavin Grove?"

"That's right."

"Mrs. Grove, we have some bad news for you. I think perhaps you'd better sit down," she said. They were treating her as if she were fragile.

"What bad news?" she asked, puzzled. She ignored the suggestion about sitting down.

"I'm afraid your husband has had an accident." They both looked at her expectantly, as if watching for her reaction.

Gavin appeared at the top of the stairs, tucking in his shirt. She called up to him, "You'd better come down, dear. This seems to be about you."

The two police officers looked at each other, evidently surprised. Gavin came downstairs. and Martha said, "This is my husband."

There was a silence, and then the policewoman said to him, "Are you Dr. Gavin Grove?"

"Yes."

"This lady's husband?"

"That's right."

The policewoman's lips trembled. "Do you mind if *I* sit down?" she asked. Martha nodded towards an armchair. She sat down and shook her head, exhaling slowly. Then she said to the young policeman, "Will you say why we're here."

He explained, "There seems to be some mistake, Mrs. Grove. We'd come to tell you that your husband was the victim of a fatal car accident."

She said, "You mean that he'd been killed?"

"That's right, Ma'am."

No one said anything for a while. Then Gavin asked, "How did you get the idea that I was killed?"

"I don't know how it happened, sir," the policeman said. "We got a report that a car had crashed and it was identified as yours. A body was found in it, and apparently documents were found identifying the body as Dr. Gavin Grove."

"Oh. I understand." He told them about his car being

stolen, and about leaving his wallet inside. "The wallet would have had my driving license and credit cards and so on. So it's the poor guy who stole the car who was killed," he said.

They reflected on this for a moment. The policeman said, "I'm afraid your car was totalled, sir." He said it as if he were handing over an item of bad news as a substitute for the other that had turned out to be a dud.

"Where was the crash? Near here?" asked Gavin. He thought he should show polite curiosity since the policeman had mentioned it.

"No, it was over in New Jersey," the policeman said. "The Palisades. It went over a cliff. Another car ran into it. A witness saw it."

"Did they catch the other driver?"

"No,"

Suddenly, Gavin wanted to know more. "Would you tell me what happened, please?"

The policeman explained, "It was about eleven o'clock at night. There was very little traffic. The car was traveling at about sixty miles an hour. That's what the witness said. And this other car came alongside it and swerved and hit it and ran it off the road. Over the cliff. Then the other car drove off at speed. Even though it must have been dented. They found your car at the bottom of the cliff. The driver was dead."

"Another car hit it and drove off?" Gavin said.

"That's what we understand happened," the policeman said.

"It sounds as if it was done deliberately."

"It does sound as if it could have been," the policeman

agreed. "We didn't talk to the witness, we've only seen the report."

They both pondered this. Martha said, "Would you two like some coffee?"

As if this were a signal, the policewoman got up and said, "Thank you, Mrs. Grove, but we've got to get back to the station. I'm very glad it's turned out as it has." They said their goodbyes and left.

Martha turned away from the door and said, "How strange. A man dead in our car, and we don't know who he is." She went into the kitchen and started putting away the breakfast plates and frying pan.

Gavin was trying not to panic. He said to Martha, "I think they were after me. I'm scared."

"What do you mean?"

"They were after me. They wanted to kill me. They thought I was driving the car."

"Who?"

"The Barreras organization. The same people who made Alan Carling disappear. The crash was deliberate. You heard what they said."

He imagined the driver going along the parkway at sixty miles an hour, and the other car - it must have been a heavy car to have hit with that impact, and it must have been going very fast - slamming into it. He imagined the driver's panic as he realized that he was going over the cliff, the impact of the fall. The seat belt would be snapped like tinsel, the body probably impaled on the steering wheel, internal organs shattered, bones splintering. He stopped his medically-trained imagination by an act of will. The other driver would have tailed the car and picked his spot and driven straight into the side of his car and then driven off, to report that the job was done.

Martha looked at him and said, "You really are frightened."

"I know. I'm sure they're after me now. I tell you, those people are ruthless. They know somehow that I was going on with Mohsin's work. They don't know how far I've got. They want to stop me. If they can't get me on to their side they'll stop me working."

"What can they do?"

"I don't know. Anything. They've got connections all over the place. Oh God, Martha, I'm sorry but I'm scared." He had a vision of this vast organization, with so many resources, with tentacles in so many areas of American life, out to kill him. There was no limit to what they could do. She sat down next to him on the couch and put her arms around him. "I've got to go into hiding. That's the answer," he said.

"What?"

"Yes. For a couple of weeks or so. After two or three weeks, it might be okay. But until then I want to stay out of sight."

"Right away?"

"They don't know I'm not dead yet. Let's see now. It'll take them a little while to find out that it wasn't me in the car. A few hours, maybe. But not long. I've got until then. I've got to get away."

"But where to?"

He was struck by an appalling thought. *"They might be bugging this house!"* he almost shouted. We can't talk here. Come outside, into the garden." And he jumped up and practically dragged her into the back. He waited until they were standing on the little lawn, away from the patio, before speaking again.

"I've got to go somewhere where nobody will find me." He could not think straight. Fear had hold of him, and he hated himself for it. "Please help me. Help me pack."

"Of course. Gavin, do you really think they'll try to kill you? It just doesn't seem possible."

"Well they did it once. Unless you think it's a coincidence that someone ran my car off the road on to some rocks."

"Do you think they'd dare try it again?"

"Yes." He talked rapidly. His fear was running away with him now and his words were following along. "They did it once and failed. I don't mean they'll shoot me down on the street. Or maybe they will. Perhaps they'll make it look as if a burglar did it. It could be an accident. Another car crash, like this one. Or maybe a sudden heart attack - they've got medical resources at their disposal. They're very powerful. They've got Mafia connections, CIA connections, who knows what else. I've got to get away, go into hiding. And quickly. Will you help me, darling?"

"Yes, if you mean it."

"Of course I mean it. Look, don't talk in the house. We'll talk out here."

"But where do you want to go? Do you want to stay with Izzy? With somebody else? You can go stay with my parents."

"No, I can't stay with anyone we know, they could find that out. I think the place to hide is New York City."

"New York City?"

"Yes. You hide in a crowd. Look, I can't explain but if I can just hide away for two weeks, I think it'll be enough. I've a reason for saying that. I'll go into the city and hide in a hotel somewhere. Help me pack some things."

She jumped up. Packing was something she could handle. They hurried upstairs and she went to the clothes cupboard and started pulling out basic clothes quickly and efficiently and putting them into a valise. Seeing her, he began to get a grip on himself. He looked around for some toilet articles. Rummaging through papers on his desk he found his credentials as an alternate delegate to the WHO meeting and threw those in the bag also. Then he took the microscope that his parents had given him when he was an undergraduate, put it in its wooden box and put that in the valise.

"Do you need to take that?" she asked.

"Yes," he said. Then he put his fingers to his lips in a gesture telling her to be silent.

When they had finished packing they went out into the back and she asked, "What should I tell people?" Martha asked.

"Tell them anything. Say I had to go away suddenly. Family business. Say I went to visit an old friend in Philadelphia. That's it, an old school friend from England who's in Philadelphia and is very ill."

"Where will you go in New York?" she asked.

"It's better that you don't know," he told her. "I shouldn't have even told you that much."

"Will you call me?"

"No. The phones here might be bugged."

"You can call my mobile. On your rmobile."

"No. They might locate my mobile."

"Is that possible?"

"Yes. I don't know. I don't want to take a chance. They can work out that it isn't in Philadelphia."

"Do you really think so? I can't believe it." She shook her head in bewilderment.

"Let's not take the chance. In fact, I think you ought to go away. They'll probably be watching you. Can you take off from the Center for a couple of weeks if you have to?"

"If I have to."

"It would be a good idea. You can go stay with your parents."

"What'll I tell them?"

"Anything. Think of something. I've got to hurry. I really think they might find out soon that I'm still alive and then follow me. I really want to get out of this house."

"Why don't you contact a newspaper? Publicity is a kind of protection."

"I've been thinking about that. I might."

"Why not contact Ted?"

"No."

"But you can trust Ted. And he's followed this story."

"I can trust Ted?" he repeated, almost shouting. "I don't want to talk to Ted!" He decided that she would guess now that he knew about her and Ted. Well, if she was stupid enough to go on about him, he could not keep it from her.

They called a taxi and went straight to Radford Station. It was twenty minutes before the next train into New York. "Time to get some money from the bank," he said. "As much as you can. I need cash. Remember, I don't have a credit card. That was in my wallet." He remained in the station sitting on a bench hiding behind a newspaper while she went to the bank. She came back and sat down next to him.

"I got twelve hundred dollars. There's not much more in the checking account. Most of it's on deposit."

"That'll do fine," he said. "But please transfer more to the checking account. I may need to take some out."

"All right. Oh darling, I'm frightened." She held her taut, anxious face up to him and gripped the lapels of his jacket tightly. "You may really be in danger."

"I'll be all right, because I'll be where nobody can find me, buried in the multitude," he told her. He had decided where he would go, and he was calmer. Now the roles were the reverse of what t0hey were a few minutes earlier. She was in the grip of fear and he was being practical.

She twisted around so that she was facing him and said, "Darling, if you're in danger, there's something I've got to tell you." She was almost whispering now. "I lied to you. I've never lied to you before about anything important. I lied to you and I want to tell you now."

He told her, "You don't have to." To himself he prayed, "Please let her stop. I don't want to hear what I already know, not now." But the prayer was only inside his head and she did not hear it..

"You probably don't remember," she went on, "but you called the Center one day and they said I'd gone home and I said they were mistaken. Well, I had gone home. I was lying. I lied to you." She repeated the word as if it were a form of flagellation. "And there was another time. Do you want to know why I lied?"

"I remember," he said. He tried to say more, to tell her that he wanted her to stop, but he could not get any words out.

"It was Grace," she went on. "She wanted to - to have an affair with me. She came home and we talked for a long time. She actually - it got to the point one time – we kissed and I nearly got into bed with her - but then I got out again right away. Nothing happened. But I didn't want you to know. I didn't want you to think that way about me. I shouldn't have lied to you."

Gavin hugged her to his chest tightly because he did not want her to feel him shaking, and turned his face away. He held her like that for some moments, until she pushed at him and mumbled, "I can't breathe."

He released her finally. "Darling, will you forgive me?" she asked.

He nodded. "Yes," he said, in a husky voice, and he kissed her.

"You don't think differently about me?" He shook his head. He could barely speak. He would never tell her what he had been thinking.

Neither of them said anything for a little while. He felt better suddenly, much, much better. His thoughts came back to his own position. The train would come any minute, and he had to hurry. "I've changed my mind," he said. "Ted can help me. Can you call him for me?"

"Sure."

He was amazed at how clearly he could think suddenly. "I asked him once whether he knew an inexpensive hotel near the center of town, and he mentioned one. Did I tell you what it was?"

"No, or if you did I don't remember."

"Good. You don't need to know the name. Tell Ted I'll

be there. I'll register under the name of - let me see." He thought of the Hotel Charles. Charles? Prince Charles. "Under the name of Mr. Prince. Have you got that? John Prince. Tell him I want to see him urgently and to come and see me there. Tell him there's a good story for him in it. And not to tell anyone else at all. That's important. I'll wait for him there. Got that?"

She nodded, and then the train was there, and they stood up and had once last fierce kiss and he climbed into the train with his case.

He had a newspaper with him but instead of reading he spent the hour and ten minutes of the journey collecting his thoughts. His life normally ran on an even keel; now it was careering around wildly. Forty-eight hours ago, he had considered leaving the Bliss Institute to work at Biotek. Now he was going into hiding from the men who owned Biotek, who were out to kill him.

He looked around the carriage. At this time of the day there were very few passengers: two women, travelling separately, and a couple of teenage boys. None of them could be working for Philip Carey. He tried to think what Carey and his team would do when they found out that he was still alive.

They would check around his friends somehow, and probably find out quickly that he had left the area. He had no car now, so to go anywhere from Melby Park he would almost certainly go by train and would almost certainly go into New York to start his journey. So they would check the station, check the trains. How? Perhaps they had private detectives, perhaps they had the co-operation of some people in the police. If someone from the CIA were involved, he could get the cooperation of the police.

This gave him his next move. It was something someone had done in a John Le Carré spy novel. It would involve causing a small scene so that people would remember him, and this went against the grain, but he would do it.

At Pennsylvania Station he came off the train and up the escalator. He looked around the concourse, which always seemed to him like a vast underground car park with shops and restaurants, with its low ceiling and supporting pillars, and he was conscious of breathing the warm, fetid air that had already been breathed by a million other rail travelers that day. He found his way to the Amtrak ticket office. He waited in line, fidgeting, and when his turn came, he asked for a ticket to Philadelphia. The man behind the grille said, "Thirty dollars."

A public scene went against his instincts and he had to steel himself to go through with the performance. He became agitated like a man in a bad state of nerves and exclaimed: "It's not that much! I've been there before. It was something like twenty-five dollars" Several people nearby heard him and turned around. He tried to make his voice very clipped and British.

"It's thirty dollars," the ticket man said, through teeth clenched with annoyance.

"You go and check." he demanded.

"I don't have to check, Mister. It's right in front of me. Now do you want a ticket to Philadelphia or not?"

Gavin slammed down two twenty-dollar bills. "All right, I'll pay it because I'm in a hurry but I'll be writing to the railway company about this."

He took his ticket and change and heard a murmuring in the line behind him. Very satisfactory. He thought this little scene would probably be remembered. But he was almost shaking from the effort. He picked up his suitcase, took a timetable from a rack and consulted it, and then after a suitable interval when no one would be looking at him any more, he walked out into the heat and dust and traffic of Seventh Avenue.

He would spend a lot of time stuck away in a hotel room, so he stopped at a news stand and bought a paperback novel and the current issue of *Scientific American*. He felt nervous walking along the street and he would be nervous until he shut himself up behind a locked door. Could there be Carey's spies among this crowd? Policemen? Passers-by? Taxi-drivers? Every other person on 33rd Street?

The burning sun of the previous day had been replaced by haze, and the humid, dusty, sunless heat that is a speciality of New York City summers. His clothes were clammy and sticking to his body as he hauled his suitcase along. But he had to get used to making his cash last, so he did not take a taxi but took a bus up to 46th Street, and walked to the Hotel Charles.

He looked around the lobby. It was spacious and the marble pillars at the four corners indicated that it had once had grandeur. Probably there was once a Mr. Charles who saw this proudly as his monument. But now its tone was seedy and shabby beyond redemption.

He registered as John Prince and took a room with a kitchenette. The kitchenette was smaller than a walk-in closet but it had a stove, a tiny oven and a fridge-freezer. He wanted to lie very low and go out as little as possible and he could make his own food there. The hotel was in the theatre district and he guessed that a lot of aspiring actors and others began their assault on New York show business in places like this, to come back after a day of knocking on doors anad take a TV dinner from the refrigerator and put it in the little oven.

The room was on the sixth floor. In It had a bed, an armchair and a straight chair, all in different shades of brown. There were also a television set and a telephone. He noted with satisfaction that the room was clean, apart from the windows, which were dulled over with the contents of big city air. He would spend his days here in this room for the next two weeks or so, venturing out only when necessary. He checked that the TV set worked.

He looked out of the window on to the backstage area of the New York spectacle The nearby buildings shimmering in the heat seemed dirty, and at street level there was only the awnings of a few small stores, a hot dog stand and a parking lot across the street.

Somewhere in this great metropolis, not too far away, there were glorious, gleaming towers, streets made beautiful by trees and waterfalls behind glass. There were piazzas with outdoor cafés with gaily colored umbrellas over the tables, where handsome men and lovely women exchanged sparkling conversation. There was a park with grass and a lake where children played in the sunshine with dogs and each other and laughed and were happy to be alive. A few blocks away there was the Hudson River, from which huge ships set out for every part of the wide world. There was, close by in this city, beauty and harmony and elegance. There was splendor and excitement and inspiration. But none of this could be seen from Room 604 of the Hotel Charles.

Gavin took off his shoes and jacket and lay down on the bed to take stock. When Ted came, he decided, he would tell him the whole story. Ted would decide how much he could print. Publicity might give him some protection. He looked forward to telling his story to Ted. He liked Ted. In fact he loved Ted, because Ted had not gone to bed with his wife.

CHAPTER ELEVEN

Ted Starowicz boarded the plane at Los Angeles Airport on Friday evening for the five-hour flight to New York. On long flights reporters traveled business class, and he settled back in his seat, stretched his legs, and enjoyed the touches of luxury and the attentions of the flight attendant as she hung up his jacket and gave him a drink and a newspaper. For dinner he ordered Cornish game hen because he had never had it before and did not know what to expect, and a Californian cabernet sauvignon to wash it down.

He had with him the Los Angeles Times and the paperback edition of a well-reviewed new novel. The in-flight movie did not look interesting so he settled down to read.

The L.A. Times reported a nationwide survey of how women felt about doing without sexual intercourse. By this time, it was estimated that most men had been sexually impotent for four months, some more, some a little less. Women between the ages of twenty and sixty across the nation were polled. Of those who answered, only 18 percent said the situation made them very unhappy. Forty-two percent said they missed sex quite a lot; 19 percent said they missed it a little; and 18 percent said they did not miss it at all. The rest could not make up their minds. Ted was surpassed to see that in a separate poll of women between twenty and thirty-five, 40 percent said they felt more comfortable now in their place of work.

When Ted turned to the novel, he found that he was reading a few lines and then just staring at the page, his mind wandering. After a while he gave up trying to read. If he had some thoughts to think, he might as well think them.

First there was the material he had gathered on the trip. He had sent back three stories for a series and had roughed out two others which he would finish when he got back, plus a couple of sidebars.

But a lot of his memories of the trip were of women. He thought of the women, and tried to keep their feel and sounds separate from one another. He smiled with satisfaction at their eagerness for him. He found he had fond feelings for every one of them: Anna, with her big, bouncy breasts, gabby Helen from Boston University talking even between gasps, Melanie, with her clever tongue. They liked him. Even progenitive Judy seemed to like him a bit. Ted decided he would send them all postcards to show that he remembered them, including Marie Zamora. He would get some of the airline's postcards, with pictures of the plane. Then he found he could not remember Helen's last name. He never knew Melanie's.

Now, and only now, he recalled something he had not allowed himself to recall before, had not dared to recall. This was a time of love - a kind of love, anyway, although it seemed more like obsession - and agony, of a humiliating conversation on the telephone, of sitting in a car outside a woman's apartment house and staring up at the light in her window, of seeing her at a party gazing up with her laughing, happy eyes into the eyes of the man she was with, and struggling to smile and make a casual remark when they were introduced, and going home and sobbing.

He was m

It was great, but it was not everything. What more was there? He thought back on that night in the hotel in New York with Didi and Ingrid, and reflected that perhaps he could have more of that kind of thing. Could he do still more with three women? As the plane flew over the Rockies he was engrossed in priapic invention.

Dinner was served. The man in the next seat, a business-suited man in his thirties, made a remark about game hen and started to chat. "Been visiting California?" he asked. Ted explained briefly what he had been doing.

"Going around the country? Me too," he said. "Been on the road three weeks." He was in software and he had been visiting computer companies. "Too long away from home. They promised me I'd get home for Labor Day weekend no matter what. I've finished on the road for a while and I'm glad. I miss my wife and kid too much."

"How long have you been married?" Ted asked, curious.

"Three years," he said. "The boy's eighteen months. Terrific little fellow. Oh, it's okay to get away for a few days, for a change of scenery. But after that, I get lonely."

"Lonely evenings after the day's work is over, huh?"

"Not always. I know people in the business, and people ask me home to dinner, or ask me out. But I miss my family. I talk to my wife on the telephone a lot, but it's not the same. You married?" Ted shook his head. They talked a little more about their travels.

Then the man said, "Can I ask you something?"

"What?"

"Do I need a shave?"

Ted looked at his face and said, "No."

"Shit! I didn't shave this morning. Just to see."

Ted was puzzled for a moment. "So what does that mean?"

"It means I'm losing my facial hair, don't you see?" the man said unhappily. "That's one of the things they said is supposed to happen when testosterones don't work. Does my voice sound normal? A bit high?"

"No, your voice sounds okay."

"How about you? Anything happening to you yet? You look pretty clean-shaven."

"Yes, maybe it's happening to me too," Ted said, and turned to his book.

But he was still thinking rather than reading. He tried to take up where he had left off. What would he do with two or even three women in bed? It could be amazing. But if something was missing from his life, this was not it. He thought of the man sitting next to him who missed his wife so much. It was not sex the man hungered for but his wife's company. It meant that he loved her. He, Ted, liked all those women, but he did not actually love any of them. So, he asked himself, what was wrong with that? Nothing at all.

What else did he want? He recalled a girl with bobbing light brown curls rehearsing a square dance, and his heart missing a beat when they passed in the high school corridor. Was it her? No, she and he were kids then.. But there was something there that should not be lost, something he should be able to feel again.

His thoughts wandered and settled on Naomi. He wanted to see her again. This came through sharp and clear.

He would call her as soon as he got back and ask her out. He wanted to make love to her again. If he could not do that because she would not let him, and he was still not quite sure why, he still wanted to see her. He found himself recalling everything they had talked about, and then the things they had not talked about. He wanted to tell her about the novel he had started reading, and people at the office, and his parents, and the feel of outdoor life in California, and what his childhood was like. He knew nothing about her childhood and he wanted to know.

He was due to spend the Labor Day weekend with his parents in Jersey City. He would come back from Jersey City on Monday and ask Naomi to come out with him on Monday evening, he decided.

He took the limo from JFK to Radford and by the time he got to his apartment it was nearly midnight, too late to call anyone. He awoke early, had coffee and a bagel, waited until nine o'clock, which seemed a decent hour for a Saturday, and then telephoned Naomi. He was nervous about what her reaction would be.

"Hi, Ted, how are you?" she said cheerily. She sounded glad to hear from him, but in the casual way she might be if he were a friendly acquaintance. This upset him right away. He had wanted something more a little passion, perhaps/0

He tried to sound more casual than he felt. "Fine, though I'm a bit tired," he said. "I've just got back from my travels." He told her a little about the trip, and then said, "I'd like to see you soon. I'm going to my parents for the weekend, but are you free on Monday evening?"

"Well gee, Ted, I'm afraid I'm going home to my folks also, and I'm due to stay over Tuesday. I'll be back then, though."

He arranged to take her out the following Wednesday. When he hung up he was dissatisfied. But what did he want? he asked himself. She said she wanted to see him. Did she have to sound desperate? Did he want her to be in love with him? Maybe.

He was in a benign mood over the weekend, and did a lot of things to please his parents. He praised his mother's cooking and told her he had missed it. He telephoned his sister Sue in Houston, and in their presence he told her that Mom and Pop were looking great and there were a lot of changes in the old neighborhood. He went with his parents to visit some of their old friends who had known him since he was a kid and reminisced with them.

When they came back from that visit, and he and his father were relaxed in armchairs and his mother was making tea in the kitchen, his father said, "Your mother always asks me to find out about girl friends. You know, all mothers want their sons to be married. She hasn't mentioned it lately. I guess there's nothing to find out about this time."

"Well, yes and no," Ted replied. He hesitated. "You see, Dad, I'm lucky, I guess. I seem to be immune. I mean - I don't have it."

"You don't - do you mean you're a *potent*?"

"Yes, that's what I mean."

"Hey, that's fantastic! Absolutely fantastic!" His father rose from his chair in excitement, grinning at the family's good fortune. He patted Ted on the arm and then looked him up and down as if he could confirm this by a visual inspection. "Fantastic!" he repeated. Then, "You really are? You're not kidding?"

"That's right," Ted confirmed. He was looking at a corner of the room awkwardly as he spoke.

His father said, "Boy, that's something." And then, "You must be having a great time. Yes? No chance of your settling down with one girl just now, huh?" And he punched him on the arm with manly jocularity.

His mother came in from the kitchen with tea and cake and he said, "Hey, Sophie. Listen to this," and he told her.

His mother stood there and rubbed her arms in perplexity. "Well, I suppose that's very good that Ted hasn't got the plague. But I don't know. Is it all right? Do you feel all right, Ted?" Any deviation from the normal made her anxious.

"All right? It's great!" his father said.

Ted began to feel uncomfortable and to wish he had not said anything. He addressed them both. "I'm quite all right, Mom, really. Do me a favor. Please keep this to yourselves. It's caused me a lot of embarrassment. I mean, a lot of people don't like it."

"Sure, sure," his father said. "It's a personal matter." But the next day, Ted heard him talking on the telephone to his brother in Patterson. "Hey, you know what? We've got a potent in the family," he heard him say. He knew it would not be long before one of them told Sue, and then Sue would telephone him and ask what it was like, excited to be the sister of such a rare creature.

He got home late on Monday evening. He awoke early on Tuesday morning, and spent some time lying in bed listening to the news on the radio.

A reporter made the point several times that Labor Day weekend road accidents were the lowest for forty years. An official questioned about this said he could only attribute it to an apparent trend towards less aggressive driving. A reduction in aggression again, Ted reflected. Some people were alive this Tuesday morning who would have been dead if sexual normalcy prevailed. He noted that the official kept clearing his throat as he spoke into the microphone. Maybe men were beginning to worry about their voice tones.

He was drinking coffee and reading the Chronicle at nine o'clock when the telephone rang and he answered it. "Hello, is that Ted Starowicz?"

"Yes." He had heard the voice before and he started to search for the memory but it identified itself before he found it.

"This is Philip Carey."

Instinctively he moved the receiver away from him, as if a fist might come out of it and punch him. "Hello," he said, surprised and wondering what was coming next.

"Do you want a story?" Carey demanded.

"Er, yes."

"Okay. If you come and see me now, I've got one for you."

"Come and see you?"

"That's right. At my home. Right now. In Walton. How soon can you get here?"

Ted thought quickly. "An hour. Is that okay?"

"Good. I'll see you then." Carey told him the address and hung up.

Ted dressed hurriedly and ran an electric shaver quickly over his face. He was thinking about what Carey might have to tell him. Did he have a conscience that was suddenly coming into its own? Was he going to tell all and repent? Humble himself before his arch-critic? That seemed improbable. Perhaps he had fallen out with Barreras Pharmaceuticals and was going to get his own back by spilling some dirt. Perhaps he had some dirt on rival pharmaceutical companies that he wanted to get into the Press. He remembered Carey's threat, uttered down the telephone: "You're going to be sorry one day!" He resolved to treat anything Carey told him skeptically.

He was w

Carey lived in a large stucco and clapboard house set back in its own lawn. Ted parked outside, and walked up the wooden steps to the porch and rang the bell. The door was answered by a blonde woman who he judged to be in her late thirties. She was slender, with pretty features, and she was wearing a halter, short shorts and sandals. She could have been attractive but she had an expression so blank and stony that any interested glance would bounce off it.

"Mrs. Carey?"

"Yes."

"I'm Ted Starowicz, from the Chronicle. I've come to see Philip Carey."

She stepped aside to let him in and as he walked into the living room, she said, "He's had to go out. He'll be back soon."

He started to say that he had only just telephoned him an hour earlier but she turned and went into the kitchen, leaving him alone in the room. He was surprised. He took off his jacket and sat down on a sofa. The previous Sunday's New York Times was on the coffee table. He started reading some parts that he had not read before. Five minutes went by.

A girl of about seventeen came down the stairs, pretty and blonde like her mother, wearing a tartan skirt and ankle socks and looked at him curiously. She stopped off in the kitchen to exchange a few words with her mother and then went out of the front door. "Give my regards to the Williams," her mother called out to her.

Ten more minutes went by. Ted read the sports section and the business section and the News of the Week in Review section. He listened to the occasional car going by but none of them stopped. A bird on the window ledge caught his attention, pecking furiously at the corner of the ledge for something that was evidently stuck there. It gave up and flew away with an empty beak. He won- dered whether he also should give up.

He got up and called out to Mrs. Carey in the kitchen, "Where's your bathroom, please?"

She appeared in the kitchen doorway just to point. "That door there," she said, and went back into the kitchen.

Ted used the toilet briefly, and then washed his hands. He spoke into the bathroom mirror:

"I'm so sorry my husband was called away, Mr. Starowicz. I'm sure he won't be long".

"Yes, it is another hot day, isn't it, Mr. Starowicz? I suppose the weather will break now that we're into September".

"Would you like some iced tea? Or would you prefer coffee? Do have some of these cookies. What a pity you're having to wait".

He went back into the living room and sat down on the sofa again. He picked up the Times and looked for items he had not read. Mrs. Carey came out of the kitchen and went upstairs without glancing at Ted.

The telephone rang, and stopped. Mrs. Carey came

downstairs, her face still an uninviting blank. "That was my husband," she said to Ted. "He won't be back. He can't see you."

Ted stood up. "That's *it*?" he said to her. He was almost speechless with fury. She had already turned her back and was going upstairs again.

He picked up his jacket, walked to the front door, turned and called out, "Thank you for your hospitality, Mrs. Carey." He did not know whether she heard. He doubted whether, even if she had heard, his sarcasm would penetrate that brick wall of a countenance. He got into his car and drove off clenching his teeth with annoyance. When he stopped at a traffic light he hit the steering wheel with the palms of both hands and swore for a while.

He drove to the office and went to his desk and looked through the hand-outs from pharmaceutical com- panies and scientific institutes that were now coming to him. There was nothing else of consequence in his mail. He was going to start on the remaining two articles about his visits to places where the plague was being tackled. He decided that first he would go and see Tom Manning to see how the articles he sent had been received. Also when he was planning to use the series. He looked across into Manning's office and saw the morning editorial conference going on, so he waited.

His telephone rang and he answered it. "Hello, this is John Dallas. Do you remember? The Playgirl Escort Agency."

"Oh yes."

"D'you remember I asked if you would let me put you on my books as a male escort?"

"I remember. 'To give physical companionship' was the

way you put it."

"Yes. Well I've got another potent on my books."

"Really?" Ted reflected that there was a heroic quality about Dallas as a businessman. He never gave up, and now he seemed to have come up with something. Lord knows how he had found a potent.

"Yes," Dallas said. "I'm going to try to build up a string. I can offer you six hundred dollars an hour. Clear. That's a lot more than any of my girls ever got. And if you want to go on being a newsman, fine. You can choose your own hours."

"Look, Mr. Dallas, I really don't think I could do that."

"Oh c'mon, you're a healthy guy. I could see that. And you won't have to do it with old bags. At that price, you'll get the cream. It won't be old women. They don't need it so much. Smart, young women. Well, not all young, maybe but not old either. College-educated. Women you can talk to about things. Relate to. Six hundred bucks an hour for that."

Ted reflected that at that rate, he could have earned several thousand dollars on the trip he had just made. The women had all seemed grateful. Compare that with his weekly salary. And he could still go on being a reporter. And more than a thousand next weekend without any strain if he wanted to. What could he do with a thousand or two thousand extra a week? Just two or three hours - good God, what was he *thinking?*

"No thanks, Mr. Dallas, definitely no!" he said, and put down the phone before the conversation could go any further. He wondered how any half-way good-looking girl kept her virtue.

He saw people leaving Manning's office so he waited

until they had gone and then went in there. "When are you - we - going to start using my series?" he asked, standing before his desk.

Manning looked up. "The stories you've sent weren't quite what I was expecting," he told Ted. Ted went cold although he tried not to show it. He had been pleased with them. Manning reached into a drawer and pulled out copies of the three that Ted had already delivered and dropped them on the desk as if they were exhibits.0

"What people want to know about this plague is if and when it's going to end," he said, in a quiet, even tone that did not invite contradiction. "What they want to know about the scientists is whether they can find a cure. You haven't told them."

"But nobody knows that," Ted protested.

Manning raised his eyebrows. "This man in St. Louis - what's his name? - " Manning looked through the copy - "Huong, Robert Huong, he knows. Or says he does."

"Yes, and I've included his view. But he's just willing to stick his neck out where others are not."

"That makes him worth quoting," Manning said. "But you've got him quoted in - let's see - about the eighth paragraph of the second story."

"Do you think I should have made him the lead? 'A Washington University scientist predicted today' and so on? I didn't think I was writing hard news. And that's not really a story."

"I'm not telling you what to put in the lead. You're writing it. But we didn't send you across the country to write about what people are wearing and what the weather's like."

This was so ridiculous and so negative that Ted knew

there was no point in arguing, but he could not stop himself. "That's just atmosphere," he said. "That's not all I'm saying. I'm trying to give a picture of who the scientists are who are fighting this thing, and how they feel about it and how they're going about it."

"Let's have a little less atmosphere and a little more about finding a cure," Manning said. "I'd like the five pieces by Thursday afternoon." He tossed the copy over to Ted and turned away indicating that the interview was at an end.

Ted went back to his desk and looked through the copy to see where he could start rewriting, and then through his notes. He could not see a way to do it, but he had been through things like this before and had always found a way. He was a pro, he told himself. He felt disappointed and rebuffed and his emotions were getting in the way. He knew from experience that the best thing now would be to put away the copy and do something else for a few hours, and turn back to it when his feelings had subsided. He might even leave it until tomorrow.

He switched on his computer terminal and ran through it. There was an article on it signed simply with the initials D.M. He started reading:

"Look at what the future holds for America. We will become a different kind of country. Something new in the world, that's what our founding fathers said we would be. Only not in the way they thought. 'A new nation, conceived in laboratories, and dedicated to the proposition that all men are emasculated equally.

"We'll be a great tourist draw. The world's freak show. Come and see America. The golden beaches where you'll see the men as well as the women with mammaries, mile after mile of subcutaneous male flesh. The land where only Santa Claus has a beard. The nation that speaks with one voice - tenor. The land of enterprise and industry, the world's biggest manufacturer of vibrators."

Caspar Kelly, who had invited him to the country club, ambled over to his desk and interrupted his reading.

"What the hell is this?" he asked Caspar indicating what was on the screen.

"Oh, it's Dan Meltzer's latest rant. He started to write it as an op ed piece and Manning said it's too downbeat. Dan's furious and thought that if we all saw it we might argue with Manning that it should go in. He's in trouble with Manning anyway."

"What's he done now?"

"Rabbi Rosen, who writes those occasional weekend columns, wrote one saying the Talmud says men have a duty to please their wives. Dan headed it 'Go Down, Moses.' The rabbi went ballistic."

"Do you think Dan could lose his job this time."

"I don't know. He's one of nature's kamikaze pilots. Anyway, how was your trip?"

"Interesting. I don't know how fruitful. I've got to do a lot more work."

"Come to lunch at Sam's and tell me about it."

"Okay, I'll tell you how the country looks west of Radford,."

A reporter he knew walked by and stopped at his desk. "I hear you had a successful trip west, Ted," he said.

"Oh really? Who did you hear that from?"

"Bob Rozhak."

"How does he know?"

"Rozhak said you met Marie Zamora.I trust the meeting was satisfactory for both parties." His tone was not friendly.

"I thought I might do a story about her."

"Rozhak said you weren't in your hotel when he called early the next morning, which is a good sign."

"Come on, this is getting rather personal," Ted pleaded.

"Perhaps you should write it up," Caspar said. "It's a pretty unusual story these days." Ted was surprised that he had joined in.

The other asked, "And if you do, are we going to get the whole truth? I think our readers deserve it."..

If only things had been different Ted would have come back with some wisecrack, or just told them to fuck off. But they were afflicted and he was the lucky one.

Caspar seemed to relent. He said, "Come on, Ted, we're only kidding." But the reporter turned on his heel and walked away.

Ted asked Caspar, "Does everyone know about Marie Zamora?"

"Everyone will soon."

"I just don't know whether I've got any friends here any more," Ted said. "It's awful."

Caspar was sympathetic. "It's hard to have friends when you're a millionaire and all the rest of us are on welfare."

Ted nodded. "It's not only women who can suffer from penis-envy. That's a point Dr. Freud missed," he said. Then he looked at Caspar's face ands wished he hadn't said it.

But Caspar simply said, "I'll stop by your desk at about twelve-fifteen. O.K.?."

Ted started wondering whether he should pretend now that the plague had caught up with him also, and whether he could. The hostility on all sides was getting him down.

His phone rang, and it was Martha Grove, with the cryptic message from Gavin. "Do you know what hotel he means?" she asked him.

"Yes, I know the hotel I recommended. It's - "

"Don't say any more. He thinks it's better I don't know. But he wants to see you right away."

"It's that urgent? Do you know what it's all about?"

"Yes, it's urgent." He could hear fear her voice. "Go today if you possibly can. He says he has a good story for you. And he says it's very important that you don't tell anyone where he is or that you're going to see him."

"He said that?"

"Yes!"

"Something's wrong?"

"Yes."

He knew the hotel was the Charles, where he had had his night of fun with Didi and Ingrid. He decided he had to go right away. It seemed urgent and he would get a break from thinking about the stories and take them up again tomorrow, when the smarting memory of Manning's rebuke was no longer so strong. He made an apology to Caspar about lunch, left word that he was going to see an important contact, and drove to Radford station. He had a sandwich in the diner opposite while he waited for a train.

::   ::   ::   ::

Gavin had often wondered what it would be like being in prison. He could not see that it would really be so bad providing the treatment was reasonable, at least for a little while. Food, clothing, bedding and so on would be simple but he would not mind that. He would not mind solitude for a while, either. He would have plenty of time to read and plenty of time to meditate, to think the kind of long-term thoughts that get crowded out by the minutae of daily living.

A long prison sentence would be one thing. It would take away a big chunk of his life. But a short one of two weeks or so would be just a break from one's workaday life. Not exactly a holiday, but a break. That's what he was having now, a break.

He did not need luxuries, he reflected, lying on the bed in his hotel room and looking at the ceiling. He really preferred a life of simple living and high thinking. True, his time in this hotel would not be simple living as Thoreau would have understood it, but simple urban living, his meals mostly carry-out food or sandwiches. He must get in some basics so that he could make himself breakfast. He would lie low, go out as little as possible, concentrate on keeping out of sight, read, keeping up with the news on television. He could think about where his life was going. He could think about the meaning of the work he was doing, not just on the impotence plague, but the whole direction in which he and his kind of science was moving.

He was reading intermittently an article on new directions in cosmology in the Scientific American, trying hard to follow it as he went along, when Ted knocked gently on the door. He got up and let him in.

"What's this all about?" Ted asked.

"Sit down and I'll tell you," Gavin said. Ted sat in the armchair and mopped his sweating face with his handkerchief, muttering about the humidity. Gavin told him the whole long story. He started with Barreras's invitation, but played down slightly his reaction to Barreras so that he did not say how near he was to accepting his offer. Then he told him about Mohsin's turnabout in his research, and the revelation that he was being blackmailed. He ended with the crash of his stolen car and his rapid departure from Melby..

Ted was sitting in the armchair, and Gavin on the bed. At the end of his account, Ted sat silent for a few moments and took a long draw on his cigarette, blew the smoke at the ceiling, and then said softly, "Those cocksuckers. That's an incredible story. Just incredible. You really think they tried to kill you?"

"Yes."

"There must be some way to nail them and get this into print. Not the car crash maybe, we can't definitely link that to them, but the rest."

"That suits me," Gavin said.

"How about your friend Mohsin? Can I tell that story?"

"No. That's confidential. I'm hoping you may be able to use it some way without mentioning names."

"We might if Izzy Rubin will talk about it. Just say there was a blackmail attempt on a member of the staff. But that wouldn't pin it on the Barreras guys."

"You might if you can link it with something else. With Philip Carey's activities."

"I'll talk to Tom Manning about it tomorrow. I'm not terribly popular at the office at the moment but he'll listen to this story all right. God, I'd like to expose those scumbags."

"Barreras and Philip Carey are quite a team."

"As a matter of fact," Ted said, "I had a curious run-in with Philip Carey myself today." And he told Gavin about his abortive visit to Carey's home.

"What do you think that was all about?" Gavin asked.

"I don't know."

"It sounds to me," Gavin said, "as if he was going to tell you something and then changed his mind. Or perhaps was persuaded to change his mind."

"That's possible," Ted acknowledged. "Although his wife wasn't exactly hospitable. Or maybe he just thought t would be fun to have me sitting on his sofa and twiddling my thumbs for an hour. Anyway, from what you say, you think they could be after you now."

"It certainly looks like it, doesn't it?"

"So a news story pointing the finger at those guys would take the heat off you. They wouldn't dare do anything to you after it appeared. That's what you have in mind, huh?"

"It would help, I think. But I think it would be wise to lay low for a while anyway."

"How long are you going to stay here?"

"Probably for two weeks."

"But what will change in two weeks?"

"Ah. That's something I haven't told you yet." As he said this, Gavin sat back on the bed so that he was leaning with his back against the wall and pondered before going on, wondering how to begin.

"You see, I sort of considered going to 00work for Biotek at one point. For several reasons, which don't do me credit, let me say. I didn't know then what Barreras was really doing. When I found out, I felt I ought to make up for it, do something to put Bliss ahead of them. So I took a short cut."

"What kind of short cut?"

"You know that they were ready to inject this thing which might produce antibodies into mice."

"Yes."

"Well that's normally the first stage. The second is to inject it into rabbits. And then into human beings. I injected it into a human being right away."

"You injected a person?"

"Yes. That was the short cut. In about two weeks, we'll be able to tell by a test whether it's producing the antibodies."

"You mean whether it's a cure?"

"Well, yes, although it's not that simple. We'll have to work out the dosage and the precise constituents before it can be bottled as medicine and sold. And in fact, a test on one subject wouldn't be acceptable as final proof, they'd have to test it on several. But in principle, yes, we could tell."

"So after two weeks you're going to leave here, get your subject to a laboratory, and test him?"

"I don't have to go anywhere. As I said, the test is very simple. These viruses cluster around red blood corpuscles along with a lot of other gunk. They create a blob, an agglutination. You can see whether they're less of them quite easily, with an ordinary microscope. Like that one there" - he gestured towards the table. "That's a 400-power microscope. I had it as a medical student. It'll do."

"I see. So you can do the test here in this room."

"That's right,"

"And you're going to get your subject to come here, is that it?"

"That won't be a problem." Gavin grinned.

There was a pause, and then Ted said, "Oh Jesus, you didn't!" Gavin nodded, still grinning.

Ted asked, "Is there any danger?"

"There's always an element of risk when you're dealing with something as new as this. But in my estimation, it's small. It would have been more prudent to go through the normal process with the mice and the rabbits and test their samples. I've done something imprudent."

Ted shook his head in wonderment. "You're a strange guy. You're scared shitless by Carey and Biotek Industries, and yet you're doing this incredibly brave thing."

"Maybe it's because in this case, the dangers are things I understand. In the other, they're lurking out there and they're unknown."

"Look, Gavin, how certain are you that they're really out to kill you?"

"For God's sake, how much evidence do you want? They tried to entice me away from Bliss and then someone ran my car off the road. And remember Alan Carling. He just disappeared."

"I suppose so. But I don't think they're likely to try again. And now that you've changed your address, you don't have to stay cooped up in here."

"Well I'm going to go out as little as possible."

"Why, do you think the whole of Manhattan is crawling with Carey's spies? That the cop on the beat, the newsboy on the corner, are all on the look-out for you? Come on."

"He's got contacts all over the place. Maybe with the police, yes. Does that sound paranoid."

"Let's say that perhaps you're more worried than you

need to be."

"Nonetheless," Gavin said, "I do intend to remain in here as much as possible. Particularly the first day or two, when they might really be looking for me. They can find out that I took a train into Pennsylvania Station."

"Well in that case let's do something. Let me take out my notebook, and go over the whole scientific background to what you did. I've got the time. I know most of it but let's get it in your own words, or at least let me check my understanding with you. \how you injected yourself. And I promise I won't use it until you tell me I can."

"You mean if the injection kills me, you'll have the exclusive story."

"I didn't exactly say that." So Gavin went over the science with him: the different tracks that might lead to a solution, and the promising denaturing process using selenium, and the consequences of injecting it into animals and people experimentally.

At the end, Ted said, "Well done, Gavin. Now let me take you out to dinner. You've earned it. We'll go to a quiet place near here and then you can come back here to your hideaway."

"Thanks, but no. I explained, I'm not leaving here any more than I have to, and certainly not this evening. But I'd be delighted if you want to have dinner with me. I suggest you go out and get us a pizza and a bottle of Scotch. I don't like pepperoni. And if you can stand it, we'll eat them right here."

"O.K."

"In fact, Ted, if you want to be a really nice guy you'll do some shopping for me. There must be a deli near here. Get me some grapefruit juice or orange juice, coffee, and sugar, and corn muffins and oleo. That'll do for breakfast. Get me also a couple of meals to last me through tomorrow. A frozen dinner I can cook in the oven.And some fresh fruit. Apples or bananas."

"Boy, you really are planning to hole up here, aren't you?"

"I told you, I'm worried about Carey and his men. And having gone this far, it would be silly to take a chance and go out when I don't have to."

"Okay, I'll do the shopping."

"And I'll tell you what else I suggest, if you've got the evening free. Have you ever seen *The Third Man?"*

"You mean the old Orson Welles movie."

"No, I mean the Carol Reed movie. He directed it and Graham Greene wrote it. Orson Welles was in it."

"No. I haven't seen it."

"It's a classic. Made in the 1950s. Black and white. I've seen it before but it's worth seeing twice. I notice that it's on television this evening. We've both had a hard day with a lot of strain. I suggest we drink some Scotch and watch it. It'll relax us."

"Okay, I'll go along with that." Ted went out, smiling for the first time that day.

He came back with the groceries and a the Scotch. The long-awaited rainstorm broke just as he arrived, and they ate their pizza and drank Scotch and watched the film to the accompaniment of thunder and lightning flashes. Afterwards, they talked about the film and its moral ambiguities, and agreed that they both felt better for watching it.

"I'll head home now," Ted said. "The rain has stopped."

"You okay for a train?" Gavin asked.

Ted took a timetable out of his pocket and held it up. "There's one at eleven-ten. I'll get a cab to Penn Station and catch it easily. If not, there's another at eleven forty-two. I'll call you in a couple of days and see how you're getting along, okay Mr. Prince?"

"From a public call box please," Gavin said. "Your phone could be bugged. They might even bug mobile phones. They know you've been close to me on this story,."

Ted said, "You've been reading too many - oh, forget it."

He left. Gavin looked around the room, planning how he would live his life here for the next two weeks. He would wash the plates and things after every meal. It would not do to let them pile up in that tiny kitchenette. He moved the armchair so that it was next to the reading lamp. He contemplated days of meals sitting in that armchair, and reading and watching television. As prison cells go, it could be worse.. He looked out of the window but there was little life in the street below.

He picked up the *Scientific American* and started again on cosmology and was soon absorbed in the subject. He had only read for a few minutes when there was a soft, urgent rapping on the door.

Gavin opened it and Ted almost fell into the room. He was clutching a newspaper. He gasped out a few strangled sounds and tried several times to begin a sentence. "They've - look at – here." He gave up the attempt to speak and thrust the newspaper into Gavin's hand..

It was the early edition of the next day's Daily News.

Gavin looked at the front page headline. It read: "Hunt Potent Suspect In Rape Bid." He opened it, and on page three there was a huge picture of Ted. He said, "My God."

Ted sat down in the armchair shaking his bowed head in what seemed like disbelief. "I don't think anyone recognized me in the lobby, thank Christ," he said.

Gavin started reading the story:

"*A Long Island housewife and former actress alleges that a man attacked her in her home yesterday and tried to rape her. The housewife, Mrs. Donna Carey, aged 40, of Treeline Drive, Walton, identified the man as Ted Starowicz, a reporter on the Long Island Chronicle, who is said by colleagues to be unaffected by the plague.*

"*Police are seeking Starowicz for questioning. They say he went to the office of the Chronicle at about eleven o'clock this morning, soon after the alleged rape attempt, and left abruptly after about an hour without telling anyone where he was going.*

"*Mrs. Carey is an attractive blonde who works part-time as a model and has played several small parts as a televisionv actress. She said Starowicz,33, gained entry to her home by saying he had come to interview her husband, Philip Carey, a senior executive of Barreras Industries. He had interviewed him in the past, in his office.*

"*According to her account, he claimed that Mr. Carey had asked to see him there. He waited until the Careys' 17-year-old daughter Elizabeth had left the house, she said, and then demanded that she have sex with him, and attacked her when she refused.*

"*She said Starowicz was only foiled because her husband came back unexpectedly. When he heard Mr. Carey getting out of his car, she said, he ran out of the house and drove away. Mr. Carey said he recognized Starowicz from the previous interview.*

"Mrs. Carey told a News reporter: 'He said he wanted to make love to me. When I refused he persisted and I told him to leave the house. He became very angry and seized hold of me and tried to drag me on to the couch. I fought back, but he grabbed me by the hair and tore at my halter so that it was half-way off.'

"Mrs. Carey paused several times in her account, forcing back tears. She turned for comfort to her husband, who was standing beside her, and he put his arm around her and patted her shoulder."

Gavin stopped reading for a moment and looked over at Ted, who was sitting in the chair and still shaking his head in what seemed like a mixture of incredulity and fear. "God, Ted," he said because he felt Ted needed him to say something.

Suddenly, Ted said, "I haven't read the whole story. What else does she say?" He got up and snatched the paper from Gavin's hand and started reading. He muttered a few oaths as he read, then threw down the paper and exploded, "That bitch. That lying, vicious, fucking, fucking bitch! "This is calculated to make me the most hated man in America. Listen. *'She said Starowicz told her - '* I can't go on. It's just awful! Here," and he pushed the paper back at Gavin. Gavin took it and read:

"She said Starowicz told her, 'What's the matter with you? Other women are begging for what I'm offering you.' She protested that she was married but he replied, 'So what?

I've had plenty of married women. I can have any woman I want. I wouldn't mind your daughter. She looks cute. '.

"Police say they have no clue as to Starowicz's whereabouts at present. Starowicz, a bachelor, has been on the staff of the Long Island Chronicle for four years. He comes from Jersey City and is a graduate of Thomas Jefferson High School in Jersey City and Rutgers, and has an M.A. from Columbia University. "

Ted was absorbed in his own thoughts now, muttering to himself. He was remembering her stony face, and sitting on that couch and reading and re-reading sections of the Sunday Times while she kept her back to him. He should have told her what he thought of her then. He wished furiously that he had. Fantasies of savage revenge came into his mind.

"It's horrible, but it's only one woman's uncorroborated testimony," Gavin said.   "I shouldn't think it'll stand up in court."

"In today's atmosphere? And who's talking about court?" yelled Ted. "I may not get to court. I could be shot resisting arrest. You could find I've committed suicide in my police cell. They've probably got contacts in the police, everywhere. Even if I do get to court, Carey could probably produce a dozen witnesses who'll say they saw me do it."

"Try to keep calm, Ted."

"Would you be calm?" Ted's voice was shrill. "You read it. 'I can have any woman I want! I've had plenty of married women.' Jesus. Any policeman in New York would be happy to beat my brains out with his night stick. They still can't find a jury to try the guy that killed Yablonsky. I could be lynched if I even walk out on to the street."

He buried his face in his hands. Gavin stared ahead and tried to think, hard. He said, half to himself, "They're certainly out to eliminate the opposition."

"'Eliminate' is right," said Ted.

"They know you're close to me on this and they don't know how much you know. Even if the story doesn't get you convicted, it'll get you out of the way for a while."

"It'll get me out of the way all right."

Then Gavin said, "I've got an idea. Could you go into the Chronicle office now, and give yourself up to the police there? Tell them you're innocent, explain the situation to the Chronicle people. They know those stories you wrote about Carey. They'll follow your case and gather evidence in your favor. But the main thing is that if you give yourself up in front of them, that'll make sure that you're arrested properly and treated properly after your arrest. The police can't beat you up or shoot you."

Ted hesitated. "It might work," he said. "But I don't see how I can even get there without being recognized. My picture's in the paper."

"You can get there in a taxi, with your face half-concealed. Or a reporter can come and get you. Is there anyone there at this time of night?"

Yes, there's a small night staff. Okay. I'm desperate, so I'll try it," he said. He took out his mobile phone and dialled a number.

Gavin heard him say, "Hello, who's that? Si? Are you on the desk? Good, this is Ted Starowicz.

"Yes. Look, I've just read about this story of rape. I'm innocent, I promise you. Hell, you know I wouldn't do anything like that. That bastard Philip Carey is framing me..... I want to give myself up, and tell you the whole story.....No, I don't want to tell you all about it now, what I want now is for somebody to come and get me. If I don't - who are you talking to, Si?"

Ted slammed down the phone and turned to Gavin. "Fuck! He was trying to keep me talking while the operator traced the call. Oh, Jesus. Everybody's against me. I'm dead."

CHAPTER TWELVE

They got through the night somehow. Ted was not going to move out of the room. Gavin went to bed and Ted sat up in the armchair all night. He said he would be comfortable. "One advantage of being my height is that I can rest my head on the back of a chair like this and go to sleep. I can sleep on airplanes," he said. Gavin slept fitfully, aware that there was someone else in the room. A couple of times when he opened his eyes he saw in the dark the glowing tip of a cigarette.

The room was not meant for two people and in the morning it smelled of sweat and tobacco. They opened the window wide and both showered in turn, and Gavin, playing host, made coffee and offered corn muffins.

Lying awake in the early morning, Gavin had worked out their next move. He thought Ted would want to stay in hiding for a while. Over coffee, he told Ted his plan. "I'll put a 'Do Not Disturb' sign on the door. That'll keep the maid out for this morning. Coming along here, I noticed a magic shop on Sixth Avenue. They sell tricks, costumes, things like that. They also sell make-up for disguises, false mustaches, beards and so on. I'll get you a false beard and some glasses."

"But that's not for serious work. That's just kids' stuff," Ted objected.

"It'll do. After all, everybody isn't going to be scrutinizing faces to see whether it's Ted Starowicz. Then, when we've given you your disguise, you go downstairs. The elevator is the other side of the lobby from the reception desk so the guy there probably won't notice you going out. He's not exactly alert. Then you come back and take a room. See if you can get one on this floor. You stay here in this hotel for a while and keep me company while we work out what to do next."

Ted hesitated anxiously, then said, "Okay. Let's try it."

Gavin went out to the magic store, hurrying along the street, and bought the beard and glasses and some rose tint as well, and got instructions on putting on the beard. He helped Ted make up his face in front of the bathroom mirror. It was a smallish, spade-shaped beard with whiskers running up the cheeks to give a wide area of concealment. With a touch of the rose tint, Gavin gave his cheeks a ruddy complexion.

Ted looked at his reflection doubtfully. "To me, I still look like me," he said.

"Yes, and I'm sure your mother would recognize you," said Gavin. "But the man who's seen your picture in the newspaper wouldn't. You know that plane accident the day before yesterday at JFK, when they got the plane down with the engine on fire so that everyone was saved?"

"Yes."

"Would you recognize the pilot if he walked in here with a beard and glasses?"

"I see what you mean. No, I guess not."

"No. But there was a big picture of him in the front of the Long Island Chronicle yesterday."

When it came time for Ted to leave the room he hesitated anxiously, like a nervous diver on the edge of a diving board. Gavin put his arm around his shoulder encouragingly and said, "If I could I'd come with you but it wouldn't look good. We're not supposed to know each other. But it'll be easy. They don't care much who takes the rooms here."

"I know," Ted said, remembering his last stay, with Didi and Ingrid. He took a deep breath and opened the door and headed out towards the elevator.

Gavin felt pleased with himself. He was finding that he was good at planning moves in this situation. Not in executing them: he recalled with a shudder the strain that the small bit of acting at Pennsylvania Station had caused him. He decided that in the John Le Carré spy novels he was George Smiley, the man who devised the schemes, rather than an agent in the field.

After a few minutes there was a knock at the door and Ted walked in holding a room key. "It worked," he reported. "I've got 610, just down the corridor. I paid a week's rent in cash."

"Good. What name did you register under?"

"Bernard King. If you're Mr. Prince, I decided that I should outrank you."

Gavin grinned, pleased at this. It was a weak joke but the touch of humor showed that Ted was loosening up a bit. "Well done," he said.

"The guy at the desk seems pretty dozy," Ted said. "He asked where my bags were and I said had a case around the corner and I'd go out and get it later. Could you go out and buy one for me please? And if I'm going to stay here for a while, I'll need a change of socks and underwear and some toilet things."

"How about going out and getting them yourself with your disguise?"

"No fucking way! I tell you, people remember a rapist. Or attempted rapist. Particularly one who says he's had lots of men's wives and can have any woman he wants. This whole city is a potential lynch mob so far as I'm concerned."

Gavin looked across at Ted and saw that he was still very frightened. So he went out and bought a cheap valise and some socks and underwear and toilet articles. He looked around nervously at the people passing by and remembered that he had planned to remain indoors himself as much as possible in the next two weeks. He went to another store and bought some ready-made meals, bread, cold cuts, fruit and milk.

"What about our mobile phones?" Ted asked.

"We shouldn't use them," Gavin said. "Maybe they can trace them. At least work out roughly where we are. Or they can find out something from whoever we call. I don't know. Just stay here and stay silent."

Those next two weeks were a strange time. Gavin had assumed that it would be a period for reflection, that he would come away with a new and clearer perspective on his life. He never worked out why it was not but he thought very little about his life and its direction. He found it difficult to think about anything but the immediate: getting food and making his cash last out and their next moves. He was surprised at how much he missed Martha. He wanted to eat a meal with her or simply see her in the same room with him. They had never spent more than a few days apart since they were married. Perhaps, he thought, when he was with her again and in his own home, then he would think about where his life was going.

The hotel became a familiar environment: the two Eastern European maids who came in alternatively to give his room a perfunctory cleaning, barely noticing him as he moved out of their way; the smell in the room after he had finished cooking his ready-made meal that lingered even with the window open; the shabby, dimly-lit corridor with its faded carpet and oatmeal-colored wallpaper; the elevator with its iron gate that had to be given an extra push to get it to shut; the two young women who spoke with a Western twang who seemed to be sharing a room on the floor and were in and out all day looking for work of some kind, and who always smiled when they passed in the corridor because that was the way to please people and get ahead; the few permanent residents, middle-aged men and women who looked as if they had come to an end of a long road; and the tired-looking room clerk to whom he paid his rent once a week.

Gavin went out every two or three evenings to shop for food, spending as little time in the street as possible. He reminded himself continually that he was still in hiding, still did not want to be recognized or to meet someone he knew. He was still afraid of Philip Carey's henchmen. If he saw a policeman he was careful not to change his pace but he walked by with his head averted. He never went eastwards towards Fifth and Madison Avenues, where people he knew were more likely to be found. If he saw a crowd of people coming out of a theater, or people waiting outside a restaurant for a taxi, he would turn and hurry off. He was relieved when he saw people he could show his face to, who could not know him by sight, a group of Afro-Americans with rasta haircuts carrying a ghetto-blaster, or some noisy men swaggering out of a bar. They might have thought it odd that this lone, slender, sober-suited WASP should walk by boldly and look them straight in the eye. Always he hurried back to the Hotel Charles and the sanctuary of Room 604. There and only there did he feel safe.

He wondered from time to time whether he needed to be here at all. Was his flight only a panic reaction? Was it really possible that Carey had people out looking for him? He always concluded that it was at least possible. The crash of his car was not likely to be a coincidence, and if Carey had tried to kill him he would try again. There was not much to be lost by staying here until the injection produced some result. He could not see himself going back home and saying it was all a mistake.

He and Ted ate most of their meals together, in one or another of their rooms, and often read or watched television together in the evenings. There was no reason for anyone to think this odd. It would be natural that once they met, in the corridor or in the elevator, they would seek each other's company, two lonely men, probably both at a way station in their lives, working out what to do next after fleeing a failed marriage.

They saw America through the newspapers, the radio and the TV screens. Ted pointed to the absence from newspapers of the usual ads for massage parlors and porno movie theaters. One enterprising porno house continued to advertise saying: "XXX-rated Adult Movies. Come in and remember what it was like."

Newspapers carried an increasing number of articles about the secondary sexual characteristics that might be expected to appear over time with the absence of functioning testosterone. There was little evidence that this was happening yet among adult males, but doctors reported a delay in boys of the onset of puberty.

Television and radio told them about the new movements that sprang up that summer. There were the tree-huggers, and in their case the term could be used literally, women and a few men who went into the woods to dance, chant ritually and embrace trees. Gavin and Ted watched film of this and a teacher - the movement rejected the term "leader" - explaining to the camera: "Living our urban lives, we've cut ourselves off from nature as a source of sustenance. We've put concrete sidewalks between out bodies and the Earth and ceilings between us and the sky. Now we're reconnecting with the Earth. We embrace trees because a tree more than any other plant draws sustenance from deep down in the earth and uses the energy to reach up towards the sky."

"Do you think she knows what a phallic symbol is?" Ted asked, watching it.

"Of course, she's not stupid," Gavin replied.

There were the witches, who gathered in increasing numbers in the woods at night for their rituals. The leader of a coven said these could not be filmed and added that some lurid newspaper accounts of what went on were guesswork or downright lies. "We worship with our spirits and our bodies," she said. "We worship the old gods, the female gods, the ones that were worshipped before men gave us the Judaeo-Christian father-figure. This is the male God who gave orders to the human race about what we were allowed to feel, frightening people out of their bodies and cramping their sexuality."

There were the emigrés, not an organized group although they were beginning to form a network, men who blamed American society for their plight and announced that they were leaving America for good, usually to live in the Far East, many of them with their families. There were the people offering unorthodox cures: fringe homeopaths, Yogis, a Nigerian who had learned witch doctor techniques from his father.

They followed on television the phenomenon of Paul Poteen, a country and western singer from rural Tennessee. He had only a few small-town gigs until July, when, promoted by an astute manager, he suddenly appeared in big city venues drawing huge crowds, trading outrageously on the implication that he was a potent. Even his stage name, which he had just adopted, suggested this, although he was at pains to point out that "poteen" was the word for the home-distilled whiskey which his Ulster Irish forbears made.

Tall and lanky, he wore suede and leather encrusted with glitter. He would sing the usual songs of love and lust and heartache playing his electric guitar, and between numbers or sometimes in the middle of one he would fling his arms out wide and call out to his audience, underlining the message of the song, "Ah love women! Ah really do love women!" His audience, which consisted almost entirely of females of all ages, would scream ecstatically, and some would run down the aisle and have to be kept back from climbing on to the stage. Some of his performances were televised.

After a little while Paul Poteen became more daring still. He would shoot glances down from the stage like darts and say, "Ah'm looking at the third row tonight. There's two or three women there who really set me a'tingling. Oh yes!" Then, looking over the whole house, he would say, "Actually, all of you ladies set me a'tingling, but I can't take you all on so ah'm looking at the third row in partic'lar." And the whole audience would scream, the third row loudest of all. Some of the younger women, writhing in their seats as they yelled out in ecstasy, seemed to be engaging in virtual intercourse with Poteen.

Gavin and Ted watched a TV report on Paul Poteen. A reporter asked him outright whether he was a potent and Poteen replied, "Well that's a part of mah innimate life. A gen'man doesn't talk about things like that." The reporter said Poteen usually left in a limousine after a show with one or two women and two bodyguards. Several town councils banned him from singing there and some TV stations refused to carry his shows.

"Even the fact that he can send out the signals makes him irresistible to women," Ted remarked. He was taking a fish pie for two out of the little oven.

Gavin said. "They can probably smell him," he said. "Like my cousin."

"People could smell your cousin?" Ted asked.

"Well, that was one theory. Women, that is. This cousin was enormously attractive to women, in the way Poteen seems to be. I mean, phenomenally. Women would throw themselves at him."

"Lucky guy."

"It was extraordinary. We decided that they could smell him. Unconsciously, of course. It was something to do with his pheromones. Those things that animals give out in their body scent that serve as a sexual stimulus. There was really something strange about it."

"So he got laid a lot."

"Oh yes. But he was irresponsible," Gavin went on. "He took anything that was going. He wasn't sex mad, it wasn't that. He just thought it wouldn't be polite to say no. He didn't like to turn people down. It got him into bad trouble."

"Men's wives?"

"Men's wives. And his aunt. That caused a family scandal. The woman next door and her daughter. Or her mother, I can't remember which. A woman who knocked at his door collecting for charity. A member of parliament who came canvassing. The entire sixth form of a Catholic girls' school. Women would stare at him in the street. Some people said a few women actually stopped him in the street and propositioned him, although I'm not sure I believe that."

"Where is he now?"

"The last I heard he was at my old college, King's College, London, Medical School."

"He's studying medicine?"

"No. They're studying him."

Ted paused, and then continued spooning the pie out on to two plates. "Your family! What gets me, you son-of-a-bitch," he said, "is that you keep a straight face when you tell these stories."

Once Gavin persuaded Ted to come out to supper with him. Ted refused at first but then admitted, "I feel I'm going stir-crazy in here. We'll just go to some quiet place."

They went to the nearby restaurant Gavin had already chosen. It was a bar and grill sort of a place, with booths around the walls. Once in there, Gavin saw Ted give an imitation of a bad actor over-doing a part as a fugitive from justice. He chose a booth in a corner and sat with his shoulders hunched as if he were trying to make his head disappear down into his neck. He gave his order in a nervous whisper, and swept the room frequently with quick glances. He flinched when two men sat down in the next booth. He wiped some gravy off his false beard with the anxious delicacy of a picture restorer cleaning an Old Master. When they got back to Gavin's room Ted sat on the bed and breathed a long sigh of relief. He did not go out again and Gavin did not suggest it.

Once, as they sat together in Ted's room, Ted contemplated its walls in morose silence for some time and then said, "Do you know what Oscar Wilde said on the morning of the day he died?"

"What?"

He was lying ill in this crummy hotel room in Paris. And he said to his friend, 'That wallpaper! One of us will have to go.'"

Ted asked Gavin a few times how he was feeling and Gavin said there seemed to be no ill-effects from the injection so far.

It appeared from the news that the plague was much less evident in Europe than in America and not at all outside Europe. The fact that it was seen nowhere in the Third World reinforced suspicions that it was something created by a terrorist organization in the Arab or Moslem world, or even by a government.

News reports were giving more space to this kind of speculation. TV programs searched around for anyone willing to talk about whether and how such a virus could be devised to stop at the shoreline, or could be limited to certain climates, and how it could be introduced into a country. Gavin was surprised to see Stephen Johns talking in a news report about the capacity for retaliation, with accompanying footage. He told Ted about meeting Johns at Bar Harbor, and about what seemed like Johns' eagerness to retaliate against somebody for something.

"That figures," Ted said.

"You think they'll find somebody to blame?"

"Somebody to blame for something. All that film of rockets taking off and those long, slim missiles homing in on their targets. What do think they signify? If we can't fuck our wives we'll fuck some other country. If somebody doesn't find a cure soon, there's a going to be a war."

"We're all supposed to be losing our macho aggressiveness some time soon," Gavin said. "Becoming less masculine. More feminine, I suppose."

"And that means being less aggressive, does it?" Ted retorted. "Like, women aren't aggressive. Like they don't quarrel, don't throw things at their husbands, and even, if they're feeling particularly irritable, kill them."

"I'm not talking about individual women," Gavin protested.

"No. We'll have a more feminine government in Washington. A gentler government. No more macho assertiveness. Run by gentle, peace-loving people like Golda Meir and Margaret Thatcher and Condoleeza Rice." Gavin decided that being cooped up was making Ted tetchy.

Gavin was working out an idea. Some part of it must have been lodged in his unconscious when he left home to go into Manhattan, for he had put his credentials as an alternate delegate to the World Health Organization meeting into his bag. If the blood test showed positive, if it showed that the new antibody was working and was fighting off the virus, then he would fly to Geneva and see that the fact was announced at the WHO meeting. Izzy could announce it. In Geneva he would be out of reach of Carey's men, at least when he arrived there. Once the announcement was made there would be no point in trying to eliminate him and he would be safe.

In fact, he thought, even if the blood test showed negative, Izzy would still have the use of the selenium culture to report. He would go to the meeting and give Izzy the slides with his blood samples so that he could tell the meeting about them. That at least would get Biotek and Philip Carey off his back.The timing would be right. The WHO meeting opened on October 1st, which would be about three weeks from the time he had gone into hiding. He told Ted about the idea over a pre-cooked chow mein supper. Ted said, "Great. I'll come too. I'll get out of the country."

They both saw the snags immediately. Ted did not have his passport with him, and even if he could get it he could be spotted and arrested the moment he presented it at the airport. But Gavin did not feel like leaving Ted. He felt he would be deserting him, and he could see that Ted was anxious at the prospect.

The next morning Ted came in to see him. "I think I can get my passport," he said. "And we can fly to Geneva from Canada. Air Canada and Swissair both go, I've made some phone calls from the pay phone in the lobby to check. We change planes at Zurich. I could get through a Canadian airport more easily than an American one. And I'm sure I could get across the border to Canada without being seen."

"Hmmm. Let me think about it," Gavin said. "I'm just washing these shirts. I'll come and see you when I've finished."

He finished washing the drip-dry shirts in the bathroom sink, which took him back to his bachelor days. He rubbed the cuffs with a nailbrush and then ran the water to rinse off the detergent, thinking about what Ted had just said, and also that he should go easy with the nailbrush because this was rubbing the surface off the shirt material. He hung the two shirts on wire hangers on the shower rail, considering as he did so the worries he had himself about leaving from an American airport, where the fact that he was traveling would go on to a computer. It might be better for him also to fly from Canada. Then he went along to Ted's room.

"Where do these flights go from?" he asked Ted.

"Toronto."

"And you say you can get your passport?"

"I'm pretty sure I can."

"Okay, here's what we do. You get your passport. We go up to Buffalo. There, I hire a car. You get into the boot - sorry, the trunk. I drive it across the border at Niagara Falls. Passport control there is bound to be rather perfunctory. Have you ever crossed the Canadian border?"

"No, I've never been to Canada."

"Neither have I. But it can't be a problem, particularly at Niagara Falls. So many people go there and cross the border all the time. We'll cross the border at night."

"Why? There won't be so many people crossing at night and it's better to be lost in a crowd."

"First, because it's still summer and you'd die of suffocation if you spent a couple of hours in the trunk of a car in the heat of the day. And second, because once we get across I'm going to park the car at the side of the road and you'll get out of the trunk, and that's a sight that's liable to arouse some curiosity. So we'll do it in the dark.

"We drive to Toronto, check into a hotel, then take the plane. Have you got your bank card?"

"Yes."

"Good. I don't have mine, it was stolen along with my car. You can get out a lot of cash. OK?"

"Yes, ok."

"We'll pay by cash at the airport for both tickets. If I buy the tickets in advance, then my name will go on the airline's computer, and who knows who has access to that? And your name also. So we'll get them at the last minute." Gavin was becoming pleased with his talent for making plans

"But I'll have to give my name at the airport."

"Not until the last moment. The only risk is when you go through passport control. Then you'll have to take off the beard so that your face looks like your passport photograph. It's not a big risk. I'll get you some sunglasses and you can wear those too. The Ted Starowicz story isn't such big news in Toronto as it is in New York, and in any case more than three weeks will have gone by and most people will have forgotten about it."

"They won't have forgotten," Ted said. "Attempted rape isn't exactly a common offense these days."

"But they'll have forgotten what you look like. And nobody will know you're in Canada so they won't be looking for you. And even if he does spot you and you're arrested, you're better off in a Canadian jail than an American one. They'll have to have extradition proceedings to take you back. But it's very unlikely."

Ted said, "There's a plus also. I've got a cousin in Toronto. Part of the Canadian branch of the Starowicz family. The more prosperous branch. He's visited us a few times when he came down to New York and we get on together. He'll believe me if I tell him I'm innocent. He could give us some logistical support if we need it."

Ted was excited at the prospect. He hated being cooped up. His missed people. He missed Naomi and thought a lot about the date they did not keep and wondered why he had waited so long to call her. Imprisoned in the hotel, he felt imprisoned also in his disguise, which became uncomfortable after a while. He would keep his beard on for two or three days but then he would have to peel it off to shave and wash his face. At those times he felt naked and vulnerable, and frightened that the maid would come in and see him. His earlier panic was replaced by a constant nagging fear. He did not sleep well.

But at least he was calm enough now to think about his next moves. He would ask Anne Broadley to get his passport. She only had to go down two floors. She said she liked him and it seemed she did. He had not telephoned anyone except a travel agent about flights to Switzerland since he saw that story about him in the Daily News, and he hesitated before dialing her number. She gasped in surprise when he spoke to her. "Ted! Where are you?" she said.

"Anne, I want you to help me," he said. "I didn't try to rape that damned woman, I swear I didn't."

"I didn't think so."

"Does it seem likely?"

"No, it doesn't. Are you all right?"

"Yes thanks, mostly. That Carey woman made it up." He wondered how much of the story about Carey and Biotek he could tell her. Without the whole background it would sound pretty fanciful.

"That's what I thought," Anne said. "There are an awful lot of frustrated women around. Things happen to their minds."

Of course, Ted thought. This was the simplest explanation. No plot to get him, just the fantasies of a frustrated woman. There was no need to tell her anything. "I suppose so," he said. "But frankly, I'm scared of being arrested. I don't know what the police will do to me. The way people are feeling and the things that are being said, they might beat me up, or kill me and say I was resisting arrest."

"Oh darling! That's terrifying."

"I don't think I can get a fair trial. There's a witch-hunt atmosphere."

"Do you want to come and hide here? We could manage it."

"No, I want to go abroad. I've got a chance to go. I'll come back and face the law eventually, when things have quieted down, but right now I want to go. That's where you come in. I want you to get my passport for me. If I mail you the keys to my apartment, will you go up there and get it?"

"Yes of course. Anything."

"Thanks. I'll mail you the keys in a padded envelope today. The passport is in the bottom drawer of my desk."

He arranged that she would mail the passport to Bernard King at the hotel. When he collected the package it contained his passport, a rabbit's foot and a note saying, "Good luck. Love, Anne."

Gavin took out a microscope and a slide. Then he sterilized a pin over the stove, pricked his finger, and dabbed at the tiny wound with the slide, smearing blood on it. He put the slide under the microscope and put his eye to the eyepiece. The blotches around the red corpuscles were smaller: he was sure. To check, he took another slide he had brought with him out of its little plastic envelope and peered at that under the microscope. He was looking at a sample of his blood taken two weeks ago. Comparing the two, he was in no doubt. The blotches, representing the virus that was damaging the testosterone receptors, were dwindling, and would soon disappear.

Then he did something that would have astonished most people who knew him if they had seen it. It was something he had learned to do many years earlier, during two uproarious nights on a summer holiday on a Greek island, and used to do when he was drunk enough at student parties. He stretched out his arms and he began whistling a Greek tune. Clicking his fingers, and circling a spot on the floor, he did a slow dance, keeping his torso straight and crossing and uncrossing his legs as he moved around.

After a while he stopped and walked down the hall to Ted's room and rapped gently on the door. "Hi," he said when Ted answered. "Do you want a story? It'll have to be off the record for the time being."

::   ::   ::

They had an argument about how to go up to Buffalo. Gavin wanted to go by train but Ted still refused to travel among the public. He wanted Gavin to rent a car so that they could drive up. He pointed out that at a station there would be policemen skilled at recognizing a disguise, particularly one put on by amateurs as this was. So Gavin agreed to rent a car. Ted's beard was getting thin and scraggly so Gavin bought him another, the same shape and color. Also, at Ted's request, he bought him a pair of shades.

. The next day, early in the morning, Ted went down and drew four thousand dollars from the bank in cash, waiting until the last possible moment before they left since the transaction and hence his presence would go on to a computer.

Then, after breakfast, he went down with his suitcase, paid his bill, collected his car, and waited outside while Gavin organized the car renta.. He felt a sense of adventure at leaving the sanctuary of the hotel for the open world. Gavin seemed to feel it also, for he had a spring in his step as he hurried out of the hotel with his face averted and crossed the road. He almost threw himself into the car. Ted said, "Let's hit the macadam."

Once they were on their way Gavin was glad they were driving. He had not realized how much he had been feeling oppressed in that hotel room. He had a feeling of liberation even driving along in the traffic, and when they were crossing the George Washington Bridge under the wide blue sky he felt exhilarated. Ted whooped and said, "Jesus, it's good to be alive!"

They drove under a sunny blue sky in a soft balmy breeze. They took the Dewey Thruway and they kept telling each other how great it was to be free and outdoors, and pointing out views to one another. "Hey, isn't that a beautiful sight? I never knew the Hudson River could look like that," Ted said looking down on the river's steep wooded banks outside Albany.

In the Mohawk Valley, Gavin pointed to the wooded hillsides, with the greenery almost glowing with occasional glimpses of russet heralding the coming of autumn. "Spruce forests. One of the glories of the American countryside," he said.

They shared the driving. Once they stopped at the roadside so they could pee behind a tree. Then, with nobody to see but the occupants of passing cars, Ted took off his shades and strolled up and down, showing his face to the world and grinning. To Gavin he looked for all the world like a little boy who is doing something he is not supposed to do and getting away with it.

They bought hamburgers and coffee and ate them in the car and Ted bought some cigarettes. Once when they stopped in a parking space to change over the driving, they saw a number of women get out of cars and start walking towards the woods. "A group of tree-huggers," Gavin remarked. The women wore long white robes, some of them diaphanous, and as they passed near them Ted looked at a couple of the younger ones. One of them returned his look and Gavin, seeing this, snapped, "Back into the car! We're on our way. Right now!"

While Ted was driving he asked, "Have you worked what we're going to do when we get to Geneva?" It seemed to be established now that Gavin was doing most of the planning.

"Yes. If we leave Toronto tomorrow night, we'll get to Geneva on Sunday morning at 11.45. We'll check in at a hotel somewhere and go find Izzy Rubin. The meeting starts on Monday. I'll talk to Izzy and explain everything and work out how to make the news public. In fact, we'll try to check in at the hotel Izzy's staying at. He's going to be pretty damned pleased. It's his work. His and Mohsin's."

"Do you know where Izzy's staying?" Ted asked.

"No, but it shouldn't be difficult to find out. The WHO must have an office open on the day before a big meeting, even on a Sunday. Delegates will be arriving."

Ted said, "Look Gavin, I may be a fugitive from justice but I'm also a reporter. I've come this far with you and God knows I've suffered through getting involved with this story. You told me how your blood samples show that you've cracked it, but that'll be announced at the conference. What say you give me an exclusive on it? Tell me what you're going to do and what Izzy's going to do. Then come out of the conference hall and tell me what happened. As soon as you know Izzy's going to announce a cure I'll phone the Chronicle telling them it's going to happen, and when the announcement is made I'll be ahead of the rest of the world." .

"I don't see why not," said Gavin. "After what you've been through, I think you deserve a scoop."

"'Scoop' is a word from the movies," Ted said. "But hell yes, it's the story of the year. The story of the century! Do you think they might give me a Pulitzer Prize when I'm in the slammer?"

"I'm hoping that once the cure is announced, the Careys will drop their complaint."

"Drop their complaint? I want them to tell the whole world it was a fucking lie!"

They drove through Buffalo and arrived in the town of Niagara Falls at seven o'clock in the evening. They had decided to stay overnight there to rest and so that Gavin could check out the border crossing area. They would go on to Toronto the following evening, Friday, and catch the Saturday evening plane.

They saw a few high-rise hotels among the garish announcements of entertainments but decided to stay in a more out-of-the-way place. They came to a string of motels along a road facing the river, advertising their suitability for honeymooners, some of them with water beds. They opted for a motel on a side street.

Gavin did the checking in and they went to their room. Ted put down his case on his bed and said, "We're still in America and I'm still nervous about going out. Every time someone looks at me I think I'm blushing. Would you do me a favor and get us a meal we can eat here"

"Okay. I'm lying low also. I didn't register here under my real name, don't worry. But I've got to check on things here. I'll probably be able to get a list of Toronto hotels."

Ted said, "I've got another idea. I'm still a bit nervous about staying in a hotel. I could be recognized. I told you I've got this cousin in Toronto, George Starowicz. I think he'll put me up. I'd rather stay there."

"You'll trust him?"

"Yes. You can come too. I imagine there's room."

"No, I think two people on the run might worry him. But you go if you like. You're sure you can count on him?"

"George will believe me if I tell him I'm innocent. I told you, he's always been fond of me. He's quite a bit older than me and a lot richer. He's often said I should come to Toronto and visit him."

"You're sure he'll put you up now? Even when the police are after you?"

"If he doesn't want me there he'll say so. At any rate, he won't turn me in, I'm sure of that."

"Okay.. I could pick you up from there and we'll go to the airport together."

"Fine."

While Gavin went to get supper for them, Ted sat on the bed and thought about his cousin George, plump, bespectacled, quiet. He had always seemed to Ted more like a smiling Buddha than a whizz-kid in the financial world. The last time they met George was visiting New York for a holiday weekend with his wife Carol, and they took him out to dinner. George was about fifty, a generation older than him, and he had always regarded Ted as a favorite nephew rather than a cousin. He seemed to think there was something glamorous about the career of a newspaper reporter, and he was tickled when Ted showed him a Chronicle story with his byline. Now Ted was frightened to be among strangers and felt he could do with the comfort of a kindly uncle.

Carol was George's second wife, several years younger than him, and Ted had met her only the once, on that evening out in New York. He recalled her as tall, good-looking and very self-possessed. George did not look like someone who could make millions in a financial jungle but she did. They told him she had been an investment analyst in George's firm and she still worked there.

He worked out what he would say when he called his uncle. "You didn't really believe that attempted rape allegation, did you? It's all connected with a story I was following. Some people are out to silence me. It's a hell of a tale. I'll tell you all about it when I get there." George would love to hear the story, with all the drama of a reporter's life.

He telephoned George from the motel room. Carol answered the phone. "Hello. This is your cousin Ted, from Long Island," he said. He thought he heard her give a little gasp of surprise but perhaps he imagined it. "Can I speak to George?" he said.

"George is in California. On business," she replied.

"Oh." He had not considered this possibility. "When will he be back?"

"In about a week."

"I see." I thought quickly. He could hang up now and forget about his Toronto cousins. But his period in hiding had been demoralizing and he looked forward to coming out of the cold into the warmth of a home. He decided to take a chance with her. "Carol, have you read about me in the newspapers?"

"Yes."

"Well I didn't do it. I didn't try to rape that damned Carey woman. I swear it. Do you believe me?"

"Yes, if you tell me so. I found it hard to believe when I first read about it."

"Of course. Why should I? She's frustrated and hysterical, that's all."

"I can well believe it."

He went on, "But I don't want to be arrested right now. I'm afraid of what will happen to me. I don't think I'll get a fair hearing and there are people who want to see me dead." He slowed down and tried to make his voice sound calm. "That sounds crazy but it's true. I can explain it, it's to do with a story I'm writing."

"Uh-huh."

"I'm on my way to Toronto. I was going to ask you and George to put me up overnight tomorrow night. Just to keep me out of sight. Can you do that?"

"I'm not sure. Wait a minute, let me think."

"It'll only be for one night because I'm on my way to somewhere else. A lot's been happening to me. You and George asked me to come and stay with you in Toronto some time. I didn't think it would be in these circumstances," he added.

She still did not answer. Sensing her reluctance, he decided to back away. "I'm sorry," he told her. "I realize that it's not fair to ask you. Forget it. Please."

But Carol seemed to make up her mind. "No. You're our cousin and I'm sure you're innocent. Do please stay here."

"Are you sure?"

"Absolutely. Please do. What time do you think you'll arrive here?"

"Around ten o'clock in the evening. Is that okay?"

"Yes. That's fine."

He stayed in the motel cabin the next day. It was like the Hotel Charles again, and after his taste of freedom he was fidgety and irritable. He watched television and ate the sandwiches that Gavin brought in. Gavin reconnoitered the crossing pointed. He came back in the early afternoon and said he had seen the falls and they were magnificent. Ted remarked sourly that this was a most original observation.

Gavin also said he had seen lots of cars crossing the border and smuggling someone across would be "a doddle." Ted said he presumed this was a quaint English phrase for a lead pipe cinch. Actually, Gavin was worried, although he did not tell Ted. At every crossing point he saw cars being stopped and the drivers' passports checked, and in some cases the cars were searched. He had not expected this. But it seemed to be happening only on the Canadian side of the border so he reckoned that if Ted was arrested, at least it would be by the Canadian police and not the American.

They came out of the motel when it was twilight and the evening cool had come. In the parking lot with nobody about, Ted crawled into the trunk. It was dark, stuffy, and uncomfortable. For once he was glad that he was not taller so that he did not have to curl up too tightly. He was anxious when the car stopped for ten minutes at what Ted assumed was the border. He was very pleased when Gavin opened the trunk and he clambered out on to the grassy verge beside broad avenue running parallel to the Niagara River which , Gavin assured him, was in the province of Ontario.

"They checked my passport and looked at my innocent face and waved me on," Gavin told him, as Ted stamped about on the grass and flexed his arms to get rid of the stiffness. "I also changed some money into Canadian dollars."

Because Ted had been cramped up in the trunk, Gavin drove all the way to Toronto. They made plans for the next day. "It's an Air Canada flight. It leaves at seven o'clock in the evenings so check-in time is five o'clock," Gavin said, speaking in the precise operational-commander voice he was acquiring. "I'll pick you up at your cousin's house and drive you there. You can still wear your beard and glasses. You can go into the men's room just before we go to passport control and take them off."

"Maybe Carol will drive me to the airport," Ted said.

"In that case I'll meet you at the Air Canada ticket desk," Gavin said. "I'm going to stay at a hotel called the Jarvis Inn. I picked it out of a tourist leaflet and called them. It seems small and central. Call me there tomorrow at twelve noon and we'll confirm arrangements. Okay?"

"Fine." Ted was tired and content to let Gavin make the plans.

They reached the city limits in two hours. They stopped at a gas station, filled up and got a map of the city. Ted located his cousin's street, Parkside Drive, and gave directions. He realized that he had hardly been out of Gavin's company for three weeks and he felt strangely nervous and excited. They stopped at the house and he got out of the car and took his valise. Gavin clapped him on the shoulder, just as he did when Ted stepped outside his room at the Charles for the first time in disguise, and said, "On your way, Ted. I'll see you tomorrow."

Ted soon on the sidewalk for a moment looking down the street. There were smart houses,most of them large, with lawns in front. It was a prosperous street, which he would have expected. Ted walked to the end of the sloping lawn and looked up at the pink brick house in the darkness, its windows ablaze with lights behind curtains. He walked up the curving path across the manicured lawn to the white door, paused for a moment and rang the bell.

Carol opened the door, wearing a blue soft wool sweater and slacks. He saw behind her an inviting brightly-lit foyer. "Come in, Ted," she said smiling, and she put out her cheek and he kissed it.

He walked in and she led him into the living room. He put down his suitcase. Two other women were sitting there. She said to them."This is George's cousin, Ted, who I told you about." And to Ted. "This is Lorraine, and this is Anne-Marie."

CHAPTER THIRTEEN

Gavin drove on into downtown Toronto through the Friday night traffic and found Jarvis Street and then the Jarvis Inn. Its lobby, like the hotel itself, was small and functional with a tiled floor. Behind the reception desk he saw pictures of the Canadian Prime Minister and Queen Elizabeth. Queen Elizabeth! The realization swept over him that he was in another country. People sounded the same but he was no longer in America, where the police might be linked to the Mafia who might be linked to people in the CIA who might be linked to a predatory corporation. This was Canada, clean, decent, halfway British. The environment was no longer threatening. God bless Queen Elizabeth!

Smiling, he walked up to the desk and registered in his own name, then looked at his signature, "Gavin Grove," bold and undisguised. He even put his home address. His room was several cuts above the last two rooms he had stayed in, small but bright with attractive, light-colored furnishings, and on the walls a photograph of the Niagara Falls he had left behind him and a painting of a bear in the Canadian Rockies..

In bed, he lay awake for a while. Now that he was no longer fearful for his safety he found himself thinking again

about the larger issue. Izzy and Mohsin had found the way to
a cure for the impotence virus. The world was waiting for it,
Biotek and a lot of other institutions were looking for it but
Izzy and Mohsin had found it. Only he knew this, and he
was on his way to tell this to an international meeting of
medical scientists, virtually to tell the world. These were
exciting thoughts. It was some time before he fell asleep.

He woke at 7.30 feeling refreshed. He ate breakfast in the
hotel's coffee shop and then walked out to see something of
Toronto. The sunny weather, comfortably warm with
zephyrs coming off the lake, matched his cheerful mood. He
walked down to the lakeside and looked out across Lake
Ontario at the islands and at the horizon beyond. It was like
the sea. He had never before seen a lake so big that you
could not see the other side. He watched some sailing craft
maneuvering to take up their positions for what was
evidently a race. Behind him were glass-sided office
buildings, some with mirror glass that reflected the blue sky
and the water. It seemed a lovely city. Perhaps he would
bring Martha here some time for a long weekend.

He strolled about the area called Harbourfront and
watched people putting up stalls, one selling copper plate
pictures, another hand-made jewellery, another drawings of
Toronto. He started a conversation with the girl at the
jewellery stall, a college-age girl wearing a smock and jeans.
He did not often talk to strangers but now he was exercising
his new freedom.

"Rather unusual this," he said to her, fingering a bead
necklace on her stall. "I'm just looking for something to take
back to my wife."

"You're visiting from England?" she asked.

"From America," he said. "I'm English but I live there. Just outside New York City."

"And how do you like Canada?" she asked.

"From what little I've seen of it, I like it very much," he replied. She showed him some more pieces of jewellery but did not ask any more questions. He was disappointed. He was ready to tell her his name, that he was a medical scientist at the Bliss Institute, even that he was working on the impotence problem. He did not have to hide anything now.

He strolled up Jarvis Street looking at the stores, stopped at a sidewalk cafe for a mid-morning cup of coffee and read the Toronto Globe and Mail, and got back to the hotel at eleven forty-five, in good time to get Ted's twelve o'clock call.

In his room he turned on the television news. The Canadian Government seemed to be facing yet another constitutional crisis over Quebec. There was a report from Geneva previewing the WHO conference. The singer Paul Poteen had arrived in Canada for a tour and a good deal of air time was devoted to him. In America, he had been attacked at concerts twice in the past week. Some Canadians wanted to ban him from the country. He gave a news conference and was asked directly whether he was a potent, and he gave his familiar reply about a gen'man not talking about such things. He gave a sly grin this time as he said it. Gavin imagined millions of men in front of their television sets swearing at this self-satisfied bastard.

After the news there was a discussion of the Problem between a Roman Catholic and a Protestant clergyman and an academic theologian. Gavin recalled that the impotence level in Canada was virtually 100 percent, as in America. The three participants agreed that a disease that cancelled out such a fundamental part of Man's nature could have theological implications but they drew back from spelling out what these were. They all, in answer to a question from the chairman, rejected the idea that it was a punishment handed down by God. Gavin was pleased by this and became absorbed in their discussion.

When he looked at his watch it was a quarter past twelve and Ted had not phoned. He dialled Ted's mobile number, and got the answering machine. "I'm at the Hotel Jarvis waiting for your call," he said. He could not understand why Ted did not answer. Then the thought came to him that he had not taken his cousin's telephone number. Damn! He looked up George Starowicz in the phone book and it was not there. He asked information and was told it was an unlisted number. Damn, damn, damn! Why had he not thought to take that number?

He could not imagine what had gone wrong. Had Ted's cousin's wife turned him over to the police? If he had been arrested, that would surely be on the news. Was he ill? Had he misunderstood the arrangement? Gavin did not see how he could, but they were both very tired and they did not spend much time on it. He waited until two o'clock for Ted to call back, and then decided to go and call for Ted and go on to the airport. Fortunately, he remembered the address on Parkside Drive.

He checked out of the hotel, put his suitcase in the car and drove to the house and rang the bell. After some time, a tall, slender, dark-haired woman with a cool, composed air answered the door. She was wearing a bright green blouse and smart pants and she stood in the doorway like a sentinel.

"Mrs. Starowicz?"

"Yes."

"I've come for my friend Ted," he said.

"You mean Ted Starowicz?" she said, still standing in the doorway.

"Yes. Your cousin."

"My husband's cousin," she corrected him. "He came last night and went away again."

"He went away again?"

"That's right."

Gavin was baffled. "But I thought - I thought he was going to stay with you."

"We decided that in the circumstances, that would not be a good idea."

"Did he say where he was going?"

"No, he didn't. It's a rather sensitive matter, as I think you'll understand. Now if you'll excuse me," and she moved to close the door.

Gavin held the door with his hand. "It's very important that I get into contact with him," he insisted.

"I'm afraid I can't help you," she said firmly, and pushed the door shut.

Gavin walked back to his car puzzled and worried. If Ted's cousin had cha0nged her mind, then why hadn't he come straight to the Jarvis Inn? And wherever he was, why hadn't he telephoned at the agreed time? The next thing was to go to the Air Canada ticket desk and hope Ted turned up. On the way to the airport, he turned on the car radio and listened to a news bulletin. The Australian Parliament had passed the quarantine bill by a narrow majority. Paul

Poteen's car had been stoned and he had received death threats. There was no report of Ted Starowicz being arrested.

At Toronto Airport he sat on a bench opposite the Air Canada check-in counter. He was going to take his one suitcase on board as hand luggage and he had it with him. He was thinking that if Ted did not turn up, the sensible thing to do would be to fly to Geneva by himself and go through with his original plan. But Ted could be in trouble and this would mean abandoning him. They had been though all this together and he did not look forward to going on without him.

He sat there looking out for Ted and debating with himself. When the last time for check-in came he found he could not go on and leave Ted. He would give him another chance. But he would definitely go the following day, with or without Ted. Even then he would get to Geneva after the WHO meeting started.

He went back to the Jarvis Inn and checked in again. "I've had to change my travel plans," he explained to the room clerk. Ted knew where he was; he did not know where Ted was. Logically, therefore, he should sit tight and hope that Ted contacted him. He paced about the room anxiously When he went out to get some supper he told the room clerk that he was expecting a call and he would be back soon. The streets were crowded with people out for Saturday night enjoyment and he felt alienated from them, as he had from people on the New York streets when he was hiding out at the Hotel Charles. He found that he was walking in the shadows and turning his face away from people again. He did not sleep well that night, and he woke early.

. He listened to the radio again for news but again there

was no mention of Ted being arrested. He tried to think what might be happening to Ted. Was he ill? Had he been mugged somewhere? He wondered whether Ted's cousin Carol had been under constraint when she sent him away. Perhaps she was mistakenly trying to shield Ted in telling him he was not there.

He had lunch in the hotel coffee shop, and decided that before going to the airport he would go back and see if he could get anything more out of that Starowicz woman. There was not much time now.

He drove to Parkside Drive and rang the bell. There was no answer. He went back to the car and sat there thinking. He looked at the house, with its clean lines, pink brick and gleaming white door and net curtains at the windows, one of a variety of architectural styles of the houses on this street, each set back behind its own lawn. The street was deserted, apart from one man pruning roses on his front hedge. Here and there, sprinklers were turning on lawns.

He stared at the Starowicz house, as if he could find some inspiration just by looking at it. He could not stay here much longer if he was going to catch that flight. Then he thought he saw something moving behind the curtains. There was someone there. He stared and waited, but he did not see any more movement.

He got out and walked quietly up to the house, across the lawn, and down the side to the back. He could not admit to himself that he was eavesdropping so he did not exactly tiptoe but he walked very quietly. He saw an open window next to what seemed like a kitchen door and he heard women's voices coming from inside. Walking softly on a flower bed, he flattened himself against the wall and moved up next to the open window and listened.

"We shouldn't have pointed the rifle at him. That's what did it."

"If we hadn't pointed the frigging gun at him, he wouldn't still be here."

"Let's try grass. Baked in brownies."

"Great idea, Lorraine. Only we haven't got any."

"We can get some."

"On a Sunday?"

"Maybe. Or at least tomorrow."

"I still say massage. I used to drive Harry wild. And if there were two of us, or even three of us, wow!"

"Okay, how about we - "

Gavin strode to the door quickly and turned the handle. It was not locked and he walked in to a large farmhouse-style kitchen. The three women were all sitting around a pinetop table. They looked up at him in surprise. One of them he recognized as Carol Starowicz.

A hunting rifle was leaning against the wall next to the door. He grabbed it and pointed it at them. "Where's Ted Starowicz?" he demanded. They stared at him, evidently dumb with amazement. He shouted, "Where is he? I'm in a hurry!"

He heard a muffled shout from somewhere in the house. He went through the kitchen into the living room and called out. An answering call came faintly from somewhere below. "Is that Gavin?" He looked around and in the hall he saw a door with a key in the lock; the sound seemed to come from behind it. He turned the key and opened the door, and saw stairs leading down to a basement, with a carpeted floor and wood panelled walls. Ted was standing there in his socks, with his shirt hanging out over his pants.

"Oh, thank God you've come," he said fervently, and hurried up the stairs.

Gavin looked around the living room and saw a belt, shoes and a jacket on a couch. He pointed to them and Ted put them on with nervous, hurrying fingers. As he did so, he shook his head and mumbled to Gavin, "Jesus, I'm glad to see you!"

"Let's hurry," Gavin said to him. "We've got to get that plane."

The three women had stood up and followed Gavin into the living room, and he turned to face them. He realized that he was still pointing the rifle at them in a threatening posture and he felt ridiculous so he dropped the barrel towards the floor.. None of the women said anything, but their faces registered defeat. Ted finished lacing his shoes, avoiding looking at anyone, and picked up his case and they started out.

The youngest of the three women, who was standing nearest the front door, a frizzy-haired brunette with glasses wearing a sweater and shorts, burst into tears. Ted stopped and turned to her. "Look, I'm sorry - " he began.

"Come *on*!" Gavin shouted, and pushed him by the shoulder out of the door." He bundled him into the car, throwing the rifle on to the ground.

In the car, Ted shook his head for a while, and muttered a couple of times, "God, that was just awful. It was just humiliating!" They drove most of the way out to the airport in silence.

At one point Gavin said, "As a matter of fact – " but Ted snarled, "If you're going to tell me that your grandfather was kidnapped by the fucking Andrews Sisters, I don't want to know." Gavin did not speak again for a while.

The Sunday flight was a Swissair flight. Gavin bought the tickets while Ted went into the men's room and took off his beard. Then they sat in the international departure lounge waiting for their flight to be called. Ted put on his shades and buried his face in a magazine.

Four policemen marched into the departure lounge. Ted looked up and ducked behind his magazine again. The thought flashed into Gavin's mind that Carol Starowicz might be vindictive and might have told the police. Did she know what flight they were catching? Did the other women? "God, after getting this far," Ted muttered. Then he said quietly to Gavin, "Look, if they're after me, don't wait, you go on alone. You've got to get to the meeting."

The policemen had split into pairs, each pair standing in a different part of the departure lounge, and they were scanning the occupants constantly. The Swissair flight to Zurich was called. "Let's wait until the last moment," Gavin whispered.

Then there was a flurry of activity at passport control and the policemen straightened up and became more alert. Two figures hurried into the departure lounge and the four policemen took up positions on either side of them. One was big and muscular, crew-cut, and looked like a football pro. The other was Paul Poteen. He had a sticking plaster on the side of his head.

Poteen and his companion stood for a few moments surrounded by the policemen, and then a flight to London was called. The pair went straight through the boarding gate along with their police escort.

A uniformed security guard, walking by, stopped and grinned at the scene, then turned to Gavin and Ted and said conversationally, "Know who that was?"

"Yes, it was Paul Poteen," said Gavin.

"That's right. With his bodyguard. He was hit on the head with a rock. He's getting the hell out. Got a booking in London."

"Guess he's decided Europe is safer," Ted said.

"Good riddance, I say," said the security man, and wandered off.

"Come on, we've got to go," Gavin said to Ted, and as they walked quickly to their boarding gate he added, "It seems you're not the only person who's in a hurry to get out of Canada."

Then they were in their seats and the plane was climbing into the evening sky, and a Swissair stewardess with blonde curls tumbling over the pale blue collar of her uniform was standing in the front of the cabin and telling the passengers in three languages about the safety precautions.

::   ::   ::

Neither slept much on the overnight flight and they were both tired when they walked down the steps at Zu0rich Airport the following morning.

The connecting flight to Geneva was a half-hour late. Switzerland was six hours later than Toronto time, and it was one-thirty by the time they left Geneva Airport in a taxi bound for the Palais des Nations. Ted put on his shades again. The building seemed to be on the outskirts of the city, set back in extensive grounds. Gavin noticed a peacock on the lawn as they drove up the driveway. Television vans and radio cars bearing media names from a dozen countries were stationed in a parking area beside the building, directing the world's attention to what was going on inside.

They hurried across the lobby and they were stopped at a barrier by a uniformed guard. Gavin showed his credentials and Ted showed his Press card. He had a brief exchange with the guard in French and then told Gavin, "Everyone's at lunch now. The meeting starts again at two-fifteen."

"Okay. We'll wait."

"He said there's a snack bar on this floor. Why don't we get something first."

Gavin shook his head. "I'm too nervous to eat. I'll just go up there and wait for Izzy to turn up. You go ahead."

"Okay, I need something. Then I'll come back and wait here, and you'll come out and tell me when an announcement's been made. Promise?"

"I will, I promise," he told Ted.

Gavin took the elevator up to the second floor where signs directed him to the WHO meeting, and he found himself hurrying along the longest corridor he had ever seen. A continuous window along one side gave a panorama of the Alps, one glorious snow-capped peak after another gleaming in the sun, stretching out in a line. Tired, nervous and preoccupied as he was, he found he enjoyed the beauty of the view and made a mental note to look at it again at leisure.

The corridor was almost deserted, with only one or two figures here and there. He came to the entrance to the conference room and sat down on a leather-cushioned bench to wait until the others returned. He would have time to collect his thoughts and work out how to tell the story to Izzy. The thing was to start with the most important: the injections, the slides in his pocket. Let the whole story of why he went into hiding wait until later. He had to be calm, to tell Izzy about the virus and the antibody and the slides in a quiet, objective tone.

He was working this out when he saw Joe Barreras standing outside the conference room, and Barreras saw him. Barreras nodded and without waiting for an answering nod he started over towards him. Another man came along the corridor and stopped him and they exchanged a few words, during which the other man glanced over at Gavin. Then the other man continued on his way.

Looking at these two well-tailored men, Gavin was suddenly conscious of his appearance, his rumpled suit, his unshaven face, and his eyes that were probably red.

Barreras said, "Hello, Gavin. I didn't expect to see you here."

Gavin said curtly, "No, I don't suppose you did." He did not get up. Then, because he was curious, he asked, "Are you on the American delegation?"

"Good Lord no," Barreras replied. "I'm not a scientist. I have observer status though, and I thought it might be interesting to look in. Also, there are one or two people here I want to see. I've just arrived from New York, a few minutes ago. I missed the opening. Are you?"

"Yes, sort of." Gavin felt he was being sucked into civility, and he did not want to be civil to Joe Barreras.

"I didn't notice your name on the list."

"No, I've been keeping rather a low profile lately. As your Mr. Carey can tell you," Gavin said, and stood up to walk away. He had intended this to be his parting shot but Barreras spoke.

"Yes, my Mr. Carey, as you call him. You referred to Philip Carey when you said you didn't want to come and work for me. It may interest you to know that he and I have now parted company. He's no longer in my employ."

Gavin was surprised. "Really?"

"That's right," Barreras assured him.

"He's found a better job?" Gavin suggested. "Strategic adviser to the mob, something like that?"

Barreras ignored this. "Our methods - our attitudes - were incompatible," he said.

"Are you going to tell me," Gavin asked, "that you didn't know what Carey was up to? That you didn't know about his dirty tricks?"

Barreras paused for a moment and then, as if deciding that he was willing to spend a little time explaining a few things, he said: "Look. I have a very big corporation to run with a lot of interests. Philip Carey had a degree of latitude in the way he went about his work, just as all my executives do."

He sat down now on the bench now and directed his full attention to Gavin, and Gavin sat down beside him almost despite himself. The man was working his charm on him again. "I think that with Carey I made a mistake. He was applying methods that he learned in a very different world. Also, he had his own agenda. He was playing another game. I found that out after a while."

"What kind of game?"

"He wanted to make sure an American organization found the cure before anyone else. And he didn't consider the Bliss Institute sufficiently American. With him it wasn't just business, it was a patriotic cause."

He said, "So Philip Carey has been put out to grass?"

"Not out to grass. He put himself on the market and he's been hired as a consultant by L.T.S. I phoned Jerry Cochrane at L.T.S. and tried to tell him that he was taking on a rogue security man. In fact - "

He stopped and looked up. Julia Hayden-Browne was standing there, smart and trim in a knee-length fawn dress with a scarf at her throat. Gavin said hello, and she smiled and said hello. It was an automatic response and a professional smile but her eyes showed curiosity at his presence.

She said to Barreras,   "Sir Peter is downstairs and he'd like to see you."

"Good," Barreras replied. Then, to Gavin, "What I was going to say was - "

Julia interrupted: "Joe, he says to tell you he's afraid he only has a few minutes before he goes back to London." She flashed a look of polite apology to Gavin.

Gavin could almost see Barreras's mind switching tracks. "Okay," he said getting up, and to Gavin, "I may see you later, then." And he left with Julia.

Gavin felt discomforted. It was nice and simple when he hated Barreras and all he stood for. Now he was not sure. Could all this about Carey have been invented? Why would Barreras bother to deceive him now?

He saw someone coming towards him, a balding, burly figure wearing horn-rimmed glasses and a dark grey suit, carrying a briefcase. He recognized him as the man who had stopped briefly to talk to Barreras.

"Dr. Gavin Grove?"

"Yes." He stood up.

"I'm John Howard. Assistant Director of the WHO. One of the assistant directors." He held out his hand and Gavin shook it. "We haven't met," he went on, "but I recognize you from the Washing- ton conference. I saw your presentation. Very able."

"Thank you. You're American?"

"Yes, but I've been with WHO here in Geneva for some years. I didn't see you at this morning's session."

"I've only just arrived."

"I see. You're with the American delegation? I like to know the delegates, at least by sight. I'm the Chairman of the conference."

"Actually, I'm an alternate delegate," Gavin explained.

"I see. Someone on the American delegation hasn't come?"

"No. I'm here because I have some important information for Israel Rubin, who's on the American delegation," Gavin continued. "Very urgent. He'll want to give it out to the conference. And I may come in and watch. I don't know whether that's allowed."

"I don't recall that Israel Rubin is down to speak today."

"Well I'm sure he'll be allowed to speak. He has a special announcement."

Howard looked doubtful. "I don't like changes in the program," he said. "Unless there's a quite exceptional reason."

"There is."

"Really?"

Gavin decided to tell him. He would know soon enough anyway because Izzy would need the Chairman's permission to break into the schedule of speakers. "The best there is," he said. "We've cracked it. We've produced a denatured virus. It works. It's a cure."

"You've done this?"

"Not me. The Bliss Institute. It's Dr. Rubin's work. His and a colleague's. But I don't think he knows how well it's succeeded. It's a long story, but basically, I did the tests and I've got the results on two slides in my pocket. I take it there's a slide projector in the conference room."

Howard asked, "And you want to announce that the Bliss Institute has denatured the virus?"

"I want Dr. Rubin to announce it. At this afternoon's session. It's important enough to break into the schedule, don't you think?"

Howard stood up. He pursed his lips and stood still for a moment, looking at the floor. Gavin watched him and decided that he was trying to work out how to reply to this astounding piece of news. After a few moments, he turned to Gavin and said, "You don't know what went on at this morning's session."

"No. I told you, I've just arrived in Geneva."

"Two Frenchmen announced that they've found the cure. They've denatured the virus. They're from the Pasteur Institute, the same place where they isolated the virus."

Gavin was stunned. "They have?"

"Yes." Howard paused to let this sink in before continuing. "The Pasteur Institute people circulated their papers. The start of this afternoon's session has been delayed by two hours so that everyone can study them."

Ted's mind reeled. He steadied it by steadying his gaze, focussing on that line of mountain tops. "Is that definite?" he asked.

"Yes, it is. I'm sorry. I guess this was going to be your big day."

"I did go to rather a lot of trouble to get here," Gavin said.

His expectations were evaporating one by one. His news to Izzy would not be exciting. It was not the Bliss Institute that had saved the American people but someone else. Izzy would not make the announcement at the conference. He would not be famous around the world. Ted would not have his big story. Hurt and disappointment went through his mind. Yet he did not feel totally defeated. He had run the race to the end. .

He looked again at the mountain peaks and suddenly he wanted to be out there, out in the fresh, clean air, out of this hermetically sealed building and away from slides and viruses and plots and competition to get there first. He felt tired. The strain of the last weeks was coming to him.

Howard interrupted his reverie. "Did you say you have slides?" he asked.

"Yes, two slides."

"Could I ask you what's on them?"

"Blood samples, with greatly reduced quantities of the virus."

"Your slides might add something."

"Uh-huh."

"What are you going to do right now?"

Gavin shook his head wearily. "I don't know. Find Israel Rubin. Get a hotel room, I thought I'd stay in the same hotel as him. Do you happen to know where he's staying?"

"No, but I can easily find out. I'd like to see your slides. I think they might have a place in the conference session later on. Would you be willing to show them?"

"Sure." He did not say what the slides had meant to him, the trump card that would astonish the world.

"I'm just going to my office now. How would like to come along with me and bring them? We can look at them and see how they relate to the French paper. And we can find out where Israel Rubin is staying, and see if we can book you a room there."

Gavin felt weighed down by disappointment and fatigue and he liked the idea of someone else taking over arrangements. "Is your office in this building?"

"No, but it's nearby. I was just going to call my car. We can get some lunch also."

"Okay," Gavin said.

Howard took a mobile phone out of his briefcase and spoke into it briefly. They walked back along the long corridor, and then Gavin thought of Ted. He said, "I came here with a friend. He'll be in the snack bar. I just want to tell him the bad - what's happened and where I'm going. I'll have to link up with him."

"Who's that?" Howard asked.

"A reporter called Ted Starowicz." The name slipped out and the moment it did he regretted it.

"Ted Starowicz?" Howard repeated. "Isn't that the man who's wanted by the police in America for trying to rape somebody?"

"Yes, but he didn't do it," Gavin said.

"Surely that's for the courts to decide," Howard said. "You say he's here?"

"Yes, but look, he'll make his peace with the authorities later. Right now I want to talk to him."

"I have an official position," Howard said. "If I find out where he is, I'll tell the police immediately. He's a wanted criminal."

Gavin did not want to see Ted arrested right now. He would either have to leave Howard or avoid Ted. He thought that perhaps he would let Ted enjoy his lunch before telling him that he would not have his big scoop. As they walked out of the door he said, "All right. If your office is near here, I could come back right after I've shown you the slides and we've sorted out some things, couldn't I?"

"Sure, no problem," Howard said.

"Okay." He would link up with Ted then.

Out in the open, Gavin noticed the weather for the first time, the same perfect autumn weather they had had driving up from New York. The lawns and flower beds in front of the building seemed to gleam, as if every blade of grass and flower petal had been cleaned separately. The peacock he had seen coming up the driveway was now accompanied by a second. The pair of them stood a little way off the path, ignoring the few people about and flaunting their finery for one another.

They walked down the path as a car appeared at the end of the driveway driven by a chauffeur in a peaked cap. "This is my car now," Howard said.

"Gavin!" The shout came from behind them and they both turned. Ted was hurrying out of the front door holding a half-eaten baguette in one hand and a bottle of beer in the other.

As he came down the path Howard said, "That's Starowicz!"

Gavin said, "Please don't call the police right away. I can

explain."

Ted reached them and said, "What the hell is - "

Howard slammed his fist into Ted's mouth. It was a hard blow and it caught Ted by surprise. Blood spurted out of his lower lip and he staggered backwards and fell down. Howard grabbed Gavin's arm and said, "Come on, let's go."

Gavin was so astonished that he let Howard propel him a few yards along the path to the driveway. He turned and looked, aghast, at Ted sitting on the path holding his hand to his mouth with blood trickling between his fingers. "Just a moment," Gavin said.

Howard was holding his arm and he tightened his hold. Gavin started to say something but suddenly his arm was being held behind his back in a painful grip. When he tried to pull away the pain increased. He wanted to protest but he could hardly breathe. Panic flooded over him along with the pain. This was insane, the Deputy-Director of the WHO twisting his arm. The grip on his arm kept him upright. No one seeing the two of them from a distance would know that one was the prisoner of the other.

The car drew up, and Gavin felt himself pressed against it with his arm in Howard's agonizing grip. Howard said quietly, through clenched teeth, "Now we'll get in the back." Gavin fought against panic.

Howard was opening the car door with his other hand, and at that moment Gavin found something to cling to. In this strange world in which he had lived these past weeks, this world of menace and subterfuge, he had held his own. He had found that he could fight back. He kicked backwards with his heel against Howard's shin. He felt Howard flinch and that was a victory, and he jerked with his arm against the grip and kicked hard again. Howard tried to tighten his grip and he wrestled to get loose gritting his teeth against the pain.

Then he heard a crash of breaking glass and the grip was loosened and he tore himself free. Howard was clutching his head and blood was trickling down from a gash on his bald patch. The shattered remains of Ted's beer bottle lay on the ground. Ted was standing now and he hurried down the path towards them. Gavin stepped away from Howard and stood there rubbing his arm and breathing hard and tried to recover his calm. The pair of peacocks were fanning their huge multi-colored tails directly behind Ted now, and they seemed to add a surreal touch to the scene.

"Still got my pitching arm," Ted said grinning, and took out a handkerchief and pressed it to his bleeding lip.

. Gavin saw that a number of people were walking across the lawn towards the entrance to the building. Among them was Izzy Rubin, deep in conversation with another man, a tall, slim, bespectacled figure who was bending down to hear what Izzy was saying. They both had plastic name tags in their lapels. He hurried away from Howard, who turned and got into his car.

They drew near and then Izzy saw him and stopped in surprise. "Good God, Gavin!" he said. "What are you doing here?" Then he saw Ted. "Ted Starowicz!" He blinked in bewilderment.

"Hello, Izzy," Gavin said, still rubbing his arm.

"I thought you were in Philadelphia," Izzy said.

"Oh yes, I forgot about Philadelphia," Gavin said.

"Actually, we were very worried when you didn't get in touch."

"I'm sorry I disappeared so suddenly."

"Martha said you were all right, but then she went away. It seemed strange. What on earth are you doing here?"

"There's a lot I've got to tell you about, Izzy. And some I haven't figured out yet. Like why that bastard just punched Ted in the face and twisted my arm behind my back."

"What bastard?" asked Izzy.

"Him," Gavin replied, indicating Howard, whose car was just driving away. "The conference chairman. I imagine he might have some odd ways of keeping order."

"Cairman my ass, 'at was Cay," said Ted, through his handkerchief. He spat a bit of tooth on to the lawn and some blood came with it.

"This is the conference Chairman," Izzy said, turning to the figure beside him. "Dr. Olaf Lindstrom, from Sweden. Dr. Lindstrom, this is a colleague of mine, Gavin Grove, who has suddenly appeared out of nowhere and is about to tell me why."

Lindstrom held out his hand and Gavin, bemused, shook it. "You're the chairman of the conference?" he asked.

"I am," Lindstrom said, giving a slight bow of assent. "And I haven't punched anyone today. Nor did I twist your arm."

"John Howard isn't the chairman?"

"Who's John Howard?" asked Izzy.

"The unexpectedly violent man I was just with," said Gavin. "There, just driving away."

Ted said, "I told you, 'at was Carey. Philip Carey," He took the handkerchief away from his lip for the moment. "You din't know?"

Gavin shook his head, and murmured, "God!"

"That was Carey," Ted said yet again. "I saw you from the window, and didn't know what the hell you were doing, going off with him. What were you doing?"

"He said he was someone else."

"He packs quite a punch," Ted said ruefully. He pressed his handkerchief to his lip again to stop the trickle of blood. "What did he say to you?"

Gavin did not answer him for the moment but he asked Lindstrom, "Tell me, did French scientists from the Pasteur Institute say anything this morning about discovering a cure?"

"No, nothing like that," Lindstrom replied.

"Is there an afternoon session?"

"Of course. We're going to it now."

"And nobody at this morning's session said they've denatured the virus? Discovered the cure?"

"Unfortunately not," replied Lindstrom.

Gavin paused, and turned away. Things were happening too fast, much too fast. Once again he stared at the landscape for a while to steady his mind, as one might getting off a carousel. He concentrated on the lawns and the hedges beyond. All the expectations that had evaporated were now acquiring substance again: telling Izzy, Izzy telling the conference, the whole world knowing about the Bliss Institute, Ted's scoop.

"What are you talking about, Gavin?" Izzy asked him. "And what are you doing here? And where have you been?"

"I've got some good news for you, Izzy," Gavin said.

::   ::   ::

On a bench in a corridor, he told Izzy first about injecting himself with the substance. He did not tell him the whole story about his weekend with Barreras - that would come later - but he said, "I owed it to the Bliss Institute to put it ahead. For reasons connected with Barreras and Biotek." When h0e had finished his account, Izzy shook his head incredulously and told him it would serve him right if he had dropped dead from an adverse reaction to the drug, doing something so damned foolish and unprofessional.

Then Gavin told him that he had a result and told him what it was, and Izzy clapped his hands gleefully, so that people in the corridor on their way to the conference hall turned around. "You've got to make the first announcement, Gavin."

"But I didn't do it. You did. You and Mohsin."

"But it's your finding you'll be reporting. You are sure about the virus, aren't you?"

"Yes. You can check the slides before we announce it if you like."

They gave in the slides to be displayed, and spoke to Lindstrom. Then they took their places in the circular conference hall, near the front row in the banked seats. Lindstrom announced a slight change in the schedule. "Before the scheduled speakers, we'll have a brief presentation by some people from the Bliss Institute in the United States that I think will be of special interest," he said.

Gavin's heart was pounding with excitement as he walked up to the rostrum. He looked out at the audience, sitting in tiers, and when he opened his mouth to speak only a croak came out at first. People looked at him curiously. Then he took a deep breath and began again: "Doctors Israel Epstein and Mohsin Ahmed of the Bliss Institute have created a denatured virus." He paused and there was a satisfying murmur of astonishment.

He continued, "Dr. Epstein is here, and he will follow me and explain the culture and the procedure that they used. I have here two slides containing blood samples, one in which the virus was present in full strength, and one in which the antibodies have had their effect, that will show the result. Dr. Epstein has not had time to prepare his presentation because he has only just learned of this success."

Later, he remembered the afternoon later as a series of explosions. An explosion of excitement among the scientists when he showed the slides. Another explosion when Izzy explained the procedure, accompanied by questions. Had any figures been calculated? How long had the denaturing taken? How many blood samples were taken? Izzy turned to Gavin to answer some of them. Some wanted to rush home immediately to start the denaturing process in their own laboratories.

There was the explosion among journalists when the conference was over, more uncontrolled and prolonged. Dr. Lindstrom gave out the news at the end of the afternoon, and then he and Izzy were surrounded by a seething mass of reporters with microphones, television cameras and notebooks, all trying to get closer, pushing microphones at them, shouting out questions frenetically. "Dr. Epstein, how long will it be before it's available as a medicine?" When will doctors have it?" "How long will it take to work?" "Would you look this way please?" "This way!" "Dr. Grove, how did you know it had worked?" "When did you tell the Bliss Institute?"

He had already left the meeting in the middle to hurry down the corridor to tell Ted, who demanded to know the exact wording of the announcement and then ran to a telephone

They fled back into the conference chamber, along with other scientists who also had to take refuge, and they did not emerge until a cordon of security guards had been organized to get them out of the building by a back door.

He took a room in Izzy's hotel and the reception were instructed to tell the Press that he was not staying there and that Dr. Epstein was not available. Then he telephoned Martha and talked to her for half an hour. She was just listening to the news from Geneva on the radio when he called. He realized how much he had missed her and longed at that moment to see her again.

He and Izzy had dinner sent up to his room, and over dinner he told Izzy the whole story of his disappearance and everything that had happened since Labor Day. As he recounted it, it all seemed more and more improbable, and more and more as if he were a man in the grip of galloping paranoia. By the time he finished, it seemed improbable to him also, and he began to think that his fears were really all imaginary. He half-expected Izzy to murmur something polite about mental strain and to say that perhaps he needed a rest. But Izzy paused for a long time after he finished his story, and then said simply, "Well I think you did damned well."

After the weeks of seclusion he could not take any more of the excitement and he remained hidden away. But he managed to contact Ted and arranged to meet him for an after-dinner drink away from the main part of town and away from the conference crowd, to share a few moments of calm after the storm. Their rendezvous was at an outdoor café perched on the hillside overlooking the lake.

It was a cloudy night, and there was no moon. The massed lights of the city glittered to the right, merging into a glow at the center. In front of them there was a black emptiness that was Lake Geneva. A stiletto blade of light that marked the Mont Blanc Bridge sliced through the blackness. Lights stretched away from the city on the far shore, thinning out. The two of them sat in silence for a while, looking out over the lake, each with a brandy in front of him, Ted smoking a Gauloise.

Gavin said, "Those lights along the shore look like a string of pearls, with diamond clusters behind."

"Not an original simile," Ted remarked. "But an apt one. Geneva's a rich person's city from what I've seen of it. I took a walk around town earlier. Diamond-studded everything. Every store window a Tiffany's. Even the cafés are four-star. Look at this place. Eleven dollars for a cognac!"

"It's a smart place. We're paying for the view," said Gavin, indicating the darkness in front of them. "So enjoy it. Do you think they have working-class people in Geneva?"

"Oh they have them. They put them in a special quarter that's not marked on any visitor's map. Only the municipal authorities know where it is."

"And poor people?"

"Poor people they ship away. Like industrial waste. They send them to more backward countries. Like America. In small bunches so that people don't notice them and complain." They were speaking softly and slowly with long pauses, relishing the absence of urgency.

"How was your evening?" Ted asked.

"Quiet. We had to hide away. The whole world wants to see Izzy, of course. And me. He's promised to give a Press conference tomorrow - I suppose you'll be there. We had a secluded dinner in my room, from room service."

"Did you tell him all about Barreras and the car crash and hiding out?"

"Yes, I told him everything. He thought we did very well. I didn't think he'd believe it all but he seemed to. But it was a lot for him to digest. He changed the subject after a while, just to get away from it. He told me some conference gossip. Did you know that the woman on the Italian group is having an affair with a woman member of the Italian parliament? And that Chou Li, the Chinese, has started angling for a job in America already? Incidentally, we ate in our room but it was an excellent meal, after all those takeaways in hotels. A splendid hors d'oeuvres selection followed by a filet mignon. And some Dole – that's the Swiss red wine. How was your dinner?"

"I had a cheese omelette," Ted replied. "I managed to chew some french fries, they were soft enough. No steak for me. Carey really packs a punch."

"Oh, I forgot. I'm sorry. How does your mouth feel?"

"Tender. I can't bite. I hope his head still hurts. I did have a delicious crème brulée for dessert."

They sat in silence. Then Gavin turned, put his hand on Ted's shoulder, and said, "Well, we did it."

Ted grinned happily and affirmed, "Yup. We did it," and they sat in silence for a few moments more, savoring that little sentence.

Gavin said, "We've got to sort out your problem with the

law. But I've an idea we can beat that now."

"I guess so," Ted said. "To tell the truth, I'm not even going to think about it until tomorrow. It's been a long day."

"It has," Gavin agreed. "We haven't been to bed since Toronto."

"I'm tired out but too strung up to sleep," said Ted. "You know the feeling?"

Gavin nodded. "I feel sort of the same way. I've kept going on adrenaline."

"Me too," Ted said. "But I'm beginning to unwind now. I'm wondering now whether another cognac would help me unwind some more or whether it would make me just come apart."

"I think another cognac is called for, for both of us." Gavin said. "Okay?" He signalled the waitress and ordered two more.

Then he asked, "Are you pleased with the story you put over?"

"Mainly, yes. I'd written a lot of in advance, of course. And my God, I'm never going to have a story as big as that again."

"How long was it?"

"The trunk story was about eighteen hundred words, I reckon. That's an awful lot. And there were two sidebars, about six hundred words each. There'll be more official pronouncements, but the paper can pick that up from the wires. One of the sidebars was a profile of you."

"Of me?"

"Of course. *'It was a tall, bespectacled British scientist with a modest manner and a house in Melby Park who gave out the news that all America has been waiting for. He* *played the self-appointed role of human guinea pig in the drama of the discov*ery.' There was a bit more of that. I said you were modest so you'd better act modest."

A lake steamer aglow with lights passed in front of them, and they both fell silent for a few moments and followed it with their eyes. Then Ted said, "Gavin, there's something I've been meaning to ask you."

"Yes?"

"You say that the antibodies are killing the virus in your bloodstream."

"That's right."

"Are there - any other signs yet of the cure working? I mean - you know - "

"Yes?"

"Well - do you feel any - do you feel anything different?"

The waitress brought their brandies. Gavin watched her as she set them down and followed her retreating form with his eyes as she threaded her way through the tables..

Then he leaned towards Ted, and speaking out of the side of his mouth he said, "Jeez, get a load of the ass on that babe!"

CHAPTER FOURTEEN

C linical trials were conducted speedily and the medicine was turned into a pill to make it easier to use. The formula was made available world-wide and it was manufactured faster and in greater quantity than any medicine before in history.

The plague traveled to other countries but nowhere was its effect as widespread as in North America. It turned out that the virus was short- lived and its effect was short-lived also. Even without the medicine, the plague would have died out soon. The virus joined the dinosaurs and the dodo in extinction..

The next few months in America became known to social historians as the "re-entry period," the term being borrowed from the language of space travel. It was only after it had been used in print a few times that its double meaning was noticed. Sexual potency came back to men, not gradually but all at once.

Nonetheless, it was a troubling time for many men. The fact that some regained their potency before others created tensions. Undercurrents of hostility grew up among groups of men where it had not been present before, in offices, factories, sports teams. Men suspected their wives of infidelity. Rows broke out because a wife mentioned, as a simple item of mealtime conversation, that so-and-so seemed to be back to normal. A man did not always know whether he was still affected by the virus or not. Many men found difficulties. Psychiatrists wrote articles in the newspapers about "performance anxiety," and the phrase became common currency.

Other terms came to have a special usage during this period. A man might ask a woman out and he might add, "I mean on a date." Or if he did not specify, or if she was just asked to go to a party with him, she might ask, "Is this a date?" If the answer was in the affirmative, it meant that he was back to normal and there was the potential, if not the promise, of sexual relations. When a couple went out on a "date," this meant that the man was sexually potent.

If a young couple said they were "going away for the weekend," their friends nodded understandingly. No one ever used the phrase if they did not mean that they were going away to enjoy their newly recovered sexuality. Most couples who said it did not actually go anywhere, but their friends did not telephone during that weekend or invite them over. Elaine's advertisement for a romantic weekend in the Adirondacks became advertisements for a weekend in the Adirondacks. No qualification was deemed to be necessary.

For most people, particularly young people, during this period sexual activity had an urgency it did not have in more normal times. Employers were likely to be indulgent if an employee said he or she wanted to take a few days off because "we want go to away for a long weekend." It was accepted tacitly that where the opportunity for sexual activity had just returned, it could take priority at first over social and even business arrangements and these might be canceled. Business discipline was slack in this period. Deadlines were often not met, appointments were cancelled at the last moment.

When Gavin telephoned his insurance company to complain that some documents had not arrived he was surprised to hear the manager at the other end, clearly harassed by a flow of complaints, reply, "I'm sorry but it's my fucking staff. And I mean that literally." A young couple canceled a date for a movie with the Groves at short notice. "She said they can't come," Martha told Gavin as she came off the telephone. "She said, 'Something has just come up,' and giggled."

At Holycroft as at other colleges, there were a lot of absences from classes. One professor drew a line saying, "I'll allow three days but no more. After that it's just an excuse. Or else boasting. If you want to go away on honeymoon, wait until the end of term."

Some people revelled in the sexuality they had recovered and there was an outbreak of promiscuous behavior. Women reported that there was more sexual pressure on them from men, and some women also were more ready than at other times to take any opportunity that presented itself. It was as if they felt that men's sexuality was not something to be taken for granted, that it could be taken away again and should be grabbed while it was there. Some husbands drove their wives to distraction and divorce by seeking every opportunity for sex with anyone they could find. Marriages broke up because of this infidelity. A few others broke up because the wife had found she preferred to do without a physical side to their relationship.

Popular magazines, and particularly women's magazines, carried even more advice than usual on sex: how to do it, when to do it, what to wear while doing it, where to do it - in the bedroom, the living room, the bathroom, the porch, the beach. There were indications that more people were taking part in orgies. One women's magazine even carried advice on etiquette for an orgy and, if it was to be held in one's own house, what facilities one could reasonably be expected to provide, what food to serve, what to tell the neighbors.

Gavin and Martha were both surprised when a rather lacklustre couple they knew said at a dinner party that they had been to an orgy, and added that it was an enriching experience and they intended to do it again. They hinted at some of the activities they had engaged in there, which the husband described as "rococo."

Gavin had always regarded this couple as very conventional and the image of them engaged in multiple sexual activities with a number of other people remained in his mind. The wife, for all her mousy little manner, had an attractive body, now that he thought about it. That night, as he was getting into his pajamas and Martha was sitting at her dressing table brushing her hair, he said thoughtfully, "You know what the Chapmans were saying."

"You mean about their orgy."

"Uh-huh. About it being an enriching experience. I've been thinking."

"Yes?"

"Maybe - perhaps it really could be - "

Martha stopped brushing her hair and cut in sharply, "You don't mean you want to - "

"Well no, I didn't necessarily mean I want - I was just thinking - "

"And you wouldn't want to have me - "

"Oh no," he replied quickly. "Good lord no. Absolutely not. I wasn't thinking that at all."

Ted Starowicz was walking along one day when he was hailed by a figure from across the street. "Hey, remember me? John Dallas, Playgirl Escort Agency."

"Oh yes, of course."

"How's the newspaper business?"

"Okay. How's yours? I guess you don't want me on your books any more."

Dallas chuckled and shook his head. "But if you know any good-looking girls who want to earn some spare cash, send them my way. I can use some more girls. I got all the business I can handle and then some."

Ted went on his way grinning. He had been flattered that morning to get a note from Anna, the flight attendant from Boston, suggesting that he call her some time because she often stayed over in New York. Evidently, with the rest of the male sex available now, she still liked him.

Gavin took Martha for a long weekend in Toronto and he showed her Harbourfront and the lake and told her again all about rescuing Ted from the three women, and the tense time at the airport. He was one of the first to take the cure, albeit with the medicine in a crude form, so the weather was still warm enough to sit at sidewalk cafés and to enjoy the browns and reds of the trees in Toronto's parks. They also enjoyed a lot of time in their hotel room in bed. Also, as a matter of fact, in an armchair and in the shower.

As he pulled her towards the bed one more time she said, "You can't get enough of it, huh?"

"I can't get enough of *you*," he replied.

"After those words, anything you want, let me know."

At the Counselling Center, Martha saw several women in tears of distress and rage because of their husbands' adultery. To some of them she said, "From what you say, you've had a pretty good marriage up to now. Why not give things a little time to work themselves out? He's not rejecting you. He's like a child who's just been given a new toy. He wants to play with it all the time."

Going home she said to Gavin, as she had said to him before after a day at the counselling center, "God, men are a shallow, stupid lot."

She continued to see Helen, the bespectacled, caring young woman that she had come to like, who had not often been dated by men before. She was making a serious effort to lose weight now and it was showing. Martha used to feel angry because life and the male sex had given Helen such a raw deal. Helen was still seeing this man, but she admitted to Martha that she was beside herself with anxiety about what would happen when he got back his sex drive. "We really like each other," she explained. "We enjoy our time together. I feel close to him. He's much more insecure than I thought, and he's got a lot of problems. You told me that other people have problems too, that I only see my own, and you're right. But I'm so frightened that when he gets it back he'll just want some conventionally beautiful girl."

"You've got your own kind of good looks," Martha told her.

Then one day she said, "Well, it's happened. He's got it back. We've been to bed together."

"And?" Martha said encouragingly.

"It was marvellous." Martha waited. Helen went on, "He says - " Her voice faltered and she stopped, and then started again. "He says that before he used to like me, and now he loves me."

Martha threw away her professional detachment and got up from her chair and hugged Helen. She went home thinking that there was a lot to be said for the sex drive and greeted Gavin at the door with a passionate kiss, to his surprise.

Things returned to normal after a time, and the months of the plague became a part of history, a memory, and no longer a part of people's daily lives.

Summer came early the following year, and with it the comfortingly familiar sounds of the season: the raised voices because a daughter has stayed out late, the noise of gunfire in woods where deer roam, the raucous shouts at a baseball game, police car sirens in the inner cities, moans of delight from a parked car.

On the Groves' patio late one afternoon, the sounds came from neighboring yards, and they were domestic ones: the laughter of children, the splash of water in a paddling pool, the clink of ice in a pitcher. The two couples were sitting on the Groves' patio with pre-dinner drinks in their hands, and they were discussing names: English names, American names, historical names.

"Gavin's got a couple of English-sounding names that are cute," said Martha. "I was looking for some among the Pilgrim Fathers since it's due at Thanks- giving."

"If it's a girl," said Naomi. "you could call her Cherry. Or Olive. I think Olive Grove is nice."

"Sort of Spanish," Ted commented.

"Whatever name you give it," said Naomi, "that kid will have a lot of competition getting into college."

"That's going to be a pretty crowded school year," agreed Martha. "In the next few months this country's going to be full of babies."

"Anyway," Gavin said, "tell us all about your honeymoon."

"God, and they say reporters are nosy," Ted murmured.

"Okay, not *all* about it. But did you enjoy Martinique?"

"It was everything we wanted," said Naomi. "Perfect weather, a good hotel, great water sports."

"I was amazed," said Ted. "They say you learn new things about each other when you get married. I learned that Naomi's good on water skis. Who knows what other talents she has?"

"It's an interesting locale," Naomi went on. "A nice cultural mix. And Ted enjoyed complaining that the waiters didn't speak proper French and he couldn't understand them most of the time."

"I didn't complain," Ted objected. "I just called it Caribbean French."

"How's the job at the Times working out?" Gavin asked.

"I think it'll be good," Ted replied. "I'm a fish in a bigger pond, of course. But they're treating me well. I'm going to ask for an overseas posting in a couple of years, when Naomi has finished her doctorate. Anyway, I had to leave the Chronicle."

"Why was that?" asked Martha.

"Gavin didn't tell you? I had a big problem. Every time I saw the managing editor, a man named Tom Manning, I wanted to kill him. Not just kill him. Pick up a chair and beat him to a bloody pulp. Or cut off his head and kick it all around the newsroom. It was a terrible strain having to resist it all the time."

"You told me you understood why he did what he did,"

said Gavin.

"Oh, I understood after I spent a few weeks calming down and thought about it," Ted said. "He explained his reasoning to me. I'm accused of attempted rape. I go on the run from the law and disappear. Nobody knows what I'm doing or what condition I'm in. Then I suddenly telephone out of the blue from Switzerland and tell them the cure has been discovered and give them the whole long story. If my story had been wrong the paper would have looked very stupid. It would have been a laughing stock. So he waited until the wire services carried the full story before using mine. Not even just the first news flash. We could have got an edition out on that before the wire services reported the whole story."

"But he ran your background story in full afterwards," Gavin pointed out. "And let you write a big series on it. You had a lot of stuff no one else had."

"Sure. That helped me get the job on the Times. As I say, I understood why he took the decision he did. But then I think that I could have beaten the whole world with that story of the discovery, and he sat on it. And I want to kill him."

"He probably feels bad about it too," Gavin suggested.

"Oh he did. He's got other problems too. I understand he had an affair and his wife's left him."

"By the way," Gavin said, "do you see the Chronicle these days?"

"Sometimes. Not regularly."

"Did you see last Saturday's by any chance?"

"No, I don't think so."

"I've saved a page for you. It'll interest you. I'll go and

get it." He went into the house and came back and handed the piece of the newspaper to Ted. That page. 'What I Learned Last Summer.'"

Ted glanced at it. "You mean," he asked, "'I Thought Bob and I Would Never Come Together Again But Now We Have a Deeper Understanding'?"

"No. There near the bottom of the page."

"Ah, yes. Mrs. Donna Carey." He read for a few moments. "I see. She learned the frailty of the human mind and the benefits of psychotherapy. And the love of her husband who stood by her. Damned nice of him, that. To stand by her. And she's sorry for all the trouble she caused. Oh yes. Mental fucking aberration. Nervous fucking breakdown. What a load of horse shit. I'm still not sure I was right to let her get away with that breakdown crap. That I shouldn't have sued her for a billion dollars."

"You had good advice. A jury would have been sympathetic to her plea of a temporary aberration. A lot of people were having a hard time. You were a potent. Your lawyer said you wouldn't have a chance."

"I suppose so," Ted grumbled.

The telephone rang. Gavin went into the house, and came back a few moments later. "Someone wants to view the house already," he reported.

"What did you say?" Martha asked.

"I told him not today, one evening in the week. He'll be the first."

While he was on his feet he offered everyone a refill of their drinks. Naomi signalled a negative with her hand, and asked them, "How do you feel about the prospect of moving?"

"I'll miss this area," Martha replied. "We've made some good friends here. We're driving up to Cambridge on Friday to spend the weekend house-hunting."

"When does the new job start?" Ted asked.

"September 1st," Gavin replied. "We should be settled in before the junior Grove comes along."

"No qualms about going into industry? You're leaving what's now about the most famous scientific institution in the world."

"I had a lot of qualms about leaving Bliss, yes. But this was a very attractive offer. And it's not really going into industry. I mean, I'll be working for an industrial corporation but it's fundamental research. I've got a project on the brain worked out that ties in with some work they're doing that's really interesting. And I'll be running my own laboratory."

"And you say there's more loot in it."

"Yes, there's substantially more money and that counts for something. We have the family coming along."

Martha stood up and straightened out her dress and said, "I think it's getting to be time for dinner."

Martha and Naomi walked in, Martha talking about her pre-natal exercises.Gavin went around collecting the glasses, and Ted lingered with him.

"You know, Gavin, I'll tell you something strange about last summer," he said.

"Uh-huh.".

"No really. Something I've been feeling lately."

"Nostalgia?"

"No. Well, yes, a bit now that you mention it. But that's not what I mean, Gavin.. My father's a lot older than me and most of his generation were all drafted, you know? He had a hernia, so he couldn't go into the service. Most of his friends, most people his age, went into the service. Some went to Vietnam. They all had that experience in common. It wasn't always a good experience. A lot of them didn't like it at all. For some it was awful. But it was something they all shared. My father told me that he missed having memories that the rest of his generation share. He felt there was a gap between him and them. Can you understand that?"

"Yes, sure."

"Well I feel sort of the same way. All the guys are talking about last summer, and how extraordinary it was, and how they feel now that they're over it and all. But I didn't go through that. I didn't have that experience. I feel sort of left out."

Gavin set down the glasses he was carrying and put his hand on Ted's shoulder. "Ted," he said, "each of us has a burden to bear in this life, and that's yours. You'll just have to be strong."

Ted sighed. "I guess I'll have to go a long way to get any sympathy," he said.

"A long way," Gavin agreed.